Bee King

by

Joanne Lewis

This book is a work of fiction. Names, characters, places and incidents are either the product of the author's imagination or are used fictitiously. Any resemblance to actual persons, living or dead, or to actual events or locales is entirely coincidental.

Bee King

Cover designed by Joanne Lewis
Visit the author website: http://www.joannelewiswrites.com

Published by Soul Attitude Press
https://www.soulattitudepress.com

ISBN: 978-1-946338-30-3 (Paperback)
ISBN: 978-1-946338-31-0 (eBook)

First Edition

A love letter to my mother

Bee King

One Point

Bee King

The honeybee (Apis mellifera L.) was one of the many animals introduced into the Americas by the European Colonists. Records are scant as to just when it was first brought to North America; however, it appears that bees were shipped to the Virginia Colony about 1622 and to New England a few years later.

Benjamin Smith Barton, "An Inquiry into the Question, Whether the Apis Mellifica, or True Honey-Bee, is a Native of America." (1861)

Chapter One

Fourteen-year-old Noble rushed uptown from the Home for Unwanted Boys, a partially renovated burned-out factory located in the Five Points downtown district of Manhattan's Sixth Ward. The newly made wood vial around his neck smacked against his chest as he headed toward Central Park in search of bee royalty. The urban plan of New York City was a steaming grid mapped out fifty years earlier with eleven major avenues and one hundred and fifty-five cross streets. Five cross streets known as Five Points, and located on the lower east side, earned the title of most notorious Manhattan neighborhood. The inhabitants of Five Points consisted of a hodgepodge of Irish immigrants who fled the Great Famine, of free blacks, mulatto children, drunks, gamblers, whores, and gang members, and of the white missionaries who hoped to save them. Here, slumming began.

Six-feet-tall, long-legged and broad shouldered, Noble wore his only shirt—frayed at the collar with the top two buttons missing—and mud-stained pants, handed down from an unknown boy who had outgrown the garments as Noble soon would. The mid-March sun reddened his shaved head and the tops of his bare feet. His skin was pale and patchy.

He wished William was by his side. His only friend had gone on many bee safaris with him but had been distant lately and disappeared for hours. When Noble questioned him as to his whereabouts and his aloofness, William claimed he was at the courthouse listening to legal arguments and, like the good lawyer he intended to be, his mind was occupied with thoughts of legal briefs and arguments.

Even without William, Noble was glad to have a few hours free of the other boys in the Home who mocked him for spending months stalking bushes and flowers in City Hall Park, and who chastised him for trudging to Central Park to search caves, rock cavities, and hollow trees for nesting sites. Each time he began a hunt for a queen, the boys ridiculed him, tried to trip him as he walked out of the Home, and threw rocks at him as he stepped on to Broadway. Still, when Noble found her he knew it was going to be worth every cruel word, every scuffle, and even the broken nose he received from the knuckles of Kid Turner when Noble was ambushed and re-strained by four other boys. He would show them he could capture a queen and bring her and her colony to the Home. He would stifle Kid's bone box and his stupid bee jokes forever.

Where does a bee sit? Kid asked.

A dirty and dusty mop of boys gathered around Kid. Where? they asked.

On his bee-hind and up Noble's ass, Kid said.

Laughs and slaps on Kid's back.

What does a bee call his girl? Honey. What does Noble call his girl? He doesn't. He ain't never gonna' have one.

On Broadway, Noble pushed his way through the crowd, the street too narrow for the pedestrians to all get where they hoped to go at the same time. He stepped over and around discarded clothes, chocolate bar wrappers, moldy cheese, broken glass, and splintered chairs tossed from windows. The stank of his city no longer offended him. It had become him. He smelled it on his clothes, and tasted it on the back of his tongue.

Most of New York City's eight hundred thousand residents crammed in below Fourteenth Street. Twelve thousand free blacks inhabited the city and lived among shipyard workers and cotton transporters, both who pretended to not earn their livings off slavery. The avenues were packed, and the pace was hectic. Hundreds of brown pigs roamed undisturbed in their duties as sanitation collectors, the only means of sewer removal. Goats munched on grass and pulled up weeds, society's early landscapers. No building extended taller than five stories, which was as high as the spray from the volunteer firemen's hand-pumped hoses could reach. Steeples knifed the horizon. Anglican, Catholic, and Lutheran church bells disharmonized in a daily trinity at six a.m., noon, and six p.m.

Fire sirens blared over the plod of horses' hooves, shouts from livery drivers, and the cries of newspaper hawkers. The brogues of Irish and German immigrants vied with the boasts of first generation Americans. Abolitionists scuffled with their rivals, the copperheads.

Like the smells, Noble was no longer disturbed by the sounds of his city. He barely heard them, and did his best to live as a singular ingredient within its stew of characters and among the hot pot that boiled and rattled on the verge of explosion.

He passed Jenny Big Stink's fish wagon and Esther, her inquisitive long-eared male mule, and walked along the curtain-covered picture windows of Doc B's clinic. As he headed uptown, the crowds, tenements, tanneries, slaughterhouses and international markets that swelled along the toes of lower Manhattan riffed into long-armed country estates. Above Forty-Second Street, he trekked near Louvre Farm, one hundred and thirty-two acres of woods bound by the Old Boston Post Road that stretched to the East River and up to Seventy-Fifth. The chatter of passersby and the clunk of carriage wheels turned to the snorts of goats and cows that grazed in weedy fields. Near Eightieth Street, the scents of marigold and lavender beckoned and he slipped into Olmstead's park.

Upon arrival at the Home three years earlier, Noble had discovered four books in the bottom drawer of a termite infested three-legged wood dresser. One on sewing, one on proper grooming for the gentleman caller, one was a Bible, and the last was a new in appearance hardback edition of Petro Prokopovych's Russian to English translated account of beekeeping.

Noble's heartbeat quickened and his hands sweated when he found Prokopovych's book and read the nineteenth century Russian beekeeper's text and studied the drawings. What was it about the bees that enraptured Noble? Their outer simplicity? Their inner complexity? He returned over and over to the section on the hierarchy of the hive, to the chapter on how no bee was ever abandoned, to the pages he had dog-eared on how to protect the queen, and to the paragraphs where Prokopovych described bee bearding, his words poetic.

The tome became Noble's How-to. He left the other books in the cockeyed drawer.

Page seven of Prokopovych's book. Beekeeping can be recreational, and there is no better pastime as it gives charming and engrossing labor in the open air, and those who love natural science find no more fascinating dilemmas than the ones unsolved in the hive.

In Central Park, shaded by cherry and magnolia trees, Noble sat in solitude. Wild horses grazed nearby. A bald eagle landed in a tree, cocked its head at the boy, and then flew away. Noble watched and waited, his breath his companion, until finally—FINALLY!—he glimpsed a stunner of a worker honeybee. Genus: Apis Mellifera. Yellow like sunshine, orange and black striped like a Bengal tiger, almost an inch long.

Her scissor-like jaws chomped through a leaf and she tore off a piece with her hind legs. She hovered over several flowers and then disappeared into one end of a severed log-like portion of a giant oak. One side of the log was charred as if struck by lightning, the other was a dark and mysterious cavern Noble yearned to light. Bees flew in and out of this end, collected pollen, and returned to the hive to their feral queen.

Chapter Twenty-Seven of Prokopovych's book. How to Capture a Queen. The queen bee is a poor flyer with a large body but only worker bee sized wings. She is not as quick as the other bees and is easily recognizable among her litter.

The queen laid hundreds of thousands of eggs over her lifetime. Female workers cleaned and nursed the brood, guarded the entrance, and foraged for pollen and nectar. Drones carried out their singular duty of fertilizing the queen. From the outside and to the uneducated, the happenings inside a hive looked like a frightening and disorganized mess, but to Noble it was a complex and loving family comprised of order, loyalty and unquestioned faith.

Noble folded his large frame until he was compact like a closed book and lay in front of the open end of the log. He dipped his right arm in. Moist and warm, thousands of bees pricked his skin. No stings, he moved slowly, lovingly, not a threat to the hive.

Page Four Hundred and Ninety-Two. Bees sting out of fear.

Slowly, Noble pulled out. His skin was covered from fingertips to elbow with sensations he had only fancied. Dreams come true! Hundreds of bees pulsated. The buzz chortled loud and brassy, euphonious. Their wings, whispered breaths against his flesh. Where was the empress?

He drew his arm in and out of the hole, a deliberate un-hurried motion as bees deserved respect. Finally, there she was, atop his wrist bone. Larger and brighter than the rest, more graceful, her body long and pointed, her hind end extended beyond the tips of her closed wings.

Page One Hundred and Fifty-Four. The queen bee may be the mother of all her subjects. Her blood is in their blood, her faults are their faults, and her weaknesses their weaknesses.

With his left index finger and thumb, he gently shuffled other bees away and gripped her lightly, only enough pressure to hold her in place. He shook his right arm and bees flew off. Those that stayed were of no hindrance. As he had practiced using beetles and spiders, he slipped the queen into the wood vial that hung around his neck and twisted the top closed.

The queen threw herself against the sides of the ampoule. Furious, like how Noble felt when he had been apprehended by the police and taken to the Home. He hesitated. Was he being unfair to the queen and her colony? Was it wrong for him to treat her as he had hated to be treated?

Page Four Hundred and Twelve. While the queen might protest being captured and relocated, she will adapt to her new surroundings rapidly and, along with her subjects, will flourish with proper love and care.

He stroked the wood container, pressed it against his heart, and trusted Prokopovych's words. He exited Central Park and made his way back to Five Points. A black cloud hummed behind him.

Chapter Two

NEW YORK TIMES. April 15, 1861. The Great Rebellion The Beginning of the End. The curtain has fallen upon the first act of this great tragedy. Fort Sumpter has surrendered. The felonious flag of the Southern Confederates has replaced the Stars and Stripes of the American Republic. Northern women moan while their men prepare for battle.

One month after capturing his first queen in Central Park—the queen having cultivated an impressive colony—Noble stood in the back yard of the Home for Unwanted Boys. He was shirtless, long arms extended, legs spread, and bare feet planted in dirt. Filth stained his toes. The wood vial hung around his neck. Inside, the queen flung her body against the curved container, maddened for being separated from her hive. Bees darted frenetically around the vessel. Female workers landed in the crooks of Noble's elbows, along his biceps, and under his armpits. Drones descended onto the backs of his hands. Bees flocked to his upper body and formed a vibrating collar around his neck, and a coat of buzzing armor across his chest.

The six o'clock morning air was unusually cold, forty-two degrees Fahrenheit. At a distance, church bells echoed. The orphans awoke to reveille each morning at five thirty. The goal being to get them up and active so they'd go to sleep early, night being the time when they immersed in the most malevolent forms of mischief. A ridiculous theory when applied to a pack of boys with no structure and no purpose, and whose leader was the boundary-less Kid.

The manager of the Home was a well-meaning twenty-five-year-old named Butchy who had grown up there and had little experience managing his own life let alone a group of homeless boys. He was short and portly and hard-working, anatomically more overcrowded factory than fancy brownstone. The palette of his unlucky facial features made beautiful by his kindness and good intentions. Butchy strived for order and well-being for his boys, but daily life was a free-for-all for those aged six to seventeen, where and when they slept, what and when they ate, how each survived.

When city workers came to inspect the Home, the boys scrubbed themselves until their skins glowed pink like rose quartz, sat on their made beds with opened books in their laps, and put forth their best innocent smiles. As soon as the social workers were gone, Kid once again was the king. Bedlam, his prince. Most of the other boys in the home, his jesters.

In the dusty backyard, the nasty smell that lodged in Noble's nose and seeped into his throat was familiar. The stench of rotted food, shit from the outhouse, and piss—the boys peed wherever they liked, some in their pants.

Page Ninety-Three of Prokopovych's book. Bee Bearding is to be attempted after the apiarist has developed a trusting relationship with the queen and her colony. Achieving a successful bee beard could take the beekeeper one month or one year depending upon how fast his relationship with the hive develops. Bearding is a sign of a healthy hive. No beekeeper should attempt bee bearding as a side show, to make money or to gain friends. It should only be done to deepen the relationship between the beekeeper and his hive.

Thirty feet from Noble, seventeen-year-old William fidgeted and wheezed. The oldest boy at the Home, his five-foot-two-inch slender body was a distinct contrast to Noble's muscled frame. William stood erect how he imagined a rich man might. He spoke cultured English, how he believed the wealthy and educated spoke.

"You sure you want to do this?" William called.

Bees pulsated, glowed and traced Noble, like the frame of a building aflame.

"They're hugging me." Noble said. "They feel like a winter coat. They smell like candy."

The grist caressed Noble, how he fantasized the sanctuary of family to feel, an eiderdown of protective love. A stunning contrast to the dark and narrow halls, the rancid and rotted wood, and the smell of burned flesh that permeated the walls of the Home. Bees landed on his head and molded a bustling helmet. They descended onto his arms, his torso and mid-section, buzzed across and down his dirty pant legs, and covered his feet. The queen continued her violent protest inside the vial.

"Are you sure you're okay?" William yelled over the hum of the workers and drones that battled to protect their queen.

"They're tickling me." Noble's voice boomed with hard consonants and swallowed vowels. His accent, the burr of lower Manhattan poor.

Four bees popped into Noble's mouth, three flew out. He clamped his lips tight. The drone that remained inside tickled his tongue like dissolving ice.

Three boys from the Home lined up next to William, a grimy firing squad. They gaped and pointed, and when they realized it was Noble disguised by honeybees, only a single hazel eye exposed, they hooted and snorted.

Kid, ghostly thin, a few inches shorter than Noble, spit into the dirt. "Bee Freak."

"He should be in the mental ward," said another.

"Leave him alone," William said.

Kid squared off in front of William. "What was that?"

The baldheaded and gritty kids snickered and William shook. Others merged with the group. Kid's fist flew without warning, hit William, how he always attacked. A chump punch, they called it. From across the yard, Noble watched with one wide opened eye as William collapsed to the dirt from the single blow, his constitution weak with asthma. Kid kicked him in the ribs and William rolled to his side. A freckled boy drove his foot into William's stomach. William regurgitated the morning's gruel. His thighs curled into his chest. Blood dripped from his nose, colored his lips, and spread across his tongue, hot like a melting bullet. His throat closed, his lungs burned, each breath difficult to draw, hard to release.

Noble froze. A bee statue. More boys surrounded William. The Bee King throbbed like an anxious heart.

Kid lifted William by his ears, dropped him to the ground, and stood over him, fists clenched. "Who's going to protect you now? Your Bee King is a coward."

Flustered, Noble didn't know what to do. Bees covered him; the one in his mouth knocked against his tongue and his palate. Inside the vial, the queen continued her hysteria. Noble had been William's protector since he arrived at the Home and now was unable to help his only friend.

Another blow girded William around the waist and his body folded like a pocket knife. Kid jumped on to William.

Bag of nails! Think! Noble demanded of himself, and then remembered what Prokopovych instructed in the book on how to get bees off the body. He bent his knees and propelled into the air, shot up like a projectile fired from a cannon. Bees took flight, and Noble sprinted across the yard. His mouth opened and the lone drone flew out. The queen swung in the vial around his neck. Attack pheromones from the Nasanoff gland at the tip of the worker bees' abdomens emitted and sent the colony into a frenzy. A vibrating cavalry charged with Noble across the yard.

In a squall of bees, Noble grabbed Kid off William and threw him to the ground. One-by-one he tried to get the boys away from his friend, but there were too many to fight. The youngest ones fled, others circled. Kid seized a stick from the ground and ran at the Bee King. Boys followed.

Feet spread, back bent and squared, Noble braced for the impact when his attackers' expressions suddenly morphed from rage to fear. Kid in front, they turned and scampered toward the Home.

Bees attacked in a throbbing and organized fast-moving haze. The five-eyed bees viewed the boys in blues and purples. Two eyes saw harried movements, and three eyes sensed their intensities through light. In a dust bowl of scummy bodies and frayed clothes, the swarm rose and dove in a stunning and visual aria. The sound, like a fast-moving river cascading and changing direction over rocks. The female bees stung, left their stingers and guts in the arms, legs and faces of the boys, sacrificed their lives for their queen. Some females died from fatigue. Wings worn out from flying. Boys scurried and panted, cried, screamed and slapped at themselves. Their skin welted. They pushed each other aside. The smaller boys shoved to the ground. The bigger ones rushed into the Home to search for safety.

Noble helped William up from the ground. The older boy swayed. His right arm shook with a tremor. His breathing calmed.

"You hurt?" Noble asked.

William spit blood, wiped tears and blood and hash from his face. "Not any worse than usual."

Noble put his arm around his shoulder. "Let me get you to bed."

He shrugged him away. "I'll walk on my own. I don't want them to think they hurt me." He wheezed and took several wobbly steps.

Noble stayed by his side, poised to catch him should he fall.

William looked up, his nose thick and swollen. Dirt edged into the corners of his dark eyes. "What about you? Are you okay?"

"Not even a sting. The bees know there's no need to fear me."

"You're crazy." William's smile was bloody. He still had all his teeth.

Noble laughed, clutched the vial around his neck and opened it. The queen jetted to the large single comb suspended from the eaves of the Home. Thousands of surviving members of her colony followed.

Chapter Three

Behind the Home for Unwanted Boys, Kid and his gang of delinquents—each soiled so badly that one could hardly be discerned from another—lit matches and set flames to newspapers that smoked and burned. Fragments of copy floated and landed as ash on their skins. The boys grew bored and so flipped matches at each other. Their adrenaline raged after Noble's bee bearding, after Kid's attack on William. The swarm of bees that hadn't died in battle, retreated.

Inside the Home, Noble and William made their way through the hallways. Bees crunched under their feet. Boys too frightened to emerge crammed into rooms, onto and under beds, and into closets. The small ones hid in cabinets and dresser drawers and disappeared into dark hall corners, crying from the multitude of bee stings that covered their bodies. Heard but nary seen, and most certainly ignored.

Noble and William's room, eight-by-eight and cell-like, smelled of the boys' sweat, pungent filth. William fell heavy on the bed, his body bruised and his pride whipped. Noble dropped to the planked floor. He pulled Prokopovych's book toward him and read about the Domino Cuckoo bee. Genus: Thyreus lugubris.

William sipped water from a cup he and Noble shared. To place his lips on the edge of the glass brought pain. He winced from bruising along his ribs. To occupy his mind, he thumbed through pages of Harper's Weekly and became engrossed in an article. He turned to the Times, folded the front page, framed the headline, and tossed it to Noble. William rolled off the bed—more slowly than he would have liked as every muscle ached—got to his feet and shoved clothes into a worn sack. Shirts and pants, underwear and socks, grayed and malodorous cotton. The only water they had to wash clothes filtered from the outhouse.

Noble picked up the paper and read.

NEW YORK TIMES. April 15, 1861. President Lincoln Calls Northerners to Enlist to Redress Wrongs Already Long Endured

He looked to William. "You're enlisting."

William stuffed his last belonging into the sack. "It's going to be hard on both of us but I can only stay here another few weeks anyway. When I turn eighteen they'll kick me out." William threw the pack over his shoulder. He teetered from the weight of the bag.

Noble looked up at William. He didn't care if his friend saw the tears that pooled at the bottom of his eyes. "That's where you've been going these past few weeks."

William nodded. "Math and civics classes. I could become an officer."

Noble scooted the bee book aside and jumped up. "I'll enlist too."

"You're only fourteen."

"I'm stronger than you, and I look older."

"They say the war will last ninety days. When I get out, I'll have money. I'll rent a room. We'll live together and you'll go to school." William limped toward the door.

"Wait," Noble said. "I don't want you to go."

William stopped but didn't look back. "You'll be okay."

"How do you know?"

William kept his back to him. "I know this is hard. It's hard for me too. You have your bees, you'll be fine. I'll be back before you know it."

"If you go, I'm not going to be here when you return."

"Yes you will." He turned and offered a half-smile.

"We'll no longer be friends."

"We'll always be friends."

"You'll be nothing to me. I won't even remember your name."

William stepped toward him, hands outstretched.

Noble leaned back as if avoiding a weak punch. "Get away from me."

"Is this how you want to say goodbye?"

Noble turned away and fingered the empty vial around his neck. William wasn't going to leave. He would never do that. They were brothers. Like the bees who fought to the death, they had to stay together.

Noble listened for William's words, the ones he wanted to hear. You're right. I won't fight in the war. I'll stay with you. But words weren't to be, only footsteps and then the thump of the front door.

Too disheartened to get out of bed, the bee book his pillow, Noble hoped William would change his mind and return but minutes turned to one hour and then to two.

He forced himself to rise, unfurled his long and broad body, and decided to check on his bees in the backyard of the Home and then walk to City Hall Park. Maybe he could find a wealthy woman who needed help carrying packages, or a businessman who would pay him to bathe and feed his horses. Last week he made two cents scrubbing dung off the wheels of a carriage.

As he neared the rear of the Home, he recognized the roar of Kid's voice.

"Stay still, Idiot," Kid said.

Noble stepped out the back door. The scene before him took seconds to decode.

Most of the thirty boys gathered in the far corner of the yard. Their skin covered in welts from bee stings. They jeered and waved sticks and table legs. The bigger ones pushed the smaller ones aside, a melee of arms and legs. Noble looked across the yard in the direction they faced and saw Kid on the shoulders of the freckled boy, a bat in Kid's hands. Kid and the freckled boy wore multiple layers of shirts and pants. Hats on their heads. Fabric tied around their faces like they were train robbers. Clothes collected, no doubt, from others in the Home since neither Kid nor the freckled boy had all those garments.

Under all the clothes, Noble knew Kid's shoulder blades and hip bones protruded from his skeletal frame. He purged after almost every meal. He couldn't be fat, not like when he was younger. It showed his weakness and lack of will power. From throwing up so often, the enamel on the back of his teeth rotted. His breath perpetually acrid. Teeth that hadn't fallen out were loose.

The freckled boy, he was non-descript. Every boy, and no boy. Imagine him as you like.

"Closer, Stupid." Kid yelled.

The freckled boy stumbled forward, regained his balance. Kid remained atop his shoulders and swung the bat toward the hive. Whooosh. A swing, and a miss.

"What are you, scared? Get closer."

The freckled boy managed two steps forward. Kid positioned the bat behind his head and wound up to gain power. The boys cheered.

"Stop," Noble yelled.

The bat met the hive in an explosion of bees, honey and combs. The hive dropped to the ground in orange and gooey chunks. Bees swarmed. The freckled boy fell backward and Kid rolled to the ground, jumped up, and whacked hunks of the hive with the stick. The other boys merged and waved their weapons. Some hit the hive, some hit the ground, and some hit each other. The queen fled and most of her bees followed. Workers became trapped under Kid and the boys' clothes. Scared, some of the bees attacked and died.

Noble sprinted across the yard. The empty wooden bee vessel banged against his chest as he ran. Kid angled the bat toward Noble, who took the first blow across his forearm.

The boys surrounded them, chanted, "Kill, kill, kill."

Kid ripped the cloth from his face. He swung the bat and taunted, "Hey Bee King, are you feeling bee-wildered?"

With a large hand, Noble snatched the wood and wrangled it away. He crashed the bat into Kid's leg, heard the eerie crunch of bone, the yelp of the boy, but didn't stop. Over and over he swung the bat. The dense wood smacked Kid, broke bone, cut flesh.

Kid squirmed on the ground, bleeding, moaning. Noble stood over him, the palms of his hands cut and bloodied from the splintered bat. He brought the bat down across Kid's back. The cap of the barrel broke off, flew across the yard. Kid's body bucked. Noble aimed the next shot for Kid's head.

Chapter Four

Noble's father, murdered during a robbery at the family's bookstore. His mother, dead a short time later. According to a doctor she died from sepsis after stepping on a rusted nail, but Noble knew the truth. He recognized the symptoms of a broken heart. He had no other family. In a matter of weeks, he was unwanted and unloved.

Eleven years old, after two years surviving on the streets, Peter Stout caught Noble rummaging for food in a garbage bin behind his saloon, Five Corner Bar. Peter Stout seized him by the nape of his neck, a lion grabbing weakened prey, and flung him into a fence. Noble fought back, a gazelle grappling for his life.

Peter Stout pinned him to the ground. "You're a tough one. I'll teach you how to survive like a man and not like an animal." The old man jumped off of him.

Noble sat up, wiped blood from his nose, and spit red into the dirt. He knew what he'd have to do in exchange. Peter Stout wasn't the first Irish man with a thick brogue and liquor on his tongue to attempt to lure him off the streets. Noble had been approached by Tammany Hall heavies plenty of times. While the lure of food and a safe place to slumber was appealing, they all wanted him to do the same thing. Use his strong and wiry frame to sneak in and out of tight places, to steal, to set off pipe bombs, and to spy. And, use his green eyes, good looks, and puckish ways to connive and manipulate. As he grew taller and stronger, they'd want him to move up the ranks, which meant hurting people who didn't repay loans or who threatened the hierarchy of Five Points.

Noble wished he could ask his father for advice. His daily thought since his father's passing.

"Fuck off." He figured that was akin to what his father would say.

Minutes later, the police arrived and hauled him to the Home for Unwanted Boys. Noble fought like a fiend but was defenseless against Officer Timothy Byrne and the Metropolitans. He wasn't fooled into believing that going to the city orphanage was to be a good thing. He had come across many a boy who had been sentenced to the Home and described it as being as ruinous as living on the streets, minus freedom. And, Noble quickly learned, living at the Home was horrendous. He planned his escape daily, and was about to put his plan into action when he met William and found the bee book. Maybe, he figured, he'd hang around for a bit.

Noble's run-ins with Peter Stout continued. Thugs bumped him as he walked through Five Points. Boys from the Home slashed his arm with shanks. All came with the same admonition. Peter Stout says hello.

♦

In the back yard of the Home, Noble held the bat over Kid's head.

The shadow of the wood darkened one side of Kid's face. "You don't have the guts."

Was he right? Did he lack the nerve to kill? Noble lowered the bat.

"You're a coward," Kid rolled onto all fours. "Peter Stout was right about you. Good thing your father is dead. He'd be embarrassed to have you as his son."

Rage built in Noble's belly. He could do this, couldn't he? Transfer his fury to his hands, through the bat, and onto Kid's skull. Right all the wrongs of this big world, wouldn't it? Indeed, it would. He aimed for Kid's head.

The freckled boy tackled him to the ground. The bat flew out of Noble's hands. The vial whipped around his neck. Other boys jumped on top of him, slid around, over, and across him. Their sweat slippery and foul-smelling. With a roar, Noble shot up as if ridding himself of bees. He ran into the Home, and to his room. He needed no bag as he had little to pack. He grabbed the book on bees and the glass he and William shared, pushed his way past the boys in the hallway who cursed and mocked him, and ran out the front door.

His stomach churned as he turned on to Broadway. A few doors away and in front of the Colored Orphan Asylum, he sat under an old oak tree and sobbed. When his ducts were dried, he walked uptown to find William. He didn't look back at Prokopovych's book of bees or the drinking glass he left under the tree. He had read the book so many times, its lessons were embossed in his brain. He pressed the bee vial to his heart.

Chapter Five

Kid hadn't cried in seven years, not since he was brought to live at the Home for Unwanted Boys as a nine-year-old. More accurately, he hadn't wept when anyone could notice. He wanted to cry often but instead strutted and pushed his way around the Home like a pugnacious rooster. He wasn't the strongest boy at the Home, that accolade belonged to Noble. He wasn't the smartest boy either, that honor went to William, but he was the meanest. He had witnessed plenty of mean of which he was certain he could mimic. What the other boys didn't know was that his anger was initially improvised—he was a character in a staged play—and with each cruel word and smack of another boy he'd know he was only playing a part, until Kid could no longer tell his role-playing from his reality. He soon learned not to show emotions, at least not positive ones. No one cared. Not the other boys. Not Butchy who was too busy trying to prevent the Home was burning down (literally and figuratively). Not from the social workers or Doc B who visited and tried but could not break through the boy's emotional barriers. Anyone who had taken interest in him, who felt he had any value, had died or disappeared.

Ten years earlier, the police raided the whorehouse where he lived with his Cousin Amy Turner, who was the madam, her voice as large and booming as her body. When the police asked his name, the chunky red-haired six-year-old responded in earnest. "My name is Kid."

He had liked living at the brothel in Five Points, a two-story wood structure with numerous bedrooms to explore and hide in. The whores mothered him, clutched him in plump embraces, rocked and lullabied him to sleep. They fed him meats and vegetables, chocolates and mints. Kid's girth widened and the whores thought his belly rolls and chubby cheeks were too cute. Cousin Amy taught him to read. A red headed painted girl, who called herself Madam Curie, showed him science experiments. He watched water flow through leaves, and learned how to start fires without matches. One woman taught him how to groom a horse. Another whore took him to the library on her day off, where they read for eight hours, the only time he didn't think about food.

Johns patted him on the head and told him how lucky he was to spend time with such lovely ladies. One day he would understand, wink wink. They called him Kid, Johns and whores alike.

Where's Kid? Has someone fed Kid today? Kid is sleeping with me tonight. No, it's my turn, Kid sleeps with me.

He never questioned the moaning and creaking that seeped out from under closed doors, or the women who ended up with blinkers or ripped bodices, or when Cousin Amy brandished a gun and shot buck into the ass of a man who ran naked from the brothel. What Kid enjoyed most, what he recalled as he lay on the ground bleeding and broken by Noble and the bat, his knees pulled into this chest, his ribs burning, was the smell of incense that drifted along the hallways of the brothel. Lavender, patchouli, nag champa. As a teenager, Kid realized that the burning of candles and the plethora of oils and perfumes twenty-four hours a day were to hide the foul smells of the women and their patrons. But to him, as a six-year-old, the symphony of scents, the aroma of sulfur from the matches, and the fusion of body odor from the painted ladies, were akin to the arms of a fat woman that smothered and protected him.

On the ground, Noble standing over him, the bat raised over his head, it was painful for Kid to take a breath. He yearned to be saved by a fat whore.

After the raid, the police took Cousin Amy to jail and he was sent to live with Martin Walsh, a police officer, and his wife, Miss Charity. The first time Kid saw Officer Martin, he was mesmerized by the short and stocky man with thick black hair and a wad of tobacco between his lips and gums that darkened his teeth like coffee grinds. When Officer Martin wasn't on duty, his dress was slovenly and whiskey fumes rose from his pores. But when he put his uniform on, Kid believed Officer Martin could safely lead a battalion into battle. The officer was rarely home but Kid cherished the memories of the few things they did together. They tossed a ball, he let him hold his billy club and touch his unloaded Colt revolver, he took him for horse and buggy rides and showed him how to fix a wagon wheel. He was the closest Kid ever had to a father.

Miss Charity, emaciated, pale, several inches taller than her husband, possessed eye sockets as drawn and dark as rain clouds. The tip of her tongue rested between her chapped lips where her front teeth were missing. She never left the house. She smelled sweet like the pee of one of his fat whores when he used the outhouse after she did.

Officer Martin and Miss Charity named Kid Silas after their infant son, dead a few weeks from a head injury after the infant fell out of his cradle. At least that's what Miss Charity told Kid had happened.

Two months after he began to live with the Walshes, Kid and Miss Charity sat side-by-side in the front parlor of the shotgun home. Kid's wide frame took up three-quarters of the loveseat. Miss Charity's narrow shell covered the rest of the couch. She wore a hand-stitched high-collared black dress. He wore trousers and a shirt Miss Charity had sewn, although his girth was too wide for the waistband, which was open. On the wood table in front of them sat a white block of cheese and a bottle of homemade red wine.

Kid wiggled to get comfortable on the poorly stuffed sofa. The rough texture poked through the thin fabric of his pants.

Miss Charity carved a slice of cheese and fed it to him. "Don't fidget."

The cheese was creamy, delicate and delicious. She handed him a glass of wine, which he chugged. He licked the bouquet of grapes from his lips. His belly was warm. He was fairly content.

Miss Charity fingered a tattered Bible. "I thought we would read Isaiah." She fed him another hunk of cheese.

Six-year-old Kid's mouth filled with the zest of goat's milk, and with the honey of wine. He reached for more.

Miss Charity smacked his hand. "You're fat."

"I'm hungry." He protested.

"You can have another piece of cheese but then no supper."

Kid considered his options. "I'll wait for supper, ma'am."

"Good. Now, Isaiah." She opened the Book.

"Can I read to you today, ma'am?"

She hit him on the leg. "No."

He recoiled. He wanted so bad to read, to learn, to meet other children and to make friends. He wanted to go to a library and sit cross-legged in a corner next to stacks of books taller than he, a fortress of words. He had a lot of friends at the brothel, even if they were mawks, but none here. Only Miss Charity, and while she said they were friends, she didn't feel like a real friend since she never taught him about anything, but the Bible.

"Can we go out and buy other books?" he dared to ask.

Miss Charity took a large gulp of wine. "Books are the work of the devil and his disciples. You will read the Bible."

"Then we can go to the library and borrow books for free. I've been there before. Trixie took me."

"Trixie? Who is Trixie?"

"My friend." He became animated thinking of the women at the brothel. "She was pretty and had bright red hair..." Miss Charity's glower unnerved him but he carried on. "...her fingernails were the same color as her hair and her eyes were purple and black depending upon if it was night or day..." His voice trailed off. He put his hands in his lap and his head down.

She said, "Look at me."

He raised his head. She picked up the carving knife and waved it at him. Kid did not flinch. She had waved knives at him before, and chipped plates and long scarves and the Bible and anything else she might be holding.

"You think I'm going to hurt you?"

"No, ma'am."

"Because if I wanted to hurt you I could." She slashed the knife through the air in an X. "Baby Silas thought I was going to hurt him too."

Kid wanted to ask, Wasn't Silas but a pap lap? How could a tiny baby have thoughts? But he said nothing. He wished to jump up from the couch but feared her reaction. He looked toward the door. Would Officer Martin be home soon? Whenever he came through the door, he yearned to run to him and become entangled in his legs to become another limb he could not leave behind.

"He's not going to save you," Miss Charity said. "When he's not here, Officer Martin doesn't exist. Do you understand what I'm saying, Silas? You think he's at work and he's a police officer but once he leaves here and you don't see him anymore he's not real."

Kid tried to grasp what she said. Does that mean the brothel never happened? Does that mean Cousin Amy and Trixie and Madam Curie are not coming to my rescue?

Miss Charity touched the point of the knife to his shirt, over his heart. "How do you know Officer Martin is real when he's not here?"

"I smell him." The scent of Officer Martin lingered for Kid. Wood, milk, sugary and sour.

"How do you know he's real when he's here?"

"I can see him."

She laughed. "You think you're smart, don't you? You want to go to the library? Is that what you want?"

"Yes, ma'am."

She removed the knife from his chest. An emphatic, "No."

"Then can I go to school?" His eyes widened. Where had he gotten the gumption to keep challenging her?

She leaned into him. Her breath hot and rancid. "You want to go to school?"

Kid yearned to jump off the couch again. Sitting so close to her was scary even without her crazy talk. The veins on her arms and hands outlined cavities where ugly blue devils hid. The lines on her face were hideaways for monsters.

"Go on." She poked him with the knife again. "Tell me why you want to go to school."

"I want to learn about everything." He spoke haltingly. "Science and math like Madam Curie showed me...history and reading like Cousin Amy taught me..."

Miss Charity ran the blade over her fingers, cutting the tips from the index to the pinkie. Kid jumped up but she grabbed his arm and pulled him down. Dark red blood seeped on to her dress and his trousers.

She drove the bloodied knife into the block of cheese. "It's too dangerous to go outside. Do you know who is out there?"

Of course, he did. Nice, fat ladies with paint on their faces and fingernails.

"No, I don't." His voice was hoarse.

"No one, that's who. The only thing that is real is this." She patted the Bible. "Don't you agree?"

He wanted to tell the truth. Wasn't lying bad? Wasn't that how you went to hell? Isn't that what Miss Charity had told him the Bible said? But he didn't know what the truth was anymore. He only knew one thing for certain.

"I think," he spoke slowly, "I really want to go to school."

She slapped him.

His cheek burned.

She cuffed him again.

He had never been hit before, not in the face, not anywhere on his body. He recalled men smacking women at the brothel, the women hitting them back, Cousin Amy retrieving the shotgun, the other whores cheering their sister on until the man fled, the celebration afterward.

Kid slapped Miss Charity across the face.

Her pigeon face turned red, her jaw slacked. She punched him in the side, pulled him in to her lap, pulled down his pants, and beat him on his bare backside and legs with an open hand. She pulled the knife from the cheese and firmly gripped the sharp end in her palm and hit him with the handle. She struck him over and over until his bottom became raw. Blood from her hand mixed with blood from his rear.

As Miss Charity pounded, she nattered about witches and evil spirits and how they never should have named him Silas after their dead son because now he possessed that boy's demons.

"Stop, stop, I'm sorry." Kid cried. "I don't want to go to school. I hate school."

"I must exorcise that demon child from you. I carried that devil for nine months. I know the evil he is capable of. Kneel!"

His bottom and the backs of his thighs raw, Kid dropped to his knees. Tears drenched his face. He looked up at her and smelled the cheese that sat on a side table, the cheese that was covered with blood. The smell of the soft curd, that had a few minutes before been glorious and soothing, revolted him.

"Do you want me to tell Officer Martin you slapped me?" she asked.

"You hit me first." He offered meekly.

Her open hand smashed into his cheek again. "If Officer Martin knew how you treated me, he would beat you too. He might even shoot you."

"I'm sorry." He repeated.

"Shut up."

Slap. Slap. Slap.

He cried. His face screwed into an abstract of cheeks and a mouth, a nose and eyes, red and runny.

She put her thumb into his mouth. "Shut up. Suck this."

Stunned, he looked up at her.

"Go on."

His lips closed on her finger. He didn't dare bite her. Her nail was long, sharp and dirty. It scratched the roof of his mouth.

◆

Two years passed, Officer Martin came home early one night and caught Miss Charity with her thumb in Kid's mouth.

"Wait outside," Officer Martin ordered.

Kid sat on the stoop and listened to their screams, threats and curses. He didn't flinch at the sound of the first gunshot, or the second.

The police reasonably deduced Miss Charity fired the first round from the Colt revolver that pierced Officer Martin's head from the rear and tore off the top of his skull. The second shot, self-inflicted, was an entry hole above her right ear, no exit.

The whorehouse had been boarded up. Cousin Amy was dead from yellow fever. Madam Curie's shriveled body was found on a street corner in Five Points and was sent to the pauper's cemetery. Trixie had become a school teacher in Colorado. The authorities laughed when the boy asked if he could go live with her. Eight-year-old Silas Walsh was taken to the Home for Unwanted Boys. When asked his name, he said, "Kid."

Chapter Six

In the back yard of the Home, dead bees littered the rocks and detritus. The bees that were breaths away from demise twitched like dusty eyes. Honey oozed from the rubble of combs.

Sprawled on his back, body bruised and fingers sprained, some broken, Kid swung his arms. "Don't touch me."

The freckled boy moved again to lift him. Bees crunched under his feet like seashells.

Kid kicked. "Get away from me."

The boy backed out of the circle of Kid's frenzy. Their leader proven fallible, one by one, then in twos and threes, the other boys left to see what else the day had to offer, until it was only the freckled boy and Kid.

"Leave me alone." Kid groaned.

The freckled boy knelt and whispered in Kid's ear. "What's my name?"

Kid thought, I don't know my own name. He shook his head.

The freckled boy plunged his knee into Kid's bruised ribs, and ran.

Kid gasped, and hoped his next breaths would be his final requiem. Pain burned throughout his body, more unbearable than a hot iron pressed to his skin, a sensation he had experienced from when he stole a case of wine from the rear of Five Corner Bar, Peter Stout's establishment.

Do not cry!

Prostrate, his right cheek and chin wedged in the dirt. The bat Noble had used to clobber him lay nearby. Kid's entire being throbbed and swelled and he felt he knew what it would be like to be a ninety-year-old man, although certain he would never live nearly that long. The memory of the smell of the spoiled cheese nauseated him. A few bewildered bees staggered by his lips, wounded, then rolled to their sides, dead.

Inches from his nose, a drone floated in a puddle. Its wings trembled. Moving slowly, as that was all he could manage, Kid brushed the bee into the palm of his hand and blew gently on the insect. Its wings dried and then fluttered.

"Don't go," Kid said.

Chapter Seven

Five Points was an embarrassment to thirty-four-year-old Alice Black as Night. Her favorite author Charles Dickens had visited nineteen years earlier in 1842, the year her daughter, Sarah High Yellow, was born. He wrote about the neighborhood in the periodical, *American Notes*: "Debauchery has made the very houses prematurely old. See how the rotten beams are tumbling down, and how the patched and broken windows seem to scowl dimly, like eyes that have been hurt in drunken frays." Although she never met Dickens, and never would, Alice was mortified that he likened her home to sin, decay and booze.

Despite this disappointment, Alice navigated the ragged streets with as much confidence and grace she could muster, even along Mulberry Bend, among the slaughterhouses, past the scruffy boys and men who wielded bats and vacant stares, among the tenements that housed the poor for whom slumming was named. Act like she was without restriction and that she shall be. She forced her steps to be light and gay like the gait of the free woman she legally was.

Behind her vigilant eyes sparkled wisdom. From her pounding heart, goodness radiated, not naiveté but an honest-to-goodness goodness, as if the hard times and bad times were no times. She was an English teacher who long ago stopped regretting her one-night stand with the Irish white man, Peter Stout. Only fifteen years of age at the time, the forbidden foray gave her the greatest gift of her life, Sarah.

Peter Stout, now nearing the fourth decade of his life, was a saloonkeeper, active in Tammany Hall and a low-level member of the Tweed Ring, Boss Tweed's group that controlled New York City's finances. Not bad for an Irish immigrant who wanted to be an actor since he was a boy but who had discovered Five Points to be a stage like none other. Peter Stout liked to think his status brought respect, but on a moonlit night when he scrubbed bloodstains away in the alley behind Five Corner Bar and recited *Hamlet*, Peter Stout delighted that respect and fear were often confused.

He had many children and might recognize some by sight. Bred from sturdy, well-meaning black women, their pregnancies signaled the end of his affiliation with them. He was building a new generation, comingling the white skin, vivaciousness, high intellect, and hard drinking ways of the Irish male, with the blackness, sharp intuition, unfailing belief in family, and determination to succeed of the African-American woman. His children would one day rule the world, at least the ones who looked white. The others, who cared what happened to them. The only thing wrong with New York City, Peter Stout believed, was its membership in the Union. Peter Stout was a proud copperhead.

On Sarah's thirteenth birthday, her mother brought her to Five Corner Bar and instructed her to peek in the front window at the handsome Caucasian who wiped the condensation from sweating beer cans off the countertop.

"That is your father," Alice said. "Stay away from him."

Sarah noted the curve of his nose and the square of his chin, and saw herself in him. She hoped the resemblance went no further than facial features. Embarrassed by the gossip she'd overhear about him, she never spoke of their blood relation but it made no difference. Everyone in Five Points knew.

Many who lived in the neighborhood were given a nickname. Some called him Peter Stout for the beer he served, others labeled him Peter Knuckles for his permanently bruised hands. Sarah preferred to think of him as Peter Doesn't Exist. It wasn't exactly recalled how this nicknaming tradition began. Some believed it was an offshoot for the way things were done back home in Ireland, but mostly the locals didn't know and didn't care, they just had a good time labeling people.

As an adult, when Sarah walked home from the school where she taught along with her mother, she often spotted a man or woman who resembled her. Long narrow noses, thick eyebrows and lips, and yellowboned. Their eyes would meet and Sarah wondered if that was her half-sibling, curious if the stranger speculated the same. She continued to walk, certain any exchange would be awkward.

"Never date a man from Five Points," Alice told Sarah. "He could be your half-brother."

Sarah wasn't interested in the boys from Five Points. Her dreams ballooned much larger than the sewer drenched and pig roaming streets. She had been saving her earnings as an elementary school marm to attend acting school in Boston. She finally had stashed enough away. All she had to do was find the gumption to tell her mother. The train ticket from New York City to Boston was folded and stuffed in a pair of stockings in her top dresser drawer.

Every Friday morning at six, as the church bells clanked, Alice and Sarah purchased fish from Jenny Big Stink. The earlier Alice and Sarah arrived to choose the fish, the better the selection. On this day, the mid-April sun fought its way around gray and heavy clouds. Mother and daughter strolled in silence, the sun climbing in the horizon, their coats buttoned tightly across their chests. Their hoop skirts swung and made it difficult to walk side-by-side, and often pulled them off balance. Ribbons adorned their bonnets. Despite the sharp differences in their skin colors, Alice as black as her favorite licorice, Sarah the light color of the beeswax sprayed on licorice to make it shine, their beauty was renowned in Five Points. When she was younger, Sarah often wished her skin darker, prejudiced within her own community for being able to pass for white. As she aged and realized her passion for the theater, she was silently pleased with the advantages her appearance afforded her.

At the convergence of Cross, Orange and Anthony Streets, dissected and oddly angled to create two triangular plats at one corner that then gave Five Points its name, Alice and Sarah trekked around pedestrian, carriage and cab traffic that started to surge. New York City streets, a never-ending carousel of pickups and deliveries, of people and of products.

"Wait." Sarah placed her hand on her mother's arm. Tell her of your dream now, she demanded of herself. For goodness sake, do it already!

Alice kept walking. "Are you okay?"

"I need to discuss something." Sarah's courage disappeared as quickly as it had reached its zenith. "It can wait."

"Now's as good as ever. Go on."

Sarah clenched her fist, as she had seen vaudeville actress Cissy Fitzgerald do on stage. "You know how I like to sing in church, Mama? And whenever Father Williams asks for a volunteer to read I'm always the first to raise my hand."

"You've always had a flair for the dramatic."

Sarah smiled and twirled. Her confidence built. "I like to perform, Mama."

Alice laughed. "Okay, okay. I know. Calm down. You've been putting on skits and singing since you were small."

"I want to be an actress," she blurted.

Alice patted her arm. "That's wonderful. It's a great hobby. Perhaps you can teach drama at your school. I am sure your students—"

"I'm going to acting school. In Boston."

There. She said it. Out for the world to hear, or at least her Mama who was bigger than any world could ever be.

Alice stopped. Her deep brown eyes turned steely. Her chin, rigid. "How are you going to do that when you teach in New York?" The words dangled in the space between mother and child.

"When you took me to see Cissy Fitzgerald at Wallack's Theatre last week, I knew I had to be like her. She was so beautiful. Did you see how the audience stood at the end and cheered? She made everyone happy. I want to make people happy."

Alice walked on, silent.

"Mama, please say something." Sarah urged.

"Oliver Twist was sold to the undertaker," Alice said. "We don't always get to do what we want in life."

"Oliver escaped, didn't he?"

Alice stopped. "Are you saying you need to escape?"

"No, no, of course not. I'm only following my dream, and it would be temporary."

"Your father wanted to be an actor," Alice said.

"My father?"

"Forget I said that."

They walked again. Hoop skirts crinkled as they bumped.

"I've given my notice at school." Sarah spoke softly. "My last day is next week. I've saved money. I've bought my train ticket."

Alice bore her eyes into Sarah's. "I won't let you do that."

"I'm nineteen years old, Mama. I don't want to say I don't need your permission but..."

Alice looked across the street. Between passing carts and taxies, and around people rushing to work. She regarded Jenny Big Stink's fish cart. Wooden planks, nailed and roped together, crisscrossed on two steel bars and four thirty-inch, twelve spoke wood wheels. Bales of hay sat atop the planks. On top of the bales was a large metal box filled with blocks of ice and rows of slimy and scaly fish, some whole, some sliced or cut into chunks.

"I hope she has catfish today," Alice said. "John Coal loves it. He's coming to dinner tonight and bringing his nephew."

"I'm not interested in Simon Black Cat."

"He's a good man. He's educated and has a steady job. Maybe Jenny has shrimp today."

Sarah grabbed her mother's hands. They were soft, the hands of an intellect and not of a laborer. Her fingers were long and thin like her own. Veins jutted from her knuckles to her wrist like a chicken's foot.

Their eyes met again. Brown upon brown, similar oval shaped lids and elegant lashes.

Sarah felt she gazed upon herself as if she looked in a mirror, plus fifteen years. "I don't want to grow old knowing I didn't try."

Alice turned away.

"I didn't mean that you're old. I don't know what to say, Mama. Please look at me. Can we start over?"

Alice turned back to her.

"I'll only be gone for a year," Sarah said. "Then I'll come home. All the acting jobs are in New York."

"Why can't you go to school here? There has to be an acting school in our city."

Sarah looked down, and mumbled. "I can't get in."

Alice lifted Sarah's chin. "That acting school in Boston let black folk in?"

Sarah shook her head, unsurprised by her mother's astuteness.

"Then how come you can get into a school in Boston but not one at home?"

"Because everyone knows me here," Sarah spewed. "They know who my mama is. They know who my papa is. No one knows me in Boston."

Alice cupped Sarah's cheek. "You're not thinking rationally."

"I am."

"This is a foolish decision."

"It's my dream."

"You can dream in New York."

"I'm going to Boston, Mama."

Alice's eyes narrowed. The lines around her face deepened. "If you must go, go as a black woman and not pretending to be white so you can get into acting school."

Sarah swung her head around. "Keep your voice down."

"I will not."

Sarah threw her shoulders back. "I'm an adult and..."

"And what?"

"I'm half white. There, I said it. I'm half white and I'm nineteen and you can't tell me what to do anymore."

Alice leaned toward her, eyes cold. "When you live on your own and have a rude daughter of your own that's when I'll stop telling you what to do."

"I've made up my mind."

"To be a white woman? Do you want your Irish blood to define who you are? You're black. That's how I raised you." Alice shook her head. "I'm not letting you make a bad decision."

Anger overtook Sarah's fear of disappointing her mother. "And what about your bad decision? You were a teenager when you got in with Peter Stout..."

Alice's hand rose quickly, too quick for Sarah to defend. The slap across Sarah's face stung. Diamond-shaped tears crowned Sarah's eyes and dropped to her cheeks.

"The only place you're going is across the street to buy fish," Alice said.

"But Cissy Fitzgerald was so beautiful up on the stage...and Oliver Twist escaped the undertaker— "

"And became a thief." Alice pointed toward Jenny's cart. "Fish. Now."

This hadn't gone any of the ways Sarah had imagined, and she thought she had considered every scenario from her mother's encouragement to her disappointment. Certainly not a slap across the face in the middle of the street. Her mother had never hit her before. But then, Sarah had never been so rude. She headed to the fish cart, determined not to cry, determined to go to Boston no matter what.

Chapter Eight

The white apron Jenny Big Stink tied around her engorged belly was splattered with blood and covered in fish guts. Never fully able to scrub the scales from under her nails and pick out the smatterings of fin and meat from between her rolls of fat, the smell followed her wherever she went. Such a strong odor, it permanently coated the insides of her nostrils. Like her father, she was adept with bamboo and string, able to hook most fish that showed even a mild interest in her line. Like her mother, who had taken in neighbors' clothes to sew and grew it into a business employing eight women, Jenny was a businesswoman. A single female who made a good, honest living and who didn't need a man. A woman by her side, now that would be nice but Jenny Big Stink didn't believe her fortunes could extend so far.

Alice and Sarah walked toward her, daughter three steps ahead of mother, bent forward at the waist, a sour expression on the child's face. Jenny wiped her sweaty brow with her forearm, left behind a streak of gunk on her face, and chewed the skin on the inside of her mouth. Esther, her old mule, pulled at hay with golden decayed teeth that chomped in a circular motion. His big triangular ears twitched as if they eavesdropped on all around him. The figure of twenty-one-year-old Metropolitan police officer Timothy Byrne reflected in the mule's dark eyes, the copper's hips distorted like in a fun house mirror.

At the wagon, Sarah rose on her tiptoes and looked inside the bed. Alice stood close, quiet, her eyes red and swollen, her lips pinched together.

Jenny always looked forward to Alice and Sarah's weekly sojourn to her fish cart. She enjoyed their friendly conversations and Esther coveted their scratches between his ears. But on this morning, Jenny wished mother and daughter would get the hell away.

◆

Alice's silence gnawed at Sarah like a regret. Sarah tried to ignore the lump in her throat and the sick feeling in her stomach and concentrate on Jenny's wagon. She hated the way the fish's vacant eyes seemed to plead for help, disliked the sight of splattered fish blood mixed with melting ice, and at times was repulsed by the smell that wafted off the back of the wagon. Sarah knew it was vital to assess Jenny's catches with her nose as much as her eyes. With the cool weather, she detected no smell of rot, only the sharp aroma of fish, the sweet draft of hay, and the pong of decay from Esther's teeth and gums. Sarah felt so saddened by the fight she had with her mother, she didn't even feel like saying hello to the old mule.

Sarah surveyed the fish, which she planned to sauté with butter and garlic. Maybe after a nice meal she could have a more civilized conversation with her mother and the result could be more like one of the scenarios she had hoped for. Not entirely pleasant but also not a slap across the face.

"What do you have today?" Sarah asked.

Jenny Big Stink didn't answer. Sarah looked around the wagon. She and her mother were the only customers. It was the reason they came so early.

Sarah pointed to a white chunk of meat. "Is that sturgeon?"

"Go away," The fish seller whispered but made no eye contact. "Now." Jenny spoke through gritted teeth.

Sarah looked to her mother who directed her gaze across the street, the track of her eyes as singular as the sight of a pistol. Sarah observed Byrne fifteen feet away. Everyone in Five Points knew the Irishman. Straight-backed and darkly dressed, blue coat buttoned to the top, cinched at the waist, and draped to above his knees. Black saliva-polished boots pulled snug over his pants to above his calves. A square cap sat askew on his head. His gold badge, buttons and belt buckle shone when sunbeams leapt in between breaks of rushing clouds. Then, shade moved over him.

Jenny realigned perfectly aligned catfish. "Buy your fish elsewhere."

"We've bought fish from you every Friday for years," Sarah said.

Alice nodded toward the officer. "Don't let him intimidate you. Five Points is free."

"Go where your people shop."

"We don't have people," Alice said. "We want to buy fish like we've always done and we'll be on our way."

"I can't sell to you today." Jenny widened her eyes, pleading with the women to leave.

Alice folded her arms over her chest. "You'll have to sell to us because we're not leaving until you do."

Sarah eyed her mother. It was hard to stay angry at her, even after she slapped her. Alice was soft spoken much of the time, yet tenacious and stubborn when necessary. As much as Sarah wanted to continue playing the petulant child, a breeze of confidence swept through her followed by showers of pride. Her mother was amazing and Sarah was sure she would acquiescence to her move to Boston once she grew accustomed to the idea. She'd come home every weekend and John would keep her mother company while Sarah was away. Sarah held back a wide smile. She was going to go to acting school in Boston with her mother's blessing, she knew it was going to happen. Even Officer Byrne's steps in their direction could not dampen Sarah's sudden hopeful mood.

"Are these people bothering you, Jenny?" Red hairs from Byrne's bushy moustache curled into his mouth.

"No, Sir."

"Move along." He swung his baton on a leather strap around his wrist.

"We are respectable citizens," Sarah said. "We were born and raised in New York. Right here in Five Points."

"Did you hear Fort Sumter was attacked and there's going to be a war?" He didn't wait for their response. "New York City is going to secede from the United States. The copperheads are going to make sure that happens."

Sarah wasn't surprised to hear Byrne invoke the copperheads, a despicable radical wing of Northern democrats who sided with the south. Byrne was known to be in the pocket of Boss Tweed and Tammany Hall.

"We are free blacks," Alice said. "Free since the day we were born."

Byrne slapped the thick end of his billy club in the palm of his hand. "Shouldn't be no such thing as a free black."

Sarah moved toward him. "How dare you."

Alice positioned herself between her daughter and the officer. The crinoline of mother and daughter's skirts mashed. Alice considered her three choices. One, two, three. (1) Walk away, (2) stand up for their rights as free women, or (3) succumb to the fall out of Lincoln's war.

What example would she be to her daughter if she didn't choose number two?

"We have as much right to shop here as anyone," Alice said.

The officer jabbed his baton into the front of Alice's wide skirt. "Are you disturbing the peace?"

Jenny Big Stink grabbed a whole fish, wrapped it in paper, and shoved it toward Alice. "No charge. Take it."

Byrne slapped Jenny's hand and the fish flopped to the ground. The mule snorted and flung his head. Passersby stopped to watch. Their skin colors fair. Some men were hugged by aprons, they were the shopkeepers, milliners and blacksmiths. Others were dressed formally and carried top hats and canes. They were the lawyers, notaries and landowners. Women, who wore crinoline skirts like Alice and Sarah, walked their children to school, and stopped to watch. The children kicked at the ground. Dust rose to their knickers.

Sarah faced the officer. "We would like to speak with your supervisor."

Byrne's lower lip trembled. "Oh no, ma'am. Please don't do that."

Sarah searched his face. Was he playing a joke on them?

Alice reevaluated their choices, and grabbed Sarah's arm. There was no way out of this without someone getting hurt, and wasn't her first responsibility to protect her child?

"Let's go, Sarah. You can try and hide from it but you'll always be a black woman."

"Please, ma'am." The officer held out his hands in mock prayer. "Please don't get me in no trouble with my massa."

Laughter and rising mumbles coursed through the crowd.

"Darkies go home." A woman yelled.

A man who wore a heavy leather apron, the blacksmith's uniform, added, "We're tired of you people taking our jobs."

Sarah was shocked by the actions of the officer and by the mood of the crowd. She had experienced pockets of prejudice but never blasts of hatred. She looked at the people who gathered and recognized many of them from the neighborhood, including one man whose facial features favored her own.

Jenny Big Stink said, "This isn't necessary, Officer Byrne. I want to give them the fish. No charge."

Byrne pointed the meaty end of the stick at her. "You will do no such thing."

"Monkey lover," a woman yelled at Jenny.

Alice pulled on Sarah's arm. "Let's go."

Incensed, she shook her mother's hand away. "This is not right. We have money. We're free. My grandfather owned a tobacco shop on Liberty Street."

"Go south where you belong, cotton-pickers," a man yelled.

Several shouted in agreement. The crowd gesticulated toward the fish wagon. The mule stepped back, tossed his head up and down.

Black faces outlined the edges of the crowd. John Coal, a mountain of a man and Alice's lover, and Simon Black Cat, smaller than his uncle, lean and muscular, pushed their way toward the front.

"Stupid blacks." Peter Stout spat.

Sarah looked at him, a quick pilfered glare. She turned away as soon as their eyes met.

"C'mon, Sarah. Let's go." Alice tried to persuade her again. "We'll file a complaint at the police department."

"You'll do no such thing." Byrne pushed Alice.

She staggered back, lost her balance and fell to the dirt.

Sarah rushed to help. "Leave her alone."

Byrne lunged toward Sarah, his stick raised in the air.

Jenny thrust the package at Alice. "Take the fish."

"Don't touch my daughter." Alice charged the officer.

"Take the fish," Jenny screamed.

Byrne crashed the club down on Alice's head. She teetered and collapsed. Blood poured from a slash across her left temple.

"Mama," Sarah yelled.

The whites scattered and a new crowd hurried forward. Their skin colors were yellowbone, redbone, brown, and black. Like the white men who had stood witness a moment earlier, the dark-toned shopkeepers, bookshop owners, and tanners wore aprons. The women, crinoline skirts. Dark skinned children shuffled their feet in the dirt. Clouds converged. Big thick drops rained on Five Points. John and Simon rushed toward Alice.

John yelled, "Out of our way! Let us through."

Sarah ran to her mother, cradled her, and screamed, "Call Doc B!"

Byrne strolled toward City Hall Park.

Chapter Nine

In her clinic at the five-pointed intersection, a few doors down from Five Corner Bar, Doctor Elizabeth Blackwell pushed a curved needle into the skin above an inebriated fellow's knee, and pulled the silk thread through. Not all that different than mending a garment, only flesh was tougher than most fabrics.

British born, pasty-hued, and the first woman to receive a medical degree in the United States, Doc B tended to the impoverished of Five Points and volunteered weekly at the Home where she treated the boys for runny noses, broken bones, typhus, yellow fever, cholera, and the pock. It had been her idea to require all boys at the Home to shave their heads to circumvent the epidemic of lice. Her brown hair was braided and tied back, long strands of gray twined with the brown. She was long-limbed, thick-skinned, swift, and strong.

As she finished suturing, Jenny Big Stink burst into her clinic.

"Alice Black as Night has been hit over the head."

Doc B nodded toward Martha, the volunteer-in-charge of the clinic, who stepped toward the drunk man with the sutured wound. Doc B grabbed a bag and dashed for the door. Jenny followed. Outside, Sarah, John Coal, and Simon Black Cat were half-a-block away. John carried Alice. Her head thrown back, her limp body bounced with John's fast-moving steps.

Doc B held the door to the clinic open. "Put her over there."

Fifteen cots were stationed five feet apart in a large open area. Most of the beds were occupied. Two rooms in the rear had been left intact with walls and a door. One was for patients with infectious diseases such as cholera. The other was the kitchen, which had a large sink, a stove for boiling water to sterilize instruments, and a system of pulleys for raising and lowering buckets filled with water.

Urine, feces, blood, and pus peppered the air like the remnants of an open-mouthed sneeze. Towels and blankets draped over drying racks, their original colors stripped by bleach. With Doc B as the only trained professional, the volunteer clinic staff worked tirelessly and diligently, and attended the many patients as best they could.

Doc B pointed. "Bed number six."

John laid Alice on the cot. John, Simon, Jenny, and Sarah stood around her.

"Move back." Doc B pushed to get close to Alice.

Jenny grabbed Sarah's hand. "I'm sorry. I didn't think…"

Sarah stared, in shock. Simon glared at Jenny.

"Byrne threatened me and Esther…I didn't think anyone would get hurt…"

"What if somebody did that to you?" Simon scowled. "You white people all think it can't happen to you but it can. Trust me. It can."

"Simon, don't be like Byrne and the rest of them," John cautioned. "Jenny, be on your way."

"But Alice…maybe I can help…"

"Go." Simon punched his hand into his fist. The slap as menacing as a gun blast.

Chapter Ten

Noble slogged his way uptown along Broadway. At Union Place he cut over to Fourth Street and trekked parallel to the Harlem Railway. Along the four-mile hike from Five Points to Jones's Wood, one hundred and thirty-two acres of farmland overlooking the East River, his feet and ankles caked with mud, manure and garbage. Intermittent drops of rain rolled into quick and numerous droplets that cut like a shiv on his arm. Dirt from his face, bare chest, shoulders, and back ran off his body.

Around him, horses plodded along the damp earth, pulled carriages, kicked up water and splashed couples who rushed arm-in-arm. The men, bedecked in morning suits and frock coats, accessorized with top hats and black gloves. The women, draped in dresses, sported short white gloves and bonnets tipped forward. Some pedestrians gripped curved wooden handles and scurried solo with umbrellas overhead. Rain hit the opened and stretched fabrics with rhythmic beats, syncopated with the clomp-clomp of horses' hooves.

Noble thought of Kid, who he had left bleeding on the ground in the back of the Home. He was sure he had broken several of his bones, and trembled when he realized how close he came to killing him.

"I am not a murderer." He spoke to no one, and no one spoke to him.

Noble traversed East Forty Second Street and cut over to Third Avenue. Jones's Wood was the nucleus for working-class New Yorkers looking to escape the urban sprawl of downtown without traveling too far. Succumbing to pressure due to the city's northward growth, the owners of Jones's Wood had leased part of the land for a hotel and other amenities. Noble and William had plotted to sneak into the dance hall or the shooting range. When word came that Lincoln needed a recruitment center in Manhattan, the Jones family donated land to the Union. Tents were erected, and Jones's Wood became overrun with boys and men looking to sign up for the fight between the States. Some in the name of freedom, others for the promise of food, clothes, a place to sleep, and a stipend.

The main entrance to Jones's Wood was framed by two boulders. A pole was wedged into the ground with an American flag atop that hung limp on the cold and windless day. Gray clouds suggested rain would continue its descent.

An immense tent constructed of black tarp, stretched and held down by ropes and pegs, was the epicenter of recruitment. It was the largest structure Noble had ever seen, at least twice as big as City Hall Park. What made it more marvelous, he thought, was that the camp could be taken down, moved, and erected again anywhere there was space.

A long line of ragged hopefuls snaked into and around the tent. No one seemed concerned by the rain that now fell with ease. As he took everything in—I am about to enlist in the United States Army and fight for freedom! —the pace of the blood that pumped through his veins, around his heart, and to his brain, accelerated. He placed his hands over his heart and pressed the bee vial to his chest. He had never been part of something so grand.

Overwhelmed, he stopped, sat on a large rock, and calmed his breathing. He couldn't lose sight of why he was there. He had to find William, he had to enlist, they had to fight together.

"Are you okay, son?" a voice called.

The tallest man in the world stood before him. He wore dark blue pants with red stitching on the sides, such fine sit-upons they looked like they could march without a body. A gray-blue coat flared over his hips. The buttons on his coat glistened. A sword in a scabbard hung at an angle off his belt.

Noble stood, his head spun, he sat again. "I think I'm dying."

The man laughed. "I don't think anyone died from excitement. That's how I felt when I first signed up. Whoever thought an oyster farmer from Long Island could become a colonel for the Union army?"

"You're a colonel?" Noble jumped up, and stood at attention.

The man laughed. Brown, thick hair jutted sideways from under his red and blue square cap. He was younger than Noble first thought, maybe the same age as Butchy, and not as tall as Noble initially believed.

"At ease. You're not enlisted yet, son. I'm Colonel Abraham Duryee. You are?"

He relaxed his posture, some. "Noble Jennings."

"That's a fine name. How old are you?"

"Eighteen, Sir."

The colonel examined Noble with his eyes, up and down, with judgment, like how Noble had seen the wealthy do at slave auctions.

"You know, you need your parents' permission to enlist if you're between eighteen and twenty years old," Duryee said.

"I'm past twenty, Sir."

"Make up your mind." The colonel laughed again.

"Twenty."

His smile retreated. "I'm not the one you need to convince, soldier. You have any other garments?"

Noble looked down at his bare chest, and then at his own sit-upons that were frayed and soaked from the rain. One pant leg reached mid-calf, the other to his ankle. He wiggled the toes on his bare feet. "No, Sir."

"When was the last time you showered?"

Noble shrugged.

"Army might be the right place for you. Make sure you figure out how old you are before you enlist."

"Yes, Sir. Thank you, Sir." Another attempt at a salute.

"No, young man. Stand up straight."

Noble flung his shoulders back and looked at the ground.

"Look at me. Always look straight ahead, eyes on the horizon, line of sight parallel to the ground. Arms flat at your sides. Palm against your leg with the fingers cupped, like you're holding three coins. The man with the lower rank initiates the salute. Understand?"

"Yes."

"Yes, what?"

"Yes, Sir."

"Good. Salute."

Noble raised his hand toward his forehead.

"No, like this." Duryee demonstrated. "Upper arm parallel to the ground, your elbow parallel to your shoulder. Try it again."

Noble put his arm back by his side. He let a long exhale loose, sensing this moment was one of paramount significance. He pulled his shoulder blades back again, stuck out his chin, and looked Duryee in the eyes. He raised his right arm in his best salute ever. Pride overcame him. He was going to be a member of the United States Army and battle evil on behalf of the Union. Excitement filled him at the prospect of being led and taught by men like Colonel Duryee. Emotion encompassed him, knowing he and William would be together. Perhaps they would even be heroes and save a battalion. Maybe they would receive medals from President Lincoln himself.

"Jennings," Duryee said.

Noble snapped back to attention.

"Where'd you go, son?"

"Nowhere, Sir."

"Make sure your wrist, hand and fingers are straight when you salute. Your middle finger should abut the outside corner of your eyebrow. Can you do that?"

"Yes, Sir."

"Excellent. You ready?"

"I'm ready to free the coloreds from slavery, Sir."

Duryee smiled. "You're an enthusiastic one."

"Yes, Sir."

"Don't get killed."

Noble lowered his arm. "Sir?"

"This isn't play time, son. Are you sure you want to enlist? Shouldn't you be in school?"

"I'm twenty," he said weakly.

"Where are your parents?"

"Dead, sir."

Noble saw the colonel's eyes again evaluate him, from his scratched and scabbed bare feet to his shaved head.

Duryee pointed toward the entrance to the black tent. "Your future is that way."

"Yes, Sir. Thank you, Sir."

Noble moved forward and scanned the crowd for William. As he searched, he practiced his story. I am twenty years old. I am twenty years old. He took his place at the end of the line that wrapped around the tent.

"Hey, Jennings."

He turned quickly.

Duryee handed him a white blousy shirt and a pair of black-laced shoes.

"Thank you, Sir."

Noble slipped on the shirt; cotton hugged him. The shoes were a little big but fit well enough. He had never had laces before and didn't know how to tie them so he left them loose. He turned to thank the colonel once more but he was gone. Tears spiked Noble's eyes. He had not received a gift since his parents were alive.

A boy walked up behind him. "Ya 'kay?"

"Yeah."

The boy knelt, and Noble jumped back.

"It's 'kay." He reached for Noble's shoes and tied the laces.

Lice roamed in the part of the boy's scalp.

"That's why I shave my head," Noble said.

The boy stood. Half-a-foot shorter than Noble, he looked up. "What ya' say?"

"Nothing. Thank you." Noble lifted one foot off the ground. The laces of his new used shoes were double knotted.

A second gift. The army was definitely for him, these people too. He was going to wear a uniform, maybe even carry a sword. He'd learn to fire a pistol, and how to load and shoot a cannon.

The boy scribbled on a piece of paper. His knuckles were crusted with dried blood. He folded the page and stuffed it in his own shoe, the left one.

"What's that?" Noble looked at the boy's foot.

The boy leaned toward him. "Can ya be a secret?"

"Be a secret?"

"Ya. Not tell anyone."

"Sure."

"When they ask ma age, I don't have ta lie." He held out his hand. "Robert Jeffries McGee the second."

"Noble Jennings, um, the first."

The underside of Robert's palms and fingers was rough but his grip was strong and confident. Noble made a note of how to shake hands, and how to look the other man in the eyes when you do so. He wanted to be like Colonel Duryee and Robert Jeffries McGee the second, and the hundreds of other boys that waited to enlist.

Robert looked him over. "How old ya?"

"Twenty."

He took the paper out of his shoe, ripped it in half, and gave the clean piece to Noble. "Write eighteen on ta." He handed the stub of a pencil toward him.

"Why eighteen?"

"You got a note from ya parents to enlist, ain't that right?"

"No."

"Well, then write twenty on ta paper."

Noble did as he was told.

"Now fold it and put it in ya shoe."

Again, he followed instructions, shoved it in without untying the laces. "Then what?" Noble asked.

"When they ask ya age ya say, 'I'm twenty and I stand on ma word.'"

"Really?"

"You wrote twenty, right?"

He nodded.

"And ya put it in your shoe?"

"Yes."

"Then ya standing on it." Robert slapped him on the back.

Noble shrugged. "How old are you?"

"Ta truth? Sixteen, but I have a note from ma parents that says I'm eighteen and I have permission ta enlist."

"They're okay with you fighting?"

"Hell, yeah. Got too many mouths ta feed at home with ma little sistas and brothas, and us McGees don't abide by slavery. It's not ta Protestant way. Ya a religious fella?"

Noble shrugged again. He had never thought much about religion, except if beekeeping was a religion he'd be a high priest.

The line moved forward until the boys were inside the tent. Noble looked for William among the crowd of fifty or sixty young men who queued toward a table where three in uniform sat. At the table, short conversations were had, documents were stamped, and boys were ordered left or right depending upon if they were accepted into the army or not.

"Well?" Robert was still behind him.

"I'm sorry? What was that?"

"I asked why ya want ta enlist?"

Noble knew he couldn't say his primary reason was to be with William for fear he would be considered immature or fay.

His secondary reason. "I believe in freedom for all men."

"Hallelujah." Robert raised his hands. "We're gonna beat ta Southern boys until they realize we are all brothers of Christ regardless of ta color of a person's skin. Praise ta Lord."

Noble nodded, figuring to agree with Robert Jeffries McGee the second was best. He would have to think about religion another time. Now, he had to stay on task. One of the tallest in the room, he looked again for William.

"You got a friend here?" Robert asked.

"I thought so, but I don't see him."

"Once we put on ta uniform, we're all friends, we're all brothas."

He now had a third reason to enlist, friends and brothers.

At the head of the line, Noble looked at the men seated at the wood table. The one in the middle with the long dark moustache and wandering eye appeared to be in charge.

Noble stepped in front of the table and mimicked what the boys in line ahead of him had said. He applied all he had learned in the short time since he arrived at Jones's Wood.

He put his shoulders back and saluted crisply. "Noble Jennings the first reporting for duty, Sirs."

The man in the middle asked, "How old are you, Son?"

"I'm twenty and I stand by my word."

The men behind the desk exchanged looks. They conferred and whispered while Noble waited. He looked back at Robert, who offered an encouraging nod and a wink.

The men separated from their short meeting. The one in the middle stood and saluted. "Congratulations, Private Jennings, you are a member of the Union army." He stamped a document.

"Noble!" William, dressed in the blue-gray of an army private, the uniform unsoiled and oversized, pushed his way past recruits. "What are you doing here?"

"I've enlisted." He beamed.

William looked to the men behind the desk. "He's only fourteen."

"He said he was twenty," the man in the middle spoke.

"I am twenty and I stand by my word, I mean, on my word," Noble said.

"You're fourteen?" Robert asked. "Ya lied before ta God?"

"No, I didn't. I mean you told me to say I was twenty...you're only sixteen..."

Robert faced the recruiters and scratched the top of his head. "I am eighteen, and I stand on ma word. Here's a letter from ma parents with permission ta enlist."

The man with the moustache ripped up Noble's stamped document. "Go to the left, young man." He took the letter from Robert.

"I'm twenty." Noble protested.

"Get him out of here, Private." One of the men behind the desk ordered William.

William saluted, grabbed Noble by the arm, and pulled.

Noble didn't move. "How could you?"

"C'mon," William said. "Don't make it worse."

"Who's going to protect you during the war?" Noble asked.

"Shh, you're embarrassing me."

Noble lowered his voice. "I have to go with you."

"Let's talk about this outside." William pulled him away.

Chapter Eleven

Outside the tent, the late morning sun hovered like a parent. Boys swarmed. Some proudly waved their acceptance papers, others stomped about, dejected.

Noble looked down at William who stood almost a foot shorter. Noble had never seen him dressed so fine. He looked like a man, and not the picked-upon boy at the Home. He seemed taller. But still, Noble was too furious to feel good for him.

"How could you do that?" he yelled.

"You're too young to go to war."

"I'm only four years younger than you."

"That's forever." His voice was stern. "Go home."

"If you mean go *to* the Home, that's not my home." A knot caught in his throat. "I thought my home was with you."

William looked away, and then back at Noble. "Lincoln says the war won't last very long."

"What if he's wrong?"

"He's not."

"How do you know?"

"Lincoln's never wrong."

"You don't even know him."

"He's our president. That's all I need to know."

"If he's so great, how come there needs to be a war? Why can't he just tell the Southerners to free all the slaves so they can be regular people?"

William pulled Noble away from the crowd. "That's ignorant talk, and you talk like that because you're a kid."

"I'm not stupid."

"You don't understand the ways of the world like I do."

"I'm not a child." Noble wrestled the tears to stay in his eyes.

William grabbed his wrist. "Nothing will happen to me. I'll join you when the war is over."

Noble's face grew hot. He turned away. Behind blurred eyes, he saw the Home, Kid, the freckled boy, and the demolished hive. He thought of his parents and could barely recall their smiles, their smells, their voices. Would William's face be only a dim memory to him one day too?

But, could William be right? The war would end soon and he'd have remuneration from fighting. They would rent a room in Five Points, Noble would go to school and work, and he'd capture another queen and start a new hive. William would study to be a lawyer, and they'd be a real family.

"Okay, I'll wait…" Noble looked back.

William was gone. He looked for him, couldn't spot him among the boys dressed alike who blended into a sea of blue, outlined with blood.

He sighed, and moved slowly forward. His toes pushed into the fronts of the oversized shoes he'd outgrow in a few months. The tail of the blousy shirt Colonel Duryee gave him fluttered in a building wind.

The sun high in the noontime sky, he began the four-mile trek back toward Five Points. A drone buzzed around him. He held out his hand and it landed in his left palm. Genus: Apis

Mellifera. Its big black compound eyes looked up, and judged him. Who's going to protect William? Noble cupped his hand around the bee. As he walked out of Jones's Wood, the American flag at the exit trembled.

Chapter Twelve

John Coal and Simon Black Cat exited Doc B's clinic at Forty-Four Orange Street. Their clothes were covered in Alice's blood from assisting Doc B. They stepped into the street and into puddles of mud. A horse, pulling a carriage, trotted past. Muck and water splashed up John and Simon's pant legs, on to their shirts and faces, and into their eyes. The downpour had stopped. The world was drenched.

Simon wiped his face, tightened his fists, and clenched his jaw. "We can't let the police get away with treating Alice and Sarah like that."

John concentrated on a fast-approaching clamor that sounded like a storm so fierce it could kick up dirt in whorls, send hats airborne, and fling women's skirts open into waist level umbrellas. Whence it came? He looked for the source. The sound grew closer, clearer. Ba-dum, ba-dum, ba-dum. A horse and carriage turned the corner and raced toward them.

Simon still complained. "It's because of Lincoln. Calling men to war."

Mud kicked up under the horse's hooves. Two white men sat atop the carriage on a cushioned seat. One slapped reins against the chestnut's neck and withers and yelled, "Giddyap. Go, go, go." The other cracked a whip over his head.

Simon was oblivious, immersed in his fury. "I'm telling you, Uncle John, those white men are going to pay for what they did to Alice."

The steed neared. Frenzy bulged in his big brown eyes and sweat winged from the chestnut's muzzle. John stared, unbelieving, quickly praying. *Father, forgive them for they do not know what they do.* Was this judgment day as in Zechariah section twelve, verse four? "I will strike every horse with panic, and its rider with madness."

Simon still yammered. "They're going to pay. Trust me that."

The horse a few feet away, John rammed his shoulder into Simon's chest. The force threw Simon into the clinic door. John moved to jump out of the way but slipped and fell. The horse's front legs trampled his chest. The steed's back hooves barreled over his legs, followed by one wagon wheel, and then another.

Chapter Thirteen

Noble moved along Orange Street. He barely noticed the people who maneuvered around him. How dare William tell the draft board he was only fourteen? William wasn't his father. They called each other brothers but they weren't even related by blood. William J. Henley was just some bob-tail he met at the Home and felt sorry for 'cause he was so little. Full of brains but weak, weak, weak. All skin and bones and no muscle, and the slightest upset got him wheezing and to bed.

Noble knew his thinking was tainted with resentment. William might be slight of body, but he was Atlas of the mind and had prevented the sky from crushing Noble.

He kicked at the dirt. William was right. He was nothing but an ignorant, stupid, and dumb kid. Getting involved in stuff he knew nothing about. He should mind his own business. Didn't he have enough trouble fending off Kid and Peter Stout? How was he going to fight in a war? What was wrong with him? Nobody liked him. Even the Union army thought he was a poltroon.

Noble felt a tickle in the palm of his left hand and realized it had been clenched since he left Jones's Wood. He recalled the bee, opened his hand and felt relief when the bee rose and took flight.

At least the bee was free.

"Go," came a cry from behind him.

Noble turned.

"Giddyap. Go, go, go."

Two men sat atop a carriage that raced down the street, toward him. The horse galloped under the persuasion of snapping reins and the whirl of an overhead whip. The large metal wheels and elliptical springs of the four-wheeled wagon groaned under the speed; the sound fierce like thunder. Noble jumped back as they sped past. The bee vial around his neck flew up, hit him in the face, bounced against his chest, and into his face again. Mud kicked up into his eyes, splattered on his new shirt.

"Hey!" He yelled after the fleeing wagon. His voice leapt into the air and thudded to the ground, unheard among the screams of others who also jumped out of the way.

Against the front door of a one-story home, Noble bent over, placed his hands on his knees. He looked up and saw the address. Fifty-Eight Orange Street.

His legs shook as he walked passed railroad homes, residences with rooms lined up from the front to the back and connected by a single hallway, communal living to accommodate the wave of immigrants to New York City. Up ahead, the horse and carriage that had almost hit him raced toward two men he recognized from Five Points: John Coal and Simon Black Cat. They stood in front of Doc B's clinic.

John had taught Noble the shell game, a short con to easy money. Noble had learned the sleight of hand trick but never had the guts to try it. John was strong with a back chiseled like marble and could move almost anything with his muscle and wit. He did the shell game to make extra cash.

Noble didn't know Simon as well but he liked to watch Simon strut along the streets, pants tight, shoes glistening, and nodding coolly to women if one wasn't already on his arm.

Up ahead, the wagon raced toward John and Simon.

"Watch out." Noble yelled.

John pushed Simon against the clinic door. John moved to jump out of the way but fell. No time to get up, the horse and the carriage careened over his body.

Chapter Fourteen

In the small, fenced yard behind Forty-Four Orange Street, pigs and goats grazed. In the kitchen, apple and blackberry pies cooled. Catfish gasped for breath in a bathtub. Payment for Miss Doctor B's services from the poor of Five Points. Doc B donated most of the knitted sweaters, scarves and gloves to the Home for Unwanted Boys and to the Colored Orphan Asylum. She barbecued the pigs, grilled the fish, milked the goats, and ate the pies. Being a generous woman, she never ate alone. Those treated by Doc B, who had nothing tangible to offer as payment, volunteered at the clinic. Her staff, therefore, was a cultural and social mishmash of the well intentioned and forever grateful.

This afternoon, nine volunteers tended to the patients. Martha was the volunteer-in-charge, half Algonquian and half English, a heavy woman with swollen legs whose diabetes was under control. Martha's staff for the day included David, a ruddy faced Jewish man with an enlarged prostate; Abigail, who was recovering from morphine addiction; and Colin, a strapping pink-skinned lad who lost an eye in a gang fight and who refused to leave the clinic.

Alice was supine on a cot in bed number six. Doc B wrapped cotton strips around her head, having to change them often as they soaked quickly with blood, the head made up of hundreds of capillaries that coursed like a river with no impediments. When the bleeding stopped, Doc B did a final swathing until Alice looked like a wounded soldier.

Sarah bent close to her unconscious mother, and looked up at the doctor. "Is she going to be all right?"

"She's lost a lot of blood." Doc B placed her index and middle fingers on the inside of Alice's wrist. "Her vitals are good. Brain injuries are unpredictable. She may not be the same person you knew. As the swelling in her brain goes down, we'll be better able to gauge her recovery."

"How long will that take?"

Doc B applied adhesive tape to the dressing. "It's hard to say. We have to see how she heals. The first few weeks are critical to assessing her long term recovery."

"Is there nothing else we can do to help her?" Alice asked.

"Only wait."

Alice hesitated, and then said, "We can pray."

"If you believe in that."

"Of course I do. Don't you?"

Doc B avoided the religion versus science conversation, especially in Five Points whose many churches were standing room only come Sunday and holidays, although the inhabitants of Five Points rarely practiced what their pastors preached.

A crash sounded by the front door and Simon and Noble backed into the clinic. They carried John, his upper body draped over their arms, his legs dragged on the floor. John screamed and thrashed. Deep red blood marked their path, and covered them.

Doc B ran toward the door. Sarah, Martha and Colin followed.

"Get a tourniquet," the doctor yelled.

Martha waddled toward a supply bin.

"Oh, no. John!" Sarah cried.

His eyes rolled in their sockets. His chin fell into his chest. His body sagged.

"He's fainted," Simon yelled.

"Get him to the bed." Doc B pointed.

Simon, Noble and Colin carried John to bed number five, next to Alice.

"One, two, three," Noble counted.

They heaved the big man on to the cot. Blood spurted from his upper thigh. Martha handed a thin leather strap to Doc B who tied it around John's leg, and stifled the geyser. Blood seeped from cuts along his mid-section and trickled out the side of his mouth and down from his nostrils.

"What is that sticking out?" Simon pointed to John's leg.

Doc B ripped off his pants, wiped gobs of brown and red, feces and blood, from John's thigh, and swept it off the table and onto the floor. Some of the mess landed on Noble's pants and splattered across the tops of his shoes. John moaned. With a mop between his hands and towels shoved in his belt, David worked to keep the floor clean and dry.

Doc B leaned closer to John. "That's bone."

Simon turned away. His last meal projected from his stomach and landed on the floor.

John's legs and arms jerked. His mid-section bucked. Noble and Colin tried to hold him still.

"Get something to put in his mouth so he doesn't bite off his tongue." The doctor yelled.

David ran and returned with a wooden tongue depressor.

"Put it between his teeth," the doctor said.

"Me?" David cried.

Noble grabbed the depressor and jammed it into John's mouth. Doc B and Martha struggled to steady his legs. Colin and David tried to hold him down. With John's teeth clenched around the depressor, Noble grabbed the big man's arms again.

Sweat from Noble's forehead dropped into his eyes. He tried to blink it away and to clear his vision. He looked up, his eyes stung, and then saw her on the other side of the table.

Tears marred her cheeks. Fear contorted her mouth. Their eyes met. Neither looked away.

"What can I do?" Sarah asked.

Noble let go of one of John's arms. "Hold him here."

She leaned on the limb, applied her body weight to try and keep him from thrashing. John's body jolted up and down. Sarah stayed with him.

Vomit dotted Simon's chin. "What's happening?"

The convulsions stopped. John's body silenced. All watched, wide eyed, waiting for the bucking to begin again.

"He's dead," Simon said.

Doc B placed two fingers on his neck. "He has a pulse. It's weak"

Martha dabbed at John's leg with a towel for the doctor to have a clear view of his injury. David mopped the floor, eyes averted from the patient. Colin held loosely to John's ankles should he convulse again. Sarah continued to lean on his arm.

Calm overcame Doc B, intuitive from years of crisis training. She inhaled deeply and then released a long and slow exhale. "There isn't a lot of time to avoid septicemia."

"Septic what?" Simon asked.

"Infection. When bone lacerates the skin, there is a high likelihood of septicity. Even if I can stop the bleeding, the infection he'll get will most likely be fatal."

"What can you do?" Sarah asked.

"Amputate. His leg won't be good anyway. There's nerve and muscle damage. I don't think I can stop the bleeding. The critical time to save his life is before infection sets in and, I promise, it will. Does he have other family?"

"Just me," Simon said.

"And me," Sarah added. "Not by blood but we're still family."

Simon grabbed her hand. Noble looked away from their clenched fingers.

"I can leave the leg but I'm certain that will be the death of him," Doc B said. "Or I can save his life." She looked up. "What will it be?"

"You're recommending amputation, Doctor?" Sarah asked.

"Clinically, it's the only option."

Simon turned to Sarah. "What should we do?"

"I wish we could ask mama." She looked over at the next table where Alice lay.

Simon looked to Noble. "What do you think?"

"You're asking me?"

"Yeah. You?"

Noble studied John, unconscious on the table. His breathing shallow. The blood around his nose and mouth oozed. Bandages applied by Martha covered the cuts on his torso but blood seeped through. The skin tone of his right leg was graying, and the leg swelled to more than double in size. The femur bone protruded. The longest bone in the body, it extended from the knee to the hip and triangled out between the ripped skin; the break in the bone like tent poles broken at the apex.

"I would do what Doc B says," Noble said.

Sarah nodded. "I agree too."

Simon's face twisted. His eyes reddened. He pulled his hand from Sarah's.

"What will it be?" Doc B asked.

Simon's eyes glazed. "Do what you have to do, doc, but you take his black leg, I'm going to get myself a white one." He raced toward the door.

Noble started after him.

"No," Doc B called to Noble. "I need you. Martha, gather the volunteers. Get towels and sheets, three buckets of water, knives, saws, thread, and a needle, and an empty carton. Grab the one that Missus Callahan brought the eggs in."

Martha, David and Colin scurried to fulfill Doc B's orders.

"You," the doctor pointed to Noble, "you're my dresser."

"Dresser?"

"My assistant."

Martha returned with a rolling cart. Doc B clamped her hand across the top of John's leg and picked up a sharp knife.

"Wait," Sarah said. "No anesthesia?"

"We don't have any," Martha said.

The doctor made an incision across his thigh. Sarah backed away.

"Tighten the tourniquet," the doctor said.

Noble pulled on the leather strap across the top of John's leg.

"Good." Doc B picked up the saw. "Pull his skin back there, until I can see more of the bone."

Noble hesitated. It was one thing to look at the wound, another to touch it. He steeled himself and placed a hand on either side of the incision. With his fingers, he drew back the skin. He looked inside and saw what he believed to be muscle and nerves, bone and fat. His stomach turned, but he had seen worse on the street. A man gutted by Boss Tweed's boys. Vultures eating the meat of a dead horse until only bones remained.

Doc B placed the jagged edge of the saw against his thigh, gripped the handle and moved the sharpened teeth back and forth. Blood poured as she sliced through skin. The saw cutting layers of skin easily, then gouging into the meat and the fat. The sound of the saw rhythmic and mild, but then she hit bone and John sat up and his eyes shot open and as quickly as he rose he was down, unconscious again, the saw meeting bone, screeching like metal upon metal.

"Sarah, put the carton here, under his leg."

Sarah hesitated.

"Now," the doctor commanded.

Sarah moved the carton next to the cot.

"Hold the leg here, right above the knee." Doc B pointed with her chin. "Lean on it to steady it. It's going to be heavy."

Sarah's hands shook. She turned away from the surgery and focused on her mother on the next cot. An angel in repose.

Doc B sawed. The muscles on her arms strained. Sweat dripped from her face and pooled in the tissue of John's leg. Noble's insides listed but he was determined not to get sick, especially with Sarah so close.

More sweat dripped down the doctor's face. Martha wiped her forehead.

Doc B stood upright. "This femur is harder to cut than I thought. Noble, switch places. Take the saw."

Noble and the doctor changed places. He hesitated. John moaned. His eyes fluttered.

"Can he feel this?" Noble asked.

"I hope not." Doc B held the incision open. "You're a strong boy. Get to it before he wakes up."

Noble began the movement back and forth, just like when he'd cut down a tree for firewood. The saw slipped through John's bone easier than he had expected. When he made the final cut and the femur was severed from the hip bone, he threw the saw down and ran to a corner and threw up.

Doc B turned to Sarah. "Let go."

Sarah was transfixed on her mother. She repeated a prayer in her mind. 'Only He has the power to heal. Only He has the power to save us. Please God, heal my mother, save John.'

"Sarah," Doc B yelled.

Sarah awoke, and looked at the blood and tissue that streamed across the cot like gobs of fish guts stuck to Jenny Big Stink's apron.

"Let. Go. Of. The. Leg." Doc B ordered again.

Pale and weakened, Sarah didn't move, couldn't. Noble, his stomach empty and feeling less queasy, approached her from behind. Gently, he reached around her and placed his hands on hers.

In her ear, he spoke softly. "One, two and three."

John's leg tumbled into the carton.

Doc B placed the middle of a line of thread in her mouth and held its ends between her fingertips. She tied off the main artery of the thigh, and then smaller ones. "Loosen the tourniquet," she told Noble.

Doc B went to Alice and checked on the bandages. The doctor then moved to the back of the house to wash John's matter from under her fingernails. Martha covered John with a blanket and sat by him, following the doctor's orders to report immediately if anything appeared wrong. David mopped. Colin wept out of his one eye.

Noble wiped his hands on his pants and realized his shirt and shoes were ruined. Could a washing save them? He turned to Sarah, who was inches from him. He teetered. From the experience he just had or from being close to the most beautiful girl he had ever seen?

Sarah grabbed his arm and rose on to her tiptoes. She leaned in to him. Her breath caressed his neck. Was this going to be his first kiss? Here, in the clinic, with John Coal's leg in a box? Was she blushing? He considered her eyes. Her look, her essence, was what he had dreamed of from another. Not generic or casual love, but deep, devoted affection for him. Yes, this was real. She was real. He leaned toward her.

Sarah put her hand on his cheek. "You're a good boy," she said.

Chapter Fifteen

Noble thundered out of the clinic and toward Five Points, not thinking of the people he'd aided but consumed with the day's rejections. Dusk settled on the dirt-lined streets like crusty sleep. The rain resumed and lightning cast a momentary glow on passersby who drew in their coats and ducked their heads. A herd of fast-moving clouds crammed the sky above the tenement homes. Ten men rushed by waving sticks, chastising Lincoln, and cursing coloreds.

They bumped Noble. "Get out of our way, young'un."

Noble spun around but maintained his footing. He glared at their backs as they jostled other pedestrians and ran toward City Hall Park. Copperheads and lushingtons, looking for a fight and more liquor.

Ahead, a woman about Sarah's age with loose blonde locks that fell about her shoulders rushed toward an overhang to escape the rowdy joes. Her foot became stuck in a puddle of yuck leftover from the earlier deluge. She jerked it out. A stockinged foot emerged, her shoe left behind. Noble fished the lone pump from the mire and handed it to her.

"Thank you, lad."

He outstretched his arms, threw his head back, looked to the darkening sky, and yelled, "I am a man."

Sharp raindrops pricked his skin. He shut his eyes. Motionless, timeless. Plymouth rock. No one to love, not deserving of love. He dropped his arms to his sides and dared to open his eyes to see all the people who stared like he belonged in the mental hospital, but no one cared. The woman with the retrieved shoe was gone. New passersby replaced the old. Ignored, he was nothing but another obstacle in their progress. A throwaway like a drone bee no longer able to fertilize the queen.

In the distance, cheers and jeers brushed the air.

He kept walking, unseeing until he neared the Home for Unwanted Boys. His chest grew tight. Would Kid and the freckled boy ambush him?

Another new crowd of faces moved past him. The lady who had lost her shoe might be home by now. His parents were surely long gone. William was off to war. Men brawled a block or two away, their tones pugilistic. A clog of smoke caught in his throat. John's blood stained his fingers.

At the stoop to the Home, he spied the front door with the wood carvings and the writings penned and etched by the hands of bored and belligerent boys.

William had chosen a portion of the words of John Brown's speech given upon his arrest for orchestrating the taking of the armory at Harper's Ferry in West Virginia to use its arsenal to end slavery. When William first read the abolitionist's final speech in the Times, and reread it numerous times, each sentence became a point of analysis.

If it is deemed necessary
that I should forfeit my life
in this slave country whose rights are disregarded
by wicked, cruel, and unjust enactments,
so let it be done!
John Brown 1800-1859

"'If it is deemed necessary'?" William queried. "By whose account, Noble? Is this John Brown's decision? Or does he refer to God? Shouldn't God decide what is deemed necessary? 'That I should forfeit my life'? He is willing to die for the freedom of strangers. Noble, do you realize how amazing this man is?"

William began the carving on the day he first read the speech, Noble whittled or read about bees on a nearby stoop. William finished one month later, one hour after John Brown's execution.

Always a contrast, Kid drew a crude picture of a painted lady with her legs spread and a man between. The whore read a book. In crooked and rushed lettering, he also cut into the wood:

Torevolutionarieswhoresandprostitutes
Boyswholovetofightgirlswhofuckallnight

Noble couldn't decide what mattered enough to him to inscribe on the door.

Butchy leaned out the door, pushed it open so quickly Noble jumped back. The twenty-five-year-old manager of the Home's paunch hung over the tops of his pants and over the frayed belt that provided no support. A dark two-days growth covered his jowls.

"Welcome home," Butchy said.

"This isn't my home."

"It's the closest thing you and me got. You can bunk with me."

Noble hesitated. "Kid?"

"Not dead. C'mon, Nobe. It's better in here than on the streets. Things have really heated up." He pointed.

Noble looked across the street. A neatly lettered sign hung in a cobbler's store. "Equality Now North and South." Next door, at a market, its competitor scrawled: "Secede = Success."

But Noble knew that's not where Butchy pointed. It was to the tops of trees from City Hall Park in the distance that drew his concern. A couple of blocks away and across the street from the courthouse, rising mannish cheers failed to obscure a feminine high-pitched cry for help.

"Get inside," Butchy said. "This ain't your fight, boy."

"Who says?"

"It's me talkin. You gotta know what you're fighting for so you know what you have to lose."

"I don't have anything to lose." Noble ran toward the fray.

◆

Everyone is given a name upon birth, Noble figured. Even Kid. A name parents lovingly and thoughtfully chose, whether to honor a deceased relative or to pay homage to a Biblical figure, or to signify their desires for the child's future. Chastity. Harmony. Faith. Hope.

But this woman, the one screaming and fighting the men that lifted her dress and grabbed at her breasts, the men who individually were sons and brothers and students and workers but collectively were a mob, the men who failed to consider that this woman was once a girl who had been a baby and had been given a name carefully chosen by her parents who, upon her birth, never imagined their baby girl to be the victim of such an attack. Maybe her name was Ruth, Miriam, Rebecca, Rachel. Noble knew her as the girl who had earlier lost her shoe. She wore two shoes now, black sensible platforms she wore to her job at the Triangle Shirtwaist Factory, the heel cracked on one, the strap torn on the other. Eighteen years old, simply pretty, a Jewish immigrant from Belarus with dark hair, pale skin, and a sharply angled nose.

In the park, Noble scrambled up a tree, the sun sinking in the horizon. Some lookers-on watched, did the math on what was occurring, and scattered. Seven-eight-nine men molested the woman. A police officer watched from the entrance to the park. Noble knew him, all right. Everyone from Five Points knew Timothy Byrne.

"Leave me alone." The woman tried to swat them away.

Like a boa that constricts the more its prey fights back, her verbal and physical objections strengthened the pack. Each man seemed to grow like a tick that filled with blood.

"Hey!" A boy atop a tree next to Noble called toward the knot of men. "Let her go."

On the ground, a slender man, receding red hair curled in a tuft above his forehead, grabbed rocks and propelled them at the boy. Another man joined in the one-sided battle, and then a second, third, and a fourth. Ten, fifteen, twenty rocks flew his way. The boy dodged a few and wrapped his arm around a branch to prevent his plummet. A rock hit him in the eye.

An errant rock, the result of poor aim and whiskey, struck Noble's bicep. He rubbed the sting away, secured himself in his tree. Another rock clipped his elbow.

"Hey!" Noble protested.

"What did you say?" the red headed man called.

Another slurred, "Come down, you cowards."

Noble looked to the kid next to him. Their eye contact brief but long enough for Noble to see the panic on his face. The boy scurried down the tree and sprinted out of the park, past the copper.

More rocks flew Noble's way, propelled like bullets, fast and feverish. A rock smacked Noble on the left shoulder, one on his chin, another on his chest. One just missed his bee necklace.

"Okay, okay." He held up his arms in surrender. A rock clouted him on the chest again.

The men stopped the barrage of rock throwing, looked up at him, waited, watched, hands on their waists. Noble climbed down, careful with his hand and foot placement, also trying to keep his eyes on the men to make sure the rock storm didn't resume. Those men had lost interest in the girl. In fact, as he looked around the park, he didn't see her at all. Had she escaped?

On the ground, Noble squared off across from six, maybe seven men. Boxed in, a couple of goons moved to rush him.

"Stand back," someone yelled.

The men stepped aside. Peter Stout treaded forward from the rear.

"What was you doing up in that tree, Noble?" Peter Stout's Irish accent boomed.

"Just watching, that's all."

"Don't you think lads oughta' have some fun?"

"Sure." Noble looked toward an exit to the park, the one where Byrne did not stand watch.

Peter Stout advanced upon him. He was a couple of inches shorter than Noble but his chest was a solid trunk and his arms dense branches. Even if Noble could knock him down long enough to get away, his cronies were sure to take up his cause.

Noble looked toward Officer Byrne, who tipped his hat and walked away.

The punch came quick, a left hook that stung Noble's cheek even though it was only a glance. Noble darted to the side, to run. Two men grabbed him and threw him at Peter Stout, who landed a gut punch that doubled Noble over. Coughing, wheezing, nauseas, he tried to straighten himself but Peter Stout's fist came up under his chin and Noble flew back. Stayed on his feet, somehow.

Noble spit blood and a couple of teeth, roots attached. "Okay, okay, stop." He leaned his hands on his knees.

Peter Stout barreled into his stomach, took Noble to the ground, hard on to his back.

Peter Stout on top, Noble's arms pinned by his knees. Noble kicked up his legs, tried to flip him off. He had to get back to his feet. No success. Punches landed, on his chest, on his face. He swallowed blood, more coughing, choking. With a tribal scream, Noble managed to roll to his side and throw Peter Stout off. Then, kicking. Noble tightened into a ball.

"Grab his arms and legs," Peter Stout ordered.

Men grabbed at him. Stretched him. Tried to pin his limbs. Noble fought like a mad man but knew his resistance was for naught. He was going to die. He closed his eyes, and continued to fight.

The gunshot was startling. Birds fluttered from the tops of trees. Peter Stout ran, his men followed.

Noble breathed, it was all he could do. No other movement. When he felt secure in the silence, he looked up. The sun set before his eyes. City Hall Park glowed like it was wrapped in honey. Butchy lifted him up and over his shoulder.

Chapter Sixteen

Pigged on a bed with Butchy, as he and William used to do, Noble curled on his side and scrunched into the smallest he could make himself. Butchy's legs didn't hang off the bed as Noble's did, but his girth took up more than half of the shabby mattress.

The shirt from Colonel Duryee, ripped and bloodied, tangled around Noble. His pants, thread bare. He stared at the wall that was inches from his nose. Cracks in lead paint were lit by a moon that cast nondiscriminatory beams through all nighttime windows across the world, including the cracked panes near the foot of the bed where Noble lay. He wished to make himself as tiny as a bee so he could fly into the chips in the paint, burrow through the wall, and shoot up into the sky, and land on the moon.

"Who lives on the moon?" he had asked William one winter's eve.

"Moon boys," William laughed.

"I bet they're nice," Noble said.

"I bet they are."

Instead of shooting up to the moon, maybe Noble would dive into the Hudson River and swim across the ocean until he washed ashore in Europe. William had taught him about places like England and Italy and Spain. France intrigued

Noble. He knew all about Ireland from neighborhood folk, and about Africa from black folks. He heard William chastise him in that faux upper crust accent he fancied. Africa isn't in Europe.

"Africa is its own continent." Noble told the wall.

"Huh?" A wave of Butchy's wicked breath hit Noble.

With a shake of the bed, Butchy flipped to his side, facing away from Noble now. He quickly fell asleep again—being able to sleep anywhere and at any time was one of Butchy's God given gifts. His deep, voluminous snores shook the bed. His ass touched Noble's. Noble tried to make himself smaller, to be absorbed by the wall.

He appreciated the little portion of the mattress he'd been allocated. It was dry and bug free and Butchy had saved him from some awful trouble three nights earlier. He still had a shiner on his left eye, and a yellow and purple bruise on his chest. He wondered how the girl who lost her shoe fared.

In the next room, the room Noble used to share with William, Kid had convalesced from the beatdown Noble had given him in the back of the Home. Through the thin walls, Noble heard Doc B declare that Kid's bruises, sprained ribs, and broken fingers would heal just dandy. Noble wanted to ask Doc B about Alice and John but didn't feel important enough to deserve her response.

The last seventy-two hours had brought Noble not sleep but rising anger toward everyone and everything, especially himself.

"Why do I have to be me?"

"What's that?" Butchy asked, and then snored again.

Noble laid in bed for a few more hours, his body smashed against the wall. Their asses touched.

♦

Noble's eyes burned. He blinked tears away. Smoke caught in his throat, in his nose. Was City Hall Park afire? No, this burning wasn't from there. It was closer. He turned over in the bed. Butchy was gone. Nice. He stretched out, his limbs and muscles happy for the space. He took inventory of his body. Not bad, some pain but bearable. He had finally gotten some sleep and started to feel like himself again. A fourteen-year-old boy who could take on the world. Perhaps this would be a day he could conquer.

"Help!" someone yelled. "There are children in there!"

Noble sat up. Tufts of gray clouds drifted into the room through the broken pane. Another cry for help, and then Butchy's panicked holler followed. Noble jumped out of bed.

Outside, two doors down from the Home, bright orange and red flames erupted from the rear of the Colored Orphan Asylum. Out front, a crowd yelled, "No war, no draft. No war, no draft." Rioters lodged logs and chairs and other furniture in front of the door to the Asylum so no one could get out, or in. Noble recognized many of the Irish, including Peter Stout.

Up ahead, Butchy tried to get to the door but was thrown to the ground. He jumped up and demanded, "If there is a person among you with a heart, come and help these poor children."

The crowd descended upon him. Butchy screamed and the gang attacked. The pack as ferocious and unforgiving as the fire.

Noble ran toward him. "Stop!"

Peter Stout punched him in the gut. Noble fell to his knees.

"Stay down!"

Noble held his stomach, and looked from Butchy to the burning building. Help Butchy, or try and get the kids out?

Think, Noble. Think! Prokopovych's book on bees flashed in his mind.

> Page three hundred and twenty-seven. Bees only attack to protect their queen or their hive as once they engage in battle and sting, they die. If given a choice between saving a singular bee who is not the queen, or saving the hive, the bee would save the hive.

Butchy struggled and fought, some men vied to hurt him, others tried to help him. Help Butchy or the children? The bees wouldn't have hesitated. They'd save the hive over the queen.

Noble leapt up and sprinted to the Asylum. Smoke billowed, gray and dense in the dusking sky. Men and women, black and white, engaged in the fray to clear the door to the orphanage. Some wrestled with Peter Stout's ruffians. Others got close to the door. Where did Simon Black Cat come from? What was Kid doing here?

Noble threw chairs and bulk from the door. A path cleared from the seething structure. Children of all ages and sizes ran out, the commonality being the dark color of their skin. Noble's lungs afire, he hacked smoke from his body. His vocal cords and his tongue swelled. Grabbed from behind, strong arms clamped around him. He struggled to be freed, coughing, fighting.

The scorched breath of Peter Stout singed his ear. "Let them burn."

With a warrior cry, Noble threw himself backwards and into Peter Stout's chest. Several steps, and they tumbled into a big oak tree. Noble sprung up, fast and wiry. Adrenaline and anger fueled him.

Peter Stout grabbed him. "It's for the best, son."

"I am not your son." The words flew out garbled. His tongue enlarged.

Noble jumped on Peter Stout. With fury, he pummeled the Irishman's face. The first blow crushed the bones in his nose, a deliberate blow to disable the bigger man. His nasal septum caved. Noble threw one-two combos. The bee vial bounced against his chest. Peter Stout's teeth tumbled into his throat. He stopped fighting back. Noble placed his hands around his neck and squeezed. Peter Stout's eyes enlarged, his mouth opened. Blood trickled out, inched along his jaw line.

"Please." A desperate whisper.

Noble squeezed more tightly. He wanted to feel his death. This man so full of hatred, who had tormented him for so long, he deserved to die. Then Noble saw them, on the ground, underneath the big oak where he had left them. Prokopovych's book on bees. The glass he and William had shared at the Home.

What was he about to do? Again? First Kid, now Peter Stout.

"I am not a murderer," he yelled.

Noble jumped up and darted past Butchy, who was upright now. Women—white, black and yellow—tended the manager. Noble joined the barricade of bodies that had formed a line to help orphans escape. His breathing labored. His lungs burned. He became a link in a chain. Genus: humanity.

The volunteer fire department arrived and a water brigade formed. Noble gripped the sides of a bucket, surprised when it was handed to him on his right from Kid. Water splashed and Noble slipped the container to Simon Black Cat on his left.

Officer Byrne stepped in front of Noble. "Let's go, boy."

"I am not a boy."

Byrne pulled him out of the line and threw him to the ground. Four-five-six police surrounded him, kicked at him, punched him, in his face, his body, his legs.

Noble covered his face with his hands, tightened into a fetal position. No need to ask what he'd done to deserve this beating. Payback for Peter Stout.

Pulled to his feet, officers held his hands behind his back. Noble could hardly see out of his swollen lids but he recognized Peter Stout. His face a blurred mess of scrapes, blood and bruises. His nose askew. Most of his front teeth gone. Blood lined his lips.

Peter Stout's first punch landed in Noble's stomach. The next one tagged him under his chin. Noble tasted bile and threw up on Peter Stout's shoes. He remained bent over, too weak to stand, held up by the officers who gripped his arms behind his back.

"I'm going to kill you," Peter Stout said.

"I've got a better idea," Byrne voiced. "Hold him." He instructed two officers, who seized Noble.

Byrne and Peter Stout quickly conversed. When they separated, Byrne grabbed Noble. "You're under arrest."

"For what?" Noble said, or tried to say. It hurt so much to speak, to breath.

"For starting the Colored Orphan Asylum fire, that's what."

Chapter Seventeen

The wood beams of the Colored Orphan Asylum exploded, buckled, and caved. Heat radiated, bare skin reddened. On the fire brigade line, Simon grabbed a bucket from the bald, skinny kid next to him. The kid smelled charred and damp and musty. A few feet away, Byrne held Noble's arms behind his back while Peter Stout beat the boy. Noble's body bucked each time Peter Stout's fist or knee connected with his face and stomach. Simon flinched, as if he too received the blows.

Simon thought of Uncle John, near death, his leg in a box at Doc B's clinic. He pictured Alice Black as Night in the bed next to him, her head wrapped in gauze. He recalled Noble helping, cutting off Uncle John's leg. Shouldn't he help Noble? He looked over his shoulder, trying to see what was going on without being seen. If he ran to Noble's rescue, they'd kill him. That's what white copperheads did to black men.

Rotating his body, Simon passed buckets along the human chain. He tried to tune out Noble's grunts, and fumed. His body felt scorched from the top of his head to his toes. Not only because of the injustice the last few days had brought, not only because of the horridness of this moment, but for his own ignorance for believing America was a land of equality.

Like his father, Simon had been born a free man and had known no shackles or iron chains. He felt safe in the confines of his life. Deliberately narrowed to family, Five Points,

Sunday morning services, the nest of the church choir, and a few friends, white and black. He worked hard at his daddy's furrier business and, while he didn't enjoy skinning animals, it was steady work that paid well. At least he didn't have to trap and kill the foxes, rabbits and opossums, as his grandfather had after he escaped a plantation in Georgia and made his way to New York City where Eugene Wheeler, an abolitionist lawyer, helped him to be declared free. Free Men, he and his descendants were. They had the paperwork to prove it.

Simon learned early that having money and freedom was an asset with the ladies. Broad shouldered and strong, more cute than handsome, what he lacked in height he made up in heart. His deep black pupils danced. Girls weakened under his polite words and gestures. After getting naked with them, he'd kiss their hands and eyelids, and make them feel as if they were his one and only, even if this might be the one and only time. He even made it with a white girl once. He discovered, with his eyes closed and his hands seeing the woman beneath him, skin color made not a lick of difference.

On the bucket brigade, anger pitched within him. Fury at Lincoln for not protecting his people, hatred for the crooked police, the copperheads, and the Tammany Hall bigots, disgust for every white person who believed he was better because when he slipped out of his mother's womb his skin was pink and not brown.

At twenty-two years old, Simon should have known his history could not be contained within the four walls of his family's brownstone. He could blame his father, who refused to share stories of the cruelties his granddaddy endured. He could fault his mother who packed his lunch each day and expected him home for supper every evening at six. But he knew there was no one to blame but himself. He was Simon Black Cat, hard-working, quick witted, and golden tongued, and he knew change began within.

Across the way, Byrne and Peter Stout lifted Noble from the ground. His head fell back. They swung him into a police wagon. The driver slapped the reins and the draft horse lunged forward.

Byrne and Peter Stout shook hands. Simon broke from the brigade.

The bald, stinky kid next to him grabbed his arm. "Where you going?"

Simon sized up the boy. Freakish, his eyes sunken like a human skeleton. His lips were outlined in grime. His face bruised. Red bumps, like bug bites and bee stings, covered his bald head and arms. Scabs on Kid's head bled, some appeared scratched until infection. His collarbones stuck out from under a dirty t-shirt.

Simon was surprised by the strength of the boy's grip. "Get off of me."

"I saw what happened to Noble."

Simon hesitated. "You know him?"

"Yeah, from the Home for Unwanted Boys."

"You his friend?"

The kid shrugged.

Simon tried to pull his arm away. "Let me go."

Kid tightened his grasp. "They'll beat you and arrest you too. You gotta wait, you gotta plan, you gotta attack when they don't expect it."

"Don't tell me what to do." Simon yanked his arm from Kid's grip, broke from the chain and ran away, where to he did not know.

◆

Hours later, the skeletal scraps of the Colored Orphan Asylum smoldered and the water brigade dispersed. Confederate supporters left to frequent the bars and brothels of Five Points. Out front of the remains of the Asylum, the anti-slavery faction bowed their heads and prayed, knowing this was but a comma in the endless paragraphs of their struggles.

◆

Kid had joined the fire brigade because he was thirsty and figured he could lap up water from the swishing buckets, besides he had grown tired of staying inside. Convafuckalescing, or whatever Doc Bitch told him he needed to do. What he needed was fresh air and a good brawl, or perhaps a cuddle with a fat whore. Either would do.

He had seen what happened to Noble, grabbed off the line by that Irish cop and the bar owner. For years Byrne and Peter Stout strutted around Five Points like a couple of rakes, people crossing the street so as not to be obscured by their shadows. Those micks didn't intimidate him. He had no use for people other than to achieve his own ends, but there was something about that colored man next to him on the fire brigade that fascinated him, always had. Kid knew him as Simon Black Cat who always hung around his uncle John Skin-black-as-shit or some name like that, a con man. Their steps light as they bounced around Five Points, tipped their hats to the ladies, and lifted their chins to the afternoon sun. Kid thought he saw the definition of the word *happy* in the shine in their eyes. He loathed and admired them for that.

To find his own happiness, Kid figured he needed to determine where he fit in. Was it with the Southern white folks who urged continued suppression of the blacks? Or with the Northern blend of whites and blacks who fought for equality? Mixing white and black, Kid believed, resulted in a darker white or a lighter black. Not even gray. Was that where he belonged? Not on the outskirts, but straddling the void in between?

Or maybe he didn't care about white or black. Let them kill each other. Let whites rule, let blacks rule, let them live side-by-side fucking each other and creating dark white and light black babies. He only cared to survive, and for that he had a plan. He'd head west to a place he heard about called Colorado where he could get land for cheap, a bunch of milking cows, and a wife. Maybe have a bunch of kids.

In front of the Asylum, abolitionists prayed near the embers while out of tune drinking songs rose and fell from nearby establishments. The police and their paddy wagons were gone, Noble tossed into the back of one of them, maybe dead. There was no more trouble for Kid to find here. He trotted off in the direction Simon had sprinted.

◆

Simon slunk through a dark lower Manhattan and along cobblestoned one-way streets framed by stores closed for the evening. As he passed each store, the smells of the regions guided him to the next storefront in a global baton hand-off. Faircloth's English Faire sold cottage pie and fish and chips. Sweeney's Market stocked corned beef with cabbage and champ. Plucked ducks hung in the large front window of the Wu's eatery.

The grooves of the cobblestones overflowed with water from the earlier rain. Each step of his leather shoes sounded like the slap of a belt against skin. Simon thought of going to the police station to try and free Noble, but he was a one-man dark-skinned band and knew that was tantamount to suicide. Noble would have to fend for himself and, with luck, would be okay. Instead, he made his way toward Peter Stout's tavern, figuring the Irish barman and the officer would be the main attractions at Five Corner Bar as they shared stories of triumph to a receptive crowd. What Simon would do once he eyeballed them, he didn't know. He'd think of something. He always did.

Perhaps, eye for an eye, tooth for a tooth. Isn't that what Matthew Chapter Five Verse Thirty-eight in the Bible instructed? Didn't Matthew and Luke both address the Golden Rule? Do unto others as they have done to you.

Sure, there were other interpretations that his parents and pastor spoke of. The Golden Rule talked of treating others as you would want to be treated, but what if others treated you with disrespect? And, eye for an eye? His pastor said while there were examples of taking a life for a life in the Bible by punishing murder with the execution of the assailant, the passage mostly applied to equity in punishment. Injure a man's hand so he cannot work, you pay his lost wages. Steal a man's animals so he cannot eat, you buy him food. But what if people acted so reprehensible that retaliation was the only justifiable response?

Simon turned the corner at Luigi's, slipped behind the Italian meat market and crept down an alley. A shard of a crescent moon softened the slate sky and illumined the street with a narrow and silvery pathway. He moved with stealth, living up to his nickname.

He approached the rear of Peter Stout's saloon and scaled a half-wall. Behind the bar, a bucket lay on its side. A broom leaned against the brick wall. The acrid smell of rag-water hit his nostrils. The stench of rotted food and spilled blood overpowered him, caught in his throat, and he hesitated. What am I doing here? What do I expect to achieve? Unaware that those seemingly simple questions were layered with complexity, he felt the answers to be obvious. I am here because God put me here. I expect to right the wrongs.

He looked toward the back door to Five Corner Bar and saw it was ajar. Mumbled, indecipherable conversations tossed about from inside, and seeped into this small courtyard. Simon peered in to the bar over the bottom sill of the rear window. Customers bustled from table to table, and tussled at the bar for another pint. Bartenders rushed to keep steins filled. Flames danced from clay sconces hung on walls. Chatter jam-packed the hall. The many seemed to speak at once, caring to be heard, but not a whit to listen.

Simon spotted Peter Stout, who raised a mug over his head. The room quieted.

"We're going to declare New York City's independence from Washington," Peter Stout announced.

"Here, here!" A man held up his mug. "And I'm declaring my independence from my wife."

"And me from my mistress." Another slurred.

Simon tuned out the nonsense and eyed the sconces. He needed a plan. He could run through the bar and knock them to the wood bar. When fire sparked and patrons panicked, he'd bash Byrne over the head with a barstool and kick Peter Stout in the leg. He imagined the chaos and destruction as Five Corner Bar seared. Singed bodies, burning flesh, blood fountaining out of Byrne's head, like what he had done to Alice. Peter Stout screaming with pain from his bashed and useless leg, like what happened to John.

Simon's stomach palpitated at the carnage he could cause. He thought of his father, who expounded non-violence, and of his mother, who believed all problems were solvable with conversation after a hot meal (no serious talk allowed at dinner). What would John Coal think of Simon's intentions? A big burly man, John never used his might to get ahead, only his wits. And Alice and Sarah, teachers and kind souls, they wouldn't agree with this sort of revenge, of that he was certain. And his pastor...? His God...?

His stomach sunk. What had he almost done?

Kid rolled over the brick wall. "Hi partner."

Simon sunk below the window. His whisper was fast and harsh. "What are you doing here?"

Kid crouched next to him. "I'll help you kill those fuckers. That's why you're here, right?" He pulled a knife from his pocket.

Simon recoiled. "Those people are like you."

"Just 'cause they're white don't mean they're right. Hey, that was a rhyme."

Weary and weakened, Simon sat. The verve to fight, to exact revenge through violence, retreated. He had never been violent before, hadn't even engaged in schoolyard brawls when he was a boy. Slink home, he thought, to my bed, to Mama's hot breakfast in the morning, to my job, and to the Five Point girls he'd yet to bed. But what about revenge for what happened to Alice and John? And for Noble? What about the black people less fortunate than he who endure slavery? What did he owe them? If he didn't do something, what would that say about him? Wasn't his inaction akin to cowardice?

Kid stuck his index finger up his nose and pulled it out. A glob of blood and snot stuck to the tip. He flicked it away. "I've seen you and your uncle around Five Points."

Simon didn't look at him.

"I'll help you get these bastards but it'll cost ya. I need money for a train ticket to Colorado. Two dollars. Better make it three." Kid waved the knife. "We'll gut them and drape their innards across Five Points."

"I've changed my mind." Simon jumped up and rolled over the wall. He ran through the maze of streets toward his home. His heart raced, not only from the sprint, but from the thought of the person he'd almost become.

♦

Kid crouched below the window, saddened Simon had run away. They could be friends, couldn't they? He recalled his efforts to make Noble his first friend at the Home. It was the day after Noble arrived and Kid had hoarded a piece of bologna from his lunch, approached Noble, and retrieved the meat from his pocket. Palm up, brown slime filled the underside of his fingers and knuckles. Noble looked down at the offering, and his eyes widened. Kid looked too, then back up at Noble, who ran off. The bologna was covered with dirt and bugs.

Kid hadn't tried to make a friend again. So much easier to hate. Now, he realized, it had been stupid to think he had a chance for Simon to be his first friend since the whores at the brothel. Why would a handsome and charming guy like Simon Black Cat ever want to hang around an ugly, stupid kid like me, one who was full of vitriol?

"Hey!" Peter Stout stood over him.

Liquor fumes gusted toward Kid.

Peter Stout grabbed him. "What are you doing here?"

"Watching."

"Watching what?"

Kid thought quick. "I hate them fucking colored people and I wanted to watch the celebration. I wish I had burned down that orphanage."

"Didn't I see you on the water brigade trying to put out the fire?"

"Not me, Sir."

"You sure?"

Kid spat. "That's the only water I'd put on that fire."

"You're lying."

"I ain't."

"You were next to Noble on the line."

"Wasn't me."

Peter Stout grabbed him by the t-shirt and pulled him up. The worn cotton tore under his grip. Peter Stout brought his fist back.

Kid held up his hands. "Wait. Don't."

"You have one second to tell me why you're here."

"Simon Black Cat."

"Who's that?"

"A negro from Five Points. He came to kill you and Byrne and everyone in your bar. I stopped him. He had a torch and a flame and he was going to set fire to the tavern."

Peter Stout let go of his shirt. "How do I know you're telling the truth?"

He pulled the knife from his pocket. "He said if anyone tried to escape, he'd cut them up. I scared him away and he dropped this knife."

Peter Stout took the blade. "You say this belongs to Simon who?"

"Simon Black Cat."

"You know where he stays?"

"Yes, Sir. I know where he lives, where he works, where he frequents."

"Tell me."

"Four dollars."

The loud crash of breaking glass sounded from inside the bar, followed by cheers. Peter Stout rushed toward the back door and looked in.

He turned to Kid. "You coming?"

Kid followed, closer to having the sharp edges of a train ticket to Colorado wedged between his fingers, nearer to owning his own plot of land, nearer to having his own wife.

Chapter Eighteen

Noble raised his head from the cold New York City jail floor. His chin dropped to the floor and splashed in vomit. Tongue inflamed, his head pounded, his muscles ached. He heard moans and thought they were his own. One eye swollen shut, the other was a slat-like peek into a dark void. Shadowy movement on the other side of the bars of the holding cell vaguely registered. Feet shuffled. The world groaned.

His body weakened, his senses heightened. Smells fouler, sounds brawnier. The nerves under his skin hyper-sensitized. His cheek, pressed against the floor, throbbed.

Byrne's nightstick scraped the iron bars. "Get up, prisoner."

Noble tried to rise but couldn't. Byrne unlocked the gate and pushed his way in. He shoved his hands under Noble's armpits and dragged him face down out of the cell. The tops of Noble's bare feet skimmed along the rough surface. His stomach scraped along the concrete. The bee necklace bounced along the ground. Where were the shirt and shoes given to him by Colonel Duryee?

Byrne pulled him to the back of the police station and outside. Three sides of the yard were enclosed by high fencing. The fourth side, a concrete wall, was dappled with bullet holes. The chilled evening air stung at Noble's raw and bloody cuts. Byrne dropped him into mud. The puddle's edges dark and dry where it had evaporated from the afternoon sun.

Byrne kicked him in the ribs. "Get up."

Noble tried.

Byrne lifted him, pushed him. Noble slammed face first against a wall. His knees buckled but he managed to stay upright. He twisted his torso, and through a partially opened eye, looked toward what was on the other side of the yard, fifteen, maybe twenty feet away. At another time, under different circumstances, fear would have flooded him, but he was too sore, too queasy, and too despondent to care.

Four men. Or were there five? Each held a rifle-musket. Was Peter Stout the third from the left?

"Ready," Byrne called.

The men raised their weapons, muzzles pointed skyward.

Byrne yelled to Noble. "Are you prepared to admit you started the fire at the Colored Orphan Asylum?"

Noble gripped the bee vessel around his neck. "I didn't...I would never..."

"This is your last chance." Byrne called.

Noble tried to weigh his choices. Concentrate! Die here now, or admit to something he didn't do. What kind of life would he have in prison? Would he be able to pilot that maze? He pictured Sarah in Doc B's clinic. How could he have been so wrong about the message in her eyes? Hadn't that been the look of love? But then she patted his cheek, and told him he was a good boy like he was some dim-witted juvenile. Maybe he'd be better off dead. Who would ever love him?

A vibrant buzz sounded by Noble's ear. He looked toward the rear of the police station and thought he saw circling bees. If they were real, the hive couldn't be far. He scanned the back of the building and a fuzzy outline of honey combs peeked out from under the eaves of the roof. More bees hovered around it. Worker bees. Inside, the queen and her drones. Genus: Apis Dorsata.

"Aim." Byrne shouted.

The firing squad squared their guns, and looked along the tops of the barrels.

Noble concentrated on the bees. Whether they were real or imagined, it didn't matter.

Page seventy-two of Prokopovych's bee bible. Bees detect changes in the air. When it is cold, they cluster in their hive to stay warm. They store the honey they make during the warm months to sustain them during the cold ones.

Since the outer temperature had dropped below fifty degrees, most of the bees huddled in the center of the hive in a "winter cluster." The queen was in the middle and the workers and drones rotated their positions to make sure no bee got too cold. Eighty degrees, the approximate temperature in the heart of the cluster. Noble wished to be there. He'd bow before the queen and ask her majesty's permission to become one of her servants. She'd agree, of course, and his arms would change into forewings and hindwings. His two legs would grow into six with pollen baskets attached to the hind ones. He'd have a stinger filled with venom.

Byrne called again. "Confess you set the Colored Orphan Asylum fire."

He could admit he did it, couldn't he? Three simple words. I did it. Or a nod that would acknowledge his guilt. They'd lower their guns and, in the moment of their victory, before they threw him back in the cell, he'd turn into a bee and sting them all. Some in their eyes, some in their hearts. Noble's abdomen, digestive tract and muscles wouldn't rupture until after the last man lay on the ground, foaming at the mouth and writhing in pain, seconds from his final breath. While

Noble might not have lived for anything, he would have died for something.

He faced the firing squad.

"Confess!" Byrne yelled.

Noble grabbed the bee necklace and clutched it against his heart. A lone bee buzzed.

Two Points

Whether true or false, what is said about men often has as much influence on their lives, and particularly on their destinies, as what they do.

Les Misérables by Victor Hugo. Published by A. Lacroix, Verboeckhoven & Cie, 1862

New York Times

CIVIL WAR DRAFT RIOTS

119 DEAD

Simon Black Cat Murdered

"It's not just about the draft."

Reported by John Coal

A Compilation of Several Articles Published in THE TIMES
from July 11 – 17, 1863

NEW YORK. On July 13, 1863, a hot, smoldering day in New York City, anti-draft violence exploded and resulted in murder, pillaging, and chaos and lasted until July 17. Governor Seymour stated the official death toll at 119. Police Superintendent John Kennedy was beaten during the riots and remains hospitalized.

"This is the bloodiest outbreak of civil disobedience in New York City history," Governor Seymour said of the Riots.

To understand the Riots, one must look back to January 1, 1863 when President Lincoln announced his Emancipation Proclamation. Two months later, a military conscription law was passed that permitted wealthy draftees to provide a substitute draftee for the fee of $300.00. Members of the Peace Wing of the Democratic Party, nicknamed the Copperheads, believed the Emancipation and the Conscription meant they would be forced to fight in Lincoln's war to free black slaves.

"If slaves are freed," Peter Stout, owner of Five Corner Bar, said, "they will move North, take our jobs, and marry our daughters. We cannot allow that to happen. It's bad enough there are free blacks to begin with."

William J. Henley, United States Army Clerk, offered this counter-position. "It's not just about the draft for the copperheads. It's about race and politics, class and religion. We should all be able to live peaceably together."

The draft lottery began on July 11. On the morning of July 13, hundreds of white workers marched in protest against the draft, the emancipation, and the conscription. They carried signs and banged on pans and drums. The crowd grew as the marchers made their way to the draft office on Third Avenue. Volunteer firemen, angry over losing their exemption from conscription, burned the draft office. Due to the violent mob, an army squadron that was to stop the violence was forced to retreat. Telegraph poles were knocked down, train tracks were uprooted, and fence rails were destroyed and used as clubs.

Rioters targeted draft supporters, Republicans, and the wealthy and their homes on Fifth Avenue. They looted and burnt homes and businesses. Irish Catholic rioters torched the Magdalene Charity and the Five Points Mission.

Rioters attacked blacks indiscriminately: men, women, and children. One elderly black man was beaten while holding his four-year-old grandson.

Simon Black Cat, a twenty-four-year-old furrier, while attempting to aid the elderly man and his grandson was knocked unconscious, carried to City Hall Park, lynched, and set afire. At least 11 other black men were murdered during the Riots. Interracial couples were particularly targeted.

No arrests have been made.

On July 13, New York City Mayor George Opdyke finally found the good sense to telegraph Secretary of War Edwin Stanton to request the assistance of federal troops. 6000 soldiers arrived in the city two days later. Fighting between the rioters and soldiers lasted until July 16 when peace was restored.

Chapter Nineteen

Court Calendar. January 15, 1867. SUPREME COURT—GENERAL
TERM. Action for Damages. Court of General Sessions. This is an action to recover $16,000, the amount of damages alleged to have been
sustained by the plaintiffs from acts of the mob during the draft riots
of July 1863. Plaintiff carried on the pork-packing business on the
corner of West Washington and Houston Streets and his establishment
was consumed by fire kindled from the burning of an adjoining lumber
yard alleged to have been set on fire by the mob. Ruling deferred.

Alice spit up. Phlegm landed on the Law Report section of
the New York Times. The quadragenarian's face turned red.
Tears followed.

"That's okay." Sarah reassured her mother. She folded the
paper, and pushed it aside.

"No cause for tears," John Coal said. "This is a celebration."

Alice's mood quickly changed when Sarah walked toward
her holding a plate with a white layer cake with bright red
strawberries and chocolate frosting on top. The cake still
warm, the frosting melted in places. Alice reached out. Although her hands were functional—they could wrap around a
fork and grip a gun—when at rest her fingers curled as if she
were ready to throw a ball.

It had only taken months after Byrne's attack on Alice for
the people of Five Points to change her name from Alice Black

as Night to Alice Knows Nothing. Six months post assault, Doc B told Sarah not to give up hope for more improvement. "The brain is unpredictable," the doctor had said. But Sarah knew there would be no further reduction of the swelling and her mother would never be her wise mama again.

Three p.m. and seated at the four-chaired folding table of the three-room tenement, Alice fidgeted with excitement. A food-stained cotton bib swayed on her elegant neck. Her dark brown eyes, as big as the moon as John liked to say, were wide with happy expectation. Despite fifteen years between mother and daughter, one might be hard pressed to identify mother from daughter. Sarah, nineteen at the time of her mother's beating, had aged in the last six years not as a woman with time as her friend, but as a woman whose dreams had been obliterated.

The people of Five Points had helped at first. Taking shifts to give Sarah needed breaks. Baking pies, frying chicken, stewing vegetables. They collected money at church. But life moved on and people administered to their own problems. Their circle of support dwindled, and disappeared. Wasn't Sarah a modern woman who could work full time, visit the market, cook dinner, keep the gas lights aglow, care for Alice and John, quilt blankets, and sew their clothes? This was the 1860s, after all, but her responsibilities proved too much. She was still Sarah High Yellow to some, but to others she became Sarah Abandoned Dreams, SAD for short. Desperate for assistance as she tried to keep her teaching job, she went to their pastor and visited neighbors and did the unthinkable: she asked for help. Promises made were promises unfulfilled.

Sarah harbored no anger toward her community. Everybody did the best they could, and the Five Points of new was different from the Five Points of old. In less than a decade, Five Points was still a world of vice and misery, as Charles

Dickens had called it, but the small town feel of community that glowed under the patina was vanishing.

Block parties with buskers and chess tables, meats slow cooking on grills, games and homemade hooch, gone. Walking along Broadway and having familiarity with each person you passed, no more. Knowing all who filled the church pews, over. Even Doc B could hardly handle the influx of people converging upon her clinic.

Since that horrific day when Alice and Sarah's lives changed irretrievably, Five Points had begun the split into the emerging neighborhoods of Little Italy, Chinatown and lower Manhattan. Little Italy was being infiltrated by gangsters from Sicily. In Chinatown, the population of johnnies greatly exceeded the Asian female population so Chinese men married Irish women. In lower Manhattan, justice was meted, and often thwarted, at the New York County Courthouse.

Stories of the gangs that roved Five Points, the brute of Boss Tweed loyalists, police corruption, overcrowded tenements, the Civil War draft riots, and the burning of the Colored Orphan Asylum continued, especially when the conversation centered on what a neighborhood should never be. One woman arrested for public drunkenness spat, "If you lived in Five Points, you'd drink whiskey for breakfast too."

Sarah and John tried to focus on the good that came from their neighborhood. They talked of Master Juba, the colored teen who'd invented tap dancing by combining Irish and African dance moves. They spoke of the intermingling of free blacks and whites. They proudly recounted how the North defeated the South, and the glory of the end of slavery. Every day, Sarah and John lit a candle in memory of Simon Black Cat, dead four years now. Each day she tried not to think of Noble Jennings.

Silly woman. She chastised herself for embracing feelings for a boy she had only briefly met. While she held John Coal's amputated leg in the crate, and her mother was unconscious in the next bed, she had looked into Noble's eyes and saw love. True, she was fortunate and surrounded by love but this differed from the affection she received from her mother, John Coal, Simon Black Cat, most of the community of Five Points, the teachers she had worked with, and her former students. The way that boy had looked at her had sent currents through her body, a feeling she had never had before and had been unable to recreate since. She was sure as she gazed into his eyes she had blushed. She wanted to kiss him so badly, right there in the clinic at that most inappropriate moment. Shameful, lustful, that's what she was.

Six years had passed, that boy would be nineteen or twenty years old now. She was twenty-five and their age difference no longer mattered. She yearned to see him, yes, to visit a prisoner. What was wrong with her? Weren't there plenty of eligible men in Five Points? She snickered, definitely not with Peter Stout's legacy. But, Sarah continued her stream of consciousness, Noble was not only a convict but a white man. Which would her mother deem worse? She looked at Alice seated at the dining room table, awaiting her birthday celebration, child-like, unaware, and knew her mother would have no feelings about Noble, good or bad or indifferent.

What if he had started the Colored Orphan Asylum fire? A boy with those eyes and the kindness he had shown to her family could never have done that. An impossibility she believed as sure as she knew the cadence of her own steps, and the intonations of her own speech.

"You okay?" John Coal asked.

Sarah snapped out of her trance. John helped around the house as much as he could, hopping here and there on his one leg, using crutches sometimes. He watched Alice while Sarah went to work. He tried to find jobs but had to rely on others to navigate the city streets and was unable to contribute financially in a meaningful way. When he had energy, he chose a busy street corner and played the shell game, but being prone to chronic pain and frequent infections, days of strength were few to none. During such times when he was incapable of caring for Alice, Sarah missed work to administer his medications and change his dressings, and to tend to her mother.

Earlier on the day of Alice's fortieth birthday, the principal had called Sarah into his office. She sat across from him and, as sure as pigs and goats roamed Five Points, she knew. His face, as malleable as clay, showed his struggle. You're fired, the words hefty on his tongue. Mister Rutherford was a kind man who suffered confrontations. He'd tell her there were budgetary considerations to be made and, as she was the youngest teacher (although not the last hired), she was the one who had to go. He'd offer a glowing reference for prospective employers, and a couple of dollars from his own pocket.

Sarah could make this hard on him by dropping to her knees in a dramatic flourish and begging him to reconsider. She'd speak of her mother, a former teacher no less, who had the capacity of a six-year-old. She'd remind Mister Rutherford of John, who had a hideous and odorous infection festering in his remaining leg. With no other source of income and no savings, what would they do without Sarah's income?

Mister Rutherford moved his mouth, but no words came out. He looked like a sad jowly dog. Sarah didn't drop to her knees and plead for her job. She was certain he was supposed to fire her weeks ago and had waited as long as he could. The principal knew her situation. They all did. She didn't want his pity, or anyone else's. In this sense, she was truly her father's daughter.

She hated Peter Stout with passion that emotionally blinded her. When she saw him, or thought of him, she could see nothing but crimson rage. Peter Stout could have prevented Byrne's attack on her mother. He could have quelled the local anger that frothed when the North entered the war, and then John wouldn't have been run over by the carriage. He could have thwarted the uprising during the draft riots and then the final scene of Simon Black Cat's story would yet to be written.

Without hearing the principal say those final words, Sarah walked out of his office, out of the school, and into the bustling street with its many carriages and pedestrians, and headed home. She stepped around pigs and goats, and over their scat. She didn't stop to scratch between Esther's long ears while the mule munched hay from Jenny Big Stink's fish wagon. She didn't want Jenny to hand her a freshly wrapped whole cod-fish or snapper. Sarah had refused Jenny's many offers of free fish, until Jenny explained taking the fish would make her feel better as she blamed herself for what happened to Alice. But today, Sarah didn't want an inch of sympathy, even Jenny's camouflaged version. She simply wanted to be able to care for her family on her own. Didn't she deserve the ability to do that?

At home, Alice's fortieth birthday, Sarah placed the warm layer cake in front of Alice. The aromas of chocolate icing and fresh strawberry mixed with the scent of the vanilla cake.

"Happy birthday, dear Mama," Sarah sang. "Happy birthday to you."

"Happy Birthday, my sweetness." John kissed her cheek.

Alice blew out the candles and clapped her hands. Sarah cut a wedge and placed it on a plate in front of her mother, along with a spoon. Alice laughed and grabbed the sweet with her hands. She bit into the dessert. Icing smeared over her face, strawberries fell into her lap, cake crumbled in her fingers, down her arms, and across her bib.

Sarah cut two additional wedges, and shoved a piece into her mouth. John mashed strawberries between his fingers and spread the mush all over his face. Alice clapped and laughed with delight.

Physical Examination of Alice Rosalie Fuller
Prepared by Doctor Elizabeth Blackwell
Testing done: January 12, 1867
Report submitted: January 15, 1867

Characteristics

Age: 40 years
Ethnicity: Negro
Height: 66 inches
Weight: 145 pounds
Resting Heart Rate: 82
Temperature: 98.2 degrees

Summary

Six years earlier, Miss Fuller suffered a brain injury of the traumatic and irreversible kind. At forty years old she presents as a small, non-school aged child. She does not speak, nor does she exhibit reactions to visual or verbal cues, nor does she offer any cues as to her needs. She seems immersed in her own world like a fish in a bowl and carries a stuffed bear that she clutches and/or a towel that she sucks. When the towel or bear is removed, she throws a tantrum that one would only expect from a child unable to communicate her distraught. As Miss Fuller's physician since the incident, I had hoped for more recovery however none is to be expected. Her daughter, Sarah Fuller, has been so informed.

Recommendations

Keep Miss Fuller clean, fed, hydrated, and safe. Continue to try and find ways to communicate with her and to determine her needs.

Chapter Twenty

take the fish take the fish take the fish

Alice smeared cake on her face. Child-like sounds emitted from her cracked lips. Her body dried up like she's been scorched while seated on the dark side of the sun. From her shriveled toes to the area between her legs where no man had gone for years, to the moonscape skin on her arms, chest and face, and her lips. Always dry, and sometimes itchy, scaly. It wasn't only age that wrinkled and desiccated, but years of her confinement.

Sarah rubbed petroleum jelly on Alice's body to help with her dry skin. But jelly cost money, money they did not have so Sarah spread it sparingly while questioning its effectiveness. The sink in the kitchen of the tenement had become a science experiment, run by John Coal in his efforts to create the perfect, affordable moisturizing cream. Oils, milk, bread, minced vegetables—whatever he could find to combine that left the skin smooth. John spread the latest concoction on his hand and watched to see if he had a reaction. Did welts form? Hives? Was his skin smoother? Miscues abounded. He had tried everything in their cupboard and ice box. Even grinding the skin and bones from Jenny Big Stink's fish. Failures, all of them. If only, he thought, I could get some honey.

Sarah and John each took a piece of Alice's birthday cake and smeared it on their faces. Alice realized she should feel appreciation at their attempts to make her feel normal when they mimicked the silly things she did. One big happy family unit, but Alice wanted to object each time they sat on the floor with her and helped her dress a doll, or when Sarah bathed her and sang—

Come up horsey, hey, hey

Come up horsey, hey, hey

Go to sleep and don't you cry

Mama's gonna make you an apple pie

—like Alice was the child and not the parent.

I'm not playing with the dolls, she wished to communicate. Stop singing to me like I'm a baby. I was not reduced to a child when Byrne cracked his club on my head. I am still Alice Black as Night. I. Am. Not. Alice. Knows. Nothing.

I just...

What?

It's just...

take the fish take the fish take the fish

She reviewed her choices. One, two, three. (1) Scream until she is heard (she has tried, doesn't work), (2) pretend everything is okay (impossible!), or (3) throw a fit.

She chose the fit.

Alice flung her body back and forth, to and fro. Her hands and arms curled toward her chest. Bits of her frosting beard flung off her face.

"There she goes," John said.

"Rocking again," Sarah said.

John reached for Alice. "I'm going to put her on the floor so she doesn't fall out of the chair."

"Wait," Sarah said. "I don't want you to fall, and you know she doesn't like to be touched. Let's watch her for a moment. Maybe she'll stop soon."

rocks dogs cats rocks dogs cats rocks dogs cats

Trapped, that's what she was. So much she understood but could not convey, such as her comprehension of the news of the day when John read The New York Times aloud. She was thrilled African-American men were permitted to vote in the District of Columbia, saddened by the Kidder massacre, and excited to ride the first elevated railcar. Would someone take her? John mistook her cooing while he read the paper as expressions of pleasure, and not as what it was. Her reaction to the news and her attempt to connect with him. Inevitably, she gave up and returned to her dolls who were the only ones who understood her.

◆

Three weeks after Alice's fortieth birthday, infection raged in John. The wet gangrene on his swollen leg was a green and black fetid fiend. With little reluctance from John—he knew the leg had to go—Doc B amputated the remaining limb. It tumbled into a box and was thrown into a garbage bin behind the clinic. Two boys filched the discarded leg from the trash, along with a kidney, a squishy benign tumor cut from a lady's neck, and the cadaver of a still born. The boys sold the remains to a body snatcher who then sold them to a medical school.

Sing Sing Prison Disciplinary Report

March 17, 1867

Re: Prisoner 752

Discipline: 30 days solitary confinement

Noble Jennings sent to solitary confinement for fighting with other inmates and general disobedience. Allow Prisoner 752 into yard once per day for no more than sixty minutes for him to tend bees and collect honey.

Benjamin Ash
Warden

Chapter Twenty-one

Sarah continued her daily charade of pretending to be an employed teacher when she actually spent ten hours each day looking for work and trying not to feel like the absolute failure she had become.

On this chilly Saint Patrick's Day, Sarah walked by Jenny Big Stink's Fish Wagon, and stopped to rub Esther's gray muzzle. The toothless mule gummed at hay, chewed in a roundabout motion, and drenched the feed with saliva. The food made compact and soft, he swallowed. Jenny was still a hefty and handsome woman, and she continued to reek of fish. Her little family had expanded from her and Esther, to her, Esther and Bertha, a German immigrant with fat fingers who threaded needles with ease and told Jenny she was wunderschön. When Bertha knit, she hummed German love songs in tune with the click of the needles.

This Friday morning, Jenny had her best piece of fish, trimmed and wrapped in paper, ready for Sarah.

"Can I pick it up later?" Sarah asked.

Jenny nodded. "I'll keep it on ice."

They smiled, knowing this cold day required no ice to preserve the fish.

Sarah gave Esther a last scratch on his sparse forelock and moved on, pretending to have somewhere to go.

In front of Saint Mary's Church on Grand Street, mounds of dirt-peaked snow lined the streets. Men tramped through slush and rushed along with collars upturned. Women burrowed hands into muffs. Boys engaged in snowball fights. Ratty dogs nuzzled the icy ground for food. Horse drawn carriages tried to traverse the streets but were blocked by snow banks. Donkeys brayed, and livery drivers cursed and spat. A block away, a crowd gathered for the start of the Saint Patrick's Day parade.

Sarah folded her arms across her chest to stave off the chill. She looked up at the brick façade of the church built in 1826 to unify and aid Irish immigrants, and eyed the bell that would soon strike twelve times.

The Angelus Bell, perched in the north spire, was cast in Ireland during the days of penal law promulgated by the English to force the Irish Roman Catholics to accept the Anglican Church. One of the laws stated it was illegal to own, possess and/or ring church bells. Fearful the three feet in diameter and almost one ton bell would be confiscated by the English government, and the bronze melted for bullets, four Irishmen secreted the bell onto a steamer ship that sailed to Argentina and then to New York Harbor. In 1833, after being stored in a dusty warehouse for several years, the bell found a home in the tower at St. Mary's Church on Manhattan's Lower East Side. It was the first bell to be hung in a Catholic church in New York. Each day the bell rang as a call to prayer and as a symbol of unity and humanity.

Inside the church, the weekly alms for the poor session was about to begin. Prayers for the unfortunate and mistreated, followed by free food and drink. For many, it was the only meal of the week that would not be begged for, stolen, or composed of picked-through discards.

The ringing of the bell began, a cacophony of dings and dongs. The clapper struck the soundbow and the bell swung back and forth with handstrokes and backstrokes. The ringer's hands, raised high above his head, pulled on the tail of the rope that caused the bell to sway. His feet left the wood landing as the weight of the bell carried him to and fro. One boom per half-second.

The peal of the bell reverberated up Sarah's long legs and to her head, and then back down and around again. How could such a beautiful sound make her feel so useless? Rent was due. It was difficult to find wood to keep the stove burning for heat. John tried to be helpful, as much as he could with no legs. Alice was oblivious to the troubles. She smiled and giggled, played with her toys, and napped. Oh, to be more like my mother, Sarah thought.

While the bell chimed, faceless and shadowy figures lurched forward, pushed past Sarah and swept into the church. Shabby coats covered rounded shoulders. Pews filled. Bodies thawed.

Outside the church, Sarah's fingers numbed. The church bell rang its final peal.

Pastor John's thick Irish accent flowed from the sanctuary, surged along the nave, sprang out the church's open door, and cut through the chill. "As we celebrate this day of the Apostle of Ireland, we step forth, letting the life-giving power of the Spirit flow through us and into the world God is out to save."

Sarah didn't know if it was the wind or the sermon that chafed her cheeks. If she went inside, would she be accepted? One-half Irish, one-half black. She had applied to teach at all the colored schools in New York City and had been turned away because she was white. She had tried to obtain tutoring and nanny jobs from well-to-do families but was rejected because she was black. She had always had a difficult time making friends, unsure if she should walk on the white or black side of the street.

If she wasn't white or black, who was she?

The asynchronous ba-boom-ba-boom of drums rose into the frosty air, coming closer. Hoots and hollers echoed along Attorney Street. Sarah looked toward the racket. Revelers turned onto Grand. A wagon became stitched in by piles of snow. The chestnut who pulled the wagon strained to move it forward under its master's whip. Trapped at the corner of Grand and Pitt, the carriage blocked the parade route. Angry marchers yelled at the driver. *Get out of the way! Move it, buster!* They descended upon him, knocked him off the seat, and rocked his carriage back and forth. The horse, wide eyed and anxious, stepped sideways and reared. A police officer attempted to placate the mob and was buried in an avalanche of snow balls, some filled with rocks. Men and boys emerged from darkened corners and waved shillelaghs and sticks. More officers converged. Additional hooligans joined. Weapons drawn: knives and sabres, bats and chains.

Sarah started for the church door but was picked up by the surge of trouble makers that heaved toward her at obtuse angles. She fought like a tigress, nails clawed, teeth bared. Near to her, a copper's scalp was cut open by the force of a club, nails driven into the barrel. His blood spurted on to her forehead.

The crowd was too big, too swift, too rough to escape. Hands fondled her breasts, and grabbed between her legs. *Show me your fun bags. Let me have a go at your giblets.* She swatted them away, tried to push through the crowd. Who will take care of Alice and John if she were dead? The image of not returning home, of Alice and John being left alone, intensified her resolve to break free of the grips and gropes.

"Noooooo!" She waved her arms, tried to hit anyone near.

A blow skidded across the back of her head, knocked her down. She jumped up and tried to escape again, this time under the crowd, through and around legs, but was still unable to get away.

Thick arms wrapped around her waist.

She fought. "Let me go!" Her legs waved in the air.

The grip tightened. "*Stoptar suas.*"

She understood the words that spilt into her ears. *Shut up*, in Gaelic. His voice was distantly familiar. His hot whiskey breath on her neck burned. She didn't recognize the feel of his rough hands that wrapped around her, or the sharpness of his elbows that bloodied mouths and noses while he pulled her through the crowd, but she knew who he was.

Chapter Twenty-two

Sarah sat on a stool at the bar and sipped beer that cooled her throat but not her mood. Her limbs shivered, not from cold and fear any longer but from anger. Anger at her loss of control, at having to have to be rescued, not just by anybody but by him.

Behind the bar, a man so slender Sarah thought he might be an apparition, swiped a dirty rag across the bar top and then reached into a box of forks and knives and shined them with the same rag. Across the wood floor, Peter Stout straightened chairs and wiped table tops. Unlit sconces, prominent like proboscises, decorated the walls. Large windows framed the front and rear of the bar.

Sarah recalled her thirteenth birthday when her mother had her peer in the windows of this very tavern.

"That is your father," Alice had said. "Stay away from him."

What would her mother think if she knew Sarah was drinking a beer at his establishment? Would she thank Peter Stout for saving her daughter from the St. Patrick's Day crush? Sarah knew exactly what her mother would think of this. Nothing. She wouldn't comprehend it.

She slid off the stool and looked out the front window and across the narrow and cobblestoned street. Signs for O'Leary's Bakery and The Cobblers Rothstein fronted stores. Five Points seemed appeased for now. Perhaps the free-for-all had ended and it was safe to go home. She headed toward the door. She'd have to stop at Jenny Big Stink's fish wagon first to get their dinner.

"Where are you going?" Peter Stout asked.

She didn't answer. He had no right to know anything about her. She reached for the door handle.

He spoke to her back. "I put the word out that no one was to hire you."

Her face reddened. She turned and faced him.

The skinny man behind the bar stopped wiping and watched.

"Why would you do that?" she asked.

"So you'd come to me for help. This is Five Points. Eventually everyone comes to me."

She glared, because he'd done nothing to help her, his own daughter. Because of him, Alice had the mental capacity of a child and John had no legs. Noble, accused by Peter Stout of causing the Orphan Asylum fire, was imprisoned. Simon Black Cat, so beautiful and innocent, had preached non-violence during the civil rights riots and died at the hands of copperheads. Peter Stout could have prevented all of that, she was sure.

She said none of this since words were no longer her weapons. They had never been enough. She wasn't a great orator like Lincoln, who could turn complex ideas into simple ones and therefore unite people from all persuasions. She didn't possess a mesmerizing baritone like John Coal. She couldn't preach and attract a crowd like Simon Black Cat had. She couldn't even get a teaching job, and had abandoned her desires to be an actress. Careers that depended upon words. Words had always failed her. It was time for action.

She lunged toward the bar and grabbed a knife. The bartender moved toward her, a ghoul in transit.

Peter Stout held up his hand. "No, Kid." He squared himself in front of Sarah.

A sound growled from her belly, an unsatiated beast. She ran at him, the blade of the knife positioned toward his chest. Anger and anguish, disappointment and regrets toppled within her. She dove for him. They fell backwards.

Sarah on top, screamed, "You're not my father."

She plunged the knife into his chest, over and over. "I hate you. I wish I had never been born." The knife plunged against him, her arm bent at the elbow, crashing back and forth like a tomahawk. Again, and again. Spit and venom leapt from her mouth, tears from her eyes, hatred from her soul.

He was silent and unmoving beneath her. She stopped, hesitated over his stillness.

Have I killed him?

She jumped off and rolled away. His eyes were closed. His lips slightly parted. Was his chest moving? No. Nothing.

I have killed him. Good.

Her nails dug into the soft skin of her palm. Her fingers closed tight around the knife. Blood? Where was the blood that spilled from his chest? She looked to the man behind the bar. Amusement lit his pale face.

Peter Stout sat up and smoothed his wrinkled yet clean shirt. Sarah leapt away, and then opened her fist. So engulfed in her fury, she hadn't noticed the knife was plastic. She held only the knife's handle, the blade had broken off.

Peter Stout didn't kill Sarah that day, nor the next. He wouldn't let Kid do it either. There weren't many codes of conduct that Peter Stout found worthy of abidance but an honorable man not offing his spawn was one of them. That, and never lie with a whore on Sundays. Just in case God was watching.

Peter Stout got Sarah a job teaching English at a local elementary school. The students were a mix of black and Irish, the first integrated school in lower Manhattan. Sarah had initially resisted his assistance, but could not do so for long. She needed the money and she loved to teach. If she didn't think about how she got the job, if she didn't think of her horrid father, she managed. The same way she handled her abandoned dreams of becoming an actress. If she didn't think about them, her reality no longer stung.

Once a month, she trekked to Sing Sing prison where she taught inmates to read. Another position Peter Stout arranged for her through his ties to the warden, Benjamin Ash, a Boss Tweed devotee and a German immigrant. Sarah had taken weeks to summon the gumption to ask Peter Stout to get this position for her. Teaching inmates to read wasn't her true motive for volunteering at the prison. It was to see Noble, whom she had been unable to get off her mind since her mother's injury. As much as she hated to ask her father for a favor, having the opportunity to see Noble was worth it. He would be twenty years old now, and no longer a boy.

Chapter Twenty-three

Imprisoned at fourteen, Noble had never known the warmth of a curved body softer than his own, and had never experienced pleasure from the hands and lips of a woman. While incarcerated, he received proposals from men, some courted him by offering their lunch or snacks from the commissary, others were more demanding. Noble turned them all down, some with stern words, the more aggressive ones with boxes to the ears.

One time during a hospital stay a nurse offered to give him a blowie. She began to touch him but the stench from her rotted teeth repulsed him. She looked so sad at his rejection that when he healed he gave her three jars of honey.

Now, twenty years of age and half-a-dozen years a prisoner, each year a ragbag of bruised knuckles and black eyes. At six-foot-five-inches tall, Noble towered over the guards and most of the other prisoners. He had to bend his head and hunch his shoulders to enter his cell, the mess hall, the library. His body was sculpted of muscle, and his arms webbed of dark blue veins that intersected like the fading streets of Five Points.

The morning sun on his face, bees and books were the pinnacle of his existence. There was reveille, meals, set times prisoners had to report in front of their lockups, exercise requirements, and lights out, but nothing mattered more to him than the sun, his bees, and books. The sun his sustenance, the books his oxygen, the bees his family. Still, he was immersed in sadness. An ache that permeated the insides of his cells. The cell he huddled in each night awaiting the morning beam of sunlight to shoot through the tiny window and warm his face, and the cells that comprised his muscles, skin and organs. Sadness: his birthright.

William visited when he could but was excelling in college and had plans to continue to law school, and so had little opportunity to make the thirty-mile trip from Columbia College at One Hundred and Sixteenth Street and Broadway to Ossining, New York and Sing Sing Correctional Facility. Other than William, Noble had no visitors.

His trial whereby he was accused of setting the Colored Orphan Asylum fire had been a twenty-day tornado from arrest to false firing squad to railroading. Noble had spent the years after his conviction burrowing through law books and treatises to discover ways to appeal his conviction. But legal gibberish was not as interesting as other books in the prison library: *Uncle Tom's Cabin, Crime and Punishment, Great Expectations, Little Women*. He even found a book on bees, although not as thorough and advanced as Petro Prokopovych's bee bible, plus the section on bee bearding had been rendered unreadable from mildew.

Noble found his first queen bee during the third year of his incarceration. He had trapped her in the same wood vial he used when he captured the queen in Central Park as a boy, the same vial he always wore around his neck. He had once come very close to killing a man who had tried to rip it from him.

In the prison yard, Noble had waited patiently for his first transplanted queen to construct a hive in one of the grand oaks. Bees don't normally nest in trees but with perseverance her congregation formed. He found two more queens in year four, another one in number five, and ordered two more that year via mail. Colonies became communities. He bottled the honey in metal containers, gifted them to guards and the warden, and sold or bartered them with other prisoners. His bees and the books and the sun became everything and he couldn't recall the value of freedom and innocence. He formed a routine. Up early, sun on face, eat, check on bees in the prison yard, read, and fight. He always fought. Some battles he started, some were begun by others but finished by Noble, some didn't involve him at all but he involved himself. Genus: Fury.

In the prison library on a rainy April afternoon, with an English translation of Victor Hugo's *Les Misérables* opened on the scratched wooden table where he sat, Noble tried to recall how he had learned to read. He yearned to craft an image of sitting on a couch, embraced by his mother who held a beginner's reader on her lap. His father seated across from them in his special armchair, the cushion depressed and dimpled to match the old man's hippy contours. A fireplace crackled and sparked. A rich, earthy fragrance akin to dried hay wafted from his father's pipe. The book his mother read was filled with simple words and primitive drawings, one sketch to a page: man, woman, dog, cat. Perhaps reading had always been natural to him, maybe he was self-taught. He couldn't recall exactly, but he did know in his grim life reading was one of his colorful gifts.

At the Home, William had helped him define the more challenging words such as abnegation, penchant, and conflagration. When Noble felt his worst, he embraced a book, imagined the blank pages before the addition of words, and pictured the author seated and about to write. He would smell its history in the turning pages, and he would find hope. He was glad to have a penchant for reading.

"Jennings."

Noble smelled the rats. Shadows clouded the pages of Jean Valjean's struggles. Four pale and husky men surrounded him. With Noble seated, Diamond Eye—named for his glass eye—was still shorter than him. This wouldn't be the first time he skirmished with the Sing Sing Sons of Dublin.

"Peter Stout says hello." Aengus, a fat jaundiced man who Noble supposed was the leader, spoke with a mighty lilt.

The pinch was on. Noble had just completed a thirty-day stint in solitary confinement (allowed out once per day to tend to his bees). Undeserved, like all the punishments meted by Ash. But Noble didn't care. He made the first move, chump punches learned from Kid. He cracked Aengus aside the head with Hugo's opus, then landed a kidney punch through rolls of skin that doubled the chub in two. A nose-ender stymied Diamond Eye and sent him flying backwards. The two other men were quicker and stronger than he had recalled from previous clashes, that's why they shared the name Muscle. They grabbed his arms, pinned them behind his back. Aengus repaid Noble with punches to his sternum and chin. Noble reeled back into Muscle One and Muscle Two. Four on the library floor—Noble, Aengus and the Muscles—hands and feet, fists and teeth, upended chairs and desks. Blood filled Noble's mouth. He spit. The punches and kicks came fast, a galloping horse, a raging fire.

Pinned to the ground, Aengus heavy on his chest, one of Noble's lungs collapsed. Diamond Eye stood over them and Noble groaned under his error. Aengus wasn't the leader. It was the little guy, Diamond Eye.

Blood covered the lower half of Diamond Eye's face like a beard, tinted his neck, mottled his prison shirt, and dripped to his hard shoes, the ones with razors lodged into the soles.

Diamond Eye stamped a plimsoll shoe into Noble's face. "We, *stomp*, said, *stomp*, Peter Stout, *stomp*, says, *stomp*, hello."

Chapter Twenty-four

Noble awoke in the infirmary. It was dark, or his eyes wouldn't open, or maybe he was dead.

Let me be dead.

It was difficult to breath. When will Aengus get off my chest? Noble tried to get up, didn't know where he wanted to go, maybe to Central Park, or to see William, or to the library. Wasn't he just in the library with his mother reading to him and his father smoking a pipe by a fireplace?

"Stop moving."

Gentle hands on his shoulders pushed him down. He could fight them off, his arms whirlybirds, but a perfume of flowers lifted from the wrists and into his nose like the scent of benevolence.

"Please, Noble, lie back."

He obeyed. Who could struggle against that honeyed voice? He thought he knew all the nurses, their rough accents, their toothless smiles, the wrinkles around their frowns, but not this one. He tried to force his eyes open. They budged, too little to see.

"It's me." Delight and hope populated the voice.

"Mother?" he asked.

He slept again. Dreamed of a man and a woman, a dog and a cat, rudimentary drawings risen to life. He awoke a few times in states of half-consciousness. That sweet voice hovered around him, those hands convinced him there was no place else he needed to be.

Aengus continued to straddle his chest. Day one, day two, day three. Sometimes he woke and it was just him and the fat man suffocating him, other times the woman who could be his mother was there too. Water caressed his lips, a cold compress soothed his forehead. Day four, day five. His stomach grumbled. Day six. Aengus lost weight. Noble breathed better. Day seven. Sight out of his right eye.

She fed him prison slop and it was the best thing he'd ever tasted. Her fingers hugged the spoon, the spoon slid between his lips, the warm mixture throbbed on his tongue, and glided down his throat.

When he had the courage to believe she was real, he said her name.

"Sarah."

Chapter Twenty-five

He drifted to sleep. It was warm and hazy and they were on a boat. Nineteen-year-old Sarah and fourteen-year-old Noble, who they were when they first met in Doc B's clinic when John Coal's leg thudded into a crate and a metal contraption screwed Alice's head together. Sarah had patted Noble on the cheek and told him he was a good boy and he felt his life was forever ruined.

The boat was small, like a row boat or a canoe, and they drifted along the East River with no oars and no direction. Indians hid in the shadows of long limbed hulking trees. President Lincoln ambled with lengthy strides amid lopsided tents strewn across Jones's Wood. Honest Abe cupped his hands around his mouth and called for able-bodied male northerners to ready for battle. William waved from the shore, a small boy who played dress up in oversized Union garb.

Seated across from him on a wooden thwart, the boat rhythmic and rocking, Sarah slipped the top of her dress to her waist. Her breasts were small and firm, perfectly round and light colored. Her nipples erect and brown, the areola pigmented chestnut. Noble was sure she'd taste like melted sugar and vanilla bean, not just her breasts but all of her.

He hardened, felt shame, and covered his growing wick. "I'm sorry."

"For what?"

"I'm too young."

"That was six years ago. You were a boy, you're a man now."

"I felt like a man then."

"We all felt like grownups. Now that we are, we want to be children." Her slender fingers covered her breasts and teased her nipples. "Do you want to touch them?"

He blushed. "Do you want me too?"

"Very much." She moved toward him in a half crouch.

The boat lolled side-to-side. She knelt in front of him. Her hands rested on his closed knees.

"Why don't you sit here?" He stood.

The boat rocked. His large erection levelled with her brown lips and he was mortified for himself, and more so for her. He swiveled his hips to get away from her. The narrow boat pitched and he spread his arms to balance. They toppled into the cool brack. He sank fast and when his feet touched the bottom of the estuary, he bent his knees and then, as if getting rid of bees that bearded his body, he pushed off and propelled to the surface.

Chapter Twenty-six

She closed the curtain around his hospital bed, and brushed her lips on his. "I've wanted to see you since the day you helped my mother and John Coal." She straddled him, drew the bottom of her dress back, and lowered herself on to him.

He placed his hands on her round and soft hips and filled her. She was wet and snug. He moved under her and they gyrated in unison, soft, deliberate thrusts. Slow at first, and then faster.

"Not yet," she said.

He watched her for guidance, ached to please her, to be whatever she needed him to be, the one who waits if that was what she required.

She moved her hips forward and back, faster, her chin tilted with grace, her eyes half-closed. He slipped his hands to her backside, one on each cheek, his fingers cocooned where she split, and guided deeper into her. He thought, as he considered her face, I didn't know eyelashes could be so long.

"Okay. Now," she said.

He exploded. She pulsated around him. She bent to him and their mouths meshed and their bodies flared. They kissed and panted and sweated, and they laughed and gathered their breaths and blushed.

She lifted off him and laid her head on his chest, stretched her damp and warm body across his as if he were her bed. He held her and caressed her and breathed her into him, and he realized he had died and found heaven because that could be the only explanation for what had occurred.

William J. Henley

Counselor at Law

300 Cherry Street

Ring #3B

New York, New York 10002

February 15, 1897

Dictated and Read

Dear Levi,

I am writing at the behest of your mother as she and I have great concern for your refusal to visit your father, although refusal to meet your father would be more precise. As my reputation is decorously a comingling of verbosity and elucidation (it is good for one to acknowledge who one is), please read this letter when you are able to concentrate in the most mundane of settings. This text requires not one-half of your attention, Levi, not three-quarters, but all.

How is it that a boy does not want the experience of looking into his father's eyes? For once, and most likely the only time in my life, I am impotent to irradiate the money and possessions I would forgo to possess the memory of my father's eyes, a memory I covet even if I were to learn that my father was the most hideous of creatures.

Five years ago, John Coal planted vanilla beans and placed the pot in the kitchen window of your mother's second floor walkup. Today, a thick and luxurious vine grows and your Uncle John has come upon the formula for John Coal's Almond, Vanilla & Honey Cream. Thanks, in no small part, to Noble's honey. The lesson, my dear boy, is that one never knows what will grow from the smallest of seeds.

The world is moving forward at a rapid pace. Modernization and expansion are rampant. By the end of this year, Queens, the Bronx, Staten Island and Brooklyn will consolidate with Manhattan to form the five-boroughs. The city that your father and I grew up in—the rough and tumble neighborhoods that one didn't leave without peril (although even remaining in Five Points during our childhoods was fraught with danger)—will soon populate with more than two million people. Where will they fit?

A vampire sits next to bedsides all over the world, thanks to Bram Stoker, and a new ordinance has gone into effect in our glorious city disallowing one to ride his bicycle not more than eight miles per hour. He must keep his feet on the pedals and his hands on the handlebars at all times. What will be legislated next? When and where we are permitted to cross streets? What days we dispose of our trash?

Ah, but as John Stuart Mill said, I am preaching to the converted. Being a man of twenty-nine years young you invite and welcome change, and, why shouldn't you? You are in the throes of your new career and your life, Doctor Levi Solomon Fuller. (If you could see my pride at this moment you would have to shield your eyes).

There are distinctions in the ages of men. As I enter my mid-fifties, a good day is quiet and one of learning and accomplishment, quite a change from the lawyer I was when I was in the early and mid-stages of my career. For you, I imagine, a good day is a sprint filled with wondrous discoveries and adventures.

As a man of a certain age knows, expectations are not always met, dreams are thwarted. That doesn't mean one should not take advantage of the opportunities that are bestowed upon him. This includes, my dear boy, the opportunity to meet your father. My friend. My brother.

I am working diligently, and have for years, to obtain your father's release. I can say emphatically and with no hesitation that he did not set the Colored Orphan Asylum Fire. (You have heard me rant in person about this many times and so will spare you the redundancy of a written tirade).

There have been nine presidents since Noble's arrest (ten if you count that Grover Cleveland led our country on two occasions, four years apart). I have petitioned each one for your father to be pardoned. Chester Arthur showed mild interest. Benjamin Harrison would not take my call. Grover Cleveland took an audience with me (during his second term) but left office without signing the pardon. William Mckinley, our current president, dear Levi, (my heart is pounding) has refused a pardon but appears willing to discuss assisting in Noble's release from prison. Have thirty years of cultivating connections finally paid off?

I am most hopeful that your father will be released from Sing Sing before this year is out, which brings me back to you. Go see him. Get to know the man for who he is, and learn, dear boy, that a man is more than how he has been (wrongfully) labeled.

Thirty-six years in prison has most certainly affected your father. While he is still physically strong (like you, Noble is naturally well-muscled and athletic), he has weakened mentally and is most forgetful. I attribute this to years of confinement and am most positive that upon his release I will come face to face with the Noble of old, or the Noble of young as the case might be. A sharp and selfless man who I love as much as I rely upon the blood that courses through my body and depend upon the breath that fills my lungs.

Don't be fooled, my boy. In this time of modernization and expansion, it is still the simple things in life that bloom into the most significant. Plant the seed now, Levi. Do not wait to grow your relationship with your father. Do not wait to look in his eyes.

I love you, dear boy.
Uncle William

Chapter Twenty-seven

As the sun rose over Five Points, the walkways and roadways glowed in gold and sepia hues that for some glorious moments fooled even the hardest hearts into believing the day held promise. Inside a brothel on Anthony Street, Kid nuzzled his face between a whore's large breasts.

She stroked his hair. "Are you sure you don't want me to do somethin'?"

"Pos'tive," came his muffled reply.

"You come here ever' week and ya never want nuthin' but ta lay all night with me. You don't even take ya clothes off, only ya shoes, and don't want me to be nekkid either. You're a strange gent, Kid Turner."

He didn't need a whore or anyone else to tell him how strange he was. His life stitched together with barbed wire. He moved from one failed opportunity to another. His reward: black eyes, broken bones, isolation. Nothing had worked out for him since he lived at Cousin Amy's brothel as a boy. Not the home of the Walshes, where Charity Walsh made him suck her thumb until the day she killed her husband and then herself, not the Home for Unwanted Boys where he ruled with his fists when all he wanted to do was make a friend, and not when he tried to team with Simon Black Cat, and then with Peter Stout, all to make a few greenbacks so he could afford a train ticket to Colorado to get himself fertile land and a fertile wife. That hadn't worked out either. Couldn't keep two bits in his pocket.

Then he borrowed seventy-five cents from the cash box at Five Corner Bar, and had been on the run ever since. Peter Stout pronounced him a marked man. All for five silver coins. Hadn't Kid done enough dirty deeds for that joe? Broke the arm of a tailor who refused to pay for protection. Threatened the girlfriend of a man who tried to home in on Peter Stout's gambling action. And so much more. He had only borrowed the money, and had every intention to pay it back. Bought a hamburger and a soda with it, and even had some coinage left over for a pack of chewing gum and a newspaper. Thing was, if he had the chance, he'd do it again.

From outside the brothel bedroom door came the throated demand. "Where is he?"

Kid shot up. How had Peter Stout found him? Kid jumped off the bed. Barefoot, he ran out of the room and smack into the hands and knees and feet of Peter Stout, who thumped him until he could barely breathe. The Irishman so adept at the beatdown, his three goons only had to stand by.

He was tossed out of the brothel, and landed on his hip inches from the swipe of a horse-haired brush. Nearing the turn-of-the-century, pigs were no longer the street cleaners of Five Points, goats no longer the landscapers. Men now had the jobs.

The street sweeper nodded toward the whorehouse. "You're not the first man to end up out here on your arse." He held out his hand. "Let me help you up." His accent, thickly Welsh.

Pain radiated down Kid's spine. His right hip throbbed like a drum beat. His face burned. There was not one spot on his body, or beneath his skin, or within his cells or in his soul, that did not ache.

"I can't move," Kid said.

The worker dropped his hand to his side. "A couple of hours with one of those women and that's to be expected. Plus, you got a helluva thrashing. You didn't pay, or something? Guess you won't be able to go back in there."

Tears blotted Kid's eyes.

The street cleaner leaned on his broom. Behind him was a wheelbarrow and a long handled dust pan. "Now, now. Don't go crying. You're a grown man here. I gotta ask you to get up though 'cause you're in my street and you landed on a pile of my dirt and it's getting to be that time when people have to go to work."

Kid wiped his eyes. "I'm not crying."

"See, you can move." The sweeper looked across the street. "I think it's best you be on your way."

Kid followed the man's line of sight, and his eyes settled on two of Peter Stout's fart catchers. Kid looked away. Let them watch him, he didn't care. What else could they do to him? Everything already hurt. The physical pain was immense, but inside he seethed unbearably. From his first breath, always the loser who didn't deserve to be loved. Why hadn't his parents thought him worthy of a name? A solid, every day first name, that was his greatest wish. David. Michael. John. He'd even take a common immigrant's name. Mikhail from Russia. Hans from Germany. Angel from Spain.

Kid looked up at the sweeper, his broom paused and held several inches off the street. He didn't want to keep the man from his job any longer. He slowly rose to his feet, shaky but upright.

"I'm Alwyn," the street cleaner said.

Kid hated this part of a conversation, not that he had many opportunities for salutations and the exchange of niceties.

Still, the man seemed kind and Kid had always been interested in the origin of names and so asked, "What kind of name is that?"

"Welsh. Means blessed."

"Do you feel blessed?" Kid asked.

"I have a job, a wife who makes the best cawl, a cup of tea each morn, and a chew of tobacco in the eve. So, yes, I am blessed. What do they call you?"

Kid scoffed. How quickly his mood changed when he was asked that question, even if he knew it was coming. Embarrassed that his name was not in fact a name but a method to describe or address every child—that kid, this kid, hey kid—or a moniker for a baby goat.

The street cleaner placed his broom's head on the ground and swept. *"Heb ei fai, heb ei ani.* He who has no faults is not born."

Kid stepped out of the way. The man pushed his pile of dirt into the dust pan. Who was this garbage man to teach him about life? Kid had no family, no woman at home to cook for him, no tea to drink, and no tobacco to chew. He had nothing but the pain in his muscles, and the agony of his failures. Not worthy of a name, not worthy of this land, not one to be saved. He walked a few steps, where to go he did not know.

The man called, "Hey."

Kid didn't turn.

"Repay evil with good, and hell will not claim you." The street cleaner said.

Kid dismissed him with a wave and walked on. Pain stabbed his stomach. He had never believed in God and heaven, and certainly did not think there was a devil and a place called hell. There was only the moment, and all his moments had stunk like a whore's twat. He was a waste of molecules and DNA and all the things that made up a human being, had always been useless, here in Five Points, and everywhere. The pigs and the goats had more purpose than he.

He crossed the street to where Peter Stout's men had lurked, and saw they were gone. He limped toward Five Corner Bar, and looked in through the large front window. Peter Stout was behind the counter, maybe ten feet from Kid, only separated by the plate glass. The barkeep poured beers for his goons, pints for breakfast.

Kid searched the ground around his feet, and found what he needed. The rock was the color of dried mud and large enough to do the job. He bent slowly, picked it up, and positioned himself in front of the window. Peter Stout looked toward him, and Kid met his blue unsmiling glare. The man Kid locked eyes with, the man who poured lager from a jug until it overflowed onto the bar, enraged him. Not because of all the wrong Peter Stout had done to him and to others, but because he realized a truth.

I am no better than Peter Stout.

Kid pulled his arm back and launched the rock as hard as he could. The slow melodic crack of glass sounded. The center of the glass shattered. Edges spidered.

Chapter Twenty-eight

Navigating the congested cross-haired intersection that gave Five Points its name, William was continually stunned by the daily witness of hardships. Not just in this fragment of Manhattan but in the many areas of the city through which he traveled on his daily walk, no matter the weather. This January day, he sported an overcoat, boots, and a hat, but many around him could not afford more than the thin clothes that entwined them.

Over there, a mound of rags, most likely a person underneath. On that corner, a mother and her young son begged. Next to that pile of garbage, rats gnawed on a dead pig. In front of Five Corner Bar, a man being beaten, the front window of Peter Stout's bar shattered.

William wondered, what other sufferings did the world offer, in America and across the sea? He had been a sensitive lad, and had matured into a sensitive man beset with shame from the successes he coveted and from the ones he achieved, and so his front right pocket held pennies for him to share with those less fortunate. Whether he carried the pennies to help the poor and mentally ill, or to assuage his guilt, he failed to analyze. Irrespective, his pockets would never be deep enough to hold all the coins life necessitated.

Coppers stood across the street from Five Corners Bar, and watched Peter Stout and three thugs kick and punch the man who lay in the street on his side, knees pulled into his chest, arms over his head. His body jumped from the blows. The man didn't try to get up, to run away, or to resist. The beating ended. Peter Stout, out-of-breath, appeared too tired to continue the assault, age sidling up next to him.

"Get him out of here," he ordered.

William debated what to do. Pennies would not help that chap. He wished Doc B's clinic was still a point on the five crossed streets. He remembered her fondly, as a beacon of his boyhood years. Doc B had returned to England and the clinic was now a boarding house.

He viewed the beaten man from a distance, and realized hospital or clinic wouldn't matter. His next stop was likely the morgue.

William crossed the street and neared the injured (dead?) man who had been dumped only a few feet from the decaying pig. No one stopped to attend him. Big black horse flies landed on his exposed skin, where his clothes had been torn away. The female flies drew blood.

William vacillated. He didn't want to be that person, the one who pretended life was fair. He could have walked in the other direction, or not crossed the street, but instead he was sent here by a force greater than himself. He pushed his hand past the pennies in his pocket and rubbed the rose quartz, its contours soft and hot. No, he couldn't be that man, the one who feigned blindness.

He knelt next to the beaten man. Flies flew away, and then returned. Among the blood that covered the man's face and matted his hair, recognition rose in William.

Kid had beaten and ridiculed most of the boys at the Home. He had brought such wrath upon them, William and Noble were certain the devil was an emaciated boy with rotted teeth. William thought of when Noble had done bee bearding,

Kid's beatdown of William, William packing up and leaving to fight the war between the states. He had to get away from Kid, and from the Home. He had to fight a meaningful fight.

Did William dare help him? Would he help me? Let him die and his body rot until the flies drained him of blood and the rats gnawed at his bones. William walked on, his hands shoved into his trouser pockets, again fingering the pennies and the rose quartz. His stomach knotted. His throat cinched. Don't be that person. Don't. Be. That. Person.

What kind of person was he? He had known poverty, and violence, and the look of blank stares from those who chose not to help. Hadn't he and Kid come from the same mold? Abandoned boys trying to survive. William had fought for the freedom of all men and had gotten an education. Kid had tried to enlist for the grub and the chance to fight without getting in trouble, but had been rejected. Not like Noble for being too young, but 4-F, for missing his four front teeth since without them he could not rip open gun powder packets. How would the trajectory of Kid's life have differed if he had fought Lincoln's war? How will the arc of William's life change if he leaves Kid to die? Would he be embattled with guilt? Would he lose his fortune?

Just take him to the hospital, he told himself.

William pivoted. "Hey."

No response.

He shook his shoulder.

Kid groaned.

William leaned close to his ear. "I'm taking you to a hospital."

"No," came the objection.

William considered his request, but could not abide. "The hospital," William repeated.

"No." Kid whimpered.

How could he feel pity for that devil? William looked toward the street. Outside Five Corner Bar, Peter Stout's retinue watched him. Metropolitans across the street eyed him too. If he took Kid to a hospital, and he survived, they'd find him and probably make sure he was properly dead the next time. Did William care if he lived or died? Walk away.

"No hospital." Kid moaned. "I want to die."

William burrowed his hand into his pocket again. Don't be a hypocrite. He looked along the street and summoned a passing carriage pulled by two lean donkeys. A sign on the side of the carriage read, "Looking for work".

He handed a fifty-cent piece to one of the two ragged-looking men aboard. "Load him into the wagon."

The men jumped down. One grabbed Kid's wrists, the other his ankles, and they loaded him into the back of the cart.

"No hospital," Kid groaned.

William directed the men to take Kid uptown and then back downtown to apartment 5C, in case they were followed. The men stared, unmoving. William reached into a back pocket and pulled out another coin, and dropped it into one of the men's hands. He watched the wagon roll away. Peter Stout and his goons watched too, as did the Metropolitans across the street.

William headed toward 5C to let Jenny know Kid would arrive soon. She could try and heal him with her special medicine. When he was well enough, William would buy him a train ticket to anyplace he wished to go with the promise he would never return to Five Points again.

Chapter Twenty-nine

"Happy birthday, dear Alice," John sang.

"Happy birthday, Mama."

Sarah looked at the two number-shaped candles on the cake. A seven and a zero. Is mama really seventy years old? How did I become fifty-five?

Alice giggled and laughed.

take the fish take the fish take the fish

The front door sailed open. Levi, gift in hand, rushed to Alice and kissed her. "Am I late? Did I miss the song? Hi Nana."

Alice shoved cake into her mouth. She grabbed the box from her grandson—icing from her hands smudged all over the wrapping paper—and opened it. She hugged the Buckner rag doll to her chest and cooed. Sarah knew that sound, like an angel's sigh. Alice's way of saying, I love you.

John cut another piece of cake, sat with Alice, sang softly to her. Sarah pulled Levi into the sitting room. Adorned with two Edwardian-style tub chairs and a two-seat sofa, upholstered in gold velvet; gifts from Harry, a local English carpenter. A finely crafted, Black Forest Oak gun cabinet sat catty-corner near a window. Deer antlers stuck up from the top. Through the glass, the recoil pad of five shotguns fit snugly into rectangular grooves cut into wood covered with green cloth. In the two drawers at the bottom of the cabinet, Colts, Walkers and Smith & Wesson revolvers and pistols lay on their sides, also on green cloth, reposing cobras in grass. The cabinet had also been constructed by Harry. Levi admired the gun cabinet, and the man who built it.

Sarah grabbed Levi's arm. "Did you talk to your uncle?"

"I did, Mama."

"What did he say?"

"Noble is getting out soon."

She released his arm and put her hands to her heart. "How soon?"

"In a few days."

"We can finally be a family."

"Is he staying here, Mama?"

"Yes."

"Are you sure that's a good idea?" Levi asked.

Sarah's expression turned stern. "He's your father."

"He's been in prison for thirty-six years. We don't know how he'll assimilate in the outside world, and you already have to care for Nana and John."

"Your father will be helpful."

"You don't know that."

"And you know he won't?" Sarah asked.

"I'm sure he's a great man, Mama, one whose been convicted of arson."

"Watch your tone. You ignored your uncle's letter, that was enough of a slap in the face."

"A jury said he did it."

"If you took the time to meet him, you'd know it wasn't true."

"Right, Mama." He turned away.

"Don't turn your back on me, Levi Solomon. Just because you're getting that fancy degree doesn't mean you can treat me or your father with disrespect. If you'd just meet him— "

"To what end, Mama?"

She took a few steps toward the gun cabinet, and then looked back at her son. "One time when I visited your father at Sing Sing...in the early days we could walk in the prison yard holding hands. It was a spectacular day and we strolled round and round with the sun shining and I tell you, for a time, I forgot where we were. I hadn't decided if I was going to tell him but without thinking I stopped and took his face in my hands. I had to stand on my tip toes because he's so tall, like you. I told him I was pregnant. Do you know what he did?"

"I don't, Mama."

"He dropped to one knee and asked me to marry him. It was such a beautiful day. He told me he had never been happier and how much he loved me and our child. That child was you, Levi."

"I figured."

"He's an amazing man."

"Feelings of optimism often create a cognitive bias that can be misleading."

Sarah shook her head. "That degree you're getting makes you sound crazy."

"I'm number one in my class, Mama."

"I know."

"And I'll be the first— "

"—negro psychiatrist in the United States." She leaned over and kissed him. "I am very proud of you. Unless Charles

Grading graduates from Columbia before you, then you'll be the second."

Levi's face drooped. "Charles Grading?"

Sarah laughed. "I made him up."

"Very funny."

"Seriously," she rubbed his day old beard, "I am very proud of you and I wish you'd meet your father, just once. You'll see that a special boy could only have come from a special man."

"I figured you were special enough on your own to produce me."

She slapped him playfully. "I don't want to hear you doubt your father's innocence again."

"You won't hear me say it."

"I want you to promise you will visit him tomorrow."

"Tomorrow?"

"Before he gets released."

"I have to study."

"Promise me, Levi."

"I can't get past that he tried to kill over one hundred black children and..."

Sarah put her hands on her hips. "Look at me Levi Solomon and say the rest of it."

"There is no rest of it," he said, sheepishly.

"Before Nana got into her...situation...she always knew what I didn't say. I never understood how she did that, but I do now."

"What's the secret?"

"Being a mother."

"What am I not saying?" Levi asked.

"You don't want to meet your father because you believed he almost killed black children."

"He is a white man."

"You are half him, and half me, which means you are only one quarter black."

"I consider myself a black man. My skin is dark. I've been raised in black culture. That's my identity. Psychologically, identity relates to one's mental image of oneself and one's individuality and— "

"—Your father is not a prejudiced man. Not one inch of him."

"I don't know how you can defend him. Byrne, a white man, cracked Nana over the head because she was black. You told me stories of Simon Black Cat and how he was lynched during the Civil War Race Riots. Uncle John was run over by a carriage driven by white men. And my father, a white man, tried to burn down the Colored Orphan Asylum— "

"—Don't they teach you in that school that it's wrong to judge others— "

"—he was found guilty at trial."

"For someone who is so smart, you're really ignorant. Juries can be corrupted, just like all men."

"Mama, I..."

"Enough. It's Nana's birthday and even if you're not happy about it I am thrilled that your father is being released."

"I don't want him staying here."

"You have no say in that, young man."

"Mama, please..."

Sarah smoothed her skirt. "I invited Peggy over for dinner. She should be here soon."

"Peggy?" Levi's back stiffened.

"Your wife, remember?"

"Of course." He forced a laugh. "Wait. Nana and John are already eating cake. You haven't had dinner yet?"

"She wanted cake first."

"She won't eat her dinner."

"What's the difference? She's happy."

Levi kissed her. "I wish I could do more to help you."

"Go see your father."

"Sarah," John called.

Sarah and Levi went into the kitchen and smelled the reason John summoned her.

"C'mon, Mama," Sarah said, "let's get you changed."

She led Alice toward the bathroom where cloth diapers were stacked by the toilet.

Levi sat next to John.

"Cake?" John asked.

"I'll wait."

"You have to live in the moment, son. That's the problem with you educated boys. Always thinking and planning. Sometimes you have to do what feels good when it feels good." He pushed the cake toward him.

Levi held up his hands. "No, thanks. I'll wait."

John stared at him. "Your mom talked to you about Noble again?"

Levi nodded.

"What are you going to do?" John asked.

"The same thing he's done for me my entire life. Nothing."

Chapter Thirty

Peggy burst through the front door, her small frame filled with energy that defied confinement. She dragged a large box.

"What's that?" Levi asked.

"For the birthday girl," Peggy said.

Alice opened the three-foot high box and pulled out a blue and white stuffed bear. She clutched it.

someone new to talk to take the fish take the fish if they'd just leave me alone for a few minutes the gun cabinet the gun cabinet

"I think she likes it," Peggy said.

"You could get her a bag of coals and she'd like it," John laughed.

Dinner was sumptuous. Cornish game hens, green beans, and rice. A second round of birthday cake. Alice sat next to Peggy, and the birthday girl balanced the rag doll on her left knee and the stuffed bear on her right. One bite for Alice, one for the doll, one for the bear.

Table cleared, Alice slept in her bed, wedged between the doll and the bear. Sarah, John, Levi and Peggy played the board game, *Round the World with Nellie Bly*. John talked of his almond, vanilla and honey cream, and how he'd perfected the formula and was seeing a difference in his own skin, and in Alice's.

After Peggy won the second game, Levi scooted his chair back.

"Leaving already?" Sarah asked.

"Peggy and I have plans."

"What plans?" Sarah asked.

"I have to study," Levi said.

"Going to hear music," Peggy said.

"Which one is it?" John smirked.

Levi placed a hand on Peggy's arm. "We're hearing music and then I have to study."

"Before you go," John said to Peggy, "grab a jar of my cream. I want you to try it."

♦

Outside, Levi and Peggy walked arm in arm. John Coal's Almond, Vanilla & Honey Cream tucked under her arm in an unlabeled glass jar.

"Why don't you try and meet someone?" Levi asked.

"Like who?"

"Like a woman."

"Do we have to have this conversation again?" she asked.

"I don't want you to feel lonely."

"I have my work."

"Being a reporter doesn't keep you warm at night."

"How do you know?"

Levi sighed. "You don't want to have sex with a man, so why not meet a woman? Sexual intimacy involves both physical and emotional closeness and is imperative to mental health and stimulation—."

"—I'm not attracted to men or women."

"I did some research and found the use of the word "asexual" in a pamphlet called "Sappho und Sokrates" by Magnus Hirschfeld. It was published last year. I've sent a letter to a doctor named Alzheimer in Germany. My professor has corresponded with Doctor Alzheimer and thinks he can obtain a copy of the pamphlet from the Bavarian State Library. I'm hopeful he'll respond. I would just have to have the pamphlet translated from German to English."

"I don't care about the pamphlet."

"But it might help us understand what you are feeling."

"There is nothing I need to understand. I'm happy with who I am, Levi. Isn't that enough? Isn't this more about your feelings than mine?"

Levi smiled. "You should be the psychiatrist."

"I'm a reporter, it's the same thing."

When they got to the corner, they kissed on their cheeks. Levi turned right. Peggy went left.

Chapter Thirty-one

Alice lay in bed, wedged between Peg-Peg and the blue and white bear, pretending to sleep. She fake slept a lot. That's what she called it. Time to go to fake sleep. If she wanted to stay up later, listen to music or conversation, she didn't know how to express it. Out came baby talk. The thoughts in her head never transferred to words, or acts. If she wanted to ask for water, out came gibberish. If she fancied to reach for something, her curled hands often refused to obey her mind's order. Her thoughts stayed trapped as prisoners. Her mind, a jail cell.

I should have taken the fish and led Sarah away. It was my job to protect my child.

take the fish take the fish take the fish

Almost four decades of regrets and replaying the incident over and over in her mind hadn't changed what Byrne had done to her, what he had done to Sarah. At least she had been the one beaten. At least she was the adult imprisoned in a child's prison. How would she have lived seeing her child like that, like this?

She recognized the wrapped package Sarah brought home weekly. Jenny Big Stink tried to make amends, to assuage her guilt. She felt responsible, and shared this with Alice when Jenny visited a couple of times each month.

"If there is anything I can do to help you..." Jenny would say, each word a teardrop.

Yes, there is something, Alice wished to communicate, and it doesn't involve bringing us fish.

Alice saw the empty cupboards and the worried look Sarah bore. She heard what Sarah and John spoke of before they quickly changed a conversation so as not to worry Alice. She sensed Sarah had lost her job and had been unemployed but now was working again. It wasn't only knowing how Sarah's life hadn't turned out the way she had expected, the way she deserved. Alice felt disheartened each time she looked at John. Not just because she still loved him and wanted him as her lover, but because of what he had also lost that day. All of this was Alice's fault. Not Jenny's. She should have taken the fish.

She had no one to discuss her feelings with other than Peg-Peg and now the blue and white bear. They read each other's thoughts. Long conversations while Alice fake slept. They tried to calm her, reasoned with her, begged her to control her anger, if not for herself, if not for them, then for Sarah and John, Levi and Peggy. But Alice was finding it harder to heed their advice, her rage ingrained as a permanent stain.

She wanted to kill Byrne. An idea she had mulled for decades. She hoped he was still alive, and she could find him. She'd already discussed the idea with Peg-Peg and now with the blue and white bear and they were formulating a plan, and it included Jenny Big Stink. If there is anything I can do to help, the fish peddler had offered many times. Yes dear, there certainly is.

There were three things Alice needed to do to put her plan into action. Each step seemed more difficult to achieve than the next. (1) Be alone, (2) communicate her plan to Jenny, and (3) get entry into John Coal's gun cabinet.

Chapter Thirty-two

In his cell, Noble tilted his face toward a high placed window. He knew the time of the day by the slant of the sun. Depending upon the season, and when clouds slid across and when they slipped away, he'd position himself within the narrow beam, angle his chin, close his eyes, and revel in the warmth like a man with something to look forward too. This being the end of April, the sun and the clouds were cooperative sundials.

He thought of William who had visited yesterday.

"I've secured your release," William said.

"You've been telling me that for months." There was no bitterness in Noble's inflection, rather resolution that his freedom would never become reality.

"The tarot cards say it's true this time."

William's tarot cards were nothing like the cards the prison guard Frankel brought to his cell to play poker with while they ate Frankel's wife's short bread and drank warm beer. The tarot cards were oversized and shiny and had pictures of constellations and planets and fairies and other mythical winged creatures, but no bees.

"When do the cards say I will be released then?" Noble asked.

"Soon. I can feel it."

Noble closed his eyes, the sun warmed his face. He would miss that ray of sunshine, the only thing he would miss other than his bees, and Frankel.

♦

Aged half-century, Noble ambled into the prison yard. He carried three feet of rolled screening. Inmates left him alone. He bothered no one and no one bothered him. He was one of the longest housed prisoners and only charged five cents for a jar of honey. They called him Sir and stepped out of his path.

He trekked along the chain link fence, the same fence he had trailed when he first arrived at Sing Sing. He stopped at a large oak on the far side of the yard, and looked up. Workers buzzed about, flew in and out of the hive.

Prison life had been an improvement over the Home for Unwanted Boys. Incarceration had its difficulties, for sure, but after the first decade or so when he achieved a calculated and cultivated place in the prison hierarchy, he no longer needed to fight for food and always had clothes and a place to sleep. He walked the grounds, visited the library for hours, went almost anywhere he wanted within the confines of the high fences and barbed wire. As long as he timely appeared at each meal and showed up in front of his cell three times a day for roll call and cell inspection.

It had been rough when he first arrived, a fourteen-year-old white boy accused of trying to murder black children and ordered to serve his sentence in an integrated prison. He was challenged daily by men bigger and older than he, men who were meaner, men who had actually committed the vicious crimes they were accused of and would do so again within the cage that housed them and upon their releases. It was different than what he had endured from Kid and his cohorts at the Home. Noble was bigger and quicker than most of those boys, and he and William had each other. They could always go for a walk through Five Points or sit under a tree in City Hall Park when things got too rough at the Home. They could even sleep out for a night or two, under the stars. In prison, he wasn't the largest man, the swiftest, or the meanest.

He walked along the fence and measured his ambivalence at being released. How does one measure uncertainty, he wondered? By time, weight, mass, temperature, by the strength of the rays of the sun? How had Jean Valjean measured his freedom after being imprisoned for nineteen years for stealing a loaf of bread?

One of Noble's favorite Jean Valjean quotes from Victor Hugo's masterpiece, the book that had transported him outside the prison parapets since its publication only one year after Noble's confinement, scuttled through his mind.

> "During the years of suffering Jean Valjean reached the conclusion that life was war in which he was one of the defeated. Hatred was his only weapon, and he resolved to sharpen it in prison and carry it with him when he left."

Noble had stumbled over those sentences, dog-eared the page, and reviewed it so often he was surprised he hadn't worn the words from the page with his eyes. He had aspired to be Jean Valjean, defined by anger, but as he aged and reread the final pages of the book, he grasped his truth. Anger was not to be his definition.

◆

Early in his incarceration, he stepped outside to feel the sun on his face. Risky since in the prison yard he was exposed to the foul mood of trapped men, but he could not stay inside all the time. In the yard, Noble learned quickly that the guards looked away when trouble arose. The prison culture was one where the guards kept order inside. Outside, they let boys be boys.

Fourteen-year-old Noble had skidded two fingers along the fence and stopped under a young oak. Noble was taller than the tree. He tried to pretend he was in Central Park.

"Hey. You. Squat."

Squat. A name for a prisoner too new or too young to have earned respect.

Noble hooked his index and middle fingers around a chain link. He turned and saw who he had already learned were Big Lion and Large Toed Max. Noble wanted to laugh at the names they gave each other in this place. In Five Points, the nicknames were more interesting and fit the person. The same couldn't be said for this prison culture, although Max had to cut the fronts of his shoes off for his feet to fit.

"I heard you called Jumbo stupid." Big Lion, a fat bald man, pointed to a worm of a man behind him.

This wasn't true, of course, but Noble knew truth had no relevancy. Not on the outside, and certainly not on the inside. Big Lion, Large Toed Max, Jumbo, others, surrounded him. He couldn't take all of them, maybe not even Jumbo who was the smallest of the lot. His ribs were still sore from when Byrne had beaten him, positive a few had been broken and hadn't healed in the three months since. He had bruising and a cut under his right eye from when someone threw a dinner tray at him. He had scratches and slashes and marks that he had already ceased to inventory and to recall from whom they came.

Their circle suffocated him. They smelled dirty and stupid. Noble was used to the stink of boys. He fit right in on that accord. What scared him was not only that they were men, but the indifference that yellowed their eyes like a waning sun. They were soldiers and anyone could be targeted as their enemy. The prison yard, their battlefield.

Sweat from their faces sprayed him as they inched closer, jawing threats, calling him names. A vibration needled his right ear. First one, then another. Soon, many. The men stepped back. The tough guys, now sissies. Noble looked to a nearby tree and saw bees crawling around a hollowed portion, and flying in and out. Honey dripped down the bark. Genus: Bombus impatiens. The common bumble bee. It amazed him how a flying insect less than two inches in length that only existed to serve its queen could frighten the meanest of beasts.

Page Seventy-eight in Prokopovych's book on bees. According to Egyptian mythology, bees formed when the tears of the sun god Ra landed on the desert sand.

Noble understood how he would survive in prison.

◆

During his incarceration, the young oak he had been taller than when he was first sentenced grew immense. Genus: Quercus of the beech family. He maintained a hive in the tree, as well as in other trees. He built several homemade hives in the eaves around the prison yard. Queen bees lived and died over the decades. Some colonies stayed intact when a new queen was born. Many bees transferred hives. Countless perished.

Wardens allowed Noble to hunt for new queen bees or to obtain them by mail order since there had been a near-riot in the twelfth year of his imprisonment when six queen bees died and Noble had no honey to sell or trade for months.

◆

Wire mesh rolled and tucked in his pants, Noble began the ascent up the old oak, hand over hand. One foot balanced on a branch, the other lunged for a higher branch; mother nature's stepladder. Bees flew around him, some buzzed across his face and neck and bumped him. None stung. The female workers and drones sent warnings to stay away from their queen but he felt no fear. He was more comfortable with bees than with humans, much preferring the insect's sting. When he scaled close to the semi-enclosed cavity, he balanced himself, removed the screening from his pants and formed it into a funnel. The circumference of one side was slightly smaller than the tree hole, and the other side even more narrow to permit only a few bees to exit at a time.

Upon his release, Noble feared other prisoners would destroy the colonies as Kid had done decades ago at the Home. He could not let that happen, and so came up with a plan. Noble knew his idea would result in his bees being displaced, but none would die and all would find a new queen and a colony. The screen cones he constructed allowed bees to exit the hive but not to enter again. Over time, perhaps a few weeks, the hollow of the big oaks would empty and his bees would be settled in their new homes.

He descended the oak and from the ground watched bees exit the hive until the swarm covered the uppermost parts of the tree. Their smell was sweet, and their music tender. Noble turned and made his way toward the next hive. He had sixteen hives well-spaced around the prison yard, fifty thousand bees in each. It would take some time to get this done. Time for him to construct, in his mind, the letter he intended to write when he returned to his cell. The letter to Levi he had wanted to write for thirty years.

Chapter Thirty-three

Bamboo cane in hand, Levi strolled along Broadway. Stars blanketed the sky like incandescent wildflowers. He imagined similarities between the vault of space above and the cerebral cortex, both auroras yet to be fully explored. The moon shone bright, its glow unencumbered by the earth and its people, and unaffected heretofore by things Levi could never guess would come—well-lit metropolises, airplanes, pollution.

He headed toward City Hall Park, ruminating on how he hated the ruse he played on his mother. Peggy was his wife, true. They had the marriage certificate to prove it, but it wasn't a marriage built from romantic love. John Coal knew of their deception. It took one con man to recognize another.

The flames that pranced in the sconces that lit the park had been doused. A cloudy sky was preferable to a clear evening but that didn't dissuade men from walking slowly through the park as if shopping in a mart. Some men strutted with a cane at their sides—digging tips into the dirt, stepping forward, moving the cane in parallel rhythm to their strides. Their signal: just browsing. Others rested the tips of their canes on their shoulders: ready and available.

The men who visited City Hall Park at night were of all colors, shapes and religions. Most had one thing in common, a beard. Not the hirsute kind, but a woman willing to pretend to be his girlfriend or, like Peggy, agreeing to be his wife. A gay man, circa 1897 New York City, could easily lose his job, his housing, his life.

Look what Assistant Chief of Police Timothy Byrne got away with. Byrne frequently lurked in the park at night, and rested his club on his shoulder to indicate he was open for business. He'd choose a feminine looking lad and lead him into a wooded area behind the Nathan Hale monument. The boy couldn't refuse. The repercussions to himself, his family, the other men in the park, were too ominous. The youngster sucked Byrne's fiddle. Hale's words the only eyewitness. I only regret that I have but one life to lose for my country.

Tangled among the low branches and bushes, the then-Assistant Chief of Police received but never gave, and most certainly never paid. Anyone who asked for remuneration received a slap, a push, even a punch.

♦

Harry sat on a bench and tied his shoe. Their sign so they could spot each other from a distance. Tall, muscular and handsome, Levi anticipated the musk of his lover's skin, the strong scent from his day's labor. A carpenter by trade, Harry immigrated from England a few years earlier. He had been the one to build and gift the Edwardian-styled chairs and sofa to his mother. He had made John Coal's gun cabinet. Sarah adored Harry and frequently invited him for dinner, the two men finding it hard to act like acquaintances during those evenings, enjoying secret looks during the dinner and belly laughs when they were later alone.

Levi and Harry met at City Hall Park two years earlier. Both had been looking for quick, non-committal contact, the reason most men frequented the park at night. They had been surprised when one meeting turned into a dozen, which then turned to love. Levi hated they couldn't live together, even to pose as roommates had turned deadly for several men they knew. He loathed that they had to meet in the park in the shadows, and couldn't eat at a restaurant or take a trip together. Too risky if one should absentmindedly rest his hand on the small of the other's back, or look at each other with eyes reserved for lovers.

He worshipped Harry's sensual lips, his thick Cockney accent, his touch, and his large uncircumcised cock. No one had ever made love to him before Harry. When they were through, breathless and sweaty, picking sticks and dirt out of each other's hair and clothes, they talked until the early morning hours. Levi then returned to his dorm room, and Harry went home to the flat above his shop.

"What are you going to do about Noble?" Harry asked.

"Nothing."

"You're not going to meet him?"

"No."

"You're stubborn."

"I thought you liked that about me," Levi teased.

"What if your mother allows him to live with them?"

"William said he could stay with him and Nancy."

Harry grabbed Levi's shoulder. "Is that...up ahead...?"

In the dark Levi saw the unmistakable outline of the second top cop surrounded by five uniformed police. Subconsciously, Levi rubbed his left bicep, the muscle never fully healed from the last time Byrne and his gorillas came into the park and beat anyone in their path. Levi hadn't moved out of the way quick enough and received a blow from a billy club to his arm.

Levi glared at the darkened figures. "He's compensating for the homosexual tendencies he struggles to hide."

"No time for your psychological speak. Let's get out of here." Harry pulled Levi toward the park's exit.

Chapter Thirty-four

At the open door to Alice's room, John watched his sweet girl. The sun's morning rays illuminated her face with gold. She sat on the floor and talked gibberish to the stuffed bear Peggy had given her the other day for her birthday. Alice's brow furrowed, her eyes steady and serious. He wondered what Alice believed to be the subject of this conversation she was having with the bear, if she believed anything at all. What goes on in your mind, my love?

Each time he looked at Alice, he had to fight not to recall the moment when she was battered by the officer, and when he was crushed by the carriage. Instead, he tried to reminisce of the days when Alice was his gorgeous lover, her body supple and soft, graceful and giving. This woman, no, this child, she was still his love, his forever love, just a different kind of love.

She reached out her arms. He swung into the room and hugged her.

"Who do you have there?" His voice was sing-song.

She held up the rag doll. "Pepepeppapa."

Peg Peg, that's what she intended to say.

The knock on the front door was soft, and expected.

"Be right back." John leaned his torso forward, landed on the palms of his hands, and then threw his hips frontward. He repeated this movement until he was at the door. There, he adjusted his sack, perpetually bruised and sore from banging and scraping along the floor. He had tried wearing several pairs of briefs, swathed his genitals close to his body, and even stuffed a pillow in his drawers, but in order to have some freedom of movement, bruising was unavoidable. Gloves safeguarded his hands but nothing protected his balls and penis.

He reached up and pulled open the door.

"Hi Pops." Levi put down the school satchel he carried, got to his knees and hugged John. "Where's Nana?"

"In her room. What happened to your hand?"

"Just a sprain."

"And the cut on your mouth?"

Levi raised his hand to his lip, touched his face, and flinched. "Nothing."

"Is Harry okay?"

"Just some bruises. He'll be fine."

"That park is not safe. One day someone is going to get killed in there."

"Pops..."

"You don't want to talk about it. Fine. For such a smart guy, you make some dumb choices."

"It's what we do for love."

Babbling lifted from Alice's room.

"Look what you've done for love," Levi said. "Peggy's downstairs, waiting."

Another hug, and Levi went to babysit his grandmother.

◆

John swung out the door and propelled his way down the stairs from the second floor flat. He leaned forward at the top of each step, endured a moment of free fall, landed on his palms, and then dragged his torso to the landing. A deep breath, repeat. Twelve stairs in all. Although there were only inches between each step, when he lunged forward and was airborne for a moment, he felt as if he were flying; those moments' bliss.

Outside the front door, Peggy held the long black handle of the deep red wooden wagon Harry built. The wagon's rectangular body sat on four ten-inch steel wheels and was large enough and deep enough for John to sit in with his widening girth and short stumps. John swung out the door and leaned his body over the side of the wagon. Peggy pushed on the opposite end to prevent the wagon from tipping. John rolled in, straightened himself, and gripped the sides.

"Ready?" Peggy asked.

"Ready," John said.

With two hands on the handle, she faced the wagon and leaned all of her body weight back.

"Hold on," she called.

Even without legs, John was a solid man who neared one hundred and fifty pounds. Once she had momentum, she turned around and pulled John along the uneven pavement.

◆

John clutched the sides of the wagon and endured the bumps and divots. The jostling caused immense pain in his stumps, his hips, and his back, but he didn't complain. Not out loud, at least. He tried to recall the feel of moving his legs and walking, the wind on his face while jogging, cool dirt on his bare feet, sand between his toes, but as time moved on so did the imageries.

Peggy steered the wagon along Broadway avoiding the passers-by and, since Harry hadn't perfected a turning mechanism on the wagon, navigating corners like a box step. Some of the passers-by gawked and pointed at the legless man being pulled in a red wagon, some tried not to look at him. Many spoke their thoughts of sorrow, perhaps not intending to speak them aloud, or for him to hear. The words "war among the states" or "civil war" murmured many times as the assumption for the cause of his missing limbs. Thirty years post-war, the veterans were men in their fifties who limped, shuffled, and often drank themselves through their daily lives. If John had lost his legs in the war, maybe, he often thought, I wouldn't feel like my life was such a waste. What John never considered was that he was one of the first casualties of the war, his injury having occurred on the day Lincoln called for Northerners to enlist, and having occurred at the hands of copperheads.

Regardless of how or why he lost his legs, whenever he emerged from the tenement, John felt to be a spectacle. A Barnum & Bailey Greatest Show on Earth sideshow. So, he often sequestered himself in the apartment, took care of Alice while Sarah taught or volunteered at the prison, and tried to pretend he was able-bodied. The reminders of his disability weren't occasional, they ignited in minute-to-minute flames of shame, a sickening deluge in the pit of his stomach that taunted him each moment he was half a man. The first leg amputated when he was smashed by the horse and carriage, the second one years later because of infection. At sixty-nine years old and three feet tall, his shoulders were broad, his biceps still hard, and his stomach muscles taut, but his wrists, forearms, neck and back muscles ached from thrusting his torso forward and back, side-to-side.

Despite decades without being full-bodied, at times he forgot and rolled out of bed and hit the floor. Pain raged on his stumps, his hips, his lower back. His relief, morphine supplied by Jenny Big Stink. The miracle drug deadened the pain and numbed his brain, which was why he only took it at night. He needed to be sharp as he tried to create the perfect moisturizer. He was not like those fast-talking hacks who whipped together milk and bread and sold bottles to women with promises to relieve their dryness and itching. With this latest formula of John Coal's Almond, Vanilla & Honey Cream, after almost three decades of trying, and with the improvement of Alice and Sarah's skin and his own from its use, he might have come upon a recipe that would make a difference.

◆

Harry's coveralls were brushed with a sandy sheen. He grabbed the wagon handle from Peggy and pulled John into his workshop. Sawdust covered the floor and dusted the air. Powdery wood particles flew up their nostrils and into their eyes.

"Where'd you get the shiner?" Peggy asked Harry.

"Fell, that's all."

John said, "I told Levi, you both need to stay out of that park."

"I know, Pops, but where else are we supposed to go?"

"How about here?"

"People see me bringing Levi to my flat and they start talking and you know what happens next."

"You're substituting one danger for another," Peggy said.

"If we looked like this after a game of rugby, everyone would have thought we sat on the sidelines the entire match." The Englishman forced a laugh. Better to change the subject, he held up a sanded piece of wood with several holes drilled through it. "Here's the body. It's two-and-a-half feet long and the deck is two feet wide. That should do, right?" He looked at John's shape and measured him with carpenter trained eyes. "Yes, that should be jolly fine."

John bowed his head. He wiped the back of his hand across his eyes and left behind a yellow streak like a comet's tail.

"Are you crying?" Peggy kneeled next to him.

"No. Maybe. I appreciate what you all do for me."

"Bullocks. I just made the deck. You're doing the rest, old man." He pointed to a broom swept section of the floor. "There's your workspace."

Eight wheels, smaller and thicker than the wagon wheels, were surrounded by nuts and bolts, nails, sandpaper, glue, and tools. Two sticks, about three feet high with flat bottoms, lay nearby. A fresh sheen of sawdust speckled the area.

Harry helped John out of the wagon. "Get to work."

Placing each palm flat on the floor, John swung forward until he was in front of the work station. He looked at the tools and the supplies, and began to put together the pieces of his self-propelled wagon, the next best thing to a pair of legs.

While John worked, Peggy pulled Harry aside. "Was it Byrne?"

"That copper is barmy on the crumpet."

"English, Harry."

"That is the Queen's English. It means he's crazy. We were in City Hall Park minding our own business when Byrne and his boys roused us."

"The man is untouchable. We've been investigating him at the Times for years and no one will talk."

"One day, he'll get his."

"Will he?" Peggy asked.

Chapter Thirty-five

Noble heard the whispers about Lonny Massacre before the killer was transferred from The Tombs to Sing Sing, and like the other convicts and the guards Noble wanted nothing to do with the maniac. Word was he had most recently ripped off a guard's ear and chewed it like salted pork. No one tried to get the ear away from him.

Noble thought he might be forced to bunk with the fella, even if just for the few days before his release. The warden often put the tough guys with Noble to see if the veteran prisoner could calm the newbie.

William had told him one week ago that the tarot cards pronounced his release would come soon. As Noble eyed Massacre on the other side of the bars—his light blue eyes jittery discs, his teeth sharpened into fangs—he knew his release was not soon enough, if it ever was going to happen.

Two guards, Frankel and Durden, shoved Massacre into the cell.

"Sorry, brother," Frankel said to Noble.

Frankel has shown up in Noble's cell for the last twenty-odd years every Sunday at four p.m. thumbing the same worn deck of cards. Ironically, or maybe by Frankel's design, the cards were called, *Bumble Bee Trading Cards*. The box proclaimed "finest quality" and "bees make the whole world sweet". The Joker had a drawing of a cowboy riding a bucking bee with the saying, "a third of all plants we eat have been pollinated by bees." Frankel also brought his wife's honey cake and a thermos of hot coffee. They played poker for hours.

The steel bars clanged shut. The guards watched from the other side, like visitors at a zoo, billy clubs palmed, even with the barrier between them and Massacre.

Massacre snarled and paced. His body slithered side to side. He didn't look at Noble, who didn't move despite the adrenaline that rushed within him. Noble was furious at this intrusion. All he wanted was write the letter to Levi he had finally formulated in his mind. He was ready to put pen to paper, and perhaps even to give it to his son. Massacre had ruined that for him. Would Noble recall what he wanted to say? The phrasing? The message he hoped to impart?

Massacre paced, mumbled. He punched the wall, blood on his knuckles, no expression of pain.

William taught Noble about intellectual pursuits, manners, and how to engage in good conversation, the bees taught him about loyalty and family, Jean Valjean instructed him on perseverance and forgiveness, but it was Kid's lessons of survival that now swirled within.

After a minute or two, Frankel and Durden exited the cell block. Noble did not hesitate. He stepped forward, propelled from his legs, and smashed his fist into Massacre's nose, a sucker punch that buckled the man's knees. Blood spurted over his face, on to Noble's cheeks and chest, in his eyes, and splattered on to the drab walls of the prison cell. When Massacre tried to pull himself up, Noble kneed him in the breadbag. He doubled over, went down again, sprung up and squared off in front of Noble. Noble reacted with a right jab, aimed for the fangs. Massacre threw up an arm to block. Undeterred, Noble was fierce. Left, right, left, right, relentless kidney punches. Bones smashed under his bloodied knuckles.

Hot liquid raged in Noble's eyes. The taste of metal filled his mouth.

Frankel and Durden reentered the cell. Noble's hands were yanked back, and he was thrown on to the bottom cot. Springs cut him like he had landed on a bed of razor blades. He was shackled.

"Just stay down, Noble," Frankel said.

On the concrete floor of the prison cell, Massacre was a coiled and gory jumble of sweat, blood and spit.

Frankel leaned closer to Noble. "Good move." Then, he stood and spoke officiously, "You're not going for him again, right?"

Noble shook his head.

They removed the cuffs. Noble wiped his nose. Blood streaked across the back of his hand.

Durden pointed toward Massacre and barked, "Clean him up or else you're going to solitary."

Guards gone again, Noble looked at the heap of the man on the floor and weighed his next move. He could kill him. Who would care if this guy was dead? A man who had only been spared Old Smoky 'cause his attorney, William J. Henley, made a deal with detectives and told them where the bodies were buried, including a couple of young squeakers who were still breathing when unearthed.

Noble thought of his own future if he killed the chap. William had been trying for years to get him out of prison and had finally succeeded. A final blow would certainly alter Noble's fate. Would it be worth it?

Noble had wondered what it would feel like to kill a man. Had come close a few times, having put men in the infirmary for weeks. He almost killed Kid in the back of the Home all those years ago, and he had fantasized of strangling Peter

Stout and watching Byrne die in front of a real firing squad. But to do the actual final deed? Fucking yes! In a life out of his control, of being power-less, ending a man's being was something he could navigate. If he had to.

But, he thought, William had never stopped championing for his release, and had finally gotten it done. Didn't he owe his best friend this freedom? William blamed himself for Noble's troubles, ruminating over what if he hadn't told the draft board he was only fourteen years old. They could have both survived the war and their lives would have been markedly different, most certainly better.

What about Sarah? Levi? The son he had yet to meet. Alice and John? What would they think, how would they feel, if he were a real murderer?

Massacre tried to get up, fell back. Noble stood, prepared to crack his boot into the guy's skull. He wouldn't kill him, just knock him out long enough for Noble to write the letter.

Massacre raised his hand, a muffled sound came from his throat, and then the formation of words from a thick tongue. "I'm in need of..." He coughed. Blood and saliva spurted from his nose and mouth.

Noble retreated from the circumference of the pinkish spray.

When Massacre's spasms ended, he tried again. "I'm in need of a cook, not a doctor. I'm fucking starving."

Noble fell back on to the bottom bunk, ignored the jab of the springs in his ass. He laughed, uncontrollably, like a fool. Massacre rose slowly. His smile was bloody. He plopped next to Noble on the bed. Noble sprung up. Massacre laid back, on his side, faced the wall, and slept for three days. When Noble wasn't tending his bees, he scrubbed blood from the walls and floor, worked on the letter to Levi, and wondered if he was really getting out this time.

♦

Massacre healed and hardly stopped talking and pacing the small cell. His fangs sparkled under the fluorescent lights during the day, and glared at night under the beam of the full moon when it shined through the porthole window. Noble didn't mind his chatter. He easily tuned him in or out and was certain Massacre told his tales even when Noble was in the prison yard or reading in the library. Massacre's voice was low in tonality and in volume, a soothing speech with a vaguely aristocratic sounding accent. Truth be told, Massacre's speak reminded Noble of the colored folks who told tales on street corners in Five Points when he was a boy. The difference being the stories Massacre told were of the men he murdered. Details that repulsed and riveted Noble, who tried not to hear but couldn't stop listening.

"You always talk this much?" Noble asked one day

His back to Noble, Massacre didn't answer.

Noble tapped him on the shoulder. Massacre turned, and watched Noble's mouth as he repeated, "You always talk this much?"

"Ain't never met someone worth talkin' to," Massacre said.

Lonny Massacre Manifesto

I wasn't born deaf, which is why my voice doesn't have that funny tinny sound to it (I think). I know sign language but not the official kind. Mon mére and me, we communicated with our hands and fingers and with the looks on our faces. We never had no problem understanding each other. As for my pére, I had to learn to read his lips 'cause if I didn't do what he wanted, even if I couldn't hear nothing, I got beaten. Papa didn't care nothing for speaking slow and enunciating so I had to learn fast. Turns out I was pretty good at lip reading. It's all about the cues and the contexts and the way the mouth forms words. I became so good at it, I didn't have to tell no one I was deaf. I just had to see their lips when they spoke, which isn't easy because people are always distracted and turning away, and burping, and chewing the inside of their mouths and pursing their lips and other stuff that takes away from language. Anyways, reading lips is the second thing I am best at.

I became deaf when I was five years old and got really sick. I was burning up, I was so tired and my whole body ached. My mouth was bone dry and I slept for an entire month. At least that's what my mama told me. She said she held me most of the time and listened to me breath. The doctor said I had mumps. Mama tried a bunch of remedies. I ate a sour pickle every day, and she tied my umbilical cord (which she had saved for this reason) around my neck. The remedials worked since I got better and the only thing different about me was that I could no longer hear. I figured that was better than being dead. Deaf is only one letter away from dead. I never minded not being able to hear since hardly no one talked to me anyway. They was always yelling, except for mama. I did miss hearing the sound of her voice but I can still hear it in my head since I have it mesmerized.

The good thing about being deaf is you can't hear no lawyers and no judges. You can't hear no one scream, or cry, or beg.

April 28, 1897

Dear Levi,

It has taken me thirty years to decide how to begin this letter to you. I have settled upon the following:

Petro Prokopovych from the Ukraine invented commercial beekeeping. Victor Hugo was a French writer. Through their books, these men have played the roles of my father who I lost at a young age. They taught me about life's challenges, and about survival. They offered the trappings to make the best decisions I could under the most intense of circumstances. It took two geniuses to take the place of my one father, a man I recall of average smarts.

I wonder, how many men have you turned to in order to take my place?

The inclination is for me to write pages and pages pleading for your forgiveness but while it took Prokopovych over seven hundred pages to share all he knew about the world of bees, and almost two thousand pages for Hugo to tell Jean Valjean's story, here I believe fewer words are suitable. And so, I will finish with these quotes.

Page ninety-three of Prokopovych's book of bees. "Don't feel anger toward the bee for his sting. He has sacrificed his life for his queen."

Les Misérables. "In all Jean Valjean's trials he felt encouraged and sometimes even upheld by a secret force within. The soul helps the body, and at certain moments raises it. It is the only bird that sustains its cage."

I love you, my son.

Your Father, Noble Jennings.

Three Points

Lunatic and Lunacy

Lunatic and lunacy include every kind of unsoundness of mind, except idiocy, including imbecility arising from old age and loss of memory and understanding.

Consolidated Laws of New York, Annotated (1906)

New York Times

All the News that's Fit to Print

FOURTH MURDER WARRANTS PANIC

BODY DISCOVERED IN FORMER FIVE POINTS

COPY KILLER?

WELL-TO-DO MEN STAY HOME!

"Have we returned to Five Points of old?"

Reported by John Coal

NEW YORK, March 12, 1906. Henry Thaw Watson, of Rye, New York, husband of Jane Rabin Watson, was brutally murdered last night in the area formerly known as Five Points. Until the turn of the century, the lower east side slum, famous for its police corruption, the Dead Rabbits riot, and the Colored Orphan Asylum fire, was the scourge of our city. The question has been asked after this fourth murder that is remarkably similar to the three other murders, "Have we returned to Five Points of old?" Said question solicited by Mayor George B. McClellan, Jr. is one that cannot be ignored.

Coroner Edmund Dooley said that the body was "twisted like the iron wheels of a sturdy carriage after a crash" and determined the cause of death to be suspicious. This reporter, who was notified immediately and hurried to the scene, saw the body and can confirm. While Coroner Dooley only said Mister Watson's death was "suspicious," it was clear from Dooley's eyes and his vigorous note taking that he knew this was murder, as did all who gathered 'round.

When referring to Mister Watson, Miss Carol Hanlon, barmaid at Five Corner Bar, said "the condition of the body is gruesome. I can barely look at it." Indeed, I stood next to Miss Hanlon in the thickening crowd and I can attest that she could barely look away from poor Mister Watson.

Missus Watson was not present. It was later determined when a reporter from THE TIMES called upon her at her Rye, New York home that while she was surprised to learn of her husband's murder, she was not overly perturbed as her first response was, "The bastard should have been at home where a husband ought to be." Missus Watson then cried, however it was believed that her tears were an act to be applauded.

Police Chief Timothy Byrne was also not present as he is suspended with pay as previously reported by THE TIMES. Chief Byrne is facing his own murder charge with the allegations that he slayed a poor chap in City Hall Park. Chief Byrne's trial is scheduled to begin next month. He is represented by the esteemed Counselor at Law, William J. Henley.

In Chief Byrne's absence, Assistant Chief Hugh Bailey took control and cleared a path around the area. This reporter had an unobstructed view and determined the following based on witness statements and police comments.

At approximately midnight on this clear and cold night, Mister Watson walked along Mulberry Street. Dirt kicked up on to Mister Watson's expensive loafers, and to the bottoms of his fine double breasted suit pants. Mister Watson looked to be "seeking companionship from a painted lady," Assistant Chief Bailey was heard to say.

The condition of the body was reminiscent of the three other murder victims found in the same area within the four corners of what was Five Points and is now comprised of the up and coming locales of China Town and Little Italy. The other victims were also men in their fifties and sixties, well-to-do, and somewhere they were not wise to be. The bodies were tangled and bent, and from each an ear had been removed as if torn by an animal. The murders have occurred over the last four months, and the police have no suspects. Or, are not revealing if they do.

As THE TIMES has been reporting, these crimes are reminiscent of Lonny Massacre, the killer of over two decades ago who has been in prison and so is not a suspect.

In 1884, Massacre confessed to police that he had murdered eight wealthy men over a span of four years, all men who he determined were disloyal to their wives and seeking the attention of younger women who agreed to be paid for their services. His capture and confession was quite a sensation and drew the attention of many New Yorkers. Some felt Massacre was engaged in a public service and so a club of sorts was formed comprised of those who condoned what he had done. Several women have proposed marriage to Mister Massacre.

Back at the scene of Mister Watson's unfortunate death, Assistant Chief Bailey commented on the similarities to the Massacre murders, and asked what THE TIMES has questioned throughout this entire ordeal. "Since Massacre is locked up, who is the copy killer?" Bailey recommends, "Well-to-do men stay home with their wives at night until the killer is apprehended and brought to justice."

A town hall meeting will be held at Saint Mary's Church on Grand Street in two days of which the police and mayor will attend to discuss the concerns of the public over the spate of murders.

Chapter Thirty-six

Lost in lower Manhattan's Sixth Ward among the alleys and rooftops, burned out buildings, and garbage bins he had conquered as a boy, fifty-nine-year-old Noble Jennings failed to recognize the corner where Jenny Big Stink sold fish from her wagon, the block where the Colored Orphan Asylum stood before it burned, and the etchings on the door to the Home for Unwanted Boys. He knew he had been a prisoner, but couldn't recall for how long, or when he had been released.

Early evening, a light snow fell. Pedestrians dashed around him on the cobbled street. Unseasonably cold for April, men hunkered into their overcoats. Women gripped their companions' arms and hid cheeks against their woolen sleeves.

Noble drew his arms across his chest, shaken by the activity. Where were all the people going? Why such a rush? Were the men off to Jones's Wood to enlist to fight in the War of the Rebellion? He shifted to close his jacket and realized he wore none, only a thin, brown-collared button-down shirt over wool slacks.

He sighed. His shoulders rounded and his once taut muscles sagged, but he was still strong like a man who had crawled the world. He fingered the wood vial that hung from a tattered string around his neck, shooed a bee away, and tried to recall the strange necklace's significance.

Had William given it to him? Noble tried to sift the memory from the contours of his mind, but it felt dim. William had bestowed many gifts upon him over the decades but his benevolences were clothes, food and drink, a place to bunk, and legal advice. Never a ratty bobble at the end of unraveling twine.

Sarah. His beautiful Sarah. It was from she! His shoulders straightened as he was momentarily transported to that day so long ago when she climbed atop him and he knew what it felt like to be free. No, her endowments were never something to wear or to hold, but were rather the way her dark eyes viewed him as the man she believed he could become.

Anger plunged into his gut, fueled by the vague recesses of his brain, some dank and dark, others still brightly torched. He searched for a pattern, but found none. One moment he'd recall minute details from long ago but not what he ate ten minutes earlier; the next he'd forget what he just remembered.

He looked around. "For goodness sakes," he cried, "where am I, and why am I here?"

The bee again buzzed near the necklace and he swat it with the back of his hand. It dropped and landed on a rectangular stone. Noble released his grip on the vial and fell to his knees lest the bee be trampled upon.

"What have I done?" Gently, he swept the insect into his palm and brought it close to his face. "How ya' doin', little fella? I'm so sorry that I hurt you."

Noble could not see as well as he used to, but he knew the outline of its furry body, its six legs, its thousands of eyes; knew it as well as he knew...wait, what did he know?

"I seem to have forgotten so many things. I think I'm here to see William." He looked at the door he crouched before, and the strange carved markings in the wood. He turned back to the bee that vibrated in the concavity of his palm. "Have you seen William?"

Noble stood, and stepped away from the door. He looked up Broadway and along the road, and gazed with watery and unfocused eyes along its cross streets. People scuttled about, carriages rolled by, an occasional car wheeled along the narrow and uneven road.

"William?" he called, louder, and looked here and there, hoping to spot the attorney's small frame in the larger canvas. Bee still in his hand, he again searched the thoroughfares.

His friend did not arrive with hand extended, a smile on his face, his eloquent tongue spilling words meant to reassure. You're okay, chap, he'd say. Let's get you a hot meal, which would be followed by William linking his fingers around Noble's arm like they were meant to be connected.

"William?" Noble asked again, softer. He looked to the bee, still sheltered in the palm of his hand. "You can go now. Fly away. Find your queen. She's out there."

The bee no longer moved.

Noble's throat tightened. "I am a murderer."

A cold wind swept along his face, light snowflakes landed on his cheeks. The loud clomp of a horse was close, the whirl of buggy gears nearby.

"Hey, buddy," a man atop a carriage yelled, "get out of the street."

Noble jumped into the safety of the door frame. He craned his neck, rotated his body and sought a point of reference, wishing himself to be a compass. Perhaps he could find a storefront he recalled. He scanned the faces that moved past him, their eyes not seeing him, as if he were part of the tapestry of the stone-block paving underfoot.

He wrapped his arms in a tighter self-hug, shivered and wondered, Where am I? He looked to his hand, to the bee for advice. His palm was empty. Frantic, he pushed his way back to the street and searched the ground, the new snow leaving a quilted blanket, the sheen dirtied by loafers and boots.

"Hey mista, outta the way." A woman pushed past him.

Noble scuttled back to the etched doorway, bent, and wrapped his forearms around his knees.

It began for Noble as it had for most. Small signs turned into billboards. An inability to match names to faces. He would walk several blocks before he realized he headed in the wrong direction. He went from one room to another inside the Henley home where he resided, and then could not recall why he had left one room to enter the other. But that wasn't so unusual. Many, of all ages, didn't readily match names to faces. Or they stared into open ice boxes and wondered, what am I looking for? But then Noble would lose his wallet and find it in the meat cold box, or he'd get dressed for work when it was three in the morning and he didn't have a job.

As Noble's memory diminished, he looked to cloak his deficiencies by lying and through tomfoolery. He felt shame and did not want to appear less of a man, stupid, or unable to care for himself. He certainly did not want to face the possibility that he had become unsound of mind.

Noble looked at the door to the brownstone of the former Home for Unwanted Boys. He cast his gaze up and down to read the carved words and reflect upon the pictures in the wood, as if seeing them for the first time, not recalling that he had been a participant in the carvings over four decades earlier.

Snowflakes landed on his eyelashes and he blinked them away. He shivered and moved to pull his winter coat more tightly around him, and discovered he only wore a button-down shirt. Hadn't he worn a coat earlier?

"William?" he called again. "Sarah?"

A cloud blocked the sun and the past eclipsed the present. He was fourteen years old and stood in the doorway to the Home for Unwanted Boys. Yes, that's where he was, in front of the door to the orphanage where he lived. Inside, seventeen-year-old William lounged in the room in the bed where they pigged together. He read the New York Times or studied the law books he pilfered. William was going to be a lawyer and president of the United States like his idol, Abraham Lincoln.

Butchy, who managed the Home, would be in there too, keeping the boys in order, or at least trying to. No one could tame Kid Turner.

Noble tried the knob, and pushed on the door with his shoulder. Funny, the door never had a working lock before. When had Butchy installed that? He knocked. No response. The bee that had fallen from his palm reduced to dust.

Commuters hurried past, oblivious to the boy. The Civil War was to begin in less than five weeks. In the back of the Home, bees clustered in the heart of the hive, consumed honey for energy, awaited warmer weather, and protected their queen. By the front door, Noble hugged himself to steal warmth amongst the frost. He cupped the aged wood vial that hung around his neck, and waited. William would fetch him soon. He always did.

**GOLDMAN SACHS BOArD OF DIrECTOrS
PrESENTS**

On this 16th day of April 1906

EMPLOYEE OF THE YEAr

THIS CErTIFICATE IS PrESENTED TO:

MISTEr JACKSON HILL

IN rECOGNITION OF YOUr DEDICATION AND COMMITMENT

Chapter Thirty-seven

Mister Jackson Hill stepped out of Fraunces Tavern, where the awards ceremony had been held for Goldman Sachs employees, and knew he should go straight home. What bores his bosses were for holding this celebration on a Monday, and then expecting him to show up in the morning clear-headed and ready to tackle the intricacies of bookkeeping. He clenched the certificate, typed using one of the ancient Adlers in the secretarial bay, the one where the R doesn't work. The new, sleek Royal Portables reserved for executive use.

Despite the light snow and the late hour, it would be a pleasant walk from Wall Street to the brownstone on Thirty-eighth and Fifth Avenue he shared with his wife and two children. Time to revel in his award, to walk off the drink. So what if he'd be tired in the morning? He'd catch up on sleep another time.

Should he be scared? There had been two town hall meetings about the murders, held at Saint Mary's Church. Maybe there had been three or four? Who could keep count? New Yorkers were alarmed, and they weren't an easy bunch to frighten. Jack hadn't attended any of the town halls; they weren't relevant to him, but all the same he promised his wife Mary he'd take a cab directly home after the awards ceremony. No walking, no dawdling. Yes, dear, he had said, and had meant it at the time. But he wasn't fearful, not him. He put up his arms and balled his hands and shadow boxed the wind. No one was going to get Jack Hill. One-two, one-two. My ear will remain attached to my head, thank you very much.

He laughed at how the chill and the drink and the compliments exhilarated him. His cheeks chafed from the wind. His hands cold—who would have thought it'd be this frigid in April? Thankfully, his insides warmed from the shots of ragwater and from the accolades. He had done it! Won Employee of the Year. Who notices accountants? Goldman Sachs does! Jack Hill, accountant *extraordinaire*.

The best part of accepting the award had been looking into the faces of the audience and seeing the gamboling men stunned and shaking their heads with disbelief. Those lowbrows of the banking division—a cluster of stupid goosecaps who had been loud with drink—became muzzled and chilled when his name was announced, and then the snide remarks began. Jack from accounting won Employee of the Year? Jack Hill? The tightwad who refused to share the sharpened pencils in his shirt pocket and viewed life as a series of algebraic equations and hyperbola? The Jack that ate lunch at his desk each day, pulled a tin container of celery soup, stuffed tomatoes, or baked beans and brown bread from his steel lunchbox, always ate fruit and drank a thermos filled with coffee for dessert? That Jack?

Yes, Sir. I'm that Jack! He laughed and waggled his fingers in front of his nose. *Nyah, nyah, nyah* to those bankers who thought they were the cat's meow. I'm the new lion in town. He released a loud roarrrrrr, and laughed. His belly cinched, and a pebble-sized release traveled down his intestines and out the back and popped like a balloon when it hit the air. He smiled at his audacity and let loose another roarrrrr. This was the real Jack, not the one tethered by the responsibilities of a wife and children and bills to pay, not the one manacled to his desk since accounting required solitude and exacting concentration.

He looked at the certificate, clinched in his fist. They hadn't even had the decency to use one of the Royal Portables. He opened his hand and tossed it to the wind. The paper lifted, and floated, and then it soared. He felt free, by gosh he certainly did, as free as that lousy certificate.

He stumbled along Water Street where the Hudson River met the southernmost tip of Manhattan. Should he have invited his wife, Mary, to the ceremony? Other VPs had brought their wives. His gay impairment turned to guilt, which swished around his insides. Golden brown like the bourbon he treasured. He had lost count at the sixth tumbler, or perhaps the seventh. Or maybe his gut hurt from the sausages. Had he consumed eight or nine slices of sausage pie? He loudly passed gas again, looked around and saw he was still alone, and laughed again. His flatulence was boss! His wife would have disciplined him for such bawdy behavior. His two young children would have laughed.

He walked along, passed a man slumped in a corner sleeping off his drink, and stepped around two pigs chewing on... He turned away. He didn't want to know. He had not invited Mary since he had craved a night to let loose. One night each year without having to sit for a family dinner, without having to fix that or move this, without having to be perfectly mannered. One evening out of three hundred and sixty-five when a woman would not reject him.

It was only once per year that he engaged the services of one that was not his wife—the last time at the previous annual Goldman Sachs award ceremony—and it saved his marriage. Statistics proved it, at least based on his unofficial data collected over the previous seven years. The hypothesis being, if a man was sexually satisfied one out of three hundred and sixty-five times each year multiplied by that man being able to pay more attention to the everydayness of life at home the remaining three hundred and sixty-four days of the year equals one hundred percent home life satisfaction.

The equation floated in front of him.

formula

So, there you go. One whore a year was the secret to a successful marriage. As long as she swallowed. Another belly laugh.

Guilt erased, gleeful impairment returned. He wasn't scared of no bad man, no sireee. He wasn't losing an ear tonight. He was saving his marriage.

Five Points wasn't far.

Chapter Thirty-eight

Noble huddled in the doorway to the Home for Unwanted Boys. No longer able to find warmth, his skin ashen from the cold. He had knocked and knocked on the door, called for William, but there was still no response. Where was Butchy? Kid? A punch in the nose from Kid would feel better than frostbite.

He gripped the vial strung around his neck, which gave him comfort although he didn't know why. He sighed. He couldn't stay in the doorway any longer. His muscles were stiff and his toes might crack off from frostbite. He'd come back in the morning when he could search out a patch of sunlight. For now, he'd find a place to stow. He thought of his hiding places when he was first on his own as a nine-year-old, when he squatted over heat that rose from grates, nestled in dry corners in abandoned buildings, and stretched out on rooftops with the moon as his cover as if he were the man. Maybe he'd even go through garbage cans and find something to eat, like he'd do as a boy. He was hungry. Wasn't he?

He stepped onto the sidewalk, the streets quieter than earlier in the evening, the light snow that had fallen in dirty disarray. He ambled along the road, along patches of earth and partially paved streets, and wondered what happened to his winter coat. Hadn't he been wearing one?

Chapter Thirty-nine

On the day Noble Jennings was to be arrested for five murders he did not commit, and one he might have, Timothy Byrne was acquitted of one he did. Before a packed courtroom and a prescient judge, on a Monday morning after twenty-three minutes of deliberations during which a professor and a clergyman discussed Van Tassel Sutphen's apocalyptic novel *The Doomsman* and other jurors talked of the blight that was Five Points, the foreman mumbled the not guilty verdict.

William, Byrne's attorney, pinched the skin on his forearm when the verdict was read lest he turn to the jurors and yell, "Cowards!"

Outside the triangular plot of the Old New York County Courthouse at Fifty-two Chamber Street, known sardonically as the Tweed Courthouse after its primary donor, horse and buggy and foot traffic clogged Broadway and City Hall Park. The crowd that waited to learn the verdict exchanged lawyer jokes. *Did you hear people are unhappy with the new subway system? Lawyers can leave town but then they're permitted to return!* Tammany thugs in knit suits stood shoulder to shoulder with Metropolitans in blue. Prostitutes' bare shoulders prickled in gusts of wind. The famished mawks rubbed their bubbies against reporters, hoping to make a date for later, money for grub. Photographers double-fisted box cameras. Anxiety corrupted the air like the brackish waters that converged into an arrowhead at the foot of Manhattan island.

William pushed his way out of the courthouse doors and to
the top of the steps. A superfluity of fanatics and judicial per-
sonnel funneled behind him. The Congregation of Byrne
swayed below him. William jammed his hand into the front
pocket of his trousers, sorted through the pennies, and rubbed
the rose quartz he always carried. A monkey could have won
this trial, William thought. Even if while on the stand Byrne
confessed to murdering that chap accused of buggery, even if
there had been a way to replay the strangulation in front of the
jurors' eyes, the verdict would have been not guilty.

William knew Byrne hired him as a formality, and felt a-
shamed he had accepted the appointment for the easy pay day.

To Byrne and his cohorts, justice was not realized in the pit
of a courtroom where lawyers engaged in intellectual battles
and word games, but in the tenement hallways and on the
jam-packed streets. Once the jurors for Byrne's trial were
seated and sworn, cops and thugs—led by Peter Stout—promised protection and groceries to agreeable jurors and their
families, and persuasively changed the minds of those jurors
inclined to abide by the legal burden imposed upon the People
of the State of New York.

Twenty-six years earlier the United States' Supreme Court
first mentioned this burden of persuasion in the court decision, <u>Miles v. United States,</u> by stating the following: "The
evidence upon which a jury is justified in returning a verdict of
guilty must be sufficient to produce a conviction of guilt, to the
exclusion of all reasonable doubt." Previously, justice had been
meted depending upon what time the judge had to be home
for dinner. While <u>Miles</u> was a leap forward for American jur-
isprudence, the highest court's ruling failed to prevent sewage
from seeping into the jury box.

On the courthouse steps, the crisp wind cooled the stubble
on The Attorney's face but offered no relief to the hot fury that
slammed his brow. He scanned the crowd for Kid, a toothless

and hefty mutt of a man with wisps of red in his gray beard. William no longer thought of their beginnings at the Home when, as children, Kid was a callous bully, but only knew their relationship of recent years when, as adults, Kid was a loyal protector. His right-hand man was out there, somewhere, camouflaged among the wash of Irish, Chinese and German immigrants who tangled with the ancestral rag tags of American-born forefathers. William scoffed at the hyperbole of the white nationalists, those megalomaniacs who believed to be more entitled than those who did not look and think like them. They were not proud descendants of the past but pathetic ascendants to the future.

Looking out over the mass that gathered to celebrate Byrne, as the corrupted jury that just set the guilty man free emerged from the courthouse, William knew one truth. Manhattan was untamed, dirty and spoiled, putrid and greedy in its backrooms and among its narrow and shadowy cobbled streets, and he loved every square inch of the island.

Byrne shook hands with some of the jurors and stepped behind The Attorney. William's right arm shook, as it has done since he was a kid, an unexplainable tremor. He shoved his hand into his pocket again and scooped the rose quartz into his palm. He rubbed the crystal at times of immense stress. It calmed him, and quieted the quiver in his arm. Even though William had sat next to The Client for four days during his trial, and they had met numerous times prior to prepare his "defense", having Byrne's negative energy crash into his aura delivered a jolt to William's chakras.

The Client was big footed with a pocked horse face and oversized saliva daubed lips. Like many of the *Famine Irish* who fled starvation, Byrne came to America on a coffin ship, the conditions as horrid as any slave ship, but he arrived with an advantage over most of the other immigrants: his education. Raised by an aunt who, despite hunger and cruelty

suffered from the hands and whips of English overlords, insisted her nephew learn to speak and write English in addition
to their native Gaelic.

When he arrived in America as a scrawny twelve-year-old,
torment wrapped his face like a bandage. He was greeted at
the pier by Tammany Hall representatives who looked to re-
cruit the in-coming wave of genetically tough and always
hungry Irish immigrants to stuff ballot boxes and to work as
muscle. The younger the better as their minds were malleable.

Men and boys who spoke English and who had above-av-
erage smarts like Byrne were made into police officers within a
few years after landing on the docks. At eighteen, Byrne married a pretty blonde German woman, had four close-in-age
tow-headed children, and moved into a three-bedroom flat on
Houston. Helga accepted that her husband worked nights as
there were many duties for a man of Byrne's up-and-coming
stature, unaware his self-proclaimed responsibilities included
skulking through City Hall Park in the thick of the night to
seek quick male companionship. Helga's refusal to nag Byrne
about his frequent absences from home—motivated by her
desire for her husband to succeed as well as by the freedom it
gave her to pursue her own affairs—aided Byrne's speedy as-
sent up the police department's ladder.

Men like Byrne never forgot how fortunate they were to
have acquired their status so quickly and shuddered at the
thought of how fast it could be snatched away. Byrne's biggest
fear used to be losing his job to free blacks who would do just
about anything for nothing. But now, as he stood at the pinnacle of the courthouse steps after his acquittal, his greatest
concern was losing the power he had so carefully cultivated
through graft and murder. As a result of a backroom deal,
Byrne had been suspended as chief of police pending trial.

Without looking behind him, William knew Byrne's posture. Four fingers folded into his palms, arms raised, thumbs

thrust high. A politician's victory stance. A unified exhale rose from his foot soldiers. Their breaths visible as puffs of tobacco-scented clouds. Applause grew like thunderclaps.

Byrne leaned toward The Attorney's ear. "I owe you one. Get a message to Peter Stout when you're ready."

William winced from the halitosis of Byrne's sour tongue and morning whiskey. He kept his head straight, his eyes moving, and noted Kid's location at a curb by a carriage. He turned toward Byrne. The whites of The Client's eyes splayed with spidery lines.

A rush of blue pushed William aside and jumped and pawed at Byrne like a scrum of happy retrievers. William scrambled and ducked through the crowd, past shiny gold buttons that fastened waistcoats, and around tightened bodices and exaggerated cleavages, and toward the road where Kid held open a carriage door.

William climbed in. "Get me the hell away from here."

Chapter Forty

Kid covered William's lap with a blanket, jumped on to the platform, and tapped the neck of the draft horse with the reins. The horse danced three half-steps, blew frustrations of cold air from his nostrils, and stopped. The crowd too thick to push through. William looked back to see Mayor George B. McClellan, Jr. place a pin on the lapel of Byrne's overcoat, returning his status to the most powerful gun slinger on the east coast.

The homosexual community knew Byrne strangled the bully trap—an effeminate and brave man-child in his late teens who had threatened to expose the police chief's proclivities. Many were witnesses, not to the actual murder but had seen the commissioner immediately before and after the crime, and had observed him frequent City Hall park in the darkness for years, rampaging the park like an under-sexed bull. Still, no one came forward.

The homosexual community's feelings about the event mirrored the reaction of the people at large. Shock when he was arrested, suspended, and prosecuted, and no surprise when he was acquitted, lauded, and reinstated as top cop on the courthouse steps.

Behind the scenes—even John Coal of the New York Times hadn't reported this—pressure had come from former New York City Police Chief President Theodore Roosevelt to the district attorney who was up for reelection. A sticky spot, stuck between local and national politics. A deal was made over whiskey at Delmonico's between the D.A. and the mayor. No need for Teddy to know. The commissioner would be suspended with pay until his trial when it would be arranged for him to be found not guilty. The trial would begin as quickly as possible, the Rough Rider would be happy, and the police would look less corrupt to the ever-growing dissatisfied public. All in all, it would be a minor hitch in Byrne's otherwise well-oiled career.

William leaned forward in the open-air cabin of the horse drawn carriage. Irritation in his voice chucked over Kid's right shoulder. "Can't you get us out of here?"

"No room for Sally to move, Sir."

William took a half-second to make his decision. He threw off the blanket and dashed from the cab.

"Sir. Wait." Kid called.

William's lungs burned as he ran. The crowd thinned on the west side of City Hall Park and dwindled to one, the way he preferred, alone with the life energies that engulfed the park—metal, fire, wood, earth and water. Even though he moved quickly, he was able to absorb the vitality of the sun that peeked through steely clouds and penetrated his fourth chakra, the heart. Wood benches, like the earth, palpitated chakra number one, his root, where the instinct "fight or flight" dwelt. Usually, William took his daily walk through this park and allowed the energies to enter and exit his body through his third eye—the sixth chakra being his favorite—but there was no time now.

Kid called from a park entrance. "Sir, please wait."

William ran faster, through the area where volunteers had staged to fight in the Civil War, and along the path where President Abraham Lincoln's funeral procession began forty years earlier. Both events of which he had participated. He rolled over a low stone wall meant to separate the park from the street and scuttled across Broadway near Trinity Church. Kid's pleas for him to stop lessened. The roar of the crowd that yelled praise and sang hallelujahs in Byrne's honor also faded. William's heart raced from the speed and from the excitement of nearing his destination. Like many of the choices he had made in his life outside a courtroom, he had chosen flight.

In his sixty-three years on earth, some spent sopped in poverty, some as a soldier in the Civil War, others cushioned by wealth, William hoarded his tendencies like the dusty tarot cards and crystals he hid in a wood box, nailed shut, and tucked under a floorboard in the kitchen of Apartment 5C. To his world, the one that stretched from the southern most points of Manhattan to the courthouse, through Five Points, and from the East River to the Hudson, he was William James Henley, Counselor at Law. He didn't know if James was actually his middle name but he liked that it made him sound like he came from somewhere special. William James Henley. William J. Henley. W.J. Henley.

W.J.H. was stitched on to the breast pockets of his tailored dress shirts. He fastened gold cufflinks to his sleeves, eighteen karat W.J.H.s that cost more than most lower east side families could scrounge together in a year. But having a middle name, or a middle initial, hadn't brought the prestige he coveted. President Theodore Roosevelt recently passed him over for a spot on the United States Supreme Court, which frustrated William as he considered them friends having worked together and hunted and fished. Instead, Teddy had announced his intention to appoint William Henry Moody. William H. Moody. W.H. Moody. W.H.M. All because of the Lizzie Borden trial, which Moody had prosecuted when he was United States Attorney for the Eastern District in Massachusetts. Thirty whacks made Borden famous, and Moody too, who after the trial found his way to congress and then to the top judge spot even though Lizzie Borden was acquitted by a jury (who had not been bribed, William noted).

While an indiscriminate choosing of clients had made William J. Henley rich, he lamented for the one case that would bring him the legal recognition that would equal his worth. While many indicted his short stature, no one dared challenge the tallness of his mind. He coveted his very own Lizzie Borden. A suitable, controversial murder that would be talked about from the growing east coast cities to the small towns that were popping up out west, and indeed across the sea. As a young man at Columbia College, William had forecast his path to the legal mountaintop, but here he was, forty years after becoming an attorney, and still no closer to a judgeship or a congressional spot than a monkey.

He slowed his pace and stopped in front of the wood door of the brownstone of the former Home for Unwanted Boys, a building he purchased after achieving financial success. He refurbished the condemned structure from roof to floorboards, and erased its smell of simmering flesh, its stench of piss, the reek of despair of abandoned boys, and the stink of who cares not a whit. Anything could be knocked down, painted over and covered, he instructed the workers, except for the front door.

Graffiti and inscriptions on the thick and wide door burned familiar. William hesitated enough to recognize the carvings. From his own hand, fastidiously engraved near the midsection of the door, a portion of a quote that inspired him as a young man eager to join Lincoln's war:

If it is deemed necessary
that I should forfeit my life
in this slave country whose rights are disregarded
by wicked, cruel, and unjust enactments,
so let it be done!

John Brown 1800-1859

Kid's contributions had been haphazardly whittled into the wood with tilts right and left. One long winding sentence sans spaces or punctuations:

Torevolutionarieswhoresandprostitutes
Boyswholovetofightgirlswhofuckallnight

Surrounding this, an array of obscenities: balls, fuck, cock-sucker, fart.

William next viewed Noble's donation to the door and his heart plunged. Life had left Noble out of its script.

"Please, Sir."

William turned, and saw a walking heap of rags, sounded like a woman from the voice but he could not be certain. He reached into his pocket, pushed a piece of ruby quartz aside, and pulled out two Indian head pennies. He placed the alms in her hand, turned back to the door, gripped the knob and pushed in.

Each time he walked through this threshold, the door felt heavier upon entering, lighter upon exiting. Electric lights flickered and burned in the hallways and up the stairwell. In the foyer, a row of mailboxes gleaned, names on each such as Levin, Goldberg and Smith, families that occupied the spit and polished apartments of the rent free six-story walk up. Rent free, which meant his tenants would feign ignorance should the law come sniffing around.

A middle-aged woman, fat cheeks flushed, approached William. Her white apron was stained with purple blotches. He pulled two pennies from his pocket and handed them to her.

She curtsied. "Mister Henley." Her voice shook. "How are you today?"

"Just fine, Missus Mulligan. Your apple pie was amazing."

She remained bowed in front of him. "Thank you for all you have done for me and my family. I have a Mulberry cooling on the stove. Your wife and children will enjoy it."

"Yes, ma'am. Thank you, ma'am." He moved past her, and up the narrow stairway.

"My husband made you a tree coat rack. It's mahogany." She yelled to his back. "Don't forget to pick up the pie and the rack before you leave."

He climbed the stairs two at a time and rested at each landing, out of breath. Fifth floor, he stood in front of Apartment 5C. Smoke seeped out from under the door. The smell, sweet. William wiped sweat from his brow, and peeled off his overcoat and suit jacket and hung them on a hook in a line of black overcoats and suit jackets, pin-striped and plain. He slipped a foot out of his right shoe, then the left, and lined them up against the floorboard along a row of scuffed and polished black leather loafers. He wet his palms with his tongue and smoothed the white hair that curled and upended from the top and sides of his head. He cursed when he remembered he forgot to have his wife shave the hair from his ears, and trim the hair from his nose.

When his pulse returned to its norm of eighty-eight beats per minute, he opened the unlocked apartment door. The creak of the hinges emitted a cranky welcome. No person greeted him, how he liked it. He yearned to be special, to be viewed as a force that shaped the laws of the United States, but not inside Apartment 5C. Here, he craved to travel through the fog without being noticed, nameless and faceless, free to inhale and inject and snort and swallow without being judged.

In a back room, Jenny Big Stink sat on a three-legged stool. Fat stacked on her sides like a cockeyed cake. She perpetually smelled like fish even though she had pushed her fish cart into the Hudson River a decade earlier. William saw her as a cartoon, himself a character in the next panel.

Jenny gestured toward a four-cushioned couch where three men sat. William stepped around the banker, past the architect, and over the judge's long legs, and sank in. His slender rear easily fit as a boy's might. Jenny pushed the pipe toward him and sparked the flame.

When William bought the brownstone, he did so not only to set up his den but to prove to those who had abandoned him and believed him to be unworthy that he was most deserving. Of course, he could not identify exactly who those people were—he had never met any blood relative—but that was of no matter. When he fixed up the brownstone, he hadn't known he would be at the forefront of the rehabilitation of Five Points, although that was a most pleasant bonus.

Jenny and her girlfriend lived in Apartment 5C. A drug parlor that provided an outlet for men akin to the local saloon, the bath house, and the whorehouse. But William wasn't a drinker, he didn't care to sit in a steam room and oblige small talk and pontificate on politics, and he wasn't a cheater. Apartment 5C was his other home. Not an escape but a dimension away from the brownstone where he resided with his wife and children in Washington Mews. A getaway from responsibility and properness. In Apartment 5C, William pursued his Orphic tendencies.

He inhaled through the long-stemmed *yen tsiang* and filled the balloons of his lungs and the cavities of his brain. He held his breath. A calm overcame him and his teeth tingled. His arm steadied. He exhaled. Smoke poured from his ears, nose and mouth.

The Attorney was convinced—along with the banker, the architect, the judge, the politicians, and the coppers in the other rooms of apartment 5C—that ingesting opioids increased intellect. In two-and-a-half months, a law would go into effect making possession of morphine, cocaine and heroin illegal, even with a prescription. The visitors to 5C possessed the financial ability and the connections to obtain the drugs on the black market, but wouldn't it be better, William believed, if reaching the zenith of one's mental capacity wasn't criminalized? At Levi's suggestion, approximately two months ago, William shipped a letter to Doctor Alois Alzheimer with the hope that the German neuropathologist would assist in proving the veracity of the following formula William had composed:

Opioid Input = Genius Output

From the Desk of

Herr Doktor Alois Alzheimer

Berlin, Germany

Sent by post via steamer

Embarked: March 30, 1906

Expected Arrival: April 16, 1906

Dear Counselor William Henley,

I trust this letter having travelled across the ocean finds you and your family in good health and spirits. I am honored to make your acquaintance and am forever grateful to Doctor Levi Solomon Fuller for our introduction. I understand you and Doctor Fuller share a close companionship, in fact that of father and son more than uncle and nephew, although you have no blood in common. Due to my affection for Doctor Fuller I thus have immediate fondness for you.

In addition, I welcome the opportunity to practice my English writing, and perhaps my English speaking if we should have the good fortune to meet one day. My father insisted I learn to speak English as he believed America, as the offspring of England, held the best opportunities. In addition to my native German, I also am fluent in Dutch, Icelandic, un peu de Français, and (naturally) psycho-speak. Although in the case of this letter, I delve into the world of psycho-scribble. Now, my new friend, enough about me.

In your correspondence, you inquired about the impact of opioids on the brain, convinced along with your colleagues that the use of the compound lends to the increase in intellectual and physical performance. Doctor Fuller, being a young psychiatrist, and perhaps due to the personal relationship you both enjoy, deferred to me, the seasoned alienist who has made it his life's endeavor to study the intricacies of the mind.

Dear Herr Lawyer, please forgive my digression as I feel it necessary to qualify my response as to the benefits of opioids. It is not the influence of tablets and powders that captivates me. My focus is on what Doctor Fuller and I deem "dementia", a term of art first used one hundred years ago and that came to mean "insanity" in the psychiatric community in the most clinical of senses. I have been working vigorously with a woman so afflicted, of the name Auguste Deter.

Doctor Fuller and I are toiling to prove the following supposition: Dementia is an unexplained and decremental change in thinking.

Now, enough about me (again) and I shall answer your inquiry. Ja, opioids increase intellectual and physical performance.

I affirm under the assumption you refer to opium and morphine, and perhaps the growing in popularity of heroin, which is created by boiling morphine. The American Medical Association recently approved heroin for general use, and is in agreement with its producer, an American company called Bayer, that it has non-addicting properties.

Opioids bind opioid receptors and reduce pain. I shan't go into too much detail as I do not wish to know the research behind the preparation of your legal briefs, but rather only care to learn your legal conclusion. I again assume that you too wish to arrive at the destination, without the need to consult a map.

Reduction in pain means people are more at ease, physically and mentally. They sleep better. They think more clearly. Their brains are not clogged with unimportant thoughts and memories and are able to concentrate on the immediate and the significant. People react more quickly and succinctly under the stimuli of opioids.

Please share with your colleagues the following: opioids indeed increase intellectual and physical performance. They are highly recommended for optimal output and advocated by the psychiatric community for our deepest thinkers. Perhaps after Doctor Fuller and I complete our study of dementia, we will tackle the opioid phenomena, although I suspect when that time arrives, heroin will already be available for purchase at your marts along with milk and eggs, and given to your children at their schools with their mid-day snacks.

Feel free to post further inquiries.

With warmth and admiration,
Herr Doktor Alzheimer

Chapter Forty-one

Five Years Former

Doctor Alois Alzheimer met Auguste Deter when he was a psychiatrist on staff at Frankfurt's Hospital for the Mentally Ill and Epileptics. Walking down the stark bleached hallway moments before their first encounter, the buttons on his lab coat strained against his protruding belly. He wore regular shoes back then, before diabetic neuropathy caused his feet to buzz like a horde of bees.

"Have you seen my spectacles?" Alois inquired of the nurse that walked beside him.

She laughed and pointed to his face. "You're wearing them, Herr Doktor."

Alois smiled, not a bit put off by his absentmindedness, attributing it to his own mind that was so filled with scientific theories and psychological conceits that it left no room in his brain to accumulate the everyday habits and courtesies of the average man. He was known to go to work wearing a robe one day, minus shoes another. He kept a separate wardrobe in his office. But while he often failed to practice social graces, he never forgot the details of his training and expertise, including the minutest particulars.

"If my head wasn't attached to my neck I'd leave it in a cupboard," he said.

The nurse smiled, affably. "Will you be needing me in the next few moments, Herr Doktor? I'd like to have lunch."

"Of course. Please do."

She veered to the right and into the staff room. Alois continued along the hallway.

Along the corridor his path tapped in a three-beat meter: metal tip of walking stick, left heel, right heel, repeat. He had been on his way to check on a patient, a man in his eighties who stared blankly and didn't speak. Locked away as mentally ill, Alois believed his catatonic state had to do with something awry in his brain unrelated to mental illness. He and Doctor Levi Solomon Fuller of the United States of America were researching memory loss, changes in muscular coordination, and the diminishment of motor functions in the aged, hoping to understand these afflictions and treat them through natural means. Those in the psychiatric field thought their pursuit foolish, especially when Alois and Levi theorized that such ailments could be lessened or reversed through exposure to the sun, human contact, and love.

He neared the intake area of the hospital.

A woman's voice labored into the hallway. "I forgot that it didn't happen."

Without seeing her, judging the tremor and pitch of her voice, Alois guessed she was in her eighties. He peered into the admission area. New patients and their family members, hospital staff, and volunteers were stitched together in a quilt of concern. The woman who spoke the nonsensical phrase sat limp in a straight back chair. Dark stringy hair fell about her long, reedy and damp face. A housedress hung on her thin frame like a postal satchel. Behind her stood a robust man, broad shouldered and straight-backed as the chair. In his fifties, Alois guessed. A young girl, maybe twelve years old, cupped her hand around his thick forearm. The woman, Alois figured, was the man's *mutter* and the girl's *oma*.

The man addressed the intake clerk. "At first Auguste's memory occasionally failed and we laughed about it. She was great around the house and with Flora, cooking, cleaning, helping with her homework, and she was attentive to me. But then she neglected her household chores and sometimes acted like Flora wasn't there. Auguste was anxious and never sat still. She stopped sleeping." He put his hands on Auguste's shoulders. Auguste had no reaction. "She throws water on me and Flora. When I ask her why, she says she's cleaning because we expect company but no one is coming."

The intake clerk pulled out a form and looked to Auguste. "What is your name?"

"Frau," she said.

"Frau what?"

"Frau Frau."

The man answered for her. "Her name is Auguste Deter."

"And you are?"

"Rolf Deter, her husband. This is our daughter."

Alois moved closer. Husband? Daughter? Not mother and grandmother?

Rolf continued, "I'm employed with the railroad authority and I can't take care of her anymore. I don't think Flora is safe alone with her."

Alois began to leave. What was it called when one spouse was significantly older than the other? Chaucer wrote in "Merchant's Tale" about Sir January, an old man who married a young girl named May. January to May romance? Yes, that was it. Alois chuckled. Good for her, nabbing a younger man.

He'd check in on the woman later. He headed toward B Ward when he heard the clerk ask, "How old is Frau Deter?"

"Fifty," Rolf said.

"Pardon me?" the clerk asked.

"My wife is fifty years old."

Alois turned back and walked into the admission bay. Fifty years old and she showed signs of dementia? Not possible.

Alois stepped next to where the clerk sat. "She looks much older than fifty."

The railroad worker looked at him sideways. "And you are?"

"Pardon me. Doctor Alois Alzheimer." He extended his hand.

Rolf did not take it. "My wife didn't look like this one year ago."

Alois raised his hand and adjusted his glasses. "When did she hit her head?"

"Never."

"No accident? She didn't fall? Hit by a pot that tumbled from a high shelf, perhaps?"

"I assure you my wife has never been injured."

"Does she suffer from Syphilis?"

"How dare you!" Rolf spat.

Alois lifted his pince nez glasses and rubbed the bridge of his nose with his thumb and forefinger. He turned to the clerk, his voice metered for calm. "I will take over from here."

The clerk hurried to assist another patient.

He extended his hand again. "Doctor Alois Alzheimer."

Rolf hesitated, and then took his hand. His tough grasp was the handshake of a man accustomed to manual labor. His nails were dirty. His skin was browned and felt gritty like sand. The contrast to Alois' soft, pale hands and manicured nails embarrassed the doctor. He gripped the man's hand, shook it with over enthusiasm, and recalled his father's derision when Alois declared his intention to attend medical school and not be a carpenter like his father and grandfather.

"Afraid to get your hands dirty?" his father jeered. "An honest day's work isn't good enough for you?"

"I am going to help people who are sick in their heads." Young Alois protested.

"Help people by building homes and schools."

"She's not right, Herr Doktor." Rolf's deep voice brought Alois back to the present. "This pains me so much, and my daughter too. We can't take care of her."

Alois forced his father's voice of disapproval from his mind, and gently placed his index finger under the woman's chin. He lifted her head. Through her stringy hair, he saw her face muscles were stiff like rawhide. Deep grooves dug into her cheeks and carved around her eyes and mouth.

The intake area was crowded with new patients and their family members but Alois failed to see or hear any of them. "Are you sure your wife is fifty years old?" Alois again rubbed the bridge of his nose.

"I know my wife's age. We grew up together." Rolf's aggravation intensified.

Alois turned to Flora. The child's eyes were tearful; her expression soulful. Was her young brain already corroded with kinks? Would she too lose her memory at fifty? He viewed each person as a patient, even the grocer and the typist. A personality kink of his own, he was well aware, amazed his wife tolerated his oddities and obsessions.

Flora leaned into her father and tightened her grip on his arm. To calm him, Alois wondered. Had the daughter assumed the role of the wife as Auguste regressed? What could that be called? Spousifying the child. Yes. Definition? When a parent treats a child like a spouse, not in the bedroom but in the child's responsibilities. Alois hid his pleasure. Could *spousify-ing* be a real condition? He made a mental note to add this to the list of his next avenues of study, along with the benefits of opioids to increase intellect, and the sun to fight sadness, and many other pursuits. His to-do list already several pages long.

"May I ask Auguste some questions?" Alois inquired.

Rolf nodded.

He pulled a chair next to the woman, and sat. With a single finger he moved hair from around her dark and hollow eyes. Eyes that studied him or looked through him, he couldn't be certain.

"Hello, dear. What is your name?" he asked.

"Auguste."

"Surname?"

"Auguste."

"What is your husband's name?"

"I believe, Auguste."

"Your husband?" Alois asked.

"I see, my husband..." Auguste said.

"Are you married?"

"To Auguste."

Alois took her thin, veined hand. "Is your name Missus Deter?"

"Yes to Auguste D."

"Do you have children?"

"I suppose I do," she said.

"How many?"

"Six, I believe."

"Is Flora your daughter?" Alois pointed toward the young girl.

Auguste looked at her. "I believe she is my oldest."

"Your oldest child?"

"Yes, my oldest."

"Mister Deter," Alois asked, "how many children do you and Auguste have?"

"Only Flora." His voice cracked.

"I see." Alois released her hand and rubbed her shoulder in a fatherly manner. "Thank you, Frau Deter."

"You're most welcome," she responded.

Alois stood. "Herr Deter, you did the right thing by bringing your wife here. I will take her into my care."

He nodded, tears in his eyes.

"Fraulein Flora," Alois said, "you are very brave."

"Thank you, Herr Doktor. Will you make my mother like she was?"

"I don't know."

Flora's eyes dimmed and he regretted his response. He should have been positive for the child, even if it wasn't true.

He cupped his hand to her cheek. "I'm sure she'll be home again and back to normal."

"Danke schoen," Flora said.

Alois turned back to Auguste. Fifty years old and she demonstrated signs he had only seen in those at least twenty-five years her senior. How many more were like her?

Five Years Later

Frankfurt News

Obituary of Auguste Deter

FRANKFURT, GERMANY, April 9, 1906.

Born: May 16, 1850 in Kassel, Germany. Died: April 8, 1906 in Frankfurt, Germany. Survived by her husband, Rolf Deter, and seventeen-year-old daughter, Flora. No services.

Chapter Forty-two

Alone in the main laboratory at the Royal Psychiatric Hospital in Munich, Germany, Herr Doktor Alzheimer contemplated a black metal box set on an operating table. The dull silver latches on the sides of the container were scratched and dented. Several of its screws were stripped. The box, scuffed and bent-in from travel, cold from refrigeration, held enough of its rectangular shape for its intended purpose. The case was large enough to fit a top hat, however what was preserved inside was of no interest to a milliner who couldn't sell a hat to a head without a body.

Alois's long fingers, elegant like the bass strings of the piano he loved to play, spread along the surface of the frigid container. He gasped, and drew his hand away. One week after her death, here she was. My darling Auguste. At least the only part of a person that mattered. Her brain.

Forty-one years old, with a balding head, ears that folded over on top, a moustache, and a light comportment, Herr Alzheimer resembled Mahatma Gandhi plus sixty pounds. He steeled himself, and again placed his uncalloused hands upon the box. Lensky's aria from Tchaikovsky's *Eugene Onegin* played in his mind. He moved his fingers along the box, and tapped out notes and chords of the piece he'd been working to master.

The clatter and conversation of surgeons and students approached outside the double doors of the operating room and he removed his hands from the box. Under his pince nez glasses, he rubbed the bridge of his nose with his thumb and forefinger.

Shortly, the doors to the laboratory would swing open. The septic smells that had become so familiar to him they felt like home would be overpowered by perfumes and colognes, and also by the scents they are meant to disguise, that of lye and fats and dirt accumulated since days-ago baths. His time alone with Auguste would be wrestled away by the presence of the interlopers, by unsolicited comments from his associates, and by questions from his students. Grief overcame him, thick like the soles of his corrective shoes. He would never be alone with Auguste again.

The doors opened and doctors and students flooded in. Lab coats buttoned around woolen three-piece suits; flexible tube stethoscopes draped over necks. Upon the inundation, Alois shielded the container, unprepared to share Auguste with the world.

"We are ready, Herr Doktor Alzheimer," Herr Doktor Kleinmann, a fellow neuropathologist (in degree only, not acclaimed, barely published), announced.

The Dullards. All of them. Bores who were interested in the spectacle of theater and not the spectacular of the craft. He pinched the bridge of his nose and then, with grave averseness as he wished not to be on stage, he pulled purple and thick gloves over his hands. He fingers stretched the rubber at the tips. One day they would make surgical gloves for doctors like him with long thin fingers, and also for short fat hands that swelled at the knuckles like knots in trees, like Kleinmann's hands. (Ha!). Perhaps Alois would invent them.

Each time Alois pulled surgical gloves on, he heard his father. Those aren't the hands of a surgeon or a pianist, he'd beseech. Those are the hands of a laborer. Until the day his father died from weariness, the old man never grasped why his only son preferred a scalpel and a microscope over a hammer and a drill.

Alois unlatched the box and removed Auguste's brain from its nest. Doctors and students moved closer, and he lifted the brain in his cupped hands. Liquid dripped. The pasty and sponge-like organ felt light in weight, as if he held a newborn bird fallen from a tree. Pallid blood vessels branched through maze-like folds and ridges and amid rows of yellowed cauliflower ears. Her brain was split by a fault line down the middle. She smelled like eternity.

Alois wasn't the tallest man in the room, maybe not the smartest, certainly not the most even-tempered, but while he held the epicenter of Auguste's intellect and motor skills he felt to be the almightiest.

He gingerly placed the brain in a large metal tray, elevated it to his chest level, and stepped among the colleagues and the students that crammed the lab. He allowed them to look through their monocles and spectacles, but not to touch.

His arms outstretched as if giving alms to the poor. "Behold Auguste Deter." His voice deepened with grandeur. "Witness the human brain, the shrine of humanity."

He loathed to sound melodramatic, but became aware that this was an instant deserving of theatrics, more so than *Tristan und Isolde*, Wagner's chromatic opera. Alois caressed this collusion of time and space, delighted and bewildered that he—a scientist who believed all occurrences could be explained through science and never by religion—faced a sacred moment. What else could explain the reverence that teemed within him? All seemed possible, and alchemical, and he knew—with scientific conviction—there indeed was a God, a discovery he loathed to share with his colleagues in the laboratory, a revelation he would contemplate until his death but never speak aloud.

"Looks like my wife's goulash," came a voice two deep in the crowd.

"Your wife's goulash after you've tossed it up," said another.

Doctoral candidates laughed, a few professors and scientists too.

Alois froze. Jokes? Were there jokes?

He brought Auguste close to his body, pivoted on his heels, and strode back to the operating table. Oh so carefully, he returned her to her metal nest. He turned again, lightning in his eyes, thunder on his tongue, and glared at the student, Siegfried something-or-other, a bright yet stupid man-child.

He bumped his chest against the joker. "Leave."

Siegfried stepped back. "Herr Doktor, I apologize for my bad manners."

"And you," Alois looked to his sidekick, another student, "exit my laboratory."

"Hold on, Doctor," said Kleinmann.

Alois glared over his glasses. "Ja?"

"They were making jokes. Bad ones, for sure, but people often bring levity to stressful circumstances through lightheartedness."

"And what," Alois asked, "might have been stressful?"

Others in the room backed away. A moat of tension formed around Alois, Siegfried and Kleinmann.

"They're sorry. Right, boys?" Kleinmann asked.

Siegfried bowed at the waist. "Right, Herr Doktor."

Alois made his way back toward Auguste. He'd let this go. He would only insure that Siegfried and his partner were never allowed in any of his classes or labs again.

"Der hat doch nicht alle Tassen im Schrank." Siegfried's voice was hushed, but not enough.

Alois stiffened. Did Siegfried just call him not right in the head? Did that child accuse the venerable Doctor Alois Alzheimer of lunacy in front of colleagues and students? And worse, so much worse, in front of Auguste?

"Everybody out!" Alois boomed.

Nobody moved, stiffened as if their brains lay in the tray.

"We didn't do anything," came a soft, reluctant voice, unspoken heretofore. "It was Siegfried and Hermann."

Alois's voice pelted and shook with fury. "The crime of one is the crime of the masses. Be gone! Now!"

Scientists and students groaned and funneled out.

◆

He and Auguste alone, he made his way to a cabinet, and swung open a door. He reached for a vile and tapped white powder on to the side of his thumb. He snorted, held his breath, waited for the spinning to stop, and exhaled. Calm tarped him.

Hands steady, mind clear, he fingered a scalpel and cut lobes from Auguste's brain. He examined her tissue under a microscope and discovered two unusual pathologies. The first was a massive amount of sticky, insoluble proteins lodged in spaces between nerve cells. The second were tangled bundles of protein threaded within neurons in a drunken cross stitch. Plaques and tangles, he thought. Not Syphilis. Not atherosclerosis. That's what caused her memory loss, her confusion, and her agitation at fifty-one years of age. Plagues and tangles in the brain.

Presenile dementia. Wunderbar.

He collected three hundred and seventeen slides and carefully labeled each.

Alois + Auguste

Like lovers who carved their names into a tree to proclaim eternal devotion.

Fire-Proof Stairs Act

An Act to Provide Against Unsafe Buildings
in the City of New York
Enacted 1856, Re-Enacted 1906
by the People of the State of New York,
represented in the State and the Assembly,
as follows

In all dwelling-houses which are built for
the residence of more than eight families,
there shall be a fire-proof stairs, in a
brick or stone, or fire-proof building, attached to the exterior walls...or if the
fire-proof stairs are not built as above,
then there must be fire-proof balconies
on each story on the outside of the building connected by fire-proof stairs.

No person shall sleep nor smoke on the
fire-proof stairs or its platforms, nor engage in sordid acts such as gambling and
imbibing upon the stairs or platforms.

Chapter Forty-three

Noble climbed the final fire-proof staircase of the five-story building, the same iron steps he'd run up as a boy to avoid the police, and the Bowery Boys, and the Daybreak Boys, and Peter Stout, and other Tammany Hall goons, and, of course, Kid. The same stairs where he'd smoke and sleep on its platforms and reign over his kingdom.

As he remembered, once he reached the top of an edifice he'd jump from roof to roof on the ration of Manhattan that tapered and drowned into the Hudson. An easy leap for a long legged boy with a running head start who, with nary a heave of his chest, would climb the iron and noisy rungs that seemed to barely cling to buildings. (Hadn't he always felt he'd plummet to the ground on every next step?). When hops-heavy coppers finally made it to the roof to nab him for stealing apples or for fighting, or a gang member would catch up to him, Noble would leap to the next building, dart down that fire escape, and disappear into the peepholes of his city.

That had happened, right?

Sometimes, five stories high, he'd square off against his pursuer knowing the rooftops were part of his education. While William instructed him on history and government, civics and economics, what the rooftops taught him were as valuable. Sometimes he'd be pummeled, other times he'd be the victor. Each bout a lesson on how to inflict and endure pain. Skills that had served him well in his almost sixty years.

He had done all that, right?

Decades removed from that boy, Noble stepped on to the rooftop and tried to remember when he first no longer trusted his thoughts. When his memory never failed him, when his actions didn't feel impetuous, when he could easily discern right from wrong. He could certainly pinpoint when he grew wary of others. That would be the day his father was killed, the semi-colon of his life. He could definitively identify when he lost faith in others. When his mother died (full stop) and he was taken to the Home for Unwanted Boys (exclamation point).

But when, he wondered, had he stopped feeling impenetrable like an island fortress? Perhaps he had never been that island. Perhaps his version of his life had never been factual, but fictional, or fact and fiction that oscillated between the broken spine of a paperback dime novel. One moment the boundary obvious, the next unclear. This was how his mind worked, or didn't work. Fog rolled in, dense and confusing, words blurred, and then abruptly the sun came out and all was well-defined.

On the rooftop, tufts of breath swelled from his mouth. He was no longer cold; the five flights winded and warmed him. That was a good thing as he knew he had been wearing a coat but now it was gone, perhaps stolen? When his breath slowed, he breathed in the smells, absorbed the sounds, and took in the sights of his city.

The moon was nearly full, lunar light bended the dark. Electric hues and flames that danced on torches glowed orange and red in the gray vista. Bonfire ash spotted the air, and fragments of newspapers drifted like disoriented confetti. Grit settled on his tongue and smoke roved into his nose. Rotating three hundred and sixty degrees, this skyline differed greatly from Lincoln's day. Of that, Noble was certain, an image of his New York-then versus his New York-now somehow perpetually sharp in his mind.

Church steeples no longer represented the tallest buildings on the island as they had when the city and its people were newborns. Forty-five years later, Manhattan had sprouted into a teenager, angst-ridden, always right, and fueled by idealism. The Met Life Tower was under construction on the corner of East Twenty-Third Street and Madison Avenue, in three years to be the tallest building in the world, at least for a time. The red veneered Hippodrome, a 5,200-seat theater on Sixth Avenue and Forty-third Street, rattled when a raised rail train passed. The Metropolitan Opera House lent early class to Times Square. Farther uptown, east and west, murkiness whelmed where the city continued its sprawl.

Noble sat on the edge of the rooftop. His feet dangled and he felt as he had in his youth, emperor of his island. The moment was stolen when the edges of the stranger's wallet in his pocket jabbed his hip bone and reminded him as to who he truly was, of his fact from his fiction. He was the dung-caked grooves of the cobbled streets of Five Points, the slippery stones and crime-ridden docks of the lower west side, the aroma of Challah and Irish Soda breads that baked on the lower east side, and the days-old water that boiled hot dogs in mid-town. He was white and black, Catholic, Protestant and Jewish, a beggar and a socialite, law abiding and law breaking. The streets and avenues of Manhattan, its good and its bad, knifed at his core like sharpened strands of DNA.

The clang of footsteps ascending the fire escape sounded and he judged the policeman was two flights down. He knew he was being chased, and could have dropped the wallet and dashed to a safe hiding spot. If he were caught he'd go back to prison. Was that what he wanted? In prison, it didn't matter what he remembered, or forgot, or if he felt confused. Routine, his bees, and the prison guards who'd gently guide him to his cell if he forgot where he was made the blurred lines inconsequential.

The copper, one flight away now. Noble removed two bills from the man's wallet and stuffed them in his pocket. He tossed the leather billfold over the side of the building and wished he could watch it float to the ground below.

Above the roofline, the officer's hat showed, then his face, his thick neck and chest, the billy club raised in his right hand, the large shiny buttons on his Metropolitan uniform. Noble couldn't see all of this in the moonlight, but he figured that's how he was dressed, envisioning him in the style of the police of his youth.

"Hey!" The cop rolled from the top step on to the roof floor. Rotund and sweaty, he wheezed. "You're under arrest."

Noble jumped up. The cop's uniform was dungier than he remembered, more gray than blue in color, the buttons smaller with no shine, the billy club short and dauntless, the officer himself nothing to shirk from. The cops of his youth had been ten-feet tall, muscled and mean. Hadn't they?

The policeman stood slowly. "Let's go."

Noble backed away.

"I'm not joking here, boy." He leaned toward him. "Hey, you're not a boy. What's on your shirt? Is that blood?"

Noble looked down. Blood?

The cop continued, "The complainant said a boy pinched his wallet. You didn't steal a wallet now, did you?"

The fog came, like a shade being drawn. Noble's brain shrinking, its byways knotting, and the sun tangled within a snarl of clouds. If Noble could recall, it began ten years earlier, one week shy of his forty-ninth birthday. The warden had ordered him to relocate a hive in the prison yard. Something about too many bees too close to a path where the warden strolled with his mistress.

Wearing a protective suit he had sewn and taped together from old prison uniforms, and a knitted hat pulled over his face with holes for the eyes and nose, Noble forgot mid-transfer what he was doing, why he was doing it, even forgot that he was the Bee King. He dropped the hive and the honeycomb and, frightened by the swarm, kicked at it and stepped on it, jumped about, and waved his arms. Bees got under his homemade suit and hat, and stung him. Many crunched beneath his prison boots. Thousands of bees flew away. Scores died. The queen was furious at him.

Noble was escorted back to his cell by the prison guard, Frankel, or so Noble was later told. The next morning, out in the prison yard, scratching at hundreds of bee stings on his skin, Noble wondered who would be so heartless as to destroy one of his hives.

"You didn't steal a wallet, did you?" The plump officer asked again.

"A wallet?"

"A billfold."

"I did what?"

"A man said a boy stole his wallet and then climbed the fire escape."

"No, Sir. I don't believe I did that. My winter coat is missing."

"Let me see."

"See what?"

"Your pockets. Pull 'em out."

Noble pulled out the front right pocket of his trousers. Two ten dollar bison bills drifted to the ground.

"Are those yours?"

"Must be."

The officer still breathed heavily. "The other pocket."

Noble upended that one too. "Nothing."

"The back ones?"

Noble turned, showed him they were empty.

"Nuts. You didn't happen to see some kid come up here, did you?"

"Kid? No, Sir, Kid isn't here."

The officer's posture softened. "I'm getting too old to be climbing fire escapes, and too fat." He laughed. "Came all this way and you ain't even the perpetrator. See, I got this bum knee. Hurts like a sonofabitch most of the time. You got a name?"

Noble was sure he did. Didn't everyone? But at that moment, with the fog thickening, he didn't know what it was. He knew a man named William. A good man. His friend. Perhaps his only friend.

"William?" he asked.

"Is that your name? See, I never met you before. There was a day I knew everyone in this neighborhood but this place is getting so big and cosmopolitan-like. I'm surrounded by strangers and most of them don't speak English too good. You got a last name?"

"William." Noble said.

"You got two first names? I knew a guy once named Johnson Johnson. We called him Johnny John. They can call you Willy Will." He laughed. "You got any identification?"

Noble looked to the side of the building and patted his pockets. Empty. Would not having ID be enough for him to go back to prison? Was that what he wanted? Had he already had this thought?

A chill overcame him. "I think someone stole my coat."

The cop waved. "I'm not arresting you. Too much paper-work. I wouldn't of arrested you anyways if you had taken that wallet, not with a little incentive if you know what I mean. I'm sure you're up here to get away from the wife for a spell. Can't blame a joe for that. I just have to catch my breath before I climb down." He sat on the ledge. "You can go if you want." He pointed sluggishly toward the fire escape.

Noble eyed the stairs and the edge of the roof. He could descend the iron steps, but he could do something more in-vigorating instead—jump to the next building like when he was a boy. He'd done that many times before. Hadn't he?

Go! Go! Go! Moving through his mind's mire, Noble jogged and then ran, toward the edge, toward darkness. He was four-teen years old again, and raced from the next ruffian who wanted to assert his authority over him. He ran from the pain of losing his parents, and dashed from his worthlessness. Swift and furious, his legs moved faster. He was going to leap, and dammit, that jump would set them free—the fourteen-year-old boy and the fifty-nine-year-old man.

The blow came from the side, hard and sudden. Noble crashed to the concrete. A heavy weight bore down on him.

"You trying to kill yourself?" the cop yelled. "What the hell is wrong with you? That's like a twenty foot leap to the next building. What were you thinking?" He rolled off of Noble and grabbed his knee. "Dammit. The damn thing popped out of its socket. Look what you did."

Noble sat up. "I'm sorry, Sir."

"I'm not gonna be able to walk for a week. You're no kinda cop if you can't walk the beat. Help me up, William." The of-ficer extended his hand.

Noble didn't move.

"C'mon, Will. Don't just stand there."

Noble stood, and pulled the man up and on to his good leg. He tucked his shoulder under the officer's armpit and helped him toward the fire escape.

"Wait." The officer nodded toward the two bison bills on the floor.

Noble picked them up.

"Ahem." The cop cleared his throat.

"Oh." Noble handed them to him.

He shoved them into his pocket.

Slowly, they descended the metal stairs. The iron shuddered and clanked, as if the rails were deciding whether to give way. The officer hopped on one foot. Noble braced himself two steps below to catch the officer should he tumble.

New York Times

All the News That's Fit to Print

CRUISE DOWN THE HUDSON

The President and Mrs. Roosevelt Return from Their Short Cruise

Reported by Peggy Fuller

New York, April 16, 1906. – President and Mrs. Roosevelt, who left here yesterday for a cruise down the Hudson on William Randolph Hearst's yacht, The Journal, returned at 8:30 o'clock this evening. The first part of the day furnished ideal weather for the outing. Clouds gathered in the afternoon and a light rain fell during the last hour of the trip. President Roosevelt wore a congenial smile that complimented his fashionable three-piece tweed suit. Mrs. Edith Roosevelt was dressed in a high collared dress affined with lace. A barmaid on the short cruise remarked, "Mrs. Roosevelt personally greeted each member of the staff on board and called us darlings and dears. She smelled like powder and poultry."

Mrs. Roosevelt will be the guest of honor at the Riverside Drive Garden Club's Orchid Extravaganza in two days hence. Thereafter, the President and the missus shall return to Washington, D.C.

Chapter Forty-four

William staggered along Broadway. Missus Mulligan's mulberry pie balanced in one hand, her husband's tree coat rack taller than he in the other. He was on his way to Washington Mews, his home between Fifth Avenue and University Place. The former row of stables converted into exclusive brownstones on a gated way. He felt giddy with cleverness. Every block or two he threw pennies into the air. Alzheimer's letter assured him his proposal was indeed correct. Opioid Intake = Genius Output. Eureka! Regular visits to Apartment 5C increased intellectual and physical prowess. Why else was he more wily and shrewd than any other attorney while embossed in the pit of a courtroom? Why else had he been able to sprint through City Hall Park like a man twenty years younger? Why else was he still able to please his wife, not once but twice? Case closed. Mystery solved.

Witness, Gentlemen of the Jury, the brilliance of the cerebral cortex. The one belonging to The Attorney, William James Henley, a beacon in a city of bright minds. Screw the lawmakers who deemed to make opioid use illegal. Many of those very lawmakers, in the secrecy of apartment 5C, inhaled opioids themselves through long bamboo pipes turned black and glossy from the opium that seeped into the wood. Hypocrites, all of them. At least The Attorney knew his truths from his lies, even if the members of the juries he addressed, the lawyers he battled, and the judges he out-cited could discern no difference.

William came upon a forming crowd, and put the coat rack down. He looked at his timepiece, a spring-driven gold pocket watch with hunter case and chain, given to him by the Rough Rider himself, President Theodore Roosevelt, and saw it was half past two in the morning. He stood on the opposite side of the street from the rabble; vagabonds and drunkards he assumed from their dress—who else was out at this hour? Then, she appeared. Darted from around a corner, a blur of audacity, the journalist wore pants!

William smiled—he loved her precociousness—Missus Peggy Fuller, wife of Doctor Levi Solomon Fuller. Missus Fuller's articles brightened the society pages of the New York Times on a weekly basis, but William and a scant others knew her best reporting of murder and other anointings was credited to a man named John Coal—a real man—Yes!—but an inventor and nary a journalist. The bogus credit judged essential by Peggy's editor, as who would ever believe a woman could reliably report on events of criminality with such accuracy and flair?

While William had come upon this scene quite by accident, Peggy had been awoken by a messenger in the night. The Five Points grapevine, well-oiled like the steel wheels of a fine carriage, notified the reporter of criminal activity before the police were summoned. Peggy kept the corner boys and the whores well fed and clothed, and they kept her up-to-date on the malevolence of the five-starred streets. She was awoken in the thick of the night so often that each evening before she went to bed she laid out her pants and shirt and shoes, the clothes arranged on the floor like a flattened version of herself.

William put the pie on a door stoop, a pig nearby sure to come upon the treat. He crossed the street. Compact and sly, the beacon of New York City slipped under the engorging crowd for a looksee and snuck to the edge of curiosity.

A tug on his pant leg and he turned. He looked down. Peggy held a note pad and a pen and knelt beside him.

Familial Asian influence shined in her eyes that glistened like diamonds rolled on their sides. Her skin was flecked with undertones of red from her American Indian heritage. She was compact, smaller than William, no fat to be found on her boyish frame. Handsome yet pretty, stylish and sporty, she was the only child of a father born during the Qing Dynasty and a native American mother who left the reservation to join her husband in his quest to start a newspaper out west that rivaled that east coast New York Times. They had hoped for a son, and had tried to have more children after their daughter was born, but Typhoid Fever took her mother's life, and then her father's. Peggy was fifteen years old when she made her way to New York where she dreamed of reporting for that east coast paper that her father so admired. Peggy was wildly ambitious and fearless, fueled by competition with the son her parents always wanted and never had.

William pointed to the side of the body's head. "Like Massacre."

The dead man's head tilted at an odd angle, his ear ripped from his head, bite marks on his face. Below the neck, the body was bent, the right leg positioned in a way only to be obtained from a broken femur and a snapped ankle bone.

William was very familiar with Massacre's calling cards. He searched the area around the body. "There it is."

Peggy followed the trajectory of his pointed finger.

William crouched and studied the page teared from its binding. It was yellowed; its edges curled. The type on top clearly delineated whence it came.

Peggy scooted next to him. "*Les Misérables* again?"

William rested on his heels. "When I was his attorney in 1884, a page from *The Adventures of Huckleberry Finn* was found at each murder."

"Massacre wants us to think he's smart."

"I suppose," William said. "Look, there are pencils scattered everywhere."

"Pencils?" Peggy squinted.

"Like the victim was a teacher."

"Or an accountant. Let me see." She angled past him, stood, and squeezed to the outskirts of the gruesome gathering. Barely five feet tall, and ninety pounds, going unnoticed in a crowd was one of the benefits of her size.

Pencils scattered among foot tracks and stamped manure patties. She bent and picked one up. Forest green A.W. Faber "Castell" Pocket Pencils. Short stubs with smooth points sharpened by a belt sander. No erasers. A person who used these pencils rarely miscued.

The first police officers arrived in black horse drawn wagons. Metropolitans jumped out. Pencils cracked and split under heavy boots. Police ordered the gawkers to step aside. No one complied with the directive. Peggy wedged herself up front, and took notes. When newly re-appointed Police Commissioner Timothy Byrne showed up, William crept away. He had enough of that man, and wished never to see him again.

Chapter Forty-five

Noble ran. Through Five Points. Into and out of City Hall Park. He wasn't fourteen years old with legs that sprinted with ease. His muscles and bones knocked on the door of sixty years. An old man according to the *Statistical Abstract of the United States*. An old man according to his swollen feet, his heaving lungs, and his diminished mind.

The command echoed among the narrow streets. "Stop. Police." Cornered. Tackled. Dragged by two coppers along Broadway.

To the firing squad?

What had he done?

Up ahead, a crowd and the unmistakable horse face of Commissioner Byrne, eerily lit by a swatch of moonlight. On the rooftop, the light cast by the full moon had offered a soft fictitious veil. On the ground, the truth beamed with hard and cruel edges.

Officers threw him to the ground, inches from Byrne's scuffed and scat-lined soles.

"Look who we have here," Byrne said. "Stand him up."

They lifted Noble. His chin dropped to his chest. His legs weak, buckled.

"Make him stand, like the soldier he never was." Byrne laughed. "Attention!"

Noble recalled the instruction of Colonel Duryee who he had met when he had tried, as a boy, to enlist to fight in the War of the Rebellion. Look at your superior. Arms flat at your sides. Fingers pointed down. Salute. Bicep parallel to the ground, elbow parallel to your shoulder.

Noble's hand rose to his forehead.

"That's the poorest salute I ever seen. No wonder the army rejected you." Byrne's eyes widened. "What's that on your shirt?"

Noble looked down. His shirt was torn and dirtied. Two buttons remained. He hastily searched to find his necklace, groped at his torso, and found it around his neck, tucked under his shirt.

Byrne pointed. "That's blood on your collar, and on your sleeve."

Noble patted his chest. "Am I bleeding?"

"Let me see your hands."

Noble held out his hands, palms down.

"Turn them over. How did your hands get bruised?"

"I've been waiting for William."

The fat officer from the rooftop shoved his way through the crowd. He looked at his commander. "I know this fellow. Followed him up on to a rooftop after a report of a stolen wallet. Don't think he did it. He got some crazy idea he could jump off the roof. He almost got himself dead. Name's William William, got two first names."

"He's Noble Jennings." Byrne grabbed Noble's arm and pulled him into the crowd, and toward the body.

Officers followed. On-lookers moved in, a scrum of those that hunted and haunted Five Points at three a.m., and surrounded them. The gawkers parted at the whack of uniformed elbows to ribs and knees to thighs, and then converged again.

Peggy saw Byrne and Noble, and stepped in front of them. She glared at Byrne. "What are you doing?"

Byrne pushed her out of the way.

"Hey," Peggy protested.

He pulled Noble by the arm until they stood over the body. "What happened to this man?"

Noble studied Jack Hill's twisted frame, looked up at a rooftop, and then back to the body. "He fell?"

Byrne tugged Noble out of the circumference of on-lookers, and threw him to the ground. The string of his necklace tore. The ampoule flew.

Peggy untangled herself from the swarm. "Leave him alone."

"Mind your own business, Missus Fuller," Byrne said.

"He didn't do this."

"Noble Jennings, you are under arrest."

"With what proof?" Peggy insisted.

"You're no lawyer." Byrne scoffed.

Peggy grabbed Byrne's arm. "Don't. He didn't. He couldn't."

Byrne looked down at her. "Remove your hand."

She stepped back.

"Arrest him." Byrne ordered the fat officer.

"Me?"

"Now," Byrne bellowed.

He took Noble's right arm and latched a snap—a round metal cuff—around his wrist. Attached to the snap was a chain that led to a larger round metal device that the officer clutched.

Noble groped at his chest. "Where's my necklace?" He swung his left arm, and hit the fat cop.

Hands grabbed him. Pinned him. A knee to the stomach.

Noble channeled curricula from the rooftops, from the Home for Unwanted Boys, from City Hall Park, and from prison. How to take pain, how to give it. Instinctive how a lion cub didn't need a tutorial to take down a gazelle since the lesson dwelt in his genes.

Noble swung out his right arm and ripped the snap from the officer's hand. He squared off, fists raised.

The officer from the rooftop held up his hands. "Steady, now." His voice was calm. "This ain't going to end well for you, Willy, if you don't cooperate."

"Get out of my way," Noble said. "Please. So I don't hurt you."

The officer stepped aside, others rushed him. Noble saw Kid at the Home, the torrential cloud of dirty boys, the Irish gangs in prison, Peter Stout in Five Points. The pages of his life contained one theme, fight to survive. He pushed and punched several away, saw them in blues and purples, but there were too many. Hands yanked behind his back, another knee to the belly, a bunch of fives in his face. Wrestled to the ground, tethered, face smashed to the concrete.

A knee in his back held him down but he wasn't moving, couldn't move. One eye closed, already swelled. The other eye looked up, and the officer from the rooftop came into view.

"My necklace?" Noble asked.

The officer looked for it. Peggy saw it, inches from a wad of spit tobacco.

"Noble Jennings, you're under arrest for murder," Byrne snarled. "Take him away."

The fat officer stepped back. Others in blue carried Noble, pulled and pushed him toward the back of a covered carriage.

The fat officer approached Peggy and held out his hand. She dropped the bee necklace into his palm.

Chapter Forty-six

Noble is not a murderer, Peggy repeated softly. Her words fell and seeped into a pile of manure.

Lonny Massacre had been in prison for nearing two decades. Was someone continuing his killing spree? Not Noble, of that she was sure. Someone else on the outside, while Massacre pulled the copyists' strings like an adroit puppeteer from the inside? Maybe one of his adoring fans? Or perhaps someone he had no contact with like an unassuming man who liked the confusion he caused by the similarities of the crimes? Hadn't Scotland Yard thought Jack the Ripper was imitated? A copycat crime, the London press dubbed it. Why was it the British always coined the best phrases?

Peggy considered the articles she had written about Massacre and his crimes. She allowed herself a moment to grouse that they had been published under the name John Coal, and then forced herself to push her resentment aside. No sense in whining. In those articles, had she revealed enough detail that somebody could then credibly mimic his crimes? Yes, of course she had. Wasn't that what a good journalist did? Recreated events through the juxtaposition of robust adjectives and verified quotes from eyewitnesses, dramatic but never melodramatic. Yes, the mark of a good article written by a skilled journalist was to not only inform but to also create arms-length emotion in the reader so he didn't abandon the news for the comics.

Under the name John Coal, she had reported on the positions of the four other bodies and the similarities in these
crimes to Massacre's victims, as well as on the early morning
hours when the murders occurred, the locations where they
were found in lower Manhattan, the victims being business-
men cheating on their wives, their chewed off ears, and the
single page of a book found near each crime scene like a mute
witness. Then there were the police reports from Massacre's
cases in the 1880s she had been able to attain from the night
sergeant in charge of record keeping. There was much in-
formation a reporter could obtain in exchange for a shot of
whiskey. Those reports contained all of the repugnant details
to aid any aper, and surely any person with gumption could
get a copy of those reports too.

The door to the covered carriage, with Noble inside,
slammed shut. The sound shook Peggy from her woolgather-
ing. The fat officer climbed on to the platform on the back of
the carriage, and slipped the ampoule and string through the
steel grated window. The bee necklace dropped into Noble's
hand. The fat officer grabbed a handle on the side and prepared for the lurch forward. Another copper leaped on to the
front seat and snapped the reins.

"Ah-ya!" the driver yelled.

The horse jumped forward, and Noble was trotted away.
Peggy watched the back of the wagon as it wobbled along the
cobblestones, and until it turned a corner and was out of her
sight. Its metal wheels click-clacked for a few more beats, and
then the sound waned into the distance. A feeling of power-
lessness took up the void in her heart that Noble's detention
left behind. How could she best help him?

She could write about Byrne's vendetta against him since
he was a boy, and where was William? Shouldn't he be here
now, as Noble's friend, as Noble's attorney? Shouldn't he have
prevented Byrne from wrongly accusing Noble, again?

The street corner where the paddy wagon had turned to take Noble to jail was empty and silent, seeming to mock her like the men she struggled to work aside at The New York Times. She thought of the article she had read earlier in the day about English women who banded together in a unified struggle for equal rights with men. Suffragettes, the London *Daily Mail* had called them. That journalist, a man, had made up the name in an attempt to insult the women. Called them SuffraGETtes, like Get Out of Town. But derision made those women more determined and more bonded, and what was going on across the ocean was happening in New York City too. Wasn't it time she made a stand for women's rights and put her own name on something more significant than articles on *La Belle Époque* who attended galas at the Met? Or what outfits the president's wife wore? Isn't that why she came to New York City over twenty years ago after her parents' deaths? To prove she was as good as the son her parents wished they had? What better place to start than by helping Noble?

Still, she'd have to write articles about Noble and Byrne's long and complicated relationship under John Coal's name. Dammit. Stay on course, she warned herself, don't be distracted by a tag. Isn't that what her editor had told her? It's not about the name, it's about the quality of the piece that you can be damned proud of. Just be damned happy you're a New York Times reporter.

Peggy tried to make that be enough, that she had achieved her dream of writing for the Times, but it never was. In one of her many attempts to persuade her editor to allow her to use her own name atop an article, she quoted Susan B. Anthony's 1872 speech; the speech Ms. Anthony gave after she was arrested for voting in the presidential election at a time when it was illegal for women to vote.

"It was we, the people; not we, the white male citizens; nor yet we, the male citizens; but we, the whole people, who formed the Union."

Anthony had been fined one hundred dollars for giving that speech, which she refused to pay. Glory be!

"Pride is for men who have families to support." The editor spat.

What a pillock!

She looked from the empty street corner and back toward the murder scene. The body was being loaded into the back of a carriage. The crowd was dispersing. Byrne was gone. Bailey and most of the other officers had left the scene. Across the street, a pig nuzzled a pie shell.

Near where a few Metropolitans with brooms and buckets scrubbed the street where the body laid, Peggy recognized a reporter from the *New York Daily Herald*, a man in his twenties who always seemed a step behind her. She had already scooped him on this one. The reporter tried to talk to the remaining officers, probably attempting to attain insight into what happened, most likely asking about Massacre.

Asking about Massacre.

Yes! That's it. She knew how she could best help Noble. Not through Byrne but through Massacre. She would interview him. What a coup that would be! Not only would she gain insight to help Noble combat this absurd accusation, but if she could interview the killer she surely would get to use her own name on the article.

Massacre was at Sing-Sing in Ossining, New York, located along the Hudson River. She would meet with Warden Benjamin Ash and request one-on-one time with the prisoner. William could help convince Ash to allow her to do this. Levi could assist in forming the best questions to ask of the killer.

Peggy would not be refused. She would suffraGETte the interview.

Chapter Forty-seven

William skidded into the interrogation room and grabbed the back of Noble's chair. It had been two days since Noble's arrest, and two days since Byrne's acquittal and reinstatement as police commissioner.

"...why choose Jack Hill as your fifth victim...?" Byrne was asking.

"Don't answer that." William put his hands on Noble's shoulders, and then looked at Byrne who sat across the table. "Peter Stout said you'd wait for me to begin."

"Hi." Noble patted William's hand.

"What did you tell Commissioner Byrne?"

"Nothing," Noble said. "I don't know."

A guard looked in. "Everything okay, Chief?"

"Fine." Byrne waved him away.

The door closed. The three, closed in by smeared gray India inked walls.

William looked at the top of the wood table that was scarred with moon-shaped burns and knife tip stabs. He saw no note pad, no writing utensil. Only the table and two chairs in this small, square windowless room of the NYPD. The room stunk of men who had sat in here to unwind and vent after long days, of their body odor, stale cigar smoke, and spilled whiskey.

Noble continued to pat William's hand.

"Aren't you going to take notes?" William asked Byrne.

"No."

"You're waiting on a secretary?"

"I'll remember what he says."

"That's against procedure, Timothy. When Teddy Roosevelt was New York police commissioner he instituted policy that required all statements be recorded on paper."

Byrne's eyes darkened. "I'm the commissioner now, which means I decide what is contrary to police procedure."

William was unfazed. "Why is the police commissioner interrogating a suspect? Isn't *that* contrary to procedure?"

Noble looked up at William, smiled.

Byrne noisily pushed his chair back and stood. He bent over, and placed his hands on the edge of the table. "What is contrary to procedure is for an attorney to be present during an interrogation."

"Not according to the Sixth Amendment to the United States Constitution."

"Perhaps a trip back to law school is in order. The Sixth Amendment only grants a defendant the right to an attorney at trial—"

"—that law will be expanded one day. The Fourteenth Amendment requires due process—"

"—until then you're a spectator and nothing more—"

"Please stop bickering." Noble fingered the necklace around his neck. The string ripped during his arrest, the officer from the rooftop had shoved the bee necklace into his hand while he was in the back of the police wagon. Noble knotted the string together, which made it the third knot of the one hundred and thirty-seventh string.

"This is my house, Counselor," Byrne spat. "You'll play by my rules."

"Since when do you follow rules?" William asked.

"I can have you ousted from this room—"

"—I can have you ousted as chief of police. President Roosevelt is a friend of mine."

Byrne put his hand on the revolver holstered to his belt. "The only friend I need is right here."

"I'm not afraid of you."

"You should be," Byrne said.

"Boys, stop. That's enough." Noble said.

William moved closer to Byrne. "You're just seeking glory before you retire, old man. You want to go out with a bang. Isn't that why you're the one interrogating Noble?"

"Get out."

"I'm not leaving. You owe me one, you said it yourself, and this is it."

Noble stood. "Please, Gentlemen. Stop."

"Sit, Noble." William put his hand on his shoulder and guided him back into the chair. He looked at Byrne. "Anyway, it's not me you owe. It's Noble."

"Me?"

"Yes," William spoke to Noble but kept his eyes on Byrne. "For arresting you for setting the Colored Orphan Asylum fire."

"I set a fire?" Noble asked.

Byrne scoffed. "He did it."

"Did not."

"What fire?" Noble pressed the ampoule to his heart.

"You were fourteen years old," William said. "Byrne and Peter Stout set you up. Tammany goons started the fire and Byrne was deep in their pockets. Peter Stout probably lit the first match."

Byrne sat. "Can I get on with the questioning now?"

"Can I go home after we're done?" Noble asked.

"You're not answering any questions," William said.

Noble looked up at him again. "Please, William. My brain hurts. I'm tired. Let me answer his questions and then we can go home."

"Fine." William looked to Byrne. "Get me a chair,"

"No more to be had." He smirked.

"In the entire police department?"

Byrne shrugged. "You can have Noble's seat."

Noble stood.

"Sit," William said.

Noble sat. William leaned against the wall.

"Now that everyone is comfortable, may I continue?" Byrne asked.

William dismissively waved his hand.

Byrne faced Noble. "You're Noble Jennings, correct?"

William scoffed. "You know who he is."

Byrne continued. "In the early mornings of the twelfth of March and the seventeenth of April, you murdered one Henry Thaw Watson and one Jackson Hill, correct?"

"Objection," William stepped forward. "Don't answer that."

Byrne sneered. "This isn't a court of law and I'm not a judge. What is your response, Noble?"

"Don't say anything," William said.

Byrne stood and stepped toward William, who met Byrne near the table and looked up at him.

Grooves aged the commissioner's mug. Thick gray hair curled around his ears and shuttled into a patchy beard. "Direct your client to answer my question."

"What was the question?" Noble asked.

Byrne's eyes remained on William. "Why did you kill Henry Thaw Watson and Jackson Hill?"

"Don't answer that." William said.

"I demand you allow him to answer all of my questions or not only will I arrest you for impeding a police investigation, but also you and your friends for partaking in illegal activity."

William stepped back, lightheaded from the immensity of Byrne's threat. His root chakra vibrated. Fight or flight, those were his options. He resisted the urge to escape into his upper chakras. He had to fight, if not for himself, than for Noble.

He shoved his hand into his pocket and rubbed a piece of rose quartz. "What we do is not illegal."

"True, opioids are not against the law when prescribed by a doctor," Byrne said. "But tell me, Counselor, are Doctors Merryweather King and Earl Highland, both frequent visitors of 5C, writing prescriptions? I doubt it. And tell me this, what do you think the public reaction will be when it's revealed that the most respected professionals of our city are drug addicts? I believe you also host visitors to 5C who are senators and representatives."

William teetered.

Byrne continued with the confidence of the only armed man in the room. "Come June thirtieth, the First Pure Food and Drug Act becomes law. Morphine, cocaine, and heroin will be illegal, even with a prescription."

"Yes," William mumbled, "I am aware,"

"Let's see how Judge James Edwards, Frank Whitmore of Hancock Financial, and the architect, Clarence Stiles, feel after they have to be bonded out of jail. Oh, and that woman who is your supplier. Jenny Big Stink? She might get a date with Old Smoky."

William was not surprised that Byrne knew the goings-on in Apartment 5C. Many police officers engaged in the benefits therein, but he was flabbergasted the chief dared to name some of the more well connected participants who had contributed generously to political campaigns, including his own.

William engaged his only move. "Several of your high ranking officers are intimately familiar with 5C." He looked for a hitch in Byrne's eyes, a shudder in his lips. Anything to suggest distress. He saw none.

"Are you referring to Assistant Chief Bailey?" Byrne asked.

William blinked. Damn, he revealed his hand. He sought to recover. "If any of your officers close down 5C, or if anyone is arrested, your assistant chief and the other officers who regularly engage in the benefits of 5C will find trouble too."

"Do you, Counselor, recall the jury from my trial?"

"All too well."

"Did you not think the evidence supported a guilty verdict?"

"I most certainly did."

"Yet I was acquitted."

Noble covered his ears with his hands. "Can I go home now?"

Byrne continued. "I am not concerned that some of my officers partake of Jenny Big Stink's poison. I feel quite certain that no members of the New York City Police Department will be troubled due to their involvement."

William understood. Tammany Hall and the boys of blue would make sure their own were protected. Did Byrne have him? Had he made a mistake by challenging him so voraciously? Wasn't Noble worth the risk of 5C being boarded and the participants being arrested? Byrne had to be bluffing. Right?

"May I now repeat my question to Mister Jennings?" the Commissioner asked.

William shrunk against the wall. If 5C were closed, and publically revealed, his career would be over. He'd be black listed, for sure. No more brain power, and no more clients.

"Well?" Byrne looked at William. "May I continue?"

Noble twisted in his chair, and looked at him too.

William merged into the gray of the wall. "Proceed."

Byrne again sat across from Noble. "Tell me about Jackson Hill."

"Who is Jackson Hill?" Noble asked.

William laughed.

"Why did you kill him?"

"I have not killed anyone, Sir."

William moved for the door. "I believe that ceases the need for any further questioning. Noble, let's go."

"He is not leaving. He is under arrest."

"You have no evidence." William sprang at him.

Byrne stared William down. "May I continue, Counselor, without your interruption?"

"Let him finish," Noble said.

William moved back against the wall.

Byrne asked Noble, "Why were you in Five Points two days afore?"

"I live there."

"I believe you live with William at Washington Mews."

"Oh, yes, of course I do."

"Then why did you say you lived in Five Points?"

"I suppose I did not understand your question."

"Very well," Byrne said. "If you live in Washington Mews, why were you in Five Points in the early morning hours?"

Noble looked at William.

Byrne said, "He cannot answer the questions for you."

"I do not remember being in Five Points."

"But you were. I arrested you there."

"Oh yes, you did."

"Then why were you there?"

"I was going for a walk."

"At two o'clock in the morning?" Byrne asked.

"I think so."

"You think you were going for a walk or you think it was two in the morning?"

"You're confusing me, Sir."

"Why did you steal a wallet? Why were you on the rooftop? Why did you try and attack my officer?"

"I didn't."

Byrne smashed his fist on the table. "You killed Jackson Hill, and the others. Just like you set the Colored Orphan Asylum fire."

"I couldn't have done that."

"Then why did you spend years in jail?"

"You're speaking too quickly. I don't understand your questions."

"He has Presenile Dementia," William interjected.

Byrne glared. "What is that?"

"According to Doctor Levi Solomon Fuller, it's when a person experiences memory loss and confusion at an unusually early age."

Byrne crossed his arms over his chest. "I never heard of it."

"Ask Doctor Fuller, he'll tell you."

"Why would I believe him? Isn't he Noble's son? And, a black man?"

"My son?" Noble questioned.

Byrne leaned forward on the table, nearly nose to nose with Noble. "Why did you do it?"

Noble moved away. "Why did I have a son?"

"Why did you commit murder?"

Noble looked down. "I confess. I murdered."

Byrne leaned closer. "Explain."

"Don't speak," William said.

Noble looked at the palm of his hand. "I murdered a bee."

"Don't say anything more," William yelled.

Byrne pointed at William. "Shut up." He looked to Noble. "Why did you kill Jackson Hill?"

"I didn't mean to," Noble cried.

"You admit to doing it and you're sorry?"

"Objection," the attorney yelled.

Byrne pointed at William. "I said shut up!"

Noble shook his head. "He was an innocent bee."

"Was it Jackson Hill's blood on your shirt?"

"Blood? On my shirt?"

"Your hands were bruised like you had been in a struggle."

"Noble, don't say anything—"

"Bruised?" Noble asked.

"Yes. Look at them."

Noble held his hands up and studied them, palms up, palms down. The skin was swollen and discolored in yellows and blacks, his knuckles scabbed.

Byrne leaned back. His facial muscles relaxed. A cop who knew he caught his criminal. "Your hands are bruised from fighting."

"Yes."

"And the three others you murdered?"

"Noble. Quit talking—"

"—Others?" Noble asked.

"Roy Allen, Philip Mattis, and David Small. Who else have you killed?"

"Thomas Pollard."

"Noble. Stop."

"Shut the fuck up," Byrne yelled at William. "Who is Thomas Pollard?"

"You'll find him under the Williamsburg Bridge at Delancey Street," Noble said.

"This interrogation is over." William grabbed Noble's shoulder. "Let's go."

"Guards," Byrne called.

The door to the interrogation room swung open.

"Remove him." Byrne pointed at William.

Two officers grabbed The Attorney and pulled him out of the room. The door slammed shut.

Noble watched the closed door. The silence in the room as thick as the fog in his brain.

"They were awfully rough with him."

Byrne jumped up, and leaned his knuckles on the table. "Thomas Pollard will be found under the Williamsburg Bridge?"

Noble's eyes remained focused on the door. "It's a suspension bridge opened on December 19, 1903."

"I know what it is. In what condition will we find Mister Pollard? Dammit! Look at me!"

Noble kept his eyes on the door.

"When did you kill Thomas Pollard and bury his body under the bridge?" Byrne yelled. "When I find his body, will he be missing an ear?"

"Missing an ear," Noble said.

Byrne took a long inhale. "Officer," he called.

A guard poked his head into the room.

Byrne made a motion as if he were taking a drink. The officer left, and then a moment later returned with a shot of whiskey. Byrne tossed it into his throat, sat, and spoke calmly. "Mister Jennings, please look at me."

Noble did so.

"You've been very helpful," Byrne said. "Before I go, tell me, what's that you're wearing around your neck? I've seen you with it since you were a boy. Is it for your trophies?"

"Trophies?"

"A prize from the people you've killed. Show me."

Noble opened the ampoule. He and Byrne looked inside. It was empty.

Byrne stood. "I'll have more questions when I return. Understood?"

"May I ask a question now?"

"Of course," Byrne said.

"When is William coming to see me?"

Chapter Forty-eight

William fumed. He had been shuttled out of the police station by one of New York's Finest like he was nothing. New York's Finest. He scoffed at the moniker. He had been there when General Joseph Hooker in 1863 claimed the Union forces were "the finest army on the planet". The Police Department's slogan was stolen from that phrase. "The finest police force on the planet" became "New York's Finest." More like New York's Lousiest, William thought as the cool air hit his face, at least with Byrne at the helm. He yearned for the days of Teddy Roosevelt as number one in blue. He had been tough, that was for certain, but also fair and honest.

Kid waited outside the police station.

William leaped into the carriage. "To the Post Office. I have a letter to compose to be sent immediately."

"Yes, Sir," Kid said.

"Call me William, for goodness sake. We've known each other for over forty years. How many times do I have to ask you that?"

"Whatever you say, Sir." Kid smiled and tapped the reins on Sally's neck. The mare pitched forward. "Who is the letter to?" Kid spoke loudly, to be heard over the clomps of Sally's horseshoes on the stone street.

"Doctor Alois Alzheimer."

The message would be sent wireless via Marconi's tele-graph, using Morse Code. William didn't understand how it was possible to transmit messages across the ocean but, fortu-nately, he didn't need to know the how, nor the why, but only the what, which came forth as a series of dits, longer sounds, and crackles that a Morse Code operator would then translate and share. William's message to Doctor Alzheimer would be short and to the point to reflect the urgency of the situation.

"What will the message say?" Kid asked.

-.-. --- -- . / - --- / .- -- . .-. .. -.-. .- .-.-.- / ... .- ...- . / .- / -- .- -.
... / .-.. .. ..-. . .-.-.-

"Come to America. Save a man's life."

Peggy Fuller, Reporter's Notebook

15 May 1906

Writing utensil: Eagle Pencil Co. wood cased slate pencil with fiber eraser

10:30 a.m. train from Grand Central Station in Manhattan to Ossining, New York and Sing Sing prison

What does a reporter wear to interview a murderer? Pants.

Lonny Massacre: born in France, came to America in 1872 (thirteen years old) with parents. Wealthy family. Little known about his parents except father Dale Massacre owned farmland in New Jersey, per tax rolls. Only child, per census. Mother, Barbara Massacre, died May 9, 1892, cholera. No record of father's death.

Paterson Evening News reported in 1892 skeletal remains on the Massacre farm dug up by coyotes. Ulnas, femurs, ear bones, jaw bones, ribs. Criminal investigation (half-hearted?). No ID of body(ies?). No arrests. No significant investigation by police. Limited coverage by Paterson Evening News? Not picked up by the Times. Note: go to Paterson Police Department and look at records, bring bottle of whiskey and cigarettes

Lonny Massacre arrested, 1884. Victim escaped and identified him. LM confessed. Ten victims, men ages 40 – 60, married, well-to-do, visited houses of ill repute, attacked upon leaving, or before arriving (possibly 3 victims on way to whorehouse?). Review previous TIMES articles written by John Coal (ha ha).

LM told police where an eleventh body was buried

William, his attorney, negotiated deal for LM to avoid death penalty. Good deal for whom?

12:45 p.m. I Arrived at Ossining Station, three mile walk to prison. Note: wear lower heeled boots next time. Waited two hours for Warden Ash to allow me to see prisoner. Thought after 3rd request when he finally agreed to let me speak to LM he'd bag out but did not. Uncle William convinced Mayor Mc-Clellan to speak to Warden Ash to allow my interview of LM. Told Ash I was John Coal's assistant. I considered wearing a skirt because warden might take to me more but that's not the way of a feminist.

Warden Benjamin Ash, thirty-nine years old, youngest warden in New York history, brother-in-law to Mayor McClellan. Ash reputation: sadistic, egomaniac, uses catocracy as punish-ment, calls Old Smoky his favorite chair, likes to sit in it and play-act electrocution (verify/get quote from reliable source), boyish appearance, floppy hair, long nose, Jewish ancestry?, dark hair, dark eyes, bushy eyebrows and moustache, taller than six-feet, skinny, would snap from an enthusiastic hug? (Who would want to hug him? Marital status? Children?). How come no prisoner has attacked him? Ash agreed to let me speak with LM for one hour. Thinks John Coal coming too.

3:45 p.m. I was brought to small room (for attorneys to meet with clients?). No windows, four chairs, narrow table that wobbles when rest elbows upon, scratches on table say, I want pussy, lick big dicks (too lewd), describe as, "obscene markings on table top"

What did I think a serial killer would look like? Act like? Black dark eyes, no whites in eyes, scowl on face, very large, seven-feet-tall, angry, manipulative, big hands, high intellect, little formal education, self-taught, mental illness? *Ask Levi about mental disorders that would cause someone to kill/would Ash and/or Massacre agree to psychological evaluation of LM? Whose permission would I need? I mean, would John Coal need? (ha, ha)

5:15 p.m. LM brought in by guard, nametag: Frankel. Friendly looking, like if he owned a corner market he'd sell milk on an IOU (use this in article)

Shackles around LM's ankles and wrists. Took short baby steps

Frankel said, "Sit"

LM sat across from me. Put our hands on table and they nearly touched. The table rocked. I placed my hands in my lap. Note: keep hands in lap

My paper and pad on the table

Frankel looked at me, hazel, kind eyes, "Do you want me to stay?"

I hesitated, what is best way to get LM to talk? What would male reporter do? "No, thank you," I didn't know if this was right response. Was I safe in this small, windowless room with a murderer?

Describe room: no personality (can a room have a personality? I think so), bland, green walls, paint peeled and mottled, floor is concrete and carroty in color (use in article, the color of rotting carrots?), heavy air, stifling, no circulation, smells unclean, like sweat, more sickening sweet smell than a foul smell, I felt a little light headed. From being so close to LM?

Frankel said, "I'll be right outside the door if you need me."

LM's chair was closest to door. I could not escape without going past him. Should I have asked Frankel to stay? Should I have sat in chair closest to the door first?

Door closed. Sounded like the seal of a tomb. A whap, or a whomp? *Try and recreate sound later so can best describe in words.

5:17 p.m. LM and I studied the other. His eyes intent on me, but he's not looking at my eyes. He watched my mouth.

Describe his eyes: Light blue. Trusting. Trustworthy? Could fool me.

He spoke first, "you don't look like a reporter."

I said, "you don't look like a killer."

Nervous laughter, ice was broken (think of other way to say not cliché)

LM leaned back in chair like he was about to read the Sunday paper. He watched my mouth the entire conversation. Odd. The trait of a killer?

"What does a killer look like?" he asked.

"What does a reporter look like?" I countered.

He smiled. "Not like a dame."

I wrote. Not like a dame…

"Are you going to subscribe down everything we say?" he asked.

Subscribe? Hadn't he meant inscribe?

I turned my notebook around to show him. He didn't look at what I wrote but kept his eyes on my lips. Was this a sexist thing? Should I be scared, or more scared than I already was. (Admit being scared in article?)

I pointed to my notepad. "It's how a reporter remembers everything."

"It's distractable."

Distractable?

I remembered the novel pages left at the crime scenes in 1880s. Huck Finn. (Les Miserables at the last crime scene). Like LM wanted everyone to think he was smart.

Trying to sound smart and unintentionally mispronouncing words.

His voice: French accent. Sounds well-educated like raised by tutors or went to private school. Voice mostly pleasant to ear with taint of hollowness in its tone. (Use in article)

I put pen down.

"Now I feel like a cad," he said. "Go ahead and write what you want. I want you to get things right too."

His face: Like an egg with eyes, nose and mouth drawn on. An afterthought of features? Plain, unadorned, functional, everything in its right place, in the right shape, but bland. Bald-headed. No facial hair. Skin is smooth. Not handsome, not ugly. Not smart looking. What does smart look like? Could be a math professor or an engineer or a mountaineer. Everyman, but he's no man (use this in article). What does he think of himself when he looks in the mirror?

I looked at his hands, fingers clasped like a weaved basket. Those hands have killed, could kill me.

"I won't hurt you," he said.

Further description of LM: Intuitive

"I know," I lied. Is it okay to lie to a murderer? Did his victims think he wouldn't hurt them before he chewed off their ears?

His neck: as wide as his head.

Also: strong arms, hands, barrel chest. Like a retired wrestler who still has a few moves.

"Tell me about your family." I sounded like Levi.

He spoke quickly, rehearsed. A pre-planned oration? "My father would make me kill to prove I was a man. I was nine when I slew my first person. Lived on an apple orchard in France at the time."

Father, no record of his death.

"You killed your father." I said. A statement, not a question. Popped out. Could I stuff it back in? Should I?

His mouth: a snarl or a smirk? thick lips, teeth carved into fangs. Very odd. *How do you carve teeth? Yellowed, brown on sides. Bad odor like ???. His tongue the color of blood. (a lazy description, think of other)

"Why didn't you tell the police you killed your father?"

He said, "I didn't want them digging him up."

I wrote again. He held up his hand.

"You said I could take notes."

"You don't need to." He pulled his hands off table and dropped them into his lap. He leaned back, shifted his hips up—I moved to call Frankel, was he going to expose himself? None of his crimes were sexual, that's what Levi told me. LM pulled something out of his pants and dropped it on the table top. Rolled paper, tied with a string. He pushed it toward me.

I untied the string and looked at the narrow scroll. Thin, cheap paper, and I realized while it's thin and cheap writing paper, it's rough tissue paper to wipe oneself. Handwritten on both sides.

"What is this?" I already knew.

"Read the title," he said.

"Lonny Massacre's Manifesto."

Note: Research manifesto. Communist Manifesto, Karl Marx outlined his plan for communism. 1840s.

"Do you know what a manifesto is?"

I did but I wanted to know what he thought it was. "No," I said.

"It's a declaratory of intent." He waggled his index finger at me. "Come closer."

"No."

He laughed. "If I wanted your ear, I'd already have it."

I was preoccupied with not showing the fear he instilled in me, partially because I knew he was right. He could have chewed on my ear at any moment.

Hindsight: How vulnerable (stupid?) I was to be alone in that room with him, not even asking the guard to stay. Journalists and their bravado.

"What is it a declaration of?" I asked.

His eyes still on my lips. "It's a declaration of me."

And that's when I realized why he agreed to speak with me, and why I still had two ears.

"You want me to write an article about you?" I asked.

"I want you to write a book," he said.

Lonny Massacre Manifesto

Don't read this if you're looking for a Dickensonian romance. My book is mountains of superior because these words are not romanticacized or dramatacized. A chockablock of truth lies between my scribbles. Can you read my writing? Don't expect no how-to neither. People write all the time and query me to share my methods. Not just how to choose a victim but how to hunt, attack, immobilize and finalize. It's not that I don't have a method. I'm just looking to trademark it or copyright it or whatever lawyers call it so I can't say nothing yet. I've sent an application to the librarian at Congress. Patent Pending. So stop sending me those requests for how-to because I fucking detest them.

The marriage proposals, you can keep those coming. Photos of the ladies in stages of undress and nondress, I like them very much, *mercy beaucoop*.

Massacre is my family name. It didn't start to mean what it ended up meaning. It related to the family business because we were apple farmers and had masses of acres. Not very creative, I know, but that's how we got names a couple of hundreds of years ago when my family sprouted.

People come over on the Mayflower or however they got to America and they was given names by some penny pinching beharried clerk. Herr Friedrich Schmidt became Fred Smith. Malachy O'Sullivan from Ireland became Michael Sullivan. Louis Chadwick was renamed Charles Lewis. It's not just that these people's names were changed by some bonehead in that isolated moment of time, but their decredants have to live with the name for all of eternity too. It's

1906 for goodness sake and where are the Schmidts and O'Sullivans and Frère Jacques? Back in Germany and Ireland and France, that's where.

But no two-bit clerk changed me and my kin's names, which is unpresidented. Me and my parents got to these United Stakes of America when I was thirteen years old. We imbarked on a boat in Paris, showed our tickets, slept in a cabin, lounged on our private balcony, ate five-star repasts, crossed the Atlantic, and embarked in New York. It was extremely civilized. When we arrived, no one changed our name or nothing like that so we're the original Massacres. You can find us in George and Charles's dictionary. They use the modern meaning.

mas·sa·cre

masəkər/

noun: massacre; plural noun: massacres

1 . . an indiscriminate and brutal slaughter of people Also to

slaughter, mass murder, mass execution, annihilation, liquidation, decimation, extermination, carnage, butchery, bloodbath, bloodletting, massacre of innocents

verb: to massacre; 3rd person present: massacres; past tense: massacred; past participle: massacred; gerund or present participle: massacring

1 . . deliberately and violently kill (a large number of people).

Origin: FRENCH late 16th century, farming family, Massacres owned mass(es) of acre(s), raised pigs and poultry, tended apple orchards.

Webster's Dictionary, Encyclopedia-Britannica, Merriam, George & Charles, 1831

Some of us Massacres remain on the slopes of Brittany today. The money is in apples, it always has been. It's a lot of work, spraying, harvesting, managing the hectors of orchards, and picking bugs off the trees.

I started in the fields one week after I was born. Not really, but it feels like that. My earliest memory of picking apples is when I was three-and-a-half. Mon père, that's my papa in French-parle, was a tall, lean and handsome son-of-a-bitch who loved the ladies, especially those that weren't mon mère.

He lifted me up toward the tops of trees and I'd use my baby hands to tug a Blue Whale off a tree and place it into the basket papa held. I had to place the fruit in very careful to make sure it didn't bruise, which I never really understood since we took all those millions of apples my family grew over the centuries and put them in pots that were bigger than me when I was a tot, covered those apples with water, boiled them, added sugar and cinnamon, and another thing that we claimed to be a family secret but I knew was ground coca leaves, and made cider. That's right, my family got rich from a beverage that's mostly consumed during winter months. That's the kind of thing you can't plan, and that's how most people grow wealth and achieve anything of substance. From the unexpected.

I never had much interest in apples. When I got bigger, I was clumsy and no good at delicacies so every apple I touched bruised. Each time I bruised an apple I was read the riot act and papa made me run really fast around the base of an apple tree until I fell down dizzy, or he'd make me sit up in a tree for an entire day and either I was too hot or too cold or ants bit me up and down my arms and legs and then I would have hives and catch colds I couldn't get rid of for days, and he'd tell me I was a goop, but he'd say it in French.

You know how you make yourself all angstious that something bad is going to happen, or something is going to be hard to do and you're going to fail and then your father beats you, and then you do it and there is nothing bad about it. That's what happened with my first kill. I was nine years old. Papa chose a field hand's son as my first target and told me I had to bring something back to prove I did it. The boy was très smaller than me. He'd follow me around all the time because I was bigger and he wanted to be like me. Always seeing this boy's face made me mad so it wasn't hard to be motivated to never see him again.

Lesson one, for all you aspirators out there. You need motivation to kill, or else what's the point? And without it you might get scared and not do it and that's when you get caught, when you are careless and act out of fear and not with control. Motivation is different than motive. Motive is your reason to kill, motivation is your drive to do it. So says Professor Massacre.

I went to an orchard where all the apples had been picked so there was no one there, and the boy followed me. What was his name? Léopold or Noel? He was a slight and short kid and so it didn't take long once I put my hands around his neck and squeezed before his eyes looked like they were going to shoot from their sockets and his face turned blue and his tongue hung out of his mouth. If he screamed or anything like that, I didn't hear it.

Lesson two from the professor. Don't hang around admiring your workmanship. I couldn't leave right away since I promised papa that I'd bring back proof. It didn't take me too long to decide what that proof would be. I didn't have a knife so I chewed off his ear and put it in my pocket.

Lesson three, choose a keepsake that has meaning to you.

I chose an ear because I am deaf.

Chapter Forty-nine

Since his arrest—was this his first arrest, his second, his third?—Noble had been the only prisoner in the Death House for the last two months. Ten subterranean cells framed a narrow, cement block hallway at Sing Sing prison. Each cell was seven feet deep and three-and-a-half feet wide, six feet, seven inches high, damp, with a bucket for a toilet, the same bucket as a sink.

Seated on a rickety cot, he looked up at the alienist who paced the cramped cell. Doctor Levi Solomon Fuller's head only a few inches away from scraping the ceiling. The heels and soles of his leather shoes clacked on the concrete floor. The sound amplified and echoed through the underground passage, bounced from wall to wall, floor to ceiling, trapped. He held a bulky manila folder.

Handsome and intelligent like a finely bound book, Levi adjusted frameless glasses along the bridge of his nose. His three-piece suit was tailor made and well-pressed. He looked at Noble. Sourness rose and burst into Levi's mouth. He swallowed and the deeply rooted bitterness burned into the nadir of the doctor's stomach. A gut-brain connection, his body's response to stress. He sighed. He was thirty-eight years old and this was the first time he met his father. He had never wanted to face the man, had never wanted to stand toe to toe and look him in the eyes. Afraid of what he might or might not see.

Yesterday, William had cornered Levi. Again! "You and Doctor Alzheimer have to help Noble."

Levi's brain motored through several retorts:

I know. You and mom have told me many times.

I know. You're presenting dementia as a defense at his murder trial.

I know. He's a perfect man who has spent decades in jail.

I know. He's never done anything wrong.

I know. I'm a lousy son who refuses to help his father.

William put his hand on Levi's shoulder, a light, fatherly touch. "You can resist me and your mother for only so long."

Sarah stood behind William.

Another response Levi could choose:

I'll do it.

He looked from his uncle to his mother. Pleasing them was high on his to-do list. Resisting had been challenging, even tiring. He thought of all his mother had done for him, raising him along with caring for Nana and Uncle John. He thought of the Sunday dinners they had shared with William, his wife and their children, and the evening William took him aside and offered to pay for his medical school.

Shouldn't that have been the role of his father? Shouldn't he have been seated at the head of the table at Sunday dinners?

"Please? For me?" his mother pled.

Okay, he succumbed, he would meet with Noble in his role as Doctor Fuller, the psychiatrist, and not as Levi, the abandoned and bitter son.

Hugs, and an arrangement was made for Doctor Levi Fuller to meet prisoner number 10642 the following day.

He believed only a few people knew Noble was his father: Sarah, his mother, of course; his uncles William and John Coal; Peggy, his wife; and Harry, his lover. Alice? His grandmother. Who could tell what she knew?

This wasn't the first time Doctor Fuller visited an inmate at Sing Sing to assess him mentally, but this was the first time he did so with shaking limbs and a twisted gut. He looked at the bucket in the cell, and hoped his stomach would calm so he wouldn't have to aim for it.

Using his fingers, Noble scooped pork and cauliflower from a metal plate that balanced on his lap. The cot he sat upon was too low, and his legs were too long, his knees leveled with his heart. He cradled gravy in crusty bread, chewed, washed it down with warm beer, and wiped his mouth with coarse paper. He sopped up the rest of the food with the bread until the gray plate sparkled.

"Have we been acquainted?" Noble asked Levi.

Levi stopped pacing, and sighed again. A habit he hated as he felt others would perceive him as feminine. Why not just say it? He thought of the advice he'd give his patients in this circumstance. Be direct, be honest.

And the truth shall set you free.

"I'm your son." Levi's breath in the cold cell shot from his mouth like a coughed up a cloud.

Noble's hazel eyes dimmed. He rubbed his hand along the silver stubble on his chin, and sighed.

Levi shivered, folded his arms across his chest, and thought of what William had told him that morning. Noble's memory has significantly worsened since his incarceration. It had been two months since Noble's arrest for the murder of Mister Jackson Hill, and, subsequently, Noble's confession to the murder of five others.

Outside the Death House, the temperature was warm yet it remained frigid within the underground block.

"Is it always this cold in here?" Levi asked.

Avoidance is a maladaptive coping mechanism to avoid dealing with a stressor. Be direct, be honest.

Noble looked up at Levi. "I can't remember ever being warm." His voice echoed through the cavern.

The lines on Noble's face rooted like a trusted tale. Remnants of the boy he used to be were evident in the child-like recesses of his failing mind. A small wood vial hung like a pendant around his neck. The Sing Sing uniform—dark and scratchy wool trousers and a stained and wrinkled once white cotton button-down shirt—hung on his diminishing frame. His clothes reeked of the bodily fluids and excrement of the inmates that had worn them before. Stenches that soap and water and time could never purge.

"Do you know Sarah?" Noble asked.

Levi found it best to say nothing when he didn't know what to say. He looked to the floor and became distracted by a dark spatter in the shape of a crescent moon. Dried blood, perhaps left behind as a warning. The prison was nicknamed House of Fear for the brutal beatings prisoners endured for often minor offenses. Cat-o-nine tails, Warden Ash's favored form of discipline.

Noble continued. "You seem familiar, like I have known you many years. Were you in the Home for Unwanted Boys with William and me?"

"No, Sir."

"You are a colored man."

"I am."

Noble put his pale hands in prayer position. His forefingers pressed against his lips. "I fought in the Civil War for the Union."

Levi opened the folder and shuffled through its pages. Even though he had its contents memorized, he scanned the sheets, not to make sure he was correct about Noble's non-military service but to give him a few seconds to formulate his response.

"No, Sir, I do not believe you fought in the Great Rebellion."

"You are mistaken, son. I am sure I am a veteran of the United States Army."

Levi gasped. He had called him son. Did he know who he was even though they had never met? Even though Noble could not recall the most recent detail?

There was no light of recognition in the older man's eyes and Levi realized he had called him son merely as a function of the differences in their ages.

"Oh yes, I remember now," Noble continued. "I served with Colonel Duryee. A fine man. We beat those Confederate boys good." Noble looked at the cleaned plate in front of him. "Have I eaten?"

Levi thought to correct him again about his military service. "You had lunch. Are you still hungry?"

"Should I be?"

"I can't say, but I can request the guard to bring more food."

"I suppose you can." Noble leaned against the wall, its stone blemished like dirty snow. "What is your profession again?"

"I am an alienist."

Noble's eyes narrowed and he seemed to digest and decipher the word. The oily steel bars and the brick walls, corroded by the seventy-eight year history of the prison, closed in on the doctor. Sing Sing was a maximum security prison and a tourist attraction. For twenty-five cents, citizens peered through a hole and watched convicts work in the prison factory. The first execution in Old Smoky had occurred ten years earlier. The claw marks of condemned men's fingernails cut grooves in the wood arms of the electric chair. Electrocutions were held on Thursdays at eleven p.m. Tickets available for purchase.

"You speak to me, why?" Noble asked.

Levi hugged the folder. Psychology one-oh-one. Never answer a question with a question. "Do you know why you are here?" Levi blanched at his rookie response.

Noble's eyes glazed, a murky algae-flecked pond. "It is always one or the other. Who carried me here?"

"Do you know where you are?" Levi asked.

"At the moment, I have temporarily, as I said, I have no means, dear me, what then is there?"

If Levi could acquire any skill, it would be the ability to see inside people's minds to determine their authenticity. Not if the person was telling the truth, but the truth of the person. Levi yearned to tunnel through his father's eyes—the same hooded shape as his own—and into his brain.

Levi watched his father. Was William correct? Did Noble have early on-set dementia? Or was Warden Ash right and Noble faked memory loss? Could the prison therapist be correct and Noble was a malingerer? What would be Alois's diagnosis? Was he really coming to America as William requested?

Levi forced a quick exhale to suppress his thoughts that sparked like from the metal wheels of a fast moving carriage, but it didn't work. Thoughts ricocheted in his mind of his medical training in Boston, of his present position as Assistant Psychiatrist at Manhattan's Hospital for the Insane, and of the position paper he and Alois have been researching in the field of dementia.

The doctors' goal? To confirm common symptoms in the elderly such as disorientation, forgetfulness, inability to do simple math, agitation, apathy, and paranoia, and to encourage their scientific peers to stop classifying senile dementia patients as lunatics to be institutionalized and restrained. What if there was a medical explanation for their symptoms other than the popular diagnoses of syphilis and insanity?

"What?" Noble asked.

Had Levi spoken all that aloud?

He looked to his father, twenty-one years his senior, and saw a physical reflection of his future self. Lines around Noble's eyes webbed with disappointment. Cheekbones cut in the shape of half hearts jutted to a resilient jaw. When his eyes did not reveal confusion, they were warm and well-meaning. Not even sixty years old and Noble exhibited symptoms of senility of those decades older.

Or was he faking it?

Repetition of questions was one method Levi and Alois found useful to discern a person's ability to recall. Levi stepped out of the robe of damaged son, and into the cloak of renowned psychiatrist. His voice deepened. He used his doctor voice.

"What is your name?" Levi asked.

"Mister Noble Jennings."

"When were you born?"

"Thirteen hundred and sixty-four, I believe."

"That would make you well over five hundred years old. In which year were you born?" Levi asked again.

"This year, no, last year."

"When were you born?

"Eighteen hundred...I don't know. Do you?"

"You were born in eighteen hundred and forty-seven."

Noble's expression blanked.

"What did I just ask you?" Levi said.

"I don't know."

"What is your name?"

"Noble."

"Your surname?"

"Noble."

"Are you married?"

"Yes."

"To whom?"

"To Noble."

"You are Noble," Levi said.

The lines around Noble's eyes and mouth eased and years erased from his face. "Sarah and I used to walk hand-in-hand in the prison yard. In those days, we were allowed to do that. We could even hug. I remember one day she stood on her tiptoes, put her hands on my face, and said, 'we're pregnant.' I was never so happy and never so in love with Sarah and with our child. I dropped to my knees and asked her to marry me, right there around all those inmates. Imagine that, in a prison yard, a white man proposing to a black woman. I didn't care the beatdown that came. I've always been color blind. Don't you think that's the way to be?"

Levi thought of his mother, and of himself as the baby who had been in her belly in the prison yard. He envisioned the scene. Noble on his knees, Sarah beaming with her hands on her still unformed baby bump.

What had his mother told him when she urged him to see Noble, and to help with his defense?

Noble Jennings is the only man I have every loved.

Levi searched his father's eyes. "What did she say when you asked her to marry you?"

Noble stared. The clarity he had just experienced, gone.

"Did she agree?" Levi persisted.

"Who?"

"Sarah."

"Sarah?" Noble looked down at the plate in his lap.

Levi sighed, and thought to skip the next line of questions but knew he must include them as they were part of his and Alois's protocol that had been patiently established through correspondences across the continents via ocean liner.

In fact, Alois was speaking on this very day in front of the Thirty-Seventh Meeting of Southwest German Psychiatrists in Germany, hoping to appeal to them to provide funding toward their research. Maybe after that, he'd come to America. Levi'd love to see the old chap again, and it would be a real lollapalooza to work together in person on Noble's defense.

William's Theory of the Case:

Noble suffers from presenile dementia. The accused unwittingly gave a confession that lacks veracity and trustworthiness. Chief of Police Byrne took advantage of Noble's weakened mind and forced a false confession. The confession must be suppressed. Noble must be found not guilty at trial.

Did Levi want his father to go free?

Levi forced the next question. "Do you have children?"

Noble's face brightened. "Oh yes. Many."

"Many?"

"One."

"A son or a daughter?"

His face screwed. "You best ask Sarah."

Levi paced again. "How long have you been at Sing Sing?"

"Three weeks."

Levi lifted a pencil from his shirt pocket. "What is this?"

"A pencil."

He dug a hand into his pants pocket. "And this?"

"A key."

"What about this?"

"A cigar."

"Good." Levi returned the items, and looked at the empty plate balanced on Noble's knees. "Did you have lunch today, Mister Jennings?"

"Yes."

"What did you have?"

"Spinach, potatoes and honey."

"I just watched you eat pork with cauliflower. Do you remember the objects I held up and asked you to identify?"

"Objects? No. You speak to me, why?"

Levi sighed. He forced his voice onward. "Do you know what is to happen to you?"

Noble looked up. "I am to die."

Levi placed his hands in his vest pockets to hide their shaking. He shook from nerves, or from the cold cell? "Why do you think you are to die? Your trial is to begin next month. I am to interview you to see if you are oriented to time and place."

"I believe I am, Sir."

"How long have you been in Sing Sing?" Levi asked again. The last response had been three weeks. What would it be now?

"Seventeen months."

Levi folded his arms across his chest. He had tried to be bigger and bolder than the cold but still, he shivered. "You have been at Sing Sing for sixty days."

"It feels longer."

"Perhaps that is because this is your second time in prison. The first time was for thirty-seven years for setting fire to the Colored Orphan Asylum."

"A fire?"

"Yes."

"When was that?"

"Eighteen sixty-one."

"And the year now?"

"Nineteen oh six."

"I am an old man?"

"You are fifty-nine years."

"Is that old?"

"To some."

"Why did you say I was in prison?"

"For setting the Colored Orphan Asylum fire."

Noble placed his hands on his knees and rocked. "If I am to now be electrocuted, I must have done something bad."

"You confessed to killing six men."

Noble stared, then asked, "Did I do it?"

Levi looked at him sideways. Textbook malingerer or diseased mind?

Noble continued to rock. His knees almost hitting his chin. The metal plate in his lap bucked. "My lawyer is William J. Henley. We were in the Home for Unwanted Boys together. He is my best friend."

Levi sat next to Noble on the cot. Metal springs jabbed through the worn mattress. He felt odd seated so close to him. Why had he sat? An attempt to form a doctor-patient bond, or a familial bond?

Noble stopped rocking, and turned toward the doctor. "And you speak to me, why?"

Levi sighed. "I am here to see if you are of unsound mind."

"And if I am, will I die?"

"Your fate has not yet been determined. Your trial is scheduled to begin next month. Do you know what a trial is?"

Noble traced the concave middle of the plate that balanced on his lap. "Pork and cauliflower, you say? Will William be visiting me today? Would you let him know I am no longer mad at him for telling the draft board I was too young when I tried to enlist in the War between the States?" Noble stared at the dank walls. "Why did you say I am here?"

"You are accused of murdering six men."

Noble grabbed Levi's bicep. "That cannot be."

Levi was surprised by the strength of his fingers that wrapped around his arm, but did not move away. "You confessed to the murders."

"I was in front of a firing squad at the time."

"That's not true. Why would you say that? You were arrested and you confessed. William was there. You gave specific details that had not been made public. You told the police where to unearth a sixth body."

"Unearth? No! I couldn't have hurt anyone." Noble stood and the plate clattered to the floor. "I couldn't have set that orphan fire. I wouldn't do that. Was anyone hurt?" He picked up the plate and set it on the cot. "William must know I am not mad at him." He put the plate back on the floor, sat and cleaned a smattering of pork from under his fingernail. "William said the War between the States would last ninety days and then we would live together."

"The Civil War lasted four years and ended in eighteen sixty-five. You didn't live with William until ninety-seven, after you were released from prison."

Noble sighed. "Why are you here?"

"I am here to determine if you are oriented to time and place."

The prisoner flicked a piece of pork off his thumb. "I am sure that I am."

Chapter Fifty

Noble sat in his cell, swathed in darkness, condemned, and listened as the alienist's footsteps echoed and dimmed along the cavernous walkway. The empty plate balanced next to him on the cot. The thick, steel door that sealed the underground chamber opened like a lid on a coffin, and clanged shut.

Who had just been to visit him?

Dammit! His body heated from inside out. Steam teemed from his pores. Why could he remember some things, but not others? Such a helpless feeling to know his mind was blank, with as many thoughts and emotions as the tin bucket he used to wash, to urinate, to defecate. He stood and pushed the plate to the floor. He kicked the pail, the toe of his shoe imprinted in the tin. He kicked out and the bucket rose into the air, hit the wall, and clinked back to the floor, another indent on its circumference. It's not fair. It's not fair. It's not fair. He sat again, his face in his hands that smelled of grease and fat, and he cried. He cried for all he wished he could not recall. The decades in prison. All the time lost with Sarah. How he's disappointed her. Having never met his son, never having the chance to raise him, to be an influence upon his life. What had become of him? Sarah had kept him apprised of their child, he was sure of that—what was his name?—but he could not evoke those details no matter how much he searched the trappings of his brain.

"I can remember a boy I met in 1861 who shook my hand, but not my own son."

He kicked the pail again. It ricochet off the side wall of the cell, to the back wall, and to the ground. He stomped it until it flattened.

Out-of-breath, panting, sweat covered him. He listened for the stillness to be broken by the sounds of Warden Ash coming to whip him with cat 'o nine tails. He'd deserve a beating. He always did.

He sat on the cement floor. The cold felt wet when it seeped to his skin through his threadbare pants. The hallway of the Death House was still.

He clenched the wood vial that hung around his neck on cotton twine. This soothed him and he tried to recall why he wore this odd necklace. If plaques and tangles didn't strangle neurons in his brain, he would remember he had carved the wood container when he was fourteen years old. A resident at the Home for Unwanted Boys at the time, he was engaged in a mission to capture his first queen bee. The ampoule he had crafted was approximately twice the size of a Minie bullet that propelled from a musket during the Civil War. Young Noble had stabbed small breathing holes through the wood, and was proud of the screw lid he devised. This was to be his queen's temporary throne, her transport until he brought her back to the Home to set up a new hive.

Noble had worn the vial every day since he was fourteen, only changing the worn string necklace for twine, and then back to string or twine or cord or woven thread, many times over the years. Inside the empty compartment was his history, all he would forget.

He released his hold on the vial and it dangled against his chest. The origin of the bee pendant was no longer important to him; he forgot he carried it most of the time as if it were a limb or an organ, forgot many times that it had the power to comfort him. Instead, the psychiatrist who had just left his cell hovered in his mind, a familiar stranger.

Had we met before?

Noble applied techniques William had taught him to improve his memory. These, he recalled.

Visualize the man. Noble closed his eyes. The doctor was tall and copper skinned. A good looking lad. What had he worn? A suit and a tie? A prison uniform?

Use word association to memorize the man's name. He had remembered his name a moment ago, hadn't he? Lewis? Lance? Lee?

Why had he been in my cell?

"Oh yes, I remember," Noble spoke aloud. "I am to be tried for murder."

He felt no fear, apprehension, or hysteria. Empty and inert like the squashed bucket, he wasn't happy or sad, not brave or scared, not anxious or relaxed. As a boy, emotions had challenged him like tsunami-fueled waves with the highest of crests and the lowest of troughs. Anger at losing his parents when he was so young. Anger at being sent to the Home for Unwanted Boys. But it wasn't all about anger. There was pleasure when he thought of Sarah, and contentment when he remembered sitting with William in their room at the Home and discussing history and politics, and elation from memories of studying the bee book. And then there was that childhood emotion, learned way too early as a matter of survival, that gave him a different kind of pleasure. An emotion that had bookended his entire life. His enjoyment of the fight and the taste of blood, his own and others.

Now, emotions rarely carried vigor. Flat as the bucket. He no longer enjoyed books. One of his favorite pastimes had been to go to the prison library. When he was released from prison in eighteen ninety—was that the year?—he had made daily visits to the Astor Public Library in the East Village. At first his reading speed slowed, then he lost track of the characters and plot points in his favorite books, books he had read many times before. Soon, he couldn't follow the shortest of sentences from capital letter to full stop. One day, he discovered, he failed to comprehend the meanings of simple words. When he forgot how to care for his bees, he cried, although he didn't know why.

The release of bolts and the shift of locks sounded and the big steel door to the prison tomb opened. Steps on the cold, concrete ground. He shivered, the sweat on his body having dried, he was cold again. He stood, his knees objecting to the movement. Was he to be whipped? So many scars having healed over other scars, he hardly felt pain.

Frankel, the prison guard, stopped in front of his cell. He held a tin tray between his husky fingers. "The doctor said you were still hungry so I brought you more grub."

Noble sighed. A habit he carried from his father who too had been a sigher. Had he passed it on to his son too?

"What doctor?" Noble asked.

"The alienist."

"Who?"

"The doctor who just left here."

"Are we playing cards today?" Noble asked.

Frankel unlocked the cell door and stepped in. "What happened to the bucket?"

Noble looked at it, a vague memory that he had been involved in its destruction. "I don't know."

"I'll get you another one." He put the tray on the cot, picked up the bucket, and tucked it under his arm like a newspaper.

Noble looked down at the plate, a brown mess. "What is it?"

"Leftovers. It was the best I could find. Warden Ash wouldn't let the boys in the mess hall make you something new." Frankel extended his hand.

Noble clasped the guard's strong grip, and flashed back to his first handshake. Eighteen sixty-one, it had to have been. He was fourteen years old and Lincoln had called for northerners to fight. Noble hurried to join William and to enlist. The boy's name whose hand he shook as they waited to register? It took him no time to recall. Robert McGee the third. Another underage kid who thought he understood what it meant to die for his country. Had he survived the war?

Frankel released his hand. "I hope that doctor can help you." Frankel looked at him, a long and hard watery stare. "You're like a brother to me. Nobe. A much older brother," he cracked, "but still like my kin."

"Are we brothers?"

Frankel reached into his pocket and retrieved a small, rectangular box. The top had a flap tucked into a closure panel, with dust flaps on either side. It fit in the palm of Noble's hand. Bees Make The Whole World Sweet, was printed on the bottom. Noble clenched his fingers around the worn box of Bumble Bee Trading Cards perched in the palm of his hand. He opened the top flap. Bee's Are "Bee"autiful, it read.

Frankel picked up the first plate that had been on the ground, and left. Noble listened to the footsteps of his departure, slow and melodious until they were swallowed by distance.

"Frankel, are we playing cards today?" Noble called, and then looked at the open door to his cell. He gazed at the second plate of food on the cot, and then looked at the door again. He stepped through the cell door and into the passageway.

"Frankel, are you there?" he asked.

Then, he realized what he had done. He had exited his cell at the Death House. His cell that was commanded by a masochistic warden who whipped prisoners for minor infractions, and who got the giggles when he strapped new detainees into Old Smoky and pretended to turn her on.

Noble looked toward a sliver of light that streamed from the end of the long corridor where the exit door was open. "Frankel," Noble called again, "you left the door open." He looked toward the light and squinted. He shielded his eyes. His mother and father vacillated in the haze.

Come here, Noble, his father said.

With tentative steps, Noble walked toward the light.

It's okay, his mother added.

Noble increased his pace, imprisoned in the ether between the boy he used to be and the man he had become.

He ran toward them. "Mother? Father?" At the door, Noble stopped. The apparitions rose, faded and disappeared.

Warden Ash and two prison guards stepped into the light, arms crossed, legs spread.

"Where you going, Noble?" the warden asked.

"Nowhere." He turned to head back to his cell.

A guard grabbed his elbow.

Ash took a page out of his pocket, unfolded it and read. "Noble Jennings, on this day, the thirteenth day of June 1906, you are hereby put to death by electrocution for the murder of six men."

Noble looked down, then at the warden. "I was right. I am to die today."

Ash returned his wife's to-do list to his pocket. "Bring him back to his cell," he ordered.

The guards grabbed Noble's elbows and pulled him down the cavernous corridor.

"Ask Frankel if he wants to play cards." Noble called to Ash.

Chapter Fifty-one

Alois and Levi were most excited to present their case studies of tangles and plaques in presenile brains at the Thirty-Seventh meeting of the Southwest German Psychiatrists, a group Alois had been a popular member of. Even though Levi could not attend, they felt certain they were about to become known as the patriarchs of dementia as Marconi was to the wireless telegraph and the Wright brothers were to flight.

Here, forthwith, are portions of the speech given by Alois on June 18, 1906 in Tübingen, Germany.

Greetings Colleagues and Scholars

Many in the psychiatric community refuse to believe P.D. or Presenile Dementia exists, and attribute the deterioration of memory and other symptoms in those under seventy years of age to disease, idiocy, lunacy, a bump on the head, or acting skills. The following Case Studies demonstrate otherwise.

Case Study #1

P.D. in the Deceased

A fifty-year-old woman named Auguste Deter was brought to the Frankfurt's Hospital for the Mentally Ill and Epileptics in

1901 by her husband who could no longer care for her. She was admitted for paranoia, memory disturbances, aggravation, and confusion. Missus Deter was not only forgetful but was often irritated, wandered the hospital halls at night, could not complete simple tasks such as tying her shoe or holding a fork. She failed to remember her husband or daughter. Toward the end of her life, Missus Deter lost the ability to speak and stared blankly. Missus Deter died on January 8, 1906. After her autopsy, with the family's permission, I dissected her brain and noted particles, like barnacles, stuck to her brain. Her brain was shriveled. Distinctive plaques and neurofibrillary tangled in the brain histology. Her brain specimens have been preserved for further research.

Case Study #2

P.D. in the Living

Noble Jennings is a fifty-nine-year-old male who spent much of his life in prison. Eight years after his release, he confessed to committing six murders he may not have committed and is awaiting trial. The prison psychiatrist opines that Mister Jennings is faking memory loss and other symptoms to avoid conviction and electrocution. Doctor Fuller believes Mister Jennings is not malingering nor delusional but rather suffers from P.D.

The Goal

We aim to aid Mister Jennings' defense to prove he suffers from P.D. and therefore did not knowingly and willingly confess to the murders. The difficult part, my colleagues, is that as shown in case study #1, P.D. has heretofore only be diagnosed post-mortem.

The Conclusion

Doctor Fuller and I implore upon the community to steer your research funds toward P.D. before it becomes an epidemic, and so that it can be diagnosed in the living and not just in the departed.

Chapter Fifty-two

Levi waited in the mailroom, a converted closet, at Manhattan's Hospital for the Insane. He was anxious for good news from Alois about his presentation, excited for the funding to begin. Their research into early onset dementia was revolutionary. Surely the psychiatric community abroad would agree.

He stood next to the Morse code operator. Levi was glad the hospital finally got the funding to obtain a telegraph machine. He no longer had to wait weeks to communicate with Alois, the letter salty and faded upon arrival.

Levi looked at his watch. It would be around midnight in Germany and the conference Alois had attended long over. Where was his promised update?

Levi watched the silent machine.

"Did a light flicker?" Levi asked. "Is a message coming in?"

"Not yet, Doctor."

Levi sighed. "Maybe he's not sending it."

The Morse code operator shrugged. "You don't have to wait. I'll write it down when it arrives and bring it to you."

A light on the machine flashed. Levi's eyes widened and he huddled close. The operator eyed him and Levi stepped back.

The operator wrote on a notepad as the message transmitted. Slow. It came across too slow for Levi. Approximately thirteen words per minute. He leaned over the operator's shoulder. The operator again showed his discomfort. Levi stepped back, paced around the closet, and listened to the dashes and dots, indecipherable to him like trying to translate the meaning of rain drops on a metal roof.

Finally, the operator ripped the deciphered page from the notebook and handed it to Levi.

Reception at meeting frigid. Overwhelmed with disappointment. Shilly-shally to continue our research. Tell Counselor Henley that I shan't be coming to America. Please forgive me.

Four Points

The evidence upon which a jury is justified in returning a verdict of guilty must be sufficient to produce a conviction of
guilt, to the exclusion of all reasonable doubt.

<u>Miles v. United States</u> 103 U.S. 304 (1880)

Chapter Fifty-three

NEW YORK. July 1, 1906. Yesterday the Hottest June 30 Here Since 1901. Fourteen persons died of the heat in this city and nearly two score prostrations were recorded on the police blotters.

Juror Number Three folded the New York Times in half, and then in half again, and fanned himself, stirring a hot wind along his sweated brow. He wondered if he stunk as much as the other twelve jurors. Like passing gas around a group of joes after bangers and mash, all hung their heads with feigned embarrassment yet no fingers dared to be pointed.

Number Three adjusted his wide rump on the wood seat of the armchair and dabbed his finger to his tongue to remove smatterings of tobacco. He flicked them to the floor, and narrowly missed the wing-tip toecap of Juror Number Four's worn brown loafer. Must have gotten those from a hand-me-down. Number Three rolled a new cigarette between his thumbs and forefingers, lit it, inhaled deeply, and focused on the courtroom. Wood floor, wood benches, wooden lawyers, immersed in stoicism and statutes. He looked at The Attorney who defended the man on trial for murder. The Attorney was slight and short—the size of a boy—and dressed as if he would be the tallest in the courtroom if he stood on his wallet.

"You may proceed," Judge Donovan Patterson spoke from his perch.

The Attorney squeezed his vacant eyed client's shoulder and walked in front of the jury box. He held no notes. Number Three placed the newspaper under his chair, blew out a large huff of smoke, and settled best he could.

Opening Statement

People of New York versus Noble Jennings

July 1, 1906

"May it please your Honor, Mister Foreman, and Gentlemen of the Jury. I am your servant, The Attorney, William J. Henley, Counselor at Law, and I want to make a private citation before referring directly to the case upon which you sit. The Defendant, Noble Jennings, is my friend. Actually, we are not related by blood yet I look upon him as my brother, no less than if we shared our blood.

"We became acquainted in an orphanage when we were boys. Together we fought for our basic needs: food, a place to sleep, and freedom from abuse. Our bond of devotion is as strong today as it was when we shared a bed as children. I speak of this as I have the benefit of over fifty-five years of friendship with Mister Jennings, who I know as a man. As you do not yet have the benefit of that history, I urge each of you to remember that one does not cease to be a man when others accuse him of a crime.

"Opening statement is not a time for argument, that will come at the end of the trial. This is the time when counselorsat-law tell you what we believe the evidence will demonstrate. You sit as the arbiter of facts on a case that is already familiar to you. You have read about it in The New York Times, The New York Herald, and The Sun. You have overheard your coworkers discuss it. You have lingered over the topic of this trial with your family during dinners of pot roast and potatoes. You have talked about it with strangers while on the train.

"As my colleague A.J. Jennings said for the defense in the trial of Lizzie Borden, 'fact and fiction have furnished many extraordinary examples of crimes that have shocked the feelings and staggered the reason of men, but I think not one of them has ever surpassed in its mystery the case that you are to consider'.

"This was true of the trial of Lizzie Borden, who was found not guilty. This is true of the trial of Noble Jennings, who I believe with the utmost of confidence that you too will swiftly acquit.

"The brutality of the crimes that have occurred is most certainly not mitigated by the actions of the victims. The practice of men stepping out on their wives to purchase the favors of young women is as old as the Roman Empire. While this behavior is most distasteful of any husband, it is surely not worthy of death, and certainly not dismemberment. Each man's body broken as if by the strength of a warrior. Each man missing an ear when his body was discovered. The ears, distinctly bitten off. Who but a lunatic—one with immense strength and determination, one more beast than human—would take part in such acts?

"The government believes they have captured their beast. My friend, Noble Jennings. However, I assure you, and the evidence shall illustrate, that Noble is not guilty, and is indeed incapable of such acts of violence.

"Ah, but you have read of his confession in the dailies, haven't you? There isn't a gentleman of any learning in New York City who has not. I feel certain that at the conclusion of the evidence you will agree to disregard this so-called confession for I shall show you that Noble was suffering of unsoundness of mind and did not know what he confessed to. Not unsoundness to be labeled lunacy, but a disease of the brain that affects his ability to reason, to understand, and to recall. A medical condition that is expected to afflict the elderly, men more than a decade older than Noble. A medical condition that heretofore has no name but has now been scientifically proven to be present in the minds of those younger, including in the mind of my friend, Noble Jennings.

"Police commissioner, Timothy Byrne, has tried to affix these murders upon Noble. A task to ruin my friend that was born more than half-a-century ago on the eve of the Civil War, born from a New York City infected with corruption.

"Mister Foreman and Gentlemen of the Jury, the law of New York draws a cloak of the presumption of innocence around the shoulders of every person accused of a crime. No juror shall find a person guilty unless he is convinced the government has proved his guilt beyond a reasonable doubt. An unwise quest that the government will fail as the truth will not permit them to succeed.

"I wish to address the two types of evidence you will consider: direct evidence and circumstantial evidence. Direct evidence is the testimony of persons who have seen, heard or felt the thing about which they testify. As an example, if this was a case of murder by stabbing, and a man should testify that he saw the defendant stab a person with a knife, that is direct evidence. Circumstantial evidence is different, and relies on the rickety trellises of inferences to connect the crime to the accused, much like the shaky spans of an unsound bridge struggle to connect masses of land.

"There is no direct evidence connecting Noble with these unfortunate deaths. No weapon. Not a drop of blood. No eyewitness. And that confession I've already mentioned? To be tossed aside and disregarded. In order to convict my friend, you must find that the shackles of justice are solid in their links. This you will be unable to do. The truth will not allow it.

"With every crime there must be motive, opportunity to commit the crime, and the ability to carry out the deed. Mister Foreman, it will be shown that my friend had no motive to commit these crimes, he did not have the opportunity to commit these crimes, nor did he have the ability to carry out such acts that require the strength of a young man coupled with the rage of a feral monster. Most certainly a man such as Noble, who is fifty-nine years of age and who is tranquil of disposition, would not ever carry the vigor nor the craving to commit such hideous acts.

"Kind Gentlemen of the Jury, to set the framework of this trial, five points of evidence shall be presented in Noble's defense that prove his indisputable innocence. Separate, each point might appear to be an excuse made by one who feels cheated by the injustices of life. But together, like the pentagonal streets that gave Five Points its name, the streets that are located not far from this very courtroom, each point has fused into an inescapable tsunami of innocence.

"Point number one. Noble, born in 1847, grew up poor, abandoned, and abused in the Home for Unwanted Boys.

"Point number two. To replace the absence of the family he never had as a boy he turned to bee tending and bee bearding.

"Point number three. Like a lone ship lost at sea, Noble navigated the streets of lower Manhattan during waves of civil unrest and divisiveness.

"Point number four. As an adult, he felt frustration at not being a proper husband to Sarah or father to Levi.

"Point number five. Just as one might have tuberculosis or diphtheria, my friend Noble suffers from a disease. Dementia of the mind.

"And so, kind Gentlemen of the Jury, the trial of the People of the State of New York versus Noble Jennings begins. The evidence will confirm that Noble is no murderer but the victim of a confluence of uncontrollable and unavoidable events. Sit back and listen astutely. I assure you there will be no sudden confession akin to a Shakespearean drama, nor shall I promise the true murderer to be revealed. But I make the following vow: you will fall in love with Five Points and its people, as I have, and your faith in humanity will be awakened.

"I, The Attorney, gift to you the past so you may untangle the present."

Chapter Fifty-four

New York. July 1, 1906. PROVED TO BE MUCH ALIVE. His Wife Had Identified His Body and Wanted Life Insurance. Coroner Peter F. Acritelli yesterday examined a live man who finally proved to the satisfaction of the county official that he was not dead.

As The Attorney neared the end of his opening statement, Juror Number Six, a retired newspaperman, focused on the defendant who watched The Attorney like a dog who followed the every move of its master lest he be abandoned.

Noble's sit bones hurt on the hard chair. It was hot in here. His feet were ablaze. Should he remove his shoes? Was he losing weight? He couldn't be sure since he wasn't certain how much he used to weigh or what he was supposed to weigh. The clothes he wore hung loosely, his shirt a burlap sack, his pants roped around his waist. Itchy, annoying, like bees swarmed between his skin and the fabric. No, not bees. Bees would have been soothing, their soft buzzes melodic. This felt more like fire ants that gripped his skin and injected their venom.

He looked to the man who just sat next to him, dapper and dressed in a woven suit with a pocket watch and chain tucked in his vest pocket. A letter stuck up from his breast pocket, thrice folded. The man in control and focused, he didn't even sweat. Two inches of the sleeve of his tailored shirt stuck out from his suit sleeve and revealed hand woven initials sewn into the cotton. WJH. The man's eyebrows scrunched and his reading glasses were perched on the end of his nose. He looked to be doing something of importance, even had stood in front of that group of men and talked and gestured, looked into their eyes, took the letter from his breast pocket and spoke of the constitution and waved the paper at them as if it were the actual document signed by our founding fathers—and now, at the desk, moved papers about, opened and closed books. WJH was important, of that Noble was sure. Even so, the man was human. His right arm shook. His hair thinned on top of his head. His handlebar moustache edges were greased and twirled, the edges yellowed. His breath, earthy like freshly picked mushrooms.

WJH's hand landed lightly on his arm like he was reassuring him, or perhaps he was seeking to be reassured.

"We did good," WJH spoke softly. "I had solid eye contact with the jurors, especially numbers three and seven. Six couldn't take his eyes off of you."

Noble wondered, where were they? Who were all these people? He looked all around, to the sides, to the front, behind him. He couldn't recall ever being in a room that looked like this before. So large, wood everywhere like a forest had collapsed, the people serious and solemn.

A meeting hall?

A man in the front of the room sat on a high branch and observed the goings-on like a raven on a tree top. Why did Noble feel like a field mouse? The Honorable Judge Donovan Patterson, the sign in front of him read. A placard next to that, "At his best, man is the noblest of animals; separated from law and justice he is the worst." Aristotle.

The judge's narrow torso was topped with a slender face and a sharp nose. Thick graying hair parted to one side. His hazel eyes barely blinked, his expression difficult to decipher.

The Hamilton collar of his finely pressed shirt peeked out from under a black robe. He ruled with aptitude, like a teacher who expected the highest of quality from his students.

Were they in a classroom?

Noble looked to his right. Twelve or thirteen—each time he counted he came up with a different number—well-dressed men sat in a box in two rows, their area cordoned off by low wood walls. The men were smoking and drinking.

Were they in college?

To Noble's left was another table perpendicular to where he and WJH sat. Two men pondered at that table, also finely dressed, one corpulent with rows of fat padding his neck, the other meaty and fit like a wrestler. Their table was also covered with books and papers, which they too opened, perused, closed, and opened again. WJH looked to be interchangeable with the fat man and the wrestler, like boys in a school yard.

Noble turned around. Behind him, rows of men and women sat, some met his eyes, some looked away. The ones in the front row wore the uniform of the New York Police Department. Their expressions grave.

Perhaps they were in church and the man in black was the minister.

The judge looked to the prosecutors. "Call your first witness."

WJH took the letter from his breast pocket and slapped it on the table.

From the Desk of
Herr Doktor Alois Alzheimer
Berlin, Germany

Dictated June 15, 1906
Anticipated receipt date July 1, 1906

Dear William,

I hope you will excuse the informality of which I address you in this post, however I feel through our correspondences that we are now more than colleagues but also friends. I too wish I could travel to America so I might help with Noble's defense (and practice my English). I appreciate your offer to send me fare however our research has been met with unanticipated resistance and so I find myself taking to bed more than I should. The ocean's journey will surely be too arduous for one in such poor health. I feel certain my circumstance is temporary. If only I could fly from Berlin to New York in one of the Wright Brothers' planes we have heard so much about in Deutschland. Flight like a bird might only take a day or two, as opposed to two weeks or more via ocean liner. I could have breakfast in my parlor with my wife in Berlin on one day, and breakfast with you and Levi at the Waldorf Hotel the following morning. Wouldn't that be newsworthy!

Ah, but writing of my fancies of flight are not responsive to your questions and concerns. Your inquiry into using Presenile Dementia as a defense is creative and apt, although I speak as a doctor and not as a jurist.

As I am sure Levi has shared with you, I have two months afore dissected the brain of a patient named Auguste Deter. I found proof in her fifty-year-old brain of senile plaques (extracellular deposits of amyloid in the gray matter of the brain) that make up neurofibrillary tangles. I also discovered amyloid deposits in the cerebral cortex and in the subcortical gray matter. Perhaps those terms are too foreign for you as most neuro-psychiatrists might not understand terminologies of your profession, so let me simplify.

In Herr Deter's brain I discovered abnormalities not normally found in the brain of a fifty-year-old person. Imagine the spots on a leopard. Leopards are mostly light colored with dark spots, or rosettes as they are called because the shape of the spots resemble roses. That is what I saw under the microscope in Auguste's brain. Black rose-like shaped spots on an orange-yellow background. Can you picture this, William? Brains dissected from people of similar ages as Auguste show no signs of these plagues and tangles. (Please note, these other subjects whose brains I've dissected died of natural causes or by accidents. I do not want you to think I killed anyone in furtherance of my scientific zeal.)

These plagues and tangles, I am one hundred percent scientifically certain, are the cause of what Levi and I term Presenile Dementia. To date Missus Deter, at fifty years old, is our youngest specimen. I am no doomsday forecaster but I would not be surprised, my friend, if Presenile Dementia is to be found in persons in their forties.

So, my friend, I feel elated to share with you the viability of the defense for your friend, even if Levi and I appear to be the only neuro-psychiatrists to feel this excitement. (Damn my non-believing colleagues, may they rot in hell as you Americans say.) You provided me with the transcript of Mister Jenning's so-called confession and your client certainly was misguided by his interrogator. Although it is a curiosity how Mister Jennings knew of a body buried under the Williamsburg

Bridge but I will leave that to your proficiency as to how to explain this to the jury.

I only wish I could be present in New York City to testify as an expert on your behalf. While Levi has not dissected a human brain, he and I have communicated about my findings in the most precise scientific terms, and he joined me in Munich in 1904 at the Royal Psychiatric Clinic at which time I shared much of my research with my esteemed colleague. I trust Doctor Fuller will make an excellent witness for the defense.

Dear William, might I be so bold as to inquire as to something on my mind? Levi is a dark skinned man, and I have heard much of prejudices in the Americas toward those of African heritage. Alas, there are few that live in Germany so I cannot boast that our citizens would not engage in the same deplorable behavior. However, when speaking of the United States of America and its recent history, slavery only fifty years erstwhile, I wonder: will an American jury trust the word of a colored psychiatrist, even one so decorated as the first African-American psychiatrist in the United States?

I know you and Levi are close; he has bragged of you being like a father to him more so than Mister Jennings who I understand has spent the majority of his life in prison. I know you are proud of Levi, as am I. I hope your jury will look past ethnicity and see that the intellect, the heart and the soul are color-less.

Good luck, Counselor. I eagerly await your next post and wish the best for Mister Jennings. I pray that one day I might visit you in your Five Points.

With warm respect,
Herr Doktor Alzheimer

Chapter Fifty-five

After three days of presenting evidence, and William's cross-examinations of the witnesses, the People of New York rested its case against Noble. Peggy sat in the second row of the pews of courtroom 201, pad on her lap. The revolutionary, non-leaking Alkin Lambert eye drop filler pen reposed in her left hand, as natural to her as a finger. She had been scribbling notes of the trial, from the opening statements to the People's witnesses: laypeople and experts the assistant district attorneys called to lay out a convincing, albeit circumstantial, tale of murder they hoped pointed to Noble.

The courtroom was chock-full. Peter Stout, eighty-four years of age, and Commissioner Byrne, sixty-six, commandeered the front row along with the assistant chief of police and a squall of Metropolitans in their finest blues. Each man equipped with a sidearm.

In the next row of the bench-like pews, Peggy wedged between John and Levi. To her right, protruding from John's torso, were legs. Yes, legs! Constructed by Harry, covered by pants, a belt attached to his waist and a rope looped around his upper thighs. Attached to the belt were hollow wooden supports rigged with springs, metal tendons, and joints. The tops of John's legs leaned on the bench, his knees bent over the seat, and his calves ran perpendicular to the wood floor and down to finely shined loafers. For those unaware of John's misfortunes, which weren't many in lower Manhattan, it would appear he would rise along with the others upon a break in the proceedings. However, John's legs were non-functional. Pomp with no circumstance. Harry was working on creating a pair of legs that used a series of ropes and pulleys that could actually make a legless man walk. So far, a man could steady his torso on a small wooden platform the size of a dinner plate from which the legs protruded. He had to have good balance, the dexterity to manipulate a complex series of ropes and springs, and patience as each step took upwards of one minute. Based on his experiments with John, after just a couple of steps, the dinner plate device resulted in agonizing pain in the lower back.

In a corner of the courtroom sat Harry's proudest and most successful creation to date. A light weight chair that wheeled. Made from Indian reed with small wheels in the back and large wheels up front, John no longer had to be pulled in a wagon but was pushed in a chair. John could even propel himself forward or backwards by rotating the wheels with his hands, although turning the chair left or right required a series of hard cut manipulations.

Next in line, and to Peggy's left, sat Levi. To his side, Alice rested her head on his shoulder and whistle-snored. A pink purse hung on her shoulder. Then sat Sarah, who twisted a handkerchief in her hand and prayed for mercy upon her Noble. Her lips moved but no sounds emitted. Kid sat at the end of the long bench of the second row behind William and Noble at the defense table; the view of his boss blocked by two broad shouldered coppers.

Three more long rows behind them were occupied by other reporters, friends, drama hopheads, and misfortune-seekers. In the back, Jenny Big Stink rearranged her large bottom on the wood bench. She wiped sweat from her brow with a handkerchief.

"Call your first witness, Mister Henley," Justice Patterson said.

The spectators tittered, some from anticipation as to who William might call, and some from the uncomfortable seats and scorching courtroom. The heatwave in New York City had already claimed more than one dozen lives. Hospitals were overrun with those delirious from dehydration. Against city ordinances, fire hydrants were pried open and children and adults alike danced in the sprays, entire families slept on fire escapes at night with the hopes of catching a breeze.

John Coal, pen and pad resting on his artificial legs, yearned for a long inhale of fresh air. The stale, crowded courtroom irked him, but he knew he could not leave. He was supposed to be taking notes. Peggy next to him jabbed him in the ribs as a reminder to keep up appearances.

"Who do you think William will call?" John whispered.

Peggy was too enthralled in the moment to respond. Like after reading the final sentence of a chapter, she couldn't wait to turn the page to find out what happened next, yet at the same time felt reluctance that the next scene might disappoint.

The judge bent forward and peered through black-rimmed Shur-on spectacles. "Call your first witness, Counselor." He repeated.

William leaned over and said something to Noble, and then stood and released a dramatic exhale. Peggy angled the point of her pen on the page. She knew he wouldn't call Levi to begin Noble's defense as William had tagged him to be the final witness, the climax of the story.

William looked to the jury, and then twisted toward the audience. His eyes caught Peggy's. He lifted one side of his lips in a half-smile.

New York Times
All the News that's Fit to Print

IN MURDER TRIAL OF NOBLE JENNINGS
DEFENSE CALLS UNEXPECTED WITNESS

"The best part of the trial so far."

Reported by John Coal

NEW YORK, July 4, 1906. On the one hundred and thirty-first an-
niversary of the ratification of the Declaration of Independence, outside the New York Courthouse sailing ships breezed through New
York Harbor and around Lady Liberty with celebratory flare and to the
cheers of thousands. Inside courtroom 201, Noble Jennings sat on trial
for the brutal murders of six men.

At Judge Donovan Patterson's behest, Counselor William Henley called
the first witness for the defense. "Mister Lonny Massacre," the
seasoned attorney announced, his voice taller than his rounded
shoulders had ever stood. His confidence was met with silence from
the peanuts in the courtroom gallery, as quiet as a congregation
ashamed to admit its sins.

The caste of the courtroom was that of anticipation. Henley spoke the
name again as if he had not been heard. This time, his voice was delicate like a thrown stone that barely sent ripples through a stream.

Heads turned at the sounds of chains clanked as loud and chaotic as
Satan's organist. Mister Massacre entered the courtroom from a side
door. Dressed in tan, loose fitting wool pants knobbed together around
his waist with knotted twine. A tan button-down shirt was finely
pressed like from a rich man's launder yet the fabric was noticeably
frayed, ripped and stained by the ghosts of prisoners past. When first
sewn the top and the bottom no doubt matched in color and quality
but were now unevenly worn and of differing shades. Mister Massacre's skin was gray, his hair thin, his eyes jaundiced, and he appeared

gaunt from the last time this reporter interviewed Mister Massacre, as previously reported in THE TIMES.

Chains wrapped around his ankles snaked up toward his wrists, which were secured in front. From his hands, the chains forked around his waist. The whole effect reminiscent of the sign of the cross. Forgive me Father, for I have sinned. Had Mister Massacre ever thought those words, or said them aloud? Two armed Metropolitans held his bent elbows, their own elbows straight and locked so their bodies stretched as far from the prisoner as possible. Four more police sentried in front of the judge's bench. A dozen or more sat in the front row of the galley and surrounded long in the tooth Police Commissioner Byrne, his assistant top cop Hugh Bailey, and Tammany Hall representative Peter Stout.

The witness stand was in the front of the wood-paneled and carpeted courtroom, situated between the judge's elevated throne and the jurors' box that was the size and shape of a small caboose. In front of the witness stand, a clearing in the pit of the room set the stage for the dramatics. The lawyers were the actors, the judge was the critic, and the jurors were the guests of honor. We, the spectators, were the second class citizens who metaphorically hung from rafters and peeked through slits in doors to witness history. As Shakespeare had said, all the world is a stage. This was certainly true of courtroom 201.

In the pit, attorneys sat at beautifully carved oak tables. Two prosecutors strategized at a table parallel to the jury box. Counselor Henley and Mister Jennings were at a right angle to the assistant district attorneys, and faced the judge. Their backs were to the spectators. The jury box was to their right, and perpendicular.

At the defense table, Henley and Jennings watched the People's witnesses and the jurors for their reactions, and evaluated their raised eyebrows, downward glances, and half-hidden sighs and gasps. As did we all.

The witness stand was a step up from where the jurors sat on wooden parables, and a flight down from where Justice Patterson towered over the plot of truth and lies.

The prisoner and his escorts stopped in front of the witness stand. Mister Massacre did not look at the judge.

"Sit," Justice Patterson said.

Mister Massacre did not move.

"Please take the witness stand," Justice Patterson said.

A guard nudged Mister Massacre's elbow and pointed to the judge. The prisoner looked up.

"Sit, Sir." The judge remained polite to the convicted killer.

It was then observed that the tightly linked bondage around Mister Massacre's ankles did not permit him to bend his knees and step up to the witness stand, nor did the binding on his wrists and around his waist give him the necessary mobility to hoist himself using his hands and arms.

Massacre eyed the judge.

Justice Patterson leaned over the top of the bench. "Guards, lift him."

"No, Sir," one said.

It was apparent the guards did not want to get too close to Massacre because they enjoyed having both of their ears, and from this I recalled a moment when I had interviewed Mister Massacre and he wished to whisper in my ear and this reporter declined.

"Shimmy," Justice Patterson ordered.

"Skinny?" Massacre asked.

The judge pointed. "Sit your buttocks down on that step and shimmy."

Mister Massacre turned and angled his backside over the step. The guards moved away and watched. Jurors leaned forward to see. The spectators, this reporter included, strained to witness and was surprised to notice the prisoner's bindings, while boisterous, were thin.

Mister Massacre fell back and landed roughly on to the witness stand platform. He winced, his boney behind surely bruised. The prisoner brought his knees to his chest, twisted his torso and leaned first his head, then his neck, followed by his shoulders on to the witness chair. All in the courtroom were rapt with attention. Slowly, Mister Massacre muscled and inched his way on to his chest, then his stomach. His hands underneath him, the chains ground together and against the wood like the brakes on a locomotive. He rested, and we all held our breaths, and then he began again and twisted and turned and grinded and flipped his body and sat with a thump in the chair. Along with the jurors, the spectators, the judge, the attorneys and Mister Noble Jennings, he was breathless. We were not sure what we had just witnessed, but felt it to be significant.

"It was painful to watch the prisoner try and get on to the witness seat with his hands and legs chained together," said Miss Jenny Big Stink. "Not that he doesn't deserve to be in pain after what he did to those people."

"I didn't think he'd make it," said another spectator who did not want to reveal his name. "It was the best part of the trial so far."

After Mister Massacre was settled in the chair, he refused water. No one would get close enough to hand it to him or help him drink it anyway. The judge then leaned over his bench, peered down at the prisoner/witness and, satisfied all was in order, pronounced, "Defense, you may proceed."

Counselor Henley stood at a lectern, no notes in hand, and the defense of Mister Noble Jennings began.

Chapter Fifty-six

Massacre settled himself on to the witness chair and Alice pretended to sleep, adding a well-rehearsed whistle-snore for realism. That had been Peg Peg's idea. She rested her head on Levi's shoulder, her face pointed toward the front of the courtroom. She kept her eyes closed for the most part, only occasionally opening them a slit to glare at the back of Byrne's head.

Three rows behind was Jenny Big Stink, beset with guilt. Alice knew this from the times Jenny swept in to her apartment with fresh trout or bass wrapped in paper and tucked under the folds of her meaty arms. Often she carried beef that Sarah threw away after Jenny left. When Jenny and Alice were alone, the fish lady wept and apologized.

When Jenny stopped selling fish and went into the pharmaceutical business, the gifts continued in the form of white powder in a small vile tucked between two rows of fat on Jenny's stomach. These gifts were for Alice and John Coal. Sarah would be furious if she knew. Jenny called the powdery substance her special vitamins and said they would give Alice brain power. Alice didn't think she was getting smarter, but she did feel like she could soar around Five Points whenever the gritty stuff tickled her nose. Jenny gave the special vitamins to John Coal to ease his pain. He only took them at night.

"If there is anything I can ever do for you..." Jenny offered each time she visited.

Alice could not think of anything Jenny could help her with other than the white powder, until she and Peg Peg and the blue and white bear had a meeting and called upon Jenny to help execute the plan they devised.

In the courtroom, Alice cuddled her pink purse. It was heavier than usual and her shoulder where it hung ached. She put the bag in her lap and rested her hand on top. She opened her eyes the width of a gash and again studied the back of Byrne's head. She hadn't seen him since that day when she didn't take the fish. When he walked into the courtroom, she stared at his patchy white beard that rusted around his lips from tobacco and bourbon, and at his bulbous and veined purple and blue nose. She supposed she could feel some vindication as he was timeworn and irrelevant to his troops, other than to honor history and pageantry, but that wasn't enough to satiate her fury.

At almost eighty years old, she had lived long enough. As far as Alice was concerned, Byrne too had lived long enough. Longer than enough. Too long for the damage he had done to her family, and to others.

She would have written a different script for her life but had to believe these had been her pages for a divine reason. She would never understand the why. Even the white powder gave her no answers, but she was old enough and wise enough to know regrets were a waste of a person's energy. Action—the what—was what counted when one took inventory of her life.

With her head on Levi's shoulder, she closed her eyes again and listened to William's questions, Massacre's responses, objections from the prosecutor, and the judge's rulings.

"Did you kill Henry Thaw Watson?" William asked.

"Yes." Massacre said.

"Roy Allen?"

"Yes."

"Philip Mattis?"

"Yes."

"David Small?"

"Him too."

Alice let go a yawn. Trials were tedious.

"What about Thomas Pollard?" William asked.

"He was mine, too," Massacre spoke with pride.

Alice opened her eyes and peered through the space between Byrne's right and Bailey's left shoulders. William walked toward the witness stand.

"It was you, and not Mister Jennings."

"That's what I said."

"Did Mister Jennings kill him or anyone else with you, or for you?"

"I did it alone."

"You've been incarcerated for thirty years, isn't that right?" William asked.

Massacre's hands were in his lap, hidden by a wood panel that fronted the witness stand. "Twenty-nine years and sixty-four days in the big house."

"When I say you've been incarcerated," William continued, "that means you've been locked in a prison and have not stepped outside of prison walls. Is that correct?"

"Except when I was transferred to Sing Sing in 1897."

"During this transfer that you mention, were you free at any time?"

"No. Not like I didn't think about escaping, you know, but those guards gave me no opportunity." He looked at the two guards that stood not too near.

"Addressing these recent murders, how was it that you killed these men while you were imprisoned?"

"I had help."

"Was Mister Jennings your helper?"

"I already told you, no." He looked at Noble. "He had nothing to do with nothing. I swear to God." He pointed his chin toward the judge. "You got a Bible?"

"Who was your helper?" William asked.

Massacre looked at The Attorney. "Huh?"

"You said Noble didn't commit these murders, but someone else did at your direction. Correct?"

"Yeah."

"Who was it?"

Massacre leaned forward and using fingers from both hands pretended to tie a knot over his lips.

William asked, "Are the jurors to interpret your action to mean you will not say who committed these murders at your behest?"

"I'll only say who it ain't."

"How did Mister Jennings know where Thomas Pollard's body was to be found if he didn't help you?"

"I told him."

"You told him?"

"Yes."

"Why would you do that?" William asked.

Massacre shrugged. "I told him everything."

Byrne jumped up. "Liar!"

Alice gripped Levi's arm.

"Sit down, Commissioner." Judge Patterson warned.

Begrudgingly, Byrne sat.

"Mister Massacre, when did you tell Mister Jennings about where Thomas Pollard's body was buried?"

"When we were cellmates in ninety-seven."

"You remember that, today, as you sit in the witness chair under oath, nine years later?"

"I told him everything about every murder I'd ever committed or been part of."

"For goodness sakes," Byrne jumped up again. "He's a liar defending a liar. Pollard was recently killed."

Assistant Chief Bailey raised his fists into the air. Police officers rose in support of their leaders.

Peter Stout yelled, "Noble Jennings is a murderer. He never should have been released from prison for setting the Orphan fire in sixty-one"

Sarah jumped up. "He's innocent of that, and of this."

Levi grabbed his mother's arm. She shook him away.

"Order," Judge Patterson banged his gavel. The placard with the Aristotle quote cockeyed. "The next person who interrupts these proceedings will be removed from the courtroom."

All sat and silenced.

"You may proceed, Mister Henley." The judge said.

"Thank you, your honor." William turned to Massacre. "Isn't it true, Mister Massacre, that Mister Jennings suffers from Presenile Dementia and so would confuse your stories with reality?"

The prosecutor shot up. "Objection. This witness is not an expert."

"This is insane," Byrne yelled. "One murderer defending another murderer."

"Yeah!" Metropolitans again joined their boss.

The banging of the gavel sounded once more. The Aristotle sign fell to the floor. Judge Patterson's voice boomed. "Order in the court."

All stood in the pews. Hollering and gesturing. Cries for Noble's freedom. Demands for his persecution. Kid tried to get to William, to protect him. Two officers pushed him back. Levi pulled Alice into him. Peggy scribbled with vigor.

The judge pointed at the guards. "Put the jury in the jury room. Secure the prisoner." He rushed out a back door.

Byrne, Bailey, Peter Stout, and uniformed officers channeled out of the courtroom.

The guards rushed the jurors into the jury room. "Lock them in," one said.

The prosecutors scurried out the rear exit.

William said to Noble, "you stay here." He ran out of the courtroom and into the hallway.

In the pews, Sarah wept softly. Levi tried to comfort her. Peggy wrote as fast as she could. John, as often happened when he sat for too long, winced in pain.

In the back of the room, Jenny Big Stink saw opportunity. She grabbed John's chair, pushed people aside with the wooden frame and large back wheels, and angled the moving seat toward him. Alice watched, knowing she too was to be included. This ballyhoo, the diversion she and Jenny, Peg Peg and the blue and white bear had hoped for but could never fully plan, was in motion.

John transferred into the wheeled chair, and Jenny beckoned toward Alice. Alice clutched her pink purse and climbed into John's lap.

From the Desk of Doctor Levi Solomon Fuller
Assistant Psychiatrist
Manhattan's Hospital for the Insane

Psychological and Physical Examination of Alice Rosalie Fuller

Testing done: May 15, 1906 - June 1, 1906
Report submitted: June 13, 1906

Memorandum to Patient File: Third periodic examination of Alice
Rosalie Fuller.

Time spent on Testing and Report Preparation: 100 hours

Patient History: At thirty-four years old, Miss Fuller was hit upon the
head by Police Officer Timothy Byrne resulting in brain damage.

Familial History: Unmarried. Daughter: Sarah Fuller. Grandson:
Doctor Levi Solomon Fuller. Companion: John Coal.

Physical Characteristics

Age: 79 years
Ethnicity: Negro
Personal Habits: non-verbal
Height: 63 inches
Weight: 115 pounds
Body Mass Index: 22.8 kg/mg
Resting Heart Rate: 78
Blood Pressure: 110/68 mm Hg
Temperature: 97.8 degrees
Head Length (chin to top of head): 7 ¾"
Head Breadth: 23 ½"
Arm Span: 58"
Length of Middle Finger: 3 ¼"
Length of Lower Arm (elbow to wrist): 9 ½"

Behavioral Characteristics
(as compared to like age and gender samples)

Hand Squeeze Strength: High

Rate of Hand Movement: Rapid
Vital Capacity of Lungs: Clear
Visual Acuity: Normal
Highest Audible Tone: Above Average
Speed of Blow: Average to High
Reaction Time to Visual Stimuli: Average to High
Reaction Time to Auditory Stimuli: Average to High
Fatigue: None Exhibited
Time for Naming Colors: Patient is non-verbal
Number of Letters Repeated Upon One Hearing: Patient is non-verbal
Degree of Pressure Needed to Cause Pain: High

Psychological Tests Utilized and Results

Experimental Memory Tests, E.N. Henderson (1903). Miss Fuller
was read a passage and asked to agree or disagree if an item was
included in said passage. For example, after reading the passage to
her three times, I asked Miss Fuller if there was a dog in the passage. The correct answer was yes, however she was unable to respond. This investigation bears on the power of learning readily and
the ability to retain what is learned.

Passage used: There was-once, in the eastern-part-of Egypt,-a
king, whose-reign-had long been-a course-of savage- tyranny; long
had he ruined-the rich and distressed-the poor. Suddenly-he
changed-his course and ruled-so well as-to be called-the just. When
asked-by a favorite-the reason-for this-change, he replied: 'I saw-a
dog.'

Result: Fail.

The Physical and Mental Measurements of the Students of
Columbia College, Clark Wissler (1901). Physical and mental characteristics of Miss Fuller were recorded.

Result: See Above.

Diagnostic Empirical Reading Assessment, Levi Solomon Fuller
(1905). To assess reading level of patient. Miss Fuller's reading level
continues to be zero.

Result: Fail.

<u>Intellectual Reaction Time of the Non-Verbal Subject</u>, Levi Solomon Fuller (1904). To determine through physical cues the patient's reaction time. Patient was asked to point to her nose after I pointed to mine. This was successful as Miss Fuller appears to have the ability to mimic. However, when asked to point to her nose without the visual clue of where a nose might be, Miss Fuller was unable to complete the task.

Result: Fail.

<u>Picture Match Mental Testing</u>, Levi Solomon Fuller (1902). Patient shown four photographs. Two matched and two did not. Miss Fuller was asked to point to the two photos that were the same.

Result: Fail

<u>Summary</u>

Miss Fuller continues to present as non-verbal and with the capacity of a child. She demonstrated frustration and anger throughout the testing, which accounted for the long hours over several days as Miss Fuller was granted many reposes. Miss Fuller appeared to want to communicate with this examiner however after many attempts to find a way for that communication to occur, this was unable to be achieved.

End of Psychological and Physical Examination of Alice Rosalie Fuller

Chapter Fifty-seven

In the hallway outside the courtroom, members of the NYPD encircled Byrne and Peter Stout, a cobalt cohort. Guns jammed into leather holsters, and clasped to leather belts that tightened around overgrown bellies and fastened over trim stomachs. They chanted, "True Blue", and nary moved out of the way when Jenny pushed John and Alice through the crowd.

"Pepepapapa," Alice said.

Jenny wheeled the chair away from the tumult of righteous anger. "Alice has to go to the bathroom," she told John.

Alice climbed off John's lap and Jenny led her toward the bathroom, but instead steered her into a stairwell. She closed the door. The protests and cries muffled. Jenny reached under her shirt, between two sweaty rows of chub, fingered a vile, and tapped out white powder on to the lower part of her thumb. She inhaled, replenished it, and held her thumb under Alice's nose. Alice breathed in deeply.

Jenny licked the residue off her thumb. "Do you have it?"

Alice opened her purse.

"Give it to me," Jenny said.

Alice shook her head furiously. "Pepepapapa!" She wanted to say, that wasn't the plan, that's not what we had agreed upon.

Jenny took Alice's face in her hands. "You being like this, it's my fault."

"Nananananana," Alice objected.

Jenny's body blocked the stairwell door. Still, Alice tried. She ran into her, to move her, or to get around her, or to go under her, but Alice was too frail and Jenny was too wide and too strong. Even with the heroin that flowed with the might of a steam engine around Alice's nervous system and into her brain, she was helpless to get passed the drug peddler. Jenny grabbed Alice's purse, pulled out the gun, and dropped the bag to the floor. The remaining contents of her pink purse scattered.

"You stay here." Jenny ran out of the stairwell.

Alice started to go after her and stopped when she realized three things. One, two, three. (1) There was nothing she could do to stop her, (2) she respected how Jenny felt, wanting to be the one to put the bullet in Byrne's heart, because Alice felt the same way, and (3) something remarkable had just occurred.

She was alone.

No one sing-sang to her, or read children's books in a high-pitched voice reserved for lunatics and imbeciles, or baby-talked, or checked on her every few minutes.

The belongings from Alice's purse shaped a mole hill on the floor. Items she had collected for decades and always carried. Ten lima beans to count when she felt anxious. A pen and pencil set Peggy had given her. A small stuffed puppy from Levi and Harry. A faded train ticket. Origination: New York City, Destination: Boston, purchased in April 1861 before Sarah's dreams of becoming an actress were dashed with the crack of Byrne's club.

Alice sat, surrounded by her stuffs, and sang a silly song.

Chapter Fifty-eight

Massacre's wrists and ankles were no longer secured having sawed at the tenuous binding while he shimmied up and over and around to maneuver into the witness chair. The chain that hung around his waist fell to the platform. A clatter sounded, to be heeded over Five Points if anyone heard, although nobody had, except Noble. The convicted killer and the defendant were the only souls present in courtroom 201, although some might opine that at least one of the men was soul-less.

Massacre stepped down, and wiggled out of the remaining chains. He jogged in place a few steps, and did some jumping jacks. His fanged smile widened and he walked to Noble who sat stony at the table for the defense. Told to stay there by WJH, Noble had done so.

"Let's go." Massacre beckoned.

With the bee necklace twined around Noble's neck, he didn't move.

Massacre dropped his hand to his side. He fidgeted. His legs jittered. He eyed the exits. The double door at the front of the courtroom led to the hallway. Too many people out there, clamorosity happening indeed, cops versus commoners. The rear door to the jury room locked by the guards.

"Come on." Massacre insisted and looked to the rear exit, the one the judge and the prosecutors rushed through. "We have to go."

"Where?" Noble asked.

"An apple orchard in France. A farm in Connecticut. The moon. Wherever we want."

Noble still did not move.

"You're going to be convicted." The speed and urgency of Massacre's words swelled. "Leapers like me and you, we're the same, we don't get the breaks others do. Together, we can conquer the world."

Noble looked up at him. "The world is a big place."

"When we were in our cells, how big was the world?"

Noble did not hesitate. "Seven feet by three feet."

"You can remember something archaic like the size of a prison cell but not what you're on trial for." Massacre laughed. "How big is your world at this moment?"

Noble looked at the paneled room, the judge's bench, the jury box. What was his question?

"This is all that exists," Massacre said, "and we're all that matters. Come with me. There's more for us to do."

"More?"

Massacre looked toward the doors again, jumped from foot to foot. "You coming or not?"

Under Noble and Massacre's matching steps, the floor creaked, the infrastructure groaned. The Old New York County Courthouse had been built over a poorhouse used to feed and shelter (hide?) the indigent and the mentally ill. They made their way, a two-man caravan across the ghostly strata of pleadings, objections, dismissals, and verdicts. Over the rubble of innocent men condemned, and guilty men set free. Across the wood floor where Grand Sachem Tweed was convicted of bilking New York City out of millions of dollars, in the very courthouse his thievery built.

Noble stopped. "WJH told me to stay at the table."

"WJH told you to come with me and do as I say."

"I don't remember that."

"You don't remember anything," Massacre said, "except the size of your cell."

"Seven feet by three feet."

Massacre drew in close to Noble. "I'm not fucking around anymore, cellmate. You're coming with me. I have plans and you're part of them."

Noble followed him again. WJH was William, of that he was certain. His lifelong friend who had fought for him, always. He had told him to wait at the table. Noble braked. Massacre's fingers closed around his bicep. Noble tried to pull his arm away. The bee necklace banged against his chest. His instinct to fight strong, powerful and innate like the desire to sleep or to eat. Noble tried to pull his arm away again, and succeeded. Freed, he squared off, fists raised.

Massacre chuckled. "Whatcha gonna do, old man?"

He didn't know. The plagues and the tangles wouldn't tell him. He froze, covered in thousands of bees. He was bee bearding behind the Home for Unwanted Boys. The grist smelled sweet like candy. Their melody a crescendo in an orchestral buzz. Across the yard, William was being pummeled by a swirl of dusty and dirty boys who rolled over him like fists of storm clouds. Noble, covered in bees, was helpless.

"As I thought," Massacre said. "You're not gonna do nothing."

Noble, a bee statue. "William." He managed.

"Your attorney ain't here. Who's going to protect you now?"

"Hey!" A voice spit from the front doors. "Bee King!"

They turned. The double doors at the back of the courtroom closed behind a toothless and hefty mutt of a man who was all at once familiar and strange to Noble. Like returning to a childhood home and ruminating, had the bedrooms always been that small, were the ceilings always that low?

Barrel chested and pock marked, Kid walked toward them. "Noble, let's go."

"He's coming with me," Massacre said.

Kid slowed, inched closer, and spoke to Noble. "William told me to come get you."

Noble saw the Home, and felt the beatings, a chump punch to his gut, a right hook to his eye. His swarm of bees attacked and died. The hive, his queen, crushed by Kid. Noble had thrashed him, hadn't he? A bat aimed for his skull. Why hadn't he killed him?

"C'mon." Massacre grabbed Noble's arm again.

Noble saw their prison cell. Seven feet by three feet. Heard the tales of murder. Bury the body under the Williamsburg Bridge, Massacre had said. The Williamsburg Bridge is under construction. They'll never find the bones. Must have repeated it while Noble slept since he imagined it in his dreams, in his sleeping dreams and in the ones he had while awake.

"We're the same," Massacre told Noble.

"No," Kid said, "we are."

A bag of nails! Think! Noble demanded of himself, and then remembered what Prokopovych instructed in the book on how to get bees off the body. He bent his knees and propelled into the air, shot up like a projectile fired from a cannon. Bees took flight, and Noble sprinted out of the courtroom. A black swarm followed, a buzzing blanket to protect against a winter's chill, a shield to defend against a firing squad.

In the hallway, the goings-on were difficult to untangle, as if Noble stepped into the chaotic workings of his own brain. Police and civilians wrestled with words. How long before they became deeds? Kid was next to him. Wanting to fight? No, his hand was on Noble's shoulder, guiding him, protecting him. Noble searched for William. There, in the middle of the coppers, in front of Byrne and Peter Stout, not William but other family faces. Jenny Big Stink stood between Sarah and Levi. Noble pushed through the crowd—Kid stayed close—and moved toward the nucleus. They would know where William was. William would tell him what to do, where to go.

Neared to Jenny, he saw a gun in her hand, by her side. Her arm started to rise.

"Don't." Noble spoke firmly.

Jenny looked at him and lowered her arm.

"Don't end up like me," Noble said.

Jenny turned toward Byrne and Peter Stout, and then looked back at Noble. Her eyes glazed. "It's too late. I'm already like you." She lifted her arm.

"No." Noble lunged and grabbed the gun. Jenny spun around, her eyes wide with surprise.

The inhabitants of the hallway quieted. All eyes on Noble with the gun in his hand, now at his side. Kid stepped in front of him, shielded him. Noble looked at Byrne and Peter Stout only a few feet away. Rage mounted in his belly. This was his chance to right all the wrongs of his world. He could do this, couldn't he? Transfer the fury and disappointment of his life, and propel a minie bullet into the hearts of Byrne and Peter Stout. Right all the wrongs they had done not only to him, but to Sarah, to Alice, to so many.

Officers moved to restrain Noble. Kid raised his fists.

"Wait," Byrne held up his hand. The officers stopped. Byrne looked at Noble. "You don't have the guts."

Was he right? Did he have the nerve to kill? He looked down at the necklace he wore, empty of a queen for decades but still worn as a reminder of when he captured his first queen in Central Park. She had been so mad at him, throwing herself against the sides of the homemade bee casket. He had been worried he was going to bring harm to her on the walk back to the Home, but they made it. He set up a hive for the queen and her colony, and it thrived until Kid destroyed it. But then Noble set up hives all over the prison yard, his very own village that buzzed and throbbed and pulsated, and he knew that despite all the challenges and losses of his life, despite his instinct to fight, he was not a murderer.

Noble opened his hand. The gun fell to the ground.

An officer grabbed it, and moved to empty the chamber. It was bullet-less. Alice would blame Peg Peg, who would blame the blue and white bear for not checking to see if the gun was loaded.

"You're a coward," Byrne said to Noble. "Good thing your father died young. He'd be embarrassed to have you as his son."

Levi stepped next to Noble and Kid, as did Jenny, Sarah, and then William. They surrounded Noble, his very own grist of bees.

When a court clerk went to check on Judge Patterson, he was unconscious and bleeding on the floor of his chambers. He was missing an ear.

Closing Argument

People of New York versus Noble Jennings

July 20, 1906

Juror Number Eleven was tired. His missed his wife, his children, and his mistress. Who knew being a juror would take so much time, and sitting in this wood chair for weeks would cause excruciating pain in his back. Even with the excitement of the serial killer getting free, and the judge being hospitalized, jury duty was arduous. He was glad the prosecution had finished its closing argument. Now, time for that bombastic little man—damn, he wish he could remember his name—to plead his case. Rather, Noble Jennings' case.

Although it seemed to Number Eleven that while Mister Jennings was the defendant and the little man was The Attorney that they were the same person. An amalgamation of the past and the present, of what was remembered and what was forgotten, and of regrets and lost opportunities. It had escaped no one seated in the jury box that this trial was not solely about determining the guilt or innocence of a man accused of murder.

Number Eleven took a sip of the whiskey on the rocks the jurors were provided with each day at half past two by the judge's secretary. In front of the jury box, the Attorney paced, seeming to be deep in thought. He clasped his hands behind his back and leaned toward the future.

"May it please your Honor, Mister Foreman, and Gentlemen of the Jury. As your servant in this search for truth, I present to you, the closing argument, when a counselor-at-law applies his education and experience to the facts, and when he mixes the legal with the logical. It is the climax of every trial, for the court, for the attorneys, and for the jurors. The moment when we hope for a revelation so we can shriek, Hallelujah!, and a light shines down and we reveal and declare the truth and we pray and have faith, from the core of our beings, that justice will be served.

"There has been much excitement over the course of this trial. Not just in the courtroom but in the halls of the courthouse.

"We are pleased to have Justice Patterson out of the hospital and back on the bench to finish this trial he has so adroitly commanded.

"We all want and deserve justice, don't we? Not only in a court of law but in our everyday lives. We yearn to be heard, to be believed, and for our words to be trusted. But we don't often get that, do we? We are often battered and wronged by those we love, and oppressed and bullied by strangers. We're falsely accused and wrongly judged.

"Why, I asked as a child, and continue to ask as I stand humbly before you, did I not know my parents? I was born in a convent, I was told. My mother, a child herself, died as I was pulled from her womb. This fact I cannot defend as I possess no evidence to the contrary. My earliest thought was, I killed my mother. Most likely, this will be my final thought too.

"Do you know what orphans are? Refuse and discards. We beg for food, we steal too and, when we don't survive, our bodies litter the streets and the people that rejected us walk a path around us. This was the truth of how I was raised, and this was how my friend, Noble Jennings, knew the world throughout his childhood for he too, like me, was raised without family.

"Noble and I met at the Home for Unwanted Boys. Let's pause here, Gentlemen of the Jury, and consider the name. Home for Unwanted Boys. Home suggests security and love, but it is made clear only two words later who is to stay in this Home. Unwanted Boys. Noble and I never spoke of this, none of the boys did, but we all knew. We were the unwanted. We never considered it possible that we should be loved.

"Ah, but Noble and I were wrong. We found love from and for each other. I was sixteen and Noble thirteen when we met. We were children who learned to fight, outsmart, negotiate, and manipulate for basic survival. As I was a diminutive lad with my nose in a book, Noble protected me from the other boys. In turn, I taught him to read. We shared our food, one bed, and our dreams.

"I was going to be a lawyer and president of the United States.

"Noble wanted to raise bees and fall in love.

"I yearned for intellectual challenges, landmark legal cases to argue, a busy life of meetings and social gatherings, and high society status in the beating heart of New York City.

"Noble desired to build a home with his hands on his own wooded property where he could live quietly with a kind, beautiful wife and happy children, raise bees, and live off the land.

"Neither of us got what we wanted.

"I am a lawyer, true, but I have not achieved the legal heights I believed to be my calling. In fact, while I possess the necessary credentials to call myself an attorney and stand before you, I am an embarrassment to my profession having chased money more than truth, having sought recognition over justice.

"Of Noble's dreams, he achieved one. He raised bees.

"As you have heard throughout this trial, on the eve of the Civil War, Noble was wrongly accused by Commissioner Byrne and Peter Stout of starting the Colored Orphan Asylum fire. At fourteen years of age, upon his arrest, he did not confess even when he believed his life was to end from the barrels of a firing squad. He was trying to save those orphaned children and did not, under any circumstance, start that fire. Rather, he helped to douse it and to remove barricades placed on the front door. Noble's innocence did not stop Byrne from lying on the witness stand to that jury. Noble's innocence did not prevent Peter Stout from using his stature as a member of the Tammany boys to threaten that jury. And Noble's innocence could not stop those same jury members who, for purposes of greed and in fear of retaliation, convicted my friend of something he did not do. As a result of their false charges and the tainted jury, he spent thirty-six years in prison.

"But that evil wasn't enough, not for Byrne and not for Peter Stout. Noble was released from prison in 1897, and less than a decade later they accused him again of still other crimes he did not commit. But this time, Byrne—now as chief of police—coerced false admissions from him. I was there, gentlemen, and I assure you this was no voluntary confession. Through the evidence you have seen and heard during this trial, you now know it, too. Just as Byrne had placed fourteen-year-old Noble in front of a firing squad to scare him into confessing—a failed approach—Byrne used another tactic on fifty-nine-year-old Noble. The tactic of suggestion. The ploy of confusion.

"You're thinking, no one can suggest to you, Mister Juror, that you committed a crime you hadn't. No one can get you, Mister Foreman, to become so confused you would admit to something you hadn't done. But what if—what if?—you suffered from a disease of the mind? What if the intricacies of your brain were as twisted and tangled as underbrush, and in that diseased mind of yours there existed confusion of such a degree that you were unable to distinguish fact from fiction, and unable to recall one moment to the next?

"That is the evidence you have heard throughout this trial. Doctor Levi Solomon Fuller testified, his hand to Bible and before God Almighty, that his work along with Doctor Alois Alzheimer of Berlin, Germany, has shown what we now know exists: Pre-senile Dementia.

"P.D. A disease of the mind, tangles in the brains of the young as if they were the old.

"If you have been fortunate enough to have your loved ones live into their seventieth and eightieth years you probably have experienced their expected memory loss, confusion, and irritability. Their minds tragically lost to the here and now. But what of those who exhibit such symptoms at a younger age? What are their diagnoses?

"Lunacy? No! Noble is no lunatic.

"Brain injury from a mule kick to the brain? No! He has suffered no knock on the head.

"Trickery? No! Noble is not so clever or diabolical as to play us for fools.

"Damnation by God for the sins of his father? No!"

He paused, and began again. "You, Gentlemen of the Jury, have heard no evidence to suggest any of these causes for Noble's memory loss and confusion. Therefore, there is only one explanation.

"Recall the testimony of Dr. Levi Solomon Fuller. The evidence has shown my friend suffers from P.D., and Byrne was so desperate to obtain evidence of Noble's pretend guilt he did the only thing he could do: he took advantage of the tangles and plagues in Noble's brain to get him to confess to crimes he did not commit.

"Byrne threatened me to achieve his goal. If, as Noble's lawyer, I was to speak out on his behalf, I would be arrested, as would my friends. In fact, Byrne had me forcibly removed from the interrogation room.

"You're thinking, what about the blood on Noble's shirt and the bruises on his hands at the time of his arrest? You heard from a police officer who told you Noble had been accused of stealing a man's wallet, near where Jack Hill's body was found. You might ask, How did Noble know about the sixth body, poor Mister Thomas Pollard, buried under the Williamsburg Bridge? How is it possible Lonny Massacre killed Mister Pollard while he was incarcerated? And if Massacre had someone on the outside do it, who is that person? And finally, as you heard on the State's case from the medical examiner, from the condition of the remains it could not be determined the date of Mister Pollard's departure.

"Damning evidence? I think not.

"As I stand before you, I offer these humble explanations. Noble had spent the previous twenty-four hours prior to his arrest lost in Five Points believing himself to be the nine-year-old boy who had lived on the streets upon his parents' murders. Noble survived as that boy had. He fought for food and a warm and dry place to sleep. The blood on his shirt was his own from a cut on his chest. The bruises on his hands received from fighting off an assailant.

"As for talk of a stolen wallet. Again, lies and falsehoods. Mister Jennings is no thief, just as he is no murderer.

"As for poor Mister Pollard, another simple explanation. Lonny Massacre, Noble's cellmate for a time, told Noble stories of his, uh, shall I say, conquests. He wrote a manifesto detailing his animalistic deeds. While Noble was being questioned by Commissioner Byrne, fact and fiction collided in Noble's jumbled mind and Massacre's facts became Noble's truth.

"What of the remains of Mister Pollard? You heard testimony that the bones found belonged to Mister Pollard, but when I asked the medical examiner if they could have been the bones of an animal, 'Yes, sir' he said. Ah, but the Williamsburg Bridge hadn't been built in 1897 when Mister Massacre told Noble about Mister Pollard's body. When under the duress of Commissioner Byrne's questioning, while stricken with P.D., Noble remembered the name Pollard, and the bridge which was in the news, and confusion in Mister Jennings mind fashioned a story. A tale created by dementia. This was verified by the expert testimony of Doctor Levi Solomon Fuller, and remains unrefuted.

"We so badly want to make sense of this difficult world, don't we? We struggle mightily for a revelation and that moment when we can yell, Hallelujah!, and a light shines and we raise our hands to heaven and with clarity we say, I understand why there is injustice, why there is poverty, starvation, and divisiveness. Why children lose their parents and are raised in orphanages, why the innocent are victimized, and yes, why decent men are wrongly accused. And then, horrors upon horrors, we spend a lifetime trying to conjure memories of the good in people and the good in ourselves but what are we left with? Often distortion, misremembrance, and self-doubt. Alas, as in the case of my friend, Noble, some have no memories as if the events of their lives had never occurred.

"How do we deal with this? Some hope and pray. I turn to drugs and the occult to unravel the secrets of this unjust world. Shocking, yes, I know, but we all have our coping devices, don't we? Some cheat on their wives, others immerse themselves in their work. I smoke heroin and ask questions of tarot cards and crystals. Noble tended his bees, until he forgot how.

"I don't paint this pathetic picture for you to feel sorry for me or for Noble, but to talk about why the human species is so remarkable. It is because no matter if we knew our parents or not, if we felt loved as a child or not, if we fought in the Great

Rebellion or not, were slaves or not, if dementia has stolen our memories, all who navigate the maze of life without succumbing to its sharp corners and dead ends have one thing in common.

"Faith. Faith makes every one of us remarkable.

"Mister Foreman and Gentlemen of the Jury, you have heard no direct evidence to link Noble Jennings to the six murders of which he is accused. What you have heard is circumstantial evidence. Fantastical theories that charade as links in a chain that cannot be looped together. You have already seen the result of weak links with the escape of Mister Massacre.

"You must throw aside every fact about which you have reasonable doubt and you must acquit Mister Jennings. Throw out the unproven and there stands the man. Not a criminal, but a man. Thomas Jefferson and John Adams declared every American is rightfully innocent unless absolutely proven guilty by hard, competent evidence. That is the law you have sworn to apply in fulfilling your duty. Noble doesn't ask for your sympathy. He has friends and clergy for that. He asks for – in fact, he demands - your justice. He doesn't ask for more, but by God, he demands nothing less."

William paused, and then stood behind Noble, hands on his shoulders. "Mister Forman and Gentlemen of the Jury, I envy you. You have the opportunity to save not one man's life, but two.

"The first life you will save with your not guilty verdict is Noble's, who will be sentenced to the electric chair if found guilty of these crimes he did not commit. Crimes he could not have committed, crimes the government has not proven motive for him to commit, crimes he had no opportunity or means to carry out. Of this, the evidence is clear.

"The other life you will save is mine. A not guilty verdict in this, the greatest trial of my career, will cap my years as a lawyer marked by underachievement. While I will never be president of the United States, and my name will never be memorialized in the annals of history, I will have nonetheless reached the zenith of my vocation—personally and professionally—in this very courtroom. I will have saved my best friend, a man who has saved me many times."

He stepped in front of the jury box. "Noble Jennings might be a defendant in this trial, but he is, before anything else, a man. A man who has been wronged his entire life by those with agendas of hurt and hatred. Being the remarkable human being that he is, like the bee who always returns to the hive knowing the queen awaits, Noble has never lost faith.

"Your job as jurors—your privilege, your duty—is to do justice. I have presented to you the five points of Noble Jennings' innocence, and by doing so have proven beyond a reasonable doubt he is no murderer. I pray you, kind and gentle men, see Five Points and its people as I do, and as Noble did. Awaken your faith in humanity.

"On behalf of my friend and my brother, I ask you return a verdict of not guilty on all counts." William bowed. "I stand humbled in your presence."

New York Times

All the News that's Fit to Print

Obituary of Justice Donovan Patterson

Reported by John Coal

NEW YORK, August 30, 1906. Sixty-seven-year-old Justice Donovan Patterson passed away at home from an infection. His wife had pre-deceased him by one year. His five children were by his side.

Donovan Patterson was born in 1839 in New York City. He attended Williams and Hobart Colleges as well as Columbia Law School. Patterson was admitted to the bar in 1860. In 1886 he received the support of Tammany Hall and was elected Justice of the Supreme Court. He is best known as having presided over the murder trial of Noble Jennings.

As reported in THE TIMES on July 5, 1906, during the trial of Mister Jennings, Justice Patterson was attacked by Lonny Massacre. He survived said assault and was able to finish presiding over the trial. Judge Patterson, however, succumbed to the viciousness of the attack on August 28, 1906 when he was no longer able to fight an infection in his ear canal.

William Henley, Attorney-and-Counselor at law who represented Noble Jennings, said about Justice Patterson, "He was well-liked. Even when he ruled against you in trial, he did so in the most affable manner. He had an unquenchable and uncompromising desire for truth and justice."

Five Points

A novel by Peggy Fuller

George M. Hill Company, Publishers (1910)

Prologue

Much of what I remembered, I have forgotten. With the dementia the doctors say wracks my brain, I knew this day was
upon me and so I placed pen to paper and documented my
story. What you are about to read of Five Points and the lives
of two extraordinary men is unfamiliar to me at this moment,
but I must have lived it and it must have occurred as the hand-
writing appears to be mine.

Chapter One

Alleys paved with mud knee-deep and freckled with lewd
crevices languished among ruined houses exposed to the
street through wide holes in walls. Thieves and murderers
squatted in abandoned tenements. All that is loathsome and
decayed lived there. This was Five Points where best friends
Nathan Jackson, a bee keeper, and Warren Henderson, an attorney, were raised in an orphanage.

January 6, 1910

New York Times
All the News that's Fit to Print
Advertisement
A Woman is as Old as she Looks

How Old Do You Look?

World Famous

John Coal's Almond, Vanilla & Honey Cream

Worn by Movie Stars, Beauty Queens and House Wives

Will Make You Look Younger

Order Now

John Coal Manufacturing Company

311 Broadway, New York, New York

Chapter Fifty-nine

Noble sat at the dining room table, between William and Sarah. His strong stature, those tough bones and muscles that had been the hardback binding of his life, had softened and atrophied. His jowls sagged, his skin grayed, patches of blue colored his legs. Few moments of clarity in several weeks had brought light to his eyes and words to his tongue. His throat swelled and so he drank broth and mashed vegetables that Sarah and Peggy prepared for him. He often failed to comprehend the simplest commands or concepts, and slept away most of his days, dreaming of being pigged in bed with Butchy, or of a Union army captain teaching him how to salute, or of a mysterious boat ride with Sarah. But at that moment, at the dining room table surrounded by those who loved him the most, as his breathing labored and his organs succumbed, he had clarity and took inventory of his sixty-three years. Like Alice while she was alive, his clarity was internal, and could not be expressed through words, or gestures, or expressions on his stony face.

"Happy birthday, dear Mama." Sarah harmonized with the hum of the electric lights. "Happy birthday to you."

Alice left to take the fish a year ago while she slept.

"Happy Birthday, my sweetness." John raised a glass.

"To Nana," Levi said, "who would have been eighty-three today."

"To Alice," William toasted.

"To Alice," Peggy said.

"And to Simon," John added.

"Don't forget Kid," William said.

Consumption had taken him.

Peggy looked at William. "What a story about how Kid tormented you and Noble when you were boys, and then became your greatest champion."

"Jenny made the difference," William said.

Jenny nodded. "Kid needed someone to be kind to him." She turned toward William. "And you needed to learn forgiveness."

William nodded, humbly.

Harry toasted. "To kindness and forgiveness."

Levi said, "May Kid rest in peace."

"To Esther," Jenny Big Stink said.

"Who was Esther?" Peggy asked.

"Her horse," Sarah said.

John shook his head. "Esther was a donkey."

"He was a mule and he was my best friend."

"Then to Esther." Peggy added, "May they all rest in peace."

Harry raised his glass. "To our loved ones who have passed away, may the winds of heaven whisper hourly benedictions over their hallowed graves."

Sarah looked at Noble. "Anything you want to say, honey?"

He had much to say. To darn the threads of his memories.

He raised a glass. Thank you—

You are my family who have stuck by me.

My wife Sarah brought me my deepest moments of happiness and the greatest gift of my life, my son.

Levi, who I only ask for forgiveness for I wish in every moment of my existence that I had been a proper father to you.

William, who courses through my body and has done so since we were boys. I never would have survived without you.

John Coal, who stepped in to care for Alice and Sarah.

Peggy, who is like my daughter, may you never stop believing you can conquer the world.

Harry, take care of Levi.

To Jenny, please, dear girl, you are not to blame.

"He's just staring," Harry said.

Levi said, "He doesn't understand."

Peggy raised her voice. "Pops, do you want to say anything?"

"He hasn't spoken in weeks." John adjusted the pillow on the chair he sat upon.

Sarah rubbed Noble's back. "I don't think he hears anymore."

Levi sighed. "It's the tangles."

"How do you know?" Jenny asked.

Levi said, "I won't know for sure until I dissect his—"

"—He understands," William said. "He's taking it all in on a deeper, cosmic level."

"Always looking to bypass scientific certainty, Uncle William." Levi said good-naturedly.

"Not everything can be explained by a formula, young man."

"Boys," Peggy said, "let's not get into the science versus spirituality discussion. You'd think you'd tire of that conversation by now."

"Never." Levi smiled.

William patted his nephew on the cheek. "Shall we begin?"

"Yes," Sarah said. "I'll shut the lights. Levi, will you light the candles?"

"Yes, Mama."

With the electric lights off, the shadows of flames from candles set on the table danced on the dining room walls. With the success of John Coal's Almond, Vanilla & Honey Cream, Sarah and John moved out of the three-room tenement in Five Points and uptown on Broadway to a lovely and spacious brownstone with an elevator. Sarah, John and Peggy had their own rooms. Levi and Harry shared a room. John Coal no longer had to lift himself up the stairs and swing himself down, a task that had gotten harder as he passed eight decades of life. Once they got the larger home, Noble moved in, to Sarah's delight, and to Levi's dissatisfaction. But over the few years Levi had gotten to know his father, four of them since Noble was found not guilty at trial, Levi had come to care for the man even if he never truly knew who he was. Sarah and William's love for Noble was evident, and that became enough for Levi to accept and respect his father.

William still resided in Washington Mews with his wife. Jenny Big Stink and Bertha lived in apartment 5C. After the First Pure Food and Drug Act became law in June oh-six, and morphine, cocaine, and heroin were deemed illegal even with prescriptions, 5C ceased to act as an opium den. Jenny returned to the sea to make her living, but instead of a mule and a wagon, William set her up with a storefront in the meat-packing district and a list of wholesale purveyors to choose from. She also sold magic mushrooms.

"Shouldn't we be holding hands?" Levi joked.

"That's enough, Levi Solomon," Sarah scolded. "Indulge your uncle."

"Yes, Ma'am."

William cleared his throat. "Ready?"

"Ready." Jenny jiggled her wide rump in the chair. "This is going to be fun."

William began. "Thank you for being here this evening to celebrate Alice's birthday, on what we're hoping might be a captivating display of the supernatural. I understand there are some nay-sayers here." He squeezed Levi's hand. "But perhaps tonight's experience will demonstrate that science and the spirit world exist on parallel planes. You can expect different experiences, such as feeling as though you are being touched, and unexpected smells. The lit candles are for us, so we can see the spirits should they choose to appear."

Peggy pointed toward the middle of the table. "Why the loaves of bread?"

"They are for the spirits who seek sustenance."

"We should have steak then," Levi said. "I hear the dead can't resist a good filet."

Sarah shot her son a look of disdain, but then smiled. She had been nicknamed Sarah High Yellow by the people of Five Points but, after her mother's brain injury and when John lost his first leg, she was tagged Sarah Abandoned Dreams. SAD, for short. A moniker she fought not to resemble.

Sarah looked at Levi, and at Harry next to him, and then to John and Jenny and William, and Noble seated to her left. Life wasn't about doing it all on your own, she had learned, but about family. She hadn't received fame and fortune, no stardom on the stage, but the greatest hobnobbed family who had stuck together during the most difficult of times. No matter their skin colors.

"Has anyone been to a séance before?" William asked.

Jenny Big Stink raised her hand.

"Anyone else?" No responses, William continued. "The purpose of a séance is to summon the dead from the spirit world so we may communicate with them, find out how they are, and to let them know we miss them. We will attempt to summon Alice and Simon Black Cat, and Kid."

"What about Esther?" Jenny asked.

"Animals often show themselves during séances, so yes, Esther too. Are we ready?"

"Ready," Peggy and Harry spoke at the same time.

"John Coal? Sarah? You ready?" William asked.

"Ready," they said.

"Good. Noble, what about you?"

Noble stared at a candle's flame. *I'm ready.*

"Okay, well, let's get started," William said. "Everyone hold hands. As it's

Alice's birthday, we will start by summoning her. Our beloved Alice, we bring you gifts from life. Commune with us. Move among us."

"Dear Alice," Jenny said, "we respectfully ask that you honor us with your presence this evening."

"Don't forget about Simon," John whispered.

"Simon, Kid, Esther, show yourselves," William said. "We mean no harm. We have no judgment. We offer only love."

Silence, a few snorts from Levi and playful slaps on his arm from Harry, and then a low moan. Soft, and then louder.

Noble spoke. "To revolutionaries, whores and prostitutes, boys who love to fight, girls who fuck all night."

"What?" Sarah looked aghast.

"That's something Kid used to say." William laughed.

Jenny added, "It's carved on the front door to my apartment building."

Noble continued, his voice as solemn now as Lincoln delivering the Gettysburg address. "If it is deemed necessary that I should forfeit my life in this slave country whose rights are disregarded by wicked, cruel, and unjust enactments, so let it be done."

William leaned toward Noble, and hugged him. "I love you, brother."

Noble cupped the wooden bee vial that hung around his neck. He took the necklace off and handed it to Levi. *The final page of Prokopovych's book of bees. Bees do not fear death. Life is far more treacherous.* He rose, bowed to his family, and walked toward the room he shared with Sarah.

Levi jumped up and switched on a light. "What was that?" He moved toward the bedroom.

"Stop," John Coal ordered.

"We have to go to him." Peggy scooted her chair back.

"Leave him alone," William said.

Silence around the table. The hum of the electric lights filled the hollowness, followed by the gentle snap of the close of the bedroom door.

Levi looped the bee pendant around his neck. "Mom?"

Sarah studied the closed bedroom door, then finally said, "Leave him alone? When he's dead, but not a moment before."

She hurried toward the bedroom. The rest followed.

Noble was under the sheets, fetal positioned on his right side. His eyes closed, his breath soft and shallow. They surrounded him. Sarah, William, Levi and Harry, Peggy, and Jenny Big Stink. John Coal swung into the room a moment later. Levi and Harry lifted him on to the foot of the bed.

"Shall we hold hands?" William asked.

They clasped hands and intertwined fingers.

William began. "Dear Spirit. Surround us with love and the light of your

protection as Noble transitions to the otherworld."

"You've got to be kidding," Levi said.

"Shh," Sarah spoke.

William continued. "Spirit, guide Noble to your greater heights..."

"You be quiet too, William," Sarah said. "Everyone, let's just be." Sarah kissed Noble on his forehead, and caressed his cheek.

Levi put his hand on Noble's back. John Coal held his leg. The rest followed, and lain their hands upon him.

Noble clustered in the center. They had called him Bee King, which pleased him. He always thought of himself as a worker bee but now knew the truth. He was, in fact, the queen, delighted to be in the heart of the hive.

Page Six Hundred and Thirty-Seven of "Bee King, the Book of Bee Keeping" by Petro Prokopovych. Translated from Russian to English, Second Edition, 1845. It is a fact of evolution that every bee colony must have a queen. Death of a queen is a most traumatic event.

Chapter Sixty

In the central laboratory at Manhattan's Hospital for the Insane, a sterile and windowless room, Levi contemplated a black metal box displayed on a table. Silver latches on the sides of the container were scratched and dented. Several of its screws were stripped. He touched the container, cold from refrigeration, and drew his hand away. His emotions bucked like a boat on a turbulent sea. He looked to the man that stood to his left. Levi gestured, gave right of way to royalty.

Alois shook his head. "This is for you."

Levi sighed and pulled on thick black rubber gloves, unlatched the box, and peered inside. He stepped back, not wanting to look but unable to avert his eyes. His hand rose dramatically to his chest, and pressed the bee necklace to his heart. Another sigh. Could he do this? Was he afraid, or was some other emotion tormenting his core? What would he instruct a student at this crossroad? Be brave. Carry on. Yes, that is what he would counsel.

"I'm shaking."

Alois smiled at his protégé. "You're human."

Levi sighed and turned back to Noble. His eyes widened at the fragility and etherealness of the brain that floated peacefully in a thick bath of cerebral spinal fluid. Had William been correct that scientific and celestial worlds co-existed and complimented the other? He shifted from one foot to the other, an anxious boy at the knee of the father he barely knew.

"He loves you unconditionally," Alois said.

Levi looked to his mentor, unabashed by the tears that deluged his eyes. "You mean loved."

"My English is not so bad. I mean what I say."

Levi studied Noble. "Is this what it feels like to..."

"What?" Alois urged.

"...to know immortality?"

"That's how I felt when I saw Auguste's brain. Take him out."

Levi removed the organ from the case and tenderly placed it in a metal tray. It was smaller than he expected for a sixty-three-year-old man, a condition Alois had also documented in Auguste's post-mortem brain. Levi took a deep breath, exhaled, and attempted to steady his hands. He lifted a scalpel and hesitated.

"Like we practiced on the melon." Alois encouraged.

Levi edged the blade into the organ, which shook like jelly. His tears fell and mixed with the matter. Here, before his clouded eyes, were the hugs he never received, the lessons a father should have passed on to his son, the balls never tossed, the first inhale on a cigar and the coughing fit that followed, the laughter of father and son, the pats of encouragement, the talks of sex.

Levi had always yearned for the ability to tunnel through people's eyes and to see into their brains. Wasn't that why he became a neuro-psychiatrist? To unveil truths? No, more pointedly, he became a psychiatrist to discover the truth of his father, and in essence, the truth of his father's son. Levi had failed to understand the man during his living years, and by extension himself, nary had the opportunity, but now with a sliver of Noble's brain on the edge of a blade held between his fingertips, none of that no longer held true. Who his father was, who he could have been, his loves, his fears, his dreams, his failures, everything a father passes down to a son, the lessons, the genetic history, they were here, in this less than three pounds of water and fat, among the gray and white matter, knotted midst jumbled neurons. Noble was not singularly his father; he was so much more, and like every person he was indeed the epicenter of humanity.

Levi sliced tissue and examined parts under a microscope. Pathologies confirmed. A massive amount of sticky, insoluble proteins lodged in spaces between nerve cells. Tangled bundles of protein threaded through neurons.

◆

Alone in his office, Levi placed a notepad on his desk. With Alois's blessing, he had been outlining a textbook on Presenile Dementia and was ready to begin writing. Where to start? With a name, perhaps. One less scientific than P.D., one that might easily tumble off the tongues of ordinary citizens, one that offered homage to the scientist who discovered the ailment.

Yes, that was it. Levi brought the tip of the pen to the page and wrote with broad cursive loops and valleys. Alzheimer's Disease. Chapter One.

New York Times

All the News that's Fit to Print

NOBLE JENNINGS
PARDONED POSTHUMOUSLY
FOR COLORED ORPHAN ASYLUM FIRE

"If only Noble had lived to see this day."

Reported by Peggy Fuller

NEW YORK, November 13, 1910. Noble Jennings, convicted of the Colored Orphan Asylum fire, has been pardoned of said crime for which he spent thirty-six years in prison. One James Fortin, a juror during the trial in 1861, revealed having been threatened and bribed, along with the other gentlemen of that jury, including the foreman, to find Mister Jennings guilty. At the behest of William J. Henley, retired Counselor-at-Law, proceedings were held before the New York City trial court in which Mister Fortin swore under oath to the following events:

"After I was chosen as a juror, Peter Stout and Officer Timothy Byrne came to my home with two other coppers. My wife and children were there. The message was clear if I did not cooperate there would be repercussions. We jurors didn't even discuss the evidence behind closed doors," Mister Fortin said, "as we were too afraid to say anything for fear word would get back to Boss Tweed. Our lives, our livelihood, and our families were at peril. Mister Jennings, forgive me. God forgive me."

Mister Fortin further testified he could no longer live with his transgression. This reporter is certain the recent deaths of former police chief Timothy Byrne and saloon owner Peter Stout in a shoot-out was a factor in Mister Fortin's atonement.

Also, testifying at the hearing to exonerate Mister Jennings were the two other surviving jurors from the Colored Orphan Asylum fire trial.

Mister Jennings, who was found not guilty of the murder of six men four years since, passed away from Alzheimer's Disease two months ago, according to his wife, Sarah Fuller Jennings, and his son, Doctor Levi Solomon Fuller.

After the court's ruling that granted the pardon of Mister Jennings, Counselor Henley said, "If only Noble had lived to see this day."

THE END

AUTHOR'S NOTE

My mother had her first transient ischemic attack (TIA) in 1998, and her second one the year after. These mini-strokes were certainly alarming but she was still our amiable mother who my siblings and I readily turned to for emotional support. She continued to work as a nurse. Mom had a good run, health-wise, until 2015 when she called my aunt and said, I don't know where I am. Turns out, mom was in a shopping plaza less than a quarter-mile from her home. How she had the presence to call her sister, and point out the stores in front of her so my aunt could find her, is unknown. What is known is mom had four small strokes that day, which caused transient global amnesia. Four days later, she had another stroke, and the following day too. All mini-strokes, the doctors said, and all ones that affected her memory. Upon her discharge from the hospital, the neurologist said she had vascular dementia, take her home and make her comfortable as there was no knowing when the final stroke might hit. A doomsday report.

Four years later, mom's still here. Life is different and the same. Although her short term memory is shot, and she is unable to offer emotional support as she once did, she is still our amiable, caring, and funny mother.

I write of this because when my father was dying—a preordained death when he voluntarily ceased dialysis—I blogged about his journey and mine. With mom, I chose not to do the same. Instead, I decided to write a love letter to my mother in the form of this novel, *Bee King*. *Bee King* is the historical fiction story of the first person diagnosed with Alzheimer's Dis-

JOANNE LEWIS

ease in the United States. *Bee King* is a story of overcoming incredible odds as well as the importance of family. Mom is a compilation of all the characters, the locations, the sights, smells and sounds. She is in each page, as she has been in all the pages of my life.

In retirement, mom was an ombudsman and would give talks to caregivers on how to approach people with dementia. I specifically remember one example where she would say, imagine you do not know where you are and who you are. In walks a stranger who tells you to take off your clothes. You are cold. You are afraid you will fall, or be harmed. You do not understand why you are being made to stand under running water that stings your skin, and made to rub a bar over your body. You don't know why a stranger is watching you during this personal moment. Mom suggested caregivers approach dementia patients from their perspectives, moving slowly, being reassuring and patient, and understanding if they lash out it is due to fear and discomfort.

While mom is still able to live in independent living, and does not require an aide, I often think of the irony of her work as an ombudsman. Mom, who used to counsel on how dementia patients must feel, now resides in that in-between zone, somewhere between here and there, between knowing and not-knowing, between empathy and indifference.

During the pages of my life, mom taught me to have compassion, patience and kindness. Now, as our roles reverse and I watch her tackle this phase of her life with courage, humility and humor, I continue to learn from her.

About the Author

Joanne Lewis is a writer and attorney living in Fort Lauderdale, Florida. She is the author of award-winning mystery and historical novels and novellas.

Please visit her website at www.joannelewiswrites.com and email her at:

jtawnylewis@gmail.com. She would love to hear from you.

If you enjoyed Bee King, please consider reading Joanne's other books:

Forbidden Room, Book 1 of the Forbidden trilogy

Forbidden Night, Book 2 of the Forbidden trilogy

Forbidden Horses, Book 3 of the Forbidden trilogy

The Lantern, a Renaissance mystery

Make Your Own Luck, a Remy Summer Woods mystery

Wicked Good, co-written with Amy Lewis Faircloth

Michelangelo & Me Series: Michelangelo & the Morgue (book 1 of 5),

Sleeping Cupid (book 2 of 5),

School of the World (book 3 of 5),

Space Between (book 4 of 5) and

Michelangelo & Me (book 5 of 5)

I miss you, Pops.

Made in the
USA
Middletown, DE